Praise for Chitra Banerjee Divakaruni

"Divakaruni's literary voice is a sensual bridge between worlds. India and America. Children and parents. Men and women. Passion and pragmatism."

—*USA Today*

"Divakaruni beautifully blends the chills of reality with the rich imaginings of a fairy tale."

—*Wall Street Journal*

"Irresistible. . . . Enchanting . . . Divakaruni shows herself to be a skilled cartographer of the heart."

—*People*

"Divakaruni's sentences dazzle. The images she creates are masterful."

—*Los Angeles Times*

"For those of us who read to escape the banalities of daily life, Chitra Divakaruni's books are oxygen. She writes about India in a way that makes the rest of the world disappear around you."

—*Chicago Tribune*

"Enchanting. . . . Divakaruni's storytelling talents put her right up there with the best."

—*Miami Herald*

"Divakaruni is an incomparable storyteller. Part of the beauty of her talent is her ability to capture the true complexity of the emotional landscape of her characters."

—*Denver Post*

"A brilliant storyteller. . . . A transplanted cultural treasure."

—*Seattle Times*

"Among contemporary writers from India, Chitra Divakaruni fills a space all her own. . . . Her fiction draws a line straight to the heart."

—*Atlanta Journal-Constitution*

"Reading Divakaruni is a pleasure. She paints worlds of complex characters and cultures with an absorbing story line and beautiful language that reads like poetry."

—*The Oregonian*

the LAST QUEEN

Also by Chitra Banerjee Divakaruni

The Forest of Enchantments

Before We Visit the Goddess

Oleander Girl

Grandma and the Great Gourd

One Amazing Thing

Shadow Land

The Palace of Illusions

The Mirror of Fire and Dreaming

Queen of Dreams

The Conch Bearer

The Vine of Desire

Neela: Victory Song

The Unknown Errors of Our Lives

Sister of My Heart

Leaving Yuba City

The Mistress of Spices

Arranged Marriage

Black Candle

the LAST QUEEN

CHITRA BANERJEE DIVAKARUNI

wm

WILLIAM MORROW

An Imprint of HarperCollins*Publishers*

This book is a work of fiction. References to real people, events, establishments, organizations, or locales are intended only to provide a sense of authenticity, and are used fictitiously. All other characters, and all incidents and dialogue, are drawn from the author's imagination and are not to be construed as real.

HarperCollins books may be purchased for educational, business, or sales promotional use. For information, please email the Special Markets Department at SPsales@harpercollins.com.

Originally published in India in 2021 by HarperCollins India.

FIRST U.S. EDITION

Library of Congress Cataloging-in-Publication Data has been applied for.

ISBN 978-0-06-316187-0

23 24 25 26 27 LBC 6 5 4 3 2

To my three kings:

Abhay, Anand, Murthy

Contents

III
QUEEN

Major Characters

Rani Jindan Kaur: the last queen of Punjab. Daughter of the royal dog trainer, Manna Singh Aulakh, she became the youngest wife of Maharaja Ranjit Singh. Mother of Maharaja Dalip Singh and queen regent during his reign

Maharaja Ranjit Singh: the greatest Sikh ruler, he built a powerful Sikh empire and protected it from the British

Maharaja Dalip Singh: youngest son of Ranjit Singh

Fakir Azizuddin: Ranjit Singh's ambassador, and adviser to Jindan during her early years in the Lahore court

Rani Guddan: one of Ranjit Singh's wives who became a close friend of Jindan

Jawahar Singh: brother of Jindan

Lal Singh: nobleman in the Lahore court

The Dogras: three brothers who rose to eminence under Ranjit Singh

Gulab Singh: the eldest brother, later became ruler of Jammu and Kashmir

Dhian Singh: the second brother, was Ranjit Singh's wazir and continued as wazir for Kharak Singh, Chand Kaur, and Sher Singh

Suchet Singh: the youngest brother

Rani Pathani: wife of Dhian Singh, she befriended Jindan

Hira Singh: son of Dhian Singh, and Jindan Kaur's first wazir

Pandit Jalla: Hira Singh's adviser

Kharak Singh: oldest son of Maharaja Ranjit Singh, he became king after Ranjit Singh

Chand Kaur: wife of Kharak Singh and mother of Naunihal

Naunihal Singh: son of Kharak Singh

Bibi Kaur: wife of Naunihal

The Sandhawalias, Ajit Singh and Lehna Singh: relatives of Chand Kaur and members of the powerful Sandhawalia clan

Mai Nakkain: chief queen of Ranjit Singh and mother of Kharak Singh

Mangla: Jindan's favorite maid

Avtar: Jindan's chief guard

Maahi: Jindan's attendant in later years

Jung Bahadur: prime minister of Nepal

Aroor: Dalip's attendant in England

Lord and Lady Login: guardians of Dalip Singh after the annexation of Punjab

Major Henry Lawrence: an agent of the British and, later, Resident at the Lahore court

Prologue

Lahore, 1839

JINDAN HASN'T SLEPT FOR TWO nights now, waiting by the sickbed of Maharaja Ranjit Singh along with his other wives. They've recited the Guru Granth Sahib until their throats are raw. *Birth and death are subject to the command of the Lord's Will. . . . He who believes in the Name becomes victorious.* They've given away their finest Kashmiri shawls, jewels, cows, horses, elephants, sacks of gold coins. Jindan doesn't own as much as the other queens. She came to her marriage empty-handed and has never cared to cajole gifts from her husband. But she, too, has gifted a triple-stranded gold necklace to the Jagannath temple hoping for the recovery of the Sarkar, as his people lovingly call him.

She kneels on the marble floor, grateful for the stone's coolness, and rests her head against the carved gold bedpost. As the maharaja's youngest wife, and his favorite, she's allowed certain liberties. The other women sit straight-spined, palms joined stiffly. Some of them send her cutting glances from under their veils. She doesn't care. It's stuffy in this room with too much whispering, too many people—Hindustani vaids, European physicians, the senior courtiers, servants, priests, punkha pullers—and of course the wives, covered from head to foot as custom dictates. Above her head, the canopy bears down, a solid sheet of beaten gold. It oppresses her. Surely it oppresses the maharaja, too. He'd prefer to lie on the roof, she knows, in sight of the stars, as was his pleasure on summer nights. He'd breathe better there in the open with the city that he conquered and made his own stretching out beneath him. The intricate, beloved tapestry of Lahore, city of myth, fashioned from the wilderness before time began by Lav, son of Ram.

But to whom can she say this? Who will listen to her? The power she possessed even a few days ago, as the Sarkar's favorite queen, has faded.

In a corner of the chamber, the chief minister, Wazir Dhian Singh, his thin, sharp face chiseled from granite, stands still and stern though he must be as exhausted as they. More so, because he has been going back and forth every hour, informing the nobles waiting in the Diwan-i-Khas of the latest developments, reminding Kanwar Kharak Singh to stay close by so he can get to the chamber right away if the king calls for his eldest son and heir. Making sure the army is kept in readiness, just in case the British decide this is a good moment to cross the Sutlej River. In the city they whisper that were it not for Dhian Singh, the day the Sarkar dies the kingdom would shatter like a mud pot dropped by a careless housewife.

Dhian watches the doctors with keen suspicion as they administer medicines and poultices. Where his master is concerned, he trusts no one. When Ranjit Singh mumbles, he's the one who interprets the sounds rightly and strides forward with a lota of water. He holds the gold pot to the maharaja's lips, raising his head as tenderly as a mother. The maharaja takes a slow sip and whispers something. Dhian's eyes widen and, for a moment, dart toward Jindan. He looks troubled, but he touches the maharaja's hand to his forehead, a gesture of fealty. What is he agreeing to?

Jindan's temples pound. The mirror-tiles on the walls glitter mockingly. Bits of Dhian's story float up in her mind: how he came from distant Jammu, young and hungry, knowing no one in the big city. A common trooper, he caught the Sarkar's attention and rose rapidly, even though he wasn't Sikh but a Hindu. Her husband was always open-minded that way—quick to spot talent and even quicker to reward it. Perhaps that is why he invoked lifelong loyalty in so many men.

Jindan wishes the Sarkar would open his eyes. *Look at me*, she wills him. *Just once.* Then she feels selfish. *You don't need to look at me. Just open your eyes, that'll be enough.* How small he appears in the bed, as though he's shrunk in these few days. The women have started a new chant: *They who practice truth and perform service shall obtain their reward*. She joins them, lips moving automatically to the familiar words, but inside her head a different litany plays: *What will happen if he dies? What will happen to my baby, my Dalip, who is not even a year old?*

She pushes away that traitorous thought. The king has weathered worse. Illnesses, accidents, injuries, hunts and battles gone wrong, his thigh clawed by a tiger, a spear tip breaking off in his chest. Didn't he survive them? The smallpox in his childhood that took his left eye. The disease in the brain, a few years back, that caused him to fall to the ground, unable to move the left side of his body for days. Didn't he triumph over them all, ruling the greatest kingdom left in Hindustan? The only man with enough power to hold back the British? That's how it's sure to be again. A few weeks and he'll be laughing that raucous bark of a laugh, asking for his favorite horse, Laila, to be brought to him, feeding her lumps of jaggery with his own hands before springing onto her back. He'll be calling for more wine, more dancing girls, fireworks, pleasure boats, wrestlers, qawwaali singers ferried all the way from Lucknow. And after they've all left, it will be just the two of them, intertwined in the cool underground chambers of the Summer Palace, her lips traveling over his body the way he likes . . .

She's reeled back into the present by Dhian Singh's announcement that the queens must return to the zenana quarters. Jindan gathers her courage and protests. "Let the others go; I need to remain. I won't be in anyone's way." She knows how to make herself small and invisible. She learned it in her village childhood from her brother, Jawahar. A useful skill when one needs to escape chastisement. "I have to be here when my Sarkar calls for me, as he surely will." She imagines her husband's hand reaching for her, finding nothing. But Dhian shakes his head, courteous, implacable.

Jindan is forced to adjust her veil and file out with the other queens. They don't look at each other. If they see their fear reflected in another's eyes, it'll become real. It'll bring the Sarkar bad luck.

The ministers have lined up in the passageway outside. The Crown Prince, Kanwar Kharak Singh, stands at their head, looking confused. He's a good-hearted man but weak and, she's heard, overfond of opium. Dhian straightens Kharak's jeweled turban for him, disapproval obvious in his fingers.

A servant rushes up with a gold bowl containing saffron paste. Jindan knows what it's for. In the presence of his courtiers, the Sarkar is going to put a tika on Kharak's forehead, binding them to the new king in loyalty so that his beloved Punjab will be safe after he's gone.

THE HAVELI THE KING gifted Jindan when she gave birth to Dalip ten months ago is her favorite place in the world. She has never owned a home before this. Her childhood was spent in a village hut belonging to a foulmouthed landlord who was always threatening to throw them out. The haveli has a few small rooms; its walls are plain yellow sandstone, its floors, slabs of gray, its windows, no more than slits. It is nothing like the palatial homes where the important ranis live, with majestic arches and domes, walls inlaid with precious stones, and mosaic floors intricate with Mughal designs. She wouldn't have felt at home there; the Sarkar, a perceptive man, and kind when statecraft allowed him to be, knew that.

But tonight she strides blindly through the house, taking no comfort in it. Her maid Mangla, who has been watching over baby Dalip, hurries forward to ask how the Sarkar, God protect him, is doing. Jindan shakes her head. She can't speak.

"Dalip is hungry," Mangla reminds her.

Jindan's breasts ache, full and heavy. It would be a relief. But no. She has only a little time. She must use it in the best way.

"You give him milk," she tells Mangla. "You lie down with him."

Usually, Jindan loves nursing Dalip. His weight in her arms, his sucking mouth, that sudden joyful release in her chest. The way his trustful limbs slacken when he falls asleep. But tonight she's glad that she started him on cow's milk a few weeks ago. He's a good baby. He mostly sleeps through the night. Even when he wakes, he will not cry for her. He's used to being with Mangla because of all the nights Jindan spends with the Sarkar. That's a good thing. If Dalip cries, she can't think. His distress cuts into her like a saw.

"Eat something," Mangla begs. "You haven't eaten since yesterday. At least drink a little buttermilk. I made it the way you like, with salt and crushed mint."

Jindan is touched by Mangla's concern. But she can't. She must stay focused. She must carry out the resolution that came to her when she was sent away from the Sarkar's chamber.

In her bedroom, she takes her thick braid and knots it to one of the bars of the window. This way, if she nods off she'll be jerked awake. Her plan is to stand at the window all night, facing the samadhi of Jhingar Shah. He was a great saint, the protector of the qila. His spirit still resides in his tomb. When Dalip had the bloody flux, she fasted and prayed there for twenty-four hours, and the next morning her baby opened his eyes and smiled at her.

She'll beg the saint for his blessing all night. Tomorrow, the Sarkar will be better.

She tightens the knot to make sure it won't come loose. She faces the samadhi and clasps her hands so hard the skin turns white. She feels the prayer pulsing in her belly.

If Jindan wants something badly enough, she can make it happen. She believes this completely. Isn't every major event in her life, all twenty-one years of it, proof of this?

How else could she, a girl from a no-name family on the outskirts of a small town, end up in Lahore, city of emperors? How else could she possess a haveli in the heart of this fortress textured by centuries of history? How else could she, the daughter of a dog trainer, become the Sarkar's favorite queen? How else could she give him what many of his wives, though they were married to him in his prime, failed to produce: a son to delight his old age?

She is about to learn how wrong she is.

I

Girl

1826–1834

I

Guavas

I'M DREAMING OF MOUNTAINS, ICY and terrifying, when a surreptitious sound wakes me. It's very early, the sun barely risen. I sit up cautiously on the frayed charpai I share with my mother and my older sister, Balbir. I must not disturb them. Once they're up, the morning will no longer be mine.

Silence all around except for Biji's mild snores. Then I hear it again, the cautious click of a wooden door. I extricate myself from under Balbir's leg. She's a greedy bedmate, a stealer of pillows in the summer and of our shared quilt in the winter, quick to pinch me if she thinks I'm being insolent, and quicker to complain that everyone treats me better because I'm prettier.

I hurry out to the yard. The charpai where my brother Jawahar sleeps is empty. But the hanging chain-latch on the outer door still sways lazily. I rush outside without changing my night salwar-kameez. I have only two other pairs anyway, both for school. I don't bother with sandals. Where we live, on the muddy edge of Gujranwala, it doesn't matter.

My brother's off on another adventure. I'm determined to share it this time.

Jawahar's adventures mostly have to do with stealing food, because we never have enough to eat. Unlike the children of poorer families, we can't beg either. That would destroy our father's reputation as a big man. Our father, Manna Singh Aulakh, works—and lives—in the Badshahi Qila in Lahore; he's told us that Maharaja Ranjit Singh, the Sarkar himself, speaks to him every day. It wouldn't do for the townspeople to see his children begging. My mother is the hardest worker I know, a skilled embroiderer of phulkari shawls. But there are many talented women in our village and not enough business. So Jawahar steals. He usually sets his spoils next to the wood-burning chulha for Biji to find: corn from a khet, grain laid out to dry, mangoes from someone's orchard. Biji accepts them wordlessly, thankful and ashamed at the same time. Jawahar always keeps aside something for me: a juicy apricot, or a handful of sweet jamuns that turn my lips purple. We sit on the bank of the grass-choked stream that stutters along behind our hut, pretty enough but sadly devoid of fish. I listen with hushed breath as he tells me how he crept into the orchard, how he managed to outrun the guard dogs. At eleven, he's only two years older than me, but there's no one in the world I admire more. I want to be a provider like him, not just a mouth to feed.

Today, I'll prove myself.

I run down the dusty path and when it forks—cornfields to the left, orchards to the right—choose the orchards, praying to Waheguru that I have chosen correctly. Is it appropriate to pray on a thieving mission? It must be, for there's Jawahar, loping along, bony-shouldered, barefoot like me because he broke his chappal straps months ago. I catch up with him, panting.

Hearing footsteps, he whirls around, fists up. When he sees me, he scowls. "Go home, Jindan. Now."

I beg. "Please, veer. Please."

Finally he gives in, mostly because time is passing. Soon the farmers will come to water the trees, and we must get away before then. I slip my delighted hand into his. We run to the guava groves.

High in the branches, we search for the riper fruits. I'm proud of how I scrambled up the tree, keeping up with Jawahar, though in the process I ripped my salwar at the knee, which is bound to earn me a beating from Biji. There are fewer guavas than I'd hoped for.

"Not the season yet," Jawahar explains, "but later you won't be able to get into the grove because the farmer will hire guards."

I bite into a fruit that's green and tart. I know I'll get the runs if I eat too many, but I'm so hungry. Jawahar's deft fingers seek out the best guavas. He drops them into his jute bag. He gives me a couple to tie into the corner of my kameez. The bag is getting respectably full. He whispers that he might be able to trade with a neighbor who's not too finicky about where things come from: a handful of guavas for a bowl of wheat. Then he stiffens. There's a green turban in the distance.

"The owner," Jawahar whispers. "Quick! Jump!"

He's down already, ready to run. But the ground looks so far.

"Come on, Jindan."

Panic freezes me. The turban bobs, closer now. I'm crying. We'll get caught because of me.

"Do what you did when you went up, only backward." His voice is calm and patient. "One foot at a time. I know you can do it."

I start down, still sobbing. But I'm too slow.

Jawahar says, "I'm going to distract him. You take the bag and run. Go by the river path. The grasses will hide you. Put the bag in our special place behind the broken kiln. Don't tell Biji anything."

He dances away from the tree, shouting derisively while holding up two guavas. The man bellows and chases after him. He's caught the farmer's attention. I slide to the ground. My knee is skinned; my salwar rips further. But I have the bag of guavas. I run and pray. *Waheguru, protect my brother.*

At home, I lie heroically to Biji. Sometimes it's better for mothers to not know the truth.

"I was at the river, trying to catch a fish. I lost track of time. No, I don't know where Jawahar has gone."

Biji twists my ear but not too hard, because she hasn't seen the torn salwar yet. Hurriedly, I wash with the leftover water at the bottom of the bucket and change into my school salwar-kameez, a too-large hand-me-down from Balbir, discolored from many washings. I don't want to be late for school which, unlike my siblings, I love. I feel lucky that Biji gave into my entreaties and let me study. Most of the families here don't believe in educating their girls. I drink the watery lassi Biji has saved from last night and pick up my slate and chalk.

Someone's banging on the door. It's green turban, dragging Jawahar by a thin arm. My brother's nose is bloody and one eye is swollen shut.

I didn't pray hard enough.

Green turban describes the thievery with dramatic gestures. Listening to him, you'd think we'd stolen a mountain of guavas. He tells Biji there was someone else with the boy, but he hasn't been able to get that information out of him. The boy wouldn't even tell him his name, but luckily one of the farmhands recognized him. He glares at all of us. "If I wasn't such a kind man, I'd have taken this thieving bastard to the village sarpanch."

Balbir, who's timid and law-abiding, starts to sniffle. I join her because it's a good strategy, but I wish I could run a kirpan through the man's fat gut instead.

When he kicks Jawahar, though, I can't control myself. I run at him and butt him hard with my head, yelling at him to leave my brother alone. Everyone is shouting now, Biji saying *get back here*, Jawahar saying *stop*. I kick at the man's shins and pull at his kurta, trying to tear it, but the cotton is too thick. He gives me a hard slap that lands me on the ground.

"Crazy bitch," he snarls. And to Biji: "A fine way you've brought up your children! Even the girl's no better than a wildcat."

Biji's face grows dark. She grabs my arm and twists it hard. But

I don't care. Jawahar has crawled under the charpai. I've saved him, at least for the moment.

Green turban shakes his fist and shouts some more insults in which he generously includes our entire ancestry. Finally, having run out of breath, he turns to leave. At the door, he tells Biji, "You'd better control your children, woman. Next time I'm going to the panchayat. I'll make sure the boy ends up in the jailkhana."

After green turban leaves, Biji slaps me hard. "Because of you, I have to hear all these gaalis from a stranger!"

Jawahar crawls out from under the charpai. "Don't punish her for my fault," he croaks.

Biji picks up a piece of firewood. "Your fault! You're right about that, kambakht! Shaming the family like this. I'll show you today."

He crouches, resigned, shielding his head as she brings the firewood down on his back. "Tell me who was with you! Which no-good loafer are you running around with? Tell me!" She hits him again. We're all crying now, Biji loudest of all. "Your father's bound to hear of this, and then what will I do?"

But I suspect a deeper reason for Biji's grief. Sure enough, she drops the firewood and crumples to the ground, sobbing. "What kind of mother am I that I can't even feed my children?"

Jawahar raises his face a little. With his good eye, he winks at me. *Smart girl. I'm proud of you.* I know that when all this is over, we'll slip away to the old kiln. He'll give me the ripest guava from the bag and call me a clever girl, and we'll laugh over the day's adventures. At night, after Biji and Balbir have gone to sleep, he'll repair my salwar because he knows how to do everything. Maybe I'll tell him about my strange mountain dream.

I'm going to remember this moment forever, and my brother's bruised, smiling face, which I love so much that it feels like someone is wringing my heart like Biji does with our laundry.

The two of us, Jawahar, against the world.

2

Manna

Manna Singh. Somehow I can't think of him as *Father.* Perhaps because he's rarely with us. He descends upon our household with a storm's whimsy, sending no notice of his coming. "Only fools waste money on messengers," he claims. But I think his real motive is to catch us off guard.

Today, loud and jovial, he flings open the courtyard door. "Hello, my bride, I'm starving! What's there to eat? Makki ki roti and saag, I hope, because no one in Lahore makes them like you."

Biji's eyes flash. She knows him too well to be taken in by his easy charm, but she speaks politely. "The grain pots are empty. You didn't send any money last month."

I marvel at how deftly she hides resentment—something I'm no good at. Biji knows that if she angers Manna, she'll get nothing out of him. He'll shout and throw things, then go and stay with his cousin, who lives in the heart of Gujranwala. They'll go carousing. Next morning, he'll stomp back to Lahore with an aching head and empty pockets.

Biji's strategy works.

"I must have forgotten," Manna says, compunction on his face. "Hard to keep track of everything when one has as many responsibilities as I do. The Sarkar counts on me for advice, you know." He scrabbles in his waistband and takes out a fistful of coins. He can be generous when the mood strikes him. He beckons to Jawahar, standing watchful by the door. We all know to be watchful when Manna is around because his laughter can suddenly become a scowl or a slap. "Here, boy, get your mother whatever she needs from the market. And tell the butcher I want goat meat tomorrow. Enough for twelve people. We'll have a feast!"

Jawahar exchanges a quick glance with Biji before he sprints away. He'll bargain hard and save as much of the money as he can. We'll hide it for leaner times.

AFTER LUNCH, MANNA RELAXES on the charpai. I've brought him all the pillows in the house. He leans on them regally and orders us to line up in front of him. He tells Balbir she's growing too fast; he's not yet ready for the expense of a daughter's wedding. Balbir hunches her shoulders to make herself smaller and stares at her feet.

"For heaven's sake!" Manna barks. "Stand up straight. I'll have even more trouble marrying off a hunchback. And you, boy, how are you doing in school?"

"Excellently," Jawahar replies, looking Manna in the eye. "Teacher ji says I have a good head for numbers."

I admire how skillfully he lies. In reality, he skips school often. I do his homework and go over his books with him before examinations. Still, last year he almost failed.

"Good, good," Manna booms. "A skill with numbers is always useful. I'll take you to Lahore one of these days. Find you a job at the palace. The Sarkar won't refuse me."

Later that night, when the rest of the household has fallen asleep, I make my way over to Jawahar, who is lying on the floor because Manna has taken his charpai.

"Will he really take you to the palace?" I want what's best for Jawahar, but I can't imagine life without him.

Jawahar shrugs. "Who knows? Half the things he says, he never does."

But I hear the longing in his voice.

TODAY, AFTER LUNCH, MANNA focuses on me. "And how's my little girl?"

"I'm well, Father," I answer, flushing with pleasure at the attention. "I've learned the times table until twelve. I've read everything in my textbook even though it's only the middle of the year. Bhai Sahib says my handwriting is the best among all his students. I can recite by heart from the Gurbani. Would you like to listen?"

"Yes, yes, why not!" Manna smiles indulgently as he settles into the pillows.

I kneel and close my eyes to create a mood of reverence. The hard ground hurts my knees, but no matter. I love the ancient words. Singing them is almost like flying. *By His Command, souls come into being; by His Command, glory and greatness are obtained. By His Command, some are high and some are low; by His Command, pain and pleasure are obtained.*

Someone taps my shoulder. Jawahar.

"You can stop now."

I open my eyes. Manna is snoring; his mouth hangs open. *Waheguru, is it very wicked of me to hope a bug flies into it?*

IN THE EVENING, THERE'S a feast. We own few vessels, so Biji sends me to borrow pots and thalis from the wives of the men who have been invited. She cooks all day until her face is red from the heat of the chulha. Karhi and rice, cauliflower, chhole, goat curry. Balbir is a better cook, so she rolls out parathas. I'm stronger, so I fetch water and firewood. Jawahar is dispatched to the sweet shop for jalebis.

"Don't let them slip you stale ones," Manna warns as he sips his sharbat. "Make sure they're fried in front of your eyes."

Manna's friends bring bamboo modhas to sit on and toddy to drink. Biji piles the platters with food, and we carry them to the guests. My mouth waters. Why must we wait until the men are done? I wolf down a jalebi when no one's looking and lick the syrup from my fingers.

After dinner the men crowd around Manna, asking about the big city and his illustrious employer. I take my time clearing away the thalis. I, too, want to hear the tales of the Sarkar. He was born here, in Gujranwala, to the rich and powerful Sukerchakia clan and, even as a child, moved in circles far removed from us. None of us have ever actually seen him. Still, we think of him proprietorially as our own.

"Does he live in that big qila in Lahore, which people say is hundreds of years old?"

Manna nods. "He does indeed, when he's not on the battlefield, routing those Afghan dogs. The Badhshahi Qila is his favorite among his many fortresses. It's so big, you could fit this entire village inside it three times over. Yes, I live there, too. Do you know how much it cost to build just the Naulakha pavilion, with its winged roof? Nine lakh! Not silver, idiot! Gold pieces. Ashrafis. No, our Sarkar didn't build it. He has too much sense to waste money like that. He snatched it from the Afghans, just like he snatched the Koh-i-Noor. You've never heard of the Koh-i-Noor? Why, it's the world's largest diamond, that's why it's called Mountain of Light. As big as my two fists put together. If it's in a dark room at midnight, you won't need lanterns—that's how powerfully it shines. The Afghan king used to wear it in his crown, but our Sarkar, he's a good Sikh, humble. He wears a turban. He's put the Koh-i-Noor on an armband and wears it only when he has foreign visitors, to show them the might of Punjab."

In the firelight, I see a rare awe on Manna's face as he lists the Sarkar's other magnificences: the fair-skinned dancing girls from the hills of Kashmir who perform all night for him in the Red Pavilion; his ghorcharhas, a cavalry made up of the bravest young men in all of Punjab, unbeaten in battle; kennels full of the fiercest hunting dogs; enclosures for the royal elephants; and stable upon stable of pedigreed horses, culled from several countries. The Sarkar loves his horses the most. More than his wives, even. He has a thousand horses right in the qila, and more outside. The most famous of them is Laila.

"I'll need a whole month to tell you the marvels of Laila and how the Sarkar got her," Manna says. "It cost him sixty lakh rupaiyas and a war. In the summer, Laila stays in Hazoori Bagh, where it's cool. She has a room of her own right next to the Sarkar's bedchamber . . ."

Is all this real, or is it spun out of Manna's longing to impress his listeners? In any case, I'll daydream about it for days to come. For now I stand and listen, my arms loaded with a stack of forgotten dinner dishes. If only I could see all these magical things, even just once.

One of Manna's friends who has drunk too much toddy remarks, "Your kudi here, what is she now? Twelve? Thirteen? She's becoming real sohni. I bet in a couple of years she'll be as pretty as any of the dancers in the Sarkar's court."

I turn away, blushing. An annoyed Manna orders me to get back to Biji. He chides the man, sternly proclaiming that the women of his household are not to be spoken of in the same breath as those Kanjaris.

But the next day, as I wash the dishes, or feed the goat, or do my schoolwork, or play hopscotch with Balbir, I feel Manna watching me. When I serve him dinner, he asks me to hold out my hands. He turns over my palms and examines them with displeased eyes. "Keep Jindan out of the sun," he tells Biji. "I don't want her getting dark. And no more scrubbing pots. It's making her hands rough, like a peasant's."

"And who will help me?" Biji demands, no longer bothering to hide her annoyance. She's upset because when, earlier in the day, she had asked him for rent money, Manna said he didn't have anything more to give her. "Why did you throw a feast, then?" she cried. But Manna merely turned away from her with a grimace of pain, massaging his aching head.

"If the girl doesn't learn housework," she continues, "who will choose her to be their daughter-in-law?"

"My Jindan? Why, anyone would be delighted to bring such a pretty girl into their family." Manna's eyes crinkle merrily as he smiles at me. "Would you like to go to Lahore sometime, beeba? Would you like to see the great palace where I live?"

"Me?"

"Yes, you!"

Waheguru, is he teasing me—because he does that sometimes—or does he really mean it?

There's a sudden flash of scarlet in the night sky. Is it the last of the sunset? A flock of foreign birds? A fire? I take it to be a sign. But of what?

In the corner of the yard, Biji, about to serve dinner to us children, becomes still as stone.

"Well? What do you say?" Manna asks.

I don't trust myself to speak. I nod vehemently.

Manna grins. His teeth are straight and white, rare in a man who grew up poor. "I'll take you soon if you're a good girl."

"And Jawahar? He'll come, too, right?"

"Yes, yes. Now go eat your dinner."

I'm not sure Manna heard me. His narrowed eyes pass through me as though he's seeing the future. Inside his head, I can sense strategies swarming like giant bees.

Raising his voice, Manna tells Biji, "Woman, make sure you give our Jindan a piece of mutton. I'm stepping out for a little while."

He's going to the village square, where his friends have gathered to play cards. He won't be back for a long time.

There are only two pieces of mutton left in the bowl, neither of them large. Biji hesitates over them.

"Why should she always get the best things?" Balbir hisses. "All of you like her better. It's not fair."

I'm suddenly tired. "Let her have the mutton," I say. I take my thali to the other end of the yard and lower myself to the ground. I dip my roti in the dal, which is cold and lumpy by now. After a few minutes, Jawahar comes and sits by me. He tears his piece of mutton in two and gives me the bigger part, the one with the bone, because I love to suck on marrow. Together, we sit and eat, chewing slowly to make the food last longer.

3

Lahore

I'M NO LONGER GOING TO school. It's the greatest tragedy, so far, of my life, but no one understands this. After all, didn't Balbir stop attending last year, telling Biji she'd had enough of books? Hadn't the other girls in my year dropped out, one by one? Several of them were betrothed now. Jawahar, too, had stopped going to class and begun hanging around the tea shops instead, though Biji doesn't know it.

Perhaps because Jawahar was no longer around, the boys at school started paying too much attention to me. Though we were in different rooms during classes, they tried to talk to me afterward, to walk me home. When I refused, they started following me, singing lewd songs. I didn't tell Jawahar. I didn't want him to get into a fight. I collected rocks in my school bag and one day, when their catcalls made me lose my temper, I threw them at the boys. By luck—good or bad, I wasn't sure which—I hit the leader's head. There was blood, a lot of shouting. I ran home while his friends milled about him.

After that, I knew I couldn't go back to school. When I told Jawahar, he slapped his thighs and snorted with laughter. *I wish I could have seen it!* He didn't understand how this abrupt end to my education broke my heart. But he did carry a letter to Bhai Sahib where I explained what had happened.

Bhai Sahib was distressed because I'd been his best student. It was why he'd kept me in the school this last year, even though I couldn't pay the fees. But he agreed that I needed to drop out. He promised to send me lessons through Jawahar. We knew he couldn't come to my house. With two young girls and no male head-of-the-household, there would be gossip.

But Jawahar soon grew tired of trudging back and forth from Bhai Sahib's home. He went once in two weeks, then once a month, and then stopped altogether. I was devastated, but what could I do? Everyone around me felt I'd had more education than was good for me. Wasn't I fifteen already? Even Biji said that too much book-learning made a girl uppity.

Now I spend my time helping Biji with phulkari work. People like my polite manners and nimble fingers and hire me to make their wedding dupattas. I bring in some money for the family this way. But each day I sense my world shrinking further.

AFTER BEING AWAY FOR almost a year, Manna shows up one day—thinner, with a sharp new crease between his brows. He hands Biji a small bag of coins and tells her there isn't any more; his eyes shift away from her consternation. He sits heavily on the charpai. I bring him water, but he drinks only a little and then stares into the tumbler. In the evening, after dinner, instead of going down to the village square, he curls up on the charpai and gazes into the flames of the cook fire until Biji comes over to check if he has a fever.

He doesn't, but something is clearly wrong.

In the morning, he beckons me to sit by him. "And how is my sweet girl?" he says with forced joviality. "What are you learning in school?"

"I'm not going to school anymore," I reply.

"Good, good. No point wasting time and money on things you have no use for."

I wonder what he'd do if I tell him why I dropped out and how I feel about it. But he's already off on another subject.

"You're looking good, beti, though you're still too thin. Doesn't your mother feed you!" He smiles to indicate that it's a joke.

Biji bangs the pots she's washing. "I'd feed her more if you sent more money. I can't cook special things just for her and leave the others to watch while she eats. She wouldn't do it, anyway. She's not that kind of girl."

Manna looks injured. "I send as much as I can. Life in the capital is expensive—but how would you understand that? Very well, I'll take Jindan back to Lahore with me when I leave. You'll have one less mouth to feed."

My heart lurches—part excitement, part surprise. "Will Jawahar go with me?"

"Sure!" Manna says airily. "Now, is anyone going to give me nashta, or should I just starve?"

Biji sets down rotis and alu sabzi in front of him. "Take Balbir, too. She's never been outside this town. A trip will do her good."

Manna pats Biji's cheek; he can be charming when he wants. "I can't leave you all alone here, can I, with no one to help?"

Inside the hut, I find Balbir sprawled facedown on the bed, crying. I touch her shoulder, feeling sorry. "I'll bring you a gift."

Balbir flings my hand off. "He's always liked you better," she spits, "just because you're pretty."

Anger takes over my mouth. "Is it my fault that you're not?"

Then I'm ashamed. *Waheguru, what kind of girl am I?*

In the morning, Manna says, "It's too expensive to take two children to Lahore. I'm only taking Jindan."

Biji is upset—but it's more than that. There's something new in her face. Fear. She pleads and then shouts, but Manna is adamant.

Biji holds me tight. "Take Jawahar instead, then."

Manna yanks at my arm. "Come on, bitiya, the bullock cart for the city will leave soon."

I look at my brother, his eyes like a kicked dog's. "I'm not going."

"What's that, girl?" Manna bellows.

My stomach cramps from dread. Manna has an iron hand, and he doesn't hesitate to use it when he loses his temper. Still I say, "If you don't take Jawahar, I'm not going."

He boxes my ears hard. "Disobedient ungrateful badtameez child! You *will* come with me."

The pain makes me gasp, but I refuse to cry. Biji curses and tries to pull me away. Jawahar grabs Manna's arm, begging him to stop. Manna throws him off, grabs my shoulders and shakes me. Blurry lights dance in my eyes. I make my body go slack and drop to the ground. "You'll have to drag me to Lahore, every step."

Manna draws back his foot, his face full of fury. He plans to kick me in the stomach. He did it to Jawahar once.

"Stop!" Biji cries. "She's a woman now. You'll hurt her childbearing parts."

Suddenly Manna laughs.

"You've got spirit, girl—I'll give you that. You're like me that way. Ah well, maybe it'll come in handy sometime. Go on then, both of you. Grab your things. Thanks to all this drama, we'll have to run all the way to the bazaar."

Along the bumpy road to Lahore, Jawahar and I are jostled in the back of the buffalo cart. Manna has negotiated a cheaper fare by squeezing us in among baskets of jackfruit. He himself is up front, conversing with the driver, affable as he always is with outsiders.

Jawahar doesn't say anything. But when no one's looking, he puts an arm around my shoulder and gives me a hug.

WHEN WE REACH LAHORE after hours of bone-rattling travel, Manna puts on a fancy turban and combs his beard. He walks differently here, holding himself tall; he is no longer the lout who farted and belched with abandon and spat wherever he wanted in our courtyard.

We enter the walled city late in the day, through a massive stone gate grander than anything I've seen.

"The Masti Darwaza," Manna says. "Lahore has twelve gates like this, all hundreds of years old. See the soldiers on the ramparts, so fine in their yellow jackets? See their toradar guns? The Sarkar gives arms to every man when he enters his service. That's why this is the safest city in the country. I almost joined the army when I first came here."

I hear him sigh, a rueful sound. For a moment I see the young man he was, arriving in the capital with his head full of dreams.

We walk through Moti Bazaar, down a narrow street flanked by buildings with friezed balconies and ground floors crowded with shops. People jostle each other, some wearing kurta pajamas, turbans and fez caps. A few are red-faced and dressed in vilayati pants and coats.

"French soldiers," Manna explains. "And these, short and slant-eyed, are Gurkhas from the mountains. All are welcome in the Sarkar's army, except for the British, whom he doesn't trust. And rightly so, I say."

Lahore makes me realize how little I've seen of life. I gawk at the wares in the shops. Elegant veils and kameezes in brilliant colors, embroidered jutis that I covet because my sandals, which I've outgrown, hurt my feet. Shawls, quilts, bolts of satin, wall hangings, lace covers, pillows like floating clouds, jewelry, spices, perfumes, goblets set with glittering stones, the slender, gleaming stems of hookahs, carpets into which my feet would probably sink all the way to my ankles if I were allowed to step on their silkiness. And food. Heaps of samosas and bhaturas, pots bubbling with alu sabzi and spicy chickpeas, multicolored sweetmeats arranged on platters so big I could curl up and sleep on them, kebabs roasting on skewers over fire pits. Saliva floods my mouth. I want to tell Manna how hungry I am, but I've used up all my favors by being so stubborn this morning.

I don't care. I'd do it again for Jawahar. I slip my hand into my brother's, and together we stare at this magical city filled with riches beyond our grasp.

A MUSTACHIOED HORSEMAN DRESSED in bright blue silks comes galloping around a corner and almost runs me over.

"Are you blind, girl?" he yells. "Don't you know to get out of the way? Allah! These bewakoof village bumpkins!"

Jawahar jumps back, startled, but I'm angry more than anything else.

"You're the bewakoof!" I shout, shaking my fist at the disappearing horseman. "Hurtling down the street like that, not caring who you might trample."

"Shut your mouth," Manna admonishes. "Talk like that'll get you in trouble here." But he isn't really angry. Lahore has put him in a happy mood. "Come, I will buy you biriyani."

I stand beside Jawahar outside a tiny stall, scooping steamy, spicy rice and pieces of meat from a leaf bowl with my fingers, copying Manna carefully because I don't want to shame him. The meat is so tender it dissolves in my mouth. It is the tastiest thing I've ever eaten. I want to ask Jawahar if he agrees, but his full attention is on his food. His jaws move with methodical efficiency. His eyes are glazed with pleasure. It would be blasphemy to disturb him.

Manna eats with easy elegance, making sure not to soil his beard, which looks more flowing and lustrous than it did back home. He exchanges pleasantries with the cook, who seems to know him well.

"You've brought your beta–beti from the village, I see."

"Yes. Time they experienced a bit of the world."

"Well, our beautiful Lahore is certainly the place for that. Will you find the boy a job here?"

"That's my plan. You know how it is. Idle hands, shaitan's tools."

"Ah yes. How about the girl?"

"Oh no, girls in our khandaan, they don't work."

The man nods his approval. "And the dogs, how are they?"

"I'll know in a while. My assistants had better have taken good care of them, or else they'll get a whipping."

"Next time around, I want to be born as those dogs. What a life!"

I'm astonished to learn that my father owns dogs who live so enviously well. And has assistants who can be whipped. In the multitude of stories he has recounted about his life in Lahore, he has never mentioned them. But why not?

I exchange a glance with Jawahar, who looks concerned.

Manna dips a ladle into a fat-bellied matka that sits on the street corner and pours out cool water for Jawahar and me to drink, and wash our hands. In Lahore, he seems kinder than in Gujranwala.

"Our Sarkar put these jars on every street. He wanted to make sure no one in his city goes thirsty."

I drink in grateful gulps. This Sarkar sounds like the perfect king.

"If only they were filled with wine instead of water!" Manna laughs, then waits until we chime in.

We walk because Manna says we ate too much and now there's no money for a cart. My bundle grows heavier by the moment. My sandal straps cut cruelly into my feet. But I'm too fascinated to care. The city is like a dream in which anyone could wander for a hundred years, and Manna is an enthusiastic guide.

"This is the Baroodkhana Masjid—you think it's a mosque, but it's really an armory. Lahore's like that—nothing in this city is what it seems. Behind these walls are the Shalimar Gardens, four hundred fountains and one lakh flowers. The common people aren't allowed inside, but I'll take you two one day."

I believe him, though I know I shouldn't.

"Those buildings painted in jewel hues, with hanging balconies and iron-spiked walls? Those are the havelis of the courtiers. That big one there, with the decorated friezes and the grand, carved roof, belongs to Wazir Dhian Singh, the most powerful man in the kingdom—after the Sarkar, of course. Look, the Sheranwala Darwaza! The live lions you see pacing on either side are to remind all who enter the city that our Sarkar is Sher-e-Punjab."

A fort looms over us, pink in the last of the evening light. Massive, gorgeous, overwhelming. Lit by hundreds of diyas, glimmering like heaven. A slender minaret, crowned with the moon, rises up. It makes my heart ache though I cannot explain why.

"The Badshahi Qila," Manna says.

"Where you live?" Jawahar asks, excited.

Manna nods. He's oddly quiet.

In front of us is a gate with stairs so wide that had someone described them to me, I'd have thought he was lying.

"The Hathi-Paer Darwaza," Manna says.

"Why's it so huge?"

Manna scowls at my ignorance. "On feast days, the royalty ride on elephants through this gate."

I imagine elephants painted with kumkum and covered in silks moving majestically down the stairs, accompanied by drummers and flower girls. Cheers erupt from the crowds waiting outside the palace. The lead elephant carries the Sarkar. I've never seen a picture of him, so I create one: tall and muscular, a swirling black mustache, a glittering gold-embroidered turban, a naked sword raised high above his head . . . No, this is a peaceful procession; I replace the sword with a jeweled scepter.

"Enough gawking. We have to get through the side door before they close the qila for the night."

Still in a trance, I follow. Uniformed men with severe beards and tall turbans guard the entrance, rifles at the ready. They scowl, pointing to Jawahar and me. Manna bows ingratiatingly, explaining. Finally, we are allowed to pass.

To one side, I notice an enormous garden full of red blooms. A sweet unfamiliar scent assails me. I risk Manna's irritation and ask the name of the flowers.

"Roses. Our Sarkar loves them, just like the Mughal emperors did. Enough questions now!"

Why is Manna so annoyed? I glance at Jawahar. He's frowning, which worries me.

Stately buildings loom in front of us. Manna recites their names, but hurriedly. The triple-domed Pearl mosque. The Diwan-i-Aam, where the Sarkar meets with commoners. The Diwan-i-Khas, where no commoners are permitted. The Sheesh Mahal, decorated with countless crystals. The zenana with covered-up windows, where queens and concubines live.

I'm confused by this rapid litany. No matter. It's not like I'll ever visit any of them.

We pass beyond the buildings to a large grassy area, lit only by open fires flickering along the edges. Here's an odor I know well: dung. Long lines of stables, a hathikhana filled with the soft snuffles of elephants. Above them, quarters for the grooms and mahouts.

Where are we going?

At the far edge of the animal compound, we turn into an alleyway echoing with frenzied barking. The dogs throw themselves so hard against their enclosures that the wooden walls shudder. They must be large and very strong. I take a step back, but Manna gives a sharp whistle and the dogs fall silent.

We stop outside a low-roofed hut, decrepit, soot-blackened, even smaller than our house in Gujranwala. This is where he lives?

Now I understand why he's been irritable. The fantasy he's created for us all these years is about to crumble.

Manna throws open the door. A rancid odor greets us.

"Home at last," he says, with a grin that's more of a grimace.

4

Hovel

I LIE ON THE FLOOR OF an alcove used to store odds and ends, on a thin mat that does little to cushion the uneven stones digging into my back. In the dark, Jawahar is an angry shape nearby, his head covered with a blanket in spite of the heat because Manna hinted at the presence of cockroaches. Manna left as soon as he'd shown us the basics: the room where he slept on the only cot, the outhouse and the cooking area in the yard. He said he needed to check on the dogs.

"He's probably with the other animal trainers, getting drunk," Jawahar spits from underneath the blanket. "I bet that's where his salary goes. That's why he lives in this shithole. All his big talk for years about how he's the Sarkar's personal friend, when he's nothing but a cleaner of dog turd. We were better off in the village. At least I had a cot to sleep on and fresh air to breathe."

I'm unwilling to write Lahore off so quickly. Yes, Manna's lies have come as a shock. But I sense mysteries all around us. Just going to the well near the stables and fetching water had been an adventure. Walking through the dark filled with whickers and intermittent trumpeting. Tomorrow I plan to visit the horses. Maybe the grooms will let me pet one of them. It'll be something to remember: I touched a horse belonging to the Sarkar.

I WAKE TO MANNA'S whistling. He's in a sunny mood. He won last night at cards, he tells us. Before he goes off to the kennels, he tosses a few coins to Jawahar. He tells him where the market is and what to buy.

"Don't let them cheat you now. Tell them whose son you are."

"Does he really think the shopkeepers care about a dog trainer?" Jawahar scoffs after Manna leaves. I want to go with him, but he says, "Let me check things out first."

I'm left to sweep and mop, roll up the sacking that covers the narrow window so a breeze can venture in, and pace the hut, worrying, until he returns. In the distance, the harsh, questioning cry of the peacocks sounds a warning: *Kya, kya, kya?*

But Jawahar returns sweaty and victorious, lugging sacks and bundles, balancing a watermelon on his head. In a good mood now, he describes how huge the bazaar is, filled with foods he's never seen. He breaks a piece off a big golden-brown tile of jaggery for me; he knows I love sweets. We submerge the watermelon in a bucket of water so it will be cool by mealtime. Jawahar lights the chulha in the backyard and helps me chop vegetables—tasks he'd have disdained as women's work back in the village.

We put together a meal that would have made Biji proud. Manna nods his satisfaction as he eats the karhi-chawal, the alu sabzi. He pronounces the watermelon to be sweet and juicy and commends Jawahar's keen eye. But when I ask if we might go and see the animals, he shakes his head.

"A rowdy, rascally lot, those grooms. Not proper for you to be anywhere near them. I don't want them making lewd comments about you. Or Jawahar picking up their bad habits. You're not to step out of the yard when I'm gone, either of you. Not even to get water. If anyone comes by, bar the door." He glares. "If I find out you've disobeyed me, I'll give you both a beating you'll remember."

Having made his point, Manna becomes cheerful. He tells us about the big hunt that's happening in a couple of weeks. Three major clans of Punjab are going to take part in it. The Sarkar's animals must perform better than theirs. The dogs need to be trained hard.

"I'll be late coming back. I'll eat with the other trainers. Finish your dinner quickly and go to sleep. Wish I could lie around the house all day like you two! Be sure to put out the lamp as soon as you've eaten. Oil doesn't fall from the sky like rain."

Once Manna has gone, Jawahar mimics him. "*If I find out you've disobeyed me* . . . Well, he won't. I'm off to explore the city."

I grab his arm. I refuse to miss out on another adventure. "I'm coming with you."

Jawahar shakes his head. "It's easy for a boy to slip away—there are plenty of them working around the qila. I'll blend in. But everyone will notice a girl."

"They'd think nothing of two boys, though," I say.

Jawahar understands right away. A grin breaks over his face. "Hurry, then. It's a good thing you're still so skinny. Look, I saved some coins from what Manna gave me. I'll buy you a treat."

I go into the alcove, wrap a dupatta tightly around my chest and put on a kurta-pajama that Jawahar has almost outgrown. He pulls my hair into a topknot, ties a turban over it, and pronounces that I make a fine boy. No one questions us as we slip out of the qila.

The hours pass in a blur of delight. Jawahar had made enquiries at the bazaar earlier. Now he takes me to one sight after another: the maidan where trainers bring their performing monkeys, the glittering jewelry shops at Anarkali Bazaar, the huge Zam-Zammeh cannon, gleaming like new though it has been standing in the open for years. The vendor from whom we buy jalebis tells us, "Even the British laats come all the way to see it. The Afghan king had it designed specially to battle us Punjabis. He attacked us with it, but our Sarkar defeated him like this." He snaps his fingers.

Our Sarkar, I think with pride as I bite into the jalebi. I imagine him twirling his glossy black mustache as he plans battle strategies.

The place that remains in my heart is the Gurdwara Lal Khoohi, where, a long time ago, Guru Arjan Dev was killed by Jahangir's henchmen. The caretaker tells us the story: "They tortured the Guru by pouring burning sand over him. But he refused to give up his Sikh faith and become a Musalman. He said, I have made this body and mind a sacrifice to my Lord. I have shaken off the fear of death. If you sit beside the well at midnight, you'll hear the Guru praying with his last breath for his people."

To love something—or someone—so much that you would willingly sacrifice yourself. I want to be brave like that.

Reentering the qila, I'm afraid someone will stop us, but the gatekeepers pay us no attention. Jubilant, we plan another excursion for tomorrow afternoon.

"BOY!" MANNA SHOUTS FROM the door when he comes home for lunch the next day. "Waheguru ji di kripa, I found you a job." He pauses to be thanked, then cuffs Jawahar on the ear when he stares back sullenly—but not too hard because he's in a good mood.

The job is at a blacksmith's shop not far from the fort. They do everything: fashion tools, shoe horses, repair swords, sharpen those newfangled bayonets that the army has started using. Manna will take Jawahar there as soon as they've eaten—no point putting off a good thing. The blacksmith, Suleiman, is a friend of Manna's. Wasn't it a stroke of luck that Manna ran into him when he came to the qila to shoe one of the Sarkar's favorite horses?

"Suleiman's strict but fair. He'll treat you well. You'll learn a good trade. War or peace, there's always work for a blacksmith. He'll give me your salary, as is right, but I'll give you a few coins each week to spend as you like."

When they leave, Manna locks the door of the hovel from the outside. "This'll keep you safe. You can use the indoor chulha to make dinner."

I protest, banging on the door, but he ignores me.

That night, Jawahar and I whisper bitterly.

"I'm nothing but a slave, making money for him. Look at the blisters on my palm just from this afternoon's shift."

"Me, I'm a maidservant and a prisoner."

"He lied about Lahore, what our life here would be like."

"You were right. He can't be trusted. Let's run away, veer."

"We'll do it tomorrow morning. I'll pretend I'm going to work. As soon as Manna leaves for the kennels, I'll hurry back. You be ready. I'll break the lock with a stone. I still have a few coins left. They'll get us part way to Gujranwala. After that, we'll walk."

But Manna is shrewder than we think. The next morning he puts an arm around Jawahar's bony shoulders and declares he'll walk him to work. He waves away protests. "Don't want you to get lost, beta. Jindan, pack him some food so the poor boy doesn't have to come all the way home for lunch."

Our canny father does this for the rest of the week. By then, things have begun to change.

When I ask Jawahar how soon we can leave, he hesitates. "Maybe we should stay for a few more weeks."

"What are you saying, veer?"

A little guiltily, he confesses that his job isn't as bad as he imagined. He's learning a lot. The older boys in the shop are showing him how to heat the forge correctly, how to shape different metals. They've offered to take him around Lahore on their next day off, which is coming up in a week. He especially likes Suleiman, a good-natured man with a belly-shaking laugh, who is kind to his workers. There's always tea by the forge, and often snacks. Yesterday Suleiman got a big basket of pakoras and they all ate it together.

I'm happy for Jawahar, but a part of me feels betrayed.

The next week, Jawahar tells me that Suleiman has had a talk with Manna about the importance of allowing young men some freedom. He's giving a third of Jawahar's salary directly to him.

"Here." He hands me a package. I open it and find a pair of jutis, the soft red leather stamped with a flowery design and decorated with beads.

I force myself to smile because he must have spent most of his earnings on the gift. At another time, I would have been whirling around the room, holding them aloft. Now I want to weep. There's no occasion in this prison for me to wear them. I put them away.

THE WEEKS CRAWL ALONG. With the hunt getting closer, Manna is harried and tight-lipped. He leaves home at sunrise—I pack lunch for him, too—and comes back only after dark. When I beg him not to lock me in, he glares. "I have a plan for you, too. I'll tell you soon. But don't add to my worries right now. Any day the Sarkar will come by to check on the dogs' progress, and I have to be ready. He's invited a group of British laats to the hunt. Our dogs must outshine theirs!"

Our simple meal takes only an hour to prepare; the rest of my day stretches ahead, endless. I feel Biji's absence like a wound in my heart. How enraged she'd be if she knew how Manna was treating me. There's nothing to read here, not even an almanac. Nothing to look at through the narrow window because no one comes to this end of the gali. I wish I'd brought my Sunder Gutka so I could at least read the prayers in it—but how could I have known that my life in Lahore would be like this? I pace until I wear a path down the middle of the hut. I grasp like a drowning person at the occasional noise. Manna has been using the field next to the house to train the dogs. I hear him yelling at the assistants, mostly young boys, sometimes hitting them. But he's always good to the dogs—I have to give him that.

When Manna talks to the dogs, there's a special fondness in his voice. Even when he scolds them, there's affection. When they perform well, he praises them in jubilant, jeweled tones he never uses toward us. *My fierce, golden boy . . . My lovely girl . . .* I press my cheek hungrily against the bars on the window. Now I know how Balbir felt.

At night, I try to talk to Jawahar about how hard my days are, but he's tired and not in the mood. Sometimes I smell toddy on his breath. I know what he's thinking. *What are you complaining about? You just lie around all day.*

Finally, I beg Manna to send me home. "Please. I miss Biji."

He smacks me on the head. "First you want to come here. Now you're sniveling to go back. Who's going to take you? Do you even know how much it costs? Am I Wazir Dhian Singh, loaded with moneybags, and one hundred servants to do my bidding? Your mother's spoiled you, that's the problem."

But perhaps he senses my desperation, because the next night, after dinner, he tousles my hair affectionately. "Be patient, bitiya. Like I said, I have a plan for you. It's just that I've been so terribly busy with this hunt. Once that's over you'll see . . ."

I lie awake in the dark, heavy with hopelessness. Male snores rise and fall around me. Tears trickle from the corners of my eyes and pool in my ears. I don't trust Manna's plans.

Please, Waheguru. Send someone to help me.

5

Horse

FROM BEHIND THE SACKING AT the window, I watch the man swing down from his horse. Slight frame, clothes simple though elegant in cut, the suspicion of a limp, a long white beard. Manna runs out, his breakfast half-eaten. He bows very low, so the man must be important. But I don't pay him much attention. I'm too busy staring at the horse.

It's the most beautiful animal I've ever seen. Tall and slim, with a sleek, glowing blackness. A proud, curved neck. A mane silky enough to rouse the envy of a queen. The two men go off, the rider calling out a quiet command to the horse, not bothering to tie it up. Perfectly trained, it doesn't move, not even to nibble at the vine spilling over a wall.

Manna and the rider are gone a long time. Surely the horse is thirsty, standing in the glaring sun? Isn't it just like men, not to think of such things! I bring out cool water in a pail, clucking as I used to do for the chickens at home, but the horse ignores me. When I come closer, it pins back its ears and paws the ground in warning.

I'm determined to make friends with it, to run my hands over that glossy mane. I remember something I'd heard in the village. I run back to our food shelf and break off a piece from the tile of jaggery. I hold it out, invitingly. The horse swivels its ears forward and allows me to approach. When I'm near enough, it takes the piece from my outstretched hand. I love its big, velvety lips on my palm. It nudges my shoulder.

I'm delighted. "You want more? I'd give you the whole piece, but I'm not sure if it's good for you. We'll ask your owner when he comes back. Meanwhile, here's some water." I bring the pail close. The horse bends its head and drinks. Greatly daring, I kiss its face and run my hands along its taut, shiny neck, telling it how beautiful it is. When it whickers, as though talking back, the ice block of depression inside me melts a little.

Suddenly, I hear yelling in the distance. "Kambakht idiot girl, what are you doing? Get away from that horse!" It is Manna. He sounds frightened. "Have you gone deaf? Can't you hear me?"

The horse is displeased by this commotion. Its ears go back. It shows the whites of its eyes. I'm a little scared. It's a huge animal. It could easily trample me. But I pat its neck, scratching along its mane, until it calms down.

The rider holds up his hand and Manna falls silent. Unhurriedly, the man walks up to the horse, who whinnies with pleasure.

"Yes, my lovely. I left you alone for a long time, didn't I? I'm sorry. I had to make sure the dogs are ready for the hunt. Anyway, it looks like you had pleasant company." He smiles at me and I see that he has kind, good-humored eyes. Eye, to be accurate; the left one is blind. On another man, it would have looked grotesque, but on him it's the mark of a warrior. His white beard flows down to his chest, over a long string of pearls. He seems a lot taller than he is, perhaps because he stands so straight. There's an aura of power around him. This is a man afraid of nothing.

Manna follows, wringing his hands. He still looks terrified. "Forgive her, janaab. She's just a stupid village girl. Doesn't know any better."

The man ignores Manna and speaks to me. "My mare doesn't take to strangers. And she never drinks water unless her groom gives it to her. What did you do?"

Now I'm scared, too. What if, in my haste to make friends, I've harmed the animal by giving it jaggery? The mare is very expensive, I can see that. *I didn't do anything*, I want to say. But the mare swishes her tail and butts her head against me trustingly, and I find it impossible to lie. I force myself to look the man in the eye.

"I gave her a lump of jaggery."

"Jaggery?"

Guiltily I explain, "They feed it to buffaloes in our village as a special treat."

"Idiot," Manna cries, slapping his forehead. "Is this a buffalo? Can't you see, it's the most expensive horse in all of Hindustan? Hazoor, I'll give her a beating she'll remember the rest of her life."

But the man is laughing. "Desi gur, hanh? Who would have thought it! And all this time I've been giving her sugar imported from Persia, because that's where she's from. Paying through the nose for it, too. And she doesn't even like it that much. Show me how you fed her."

I bring out the last piece of gur, ashamed because it's so small, and offer it to him.

"No. I want to see how you do it."

I hold out the lump. Again, that wide, gentle mouth. I can't stop smiling. The mare nuzzles me and I lay my cheek shyly against its neck.

"Amazing," the man marvels. "I've never seen her so friendly with a stranger. Have you grown up around horses?"

Manna says, "Hai, janaab, we're poor peasants! The child's never even seen a horse up close until today."

I'm ashamed of my ignorance. Will the rider look down on me now? Suddenly, his opinion matters very much.

"You must know some jaadu, then."

I feel myself blushing under his gaze. There's something about him, a wild magnetism. His face breaks into a smile. I'm astonished at how handsome it makes him look.

No. Handsome is too light a word. Here is a man whose attraction lies in the power he carries so naturally.

"Would you like to ride her sometime?"

Waheguru, is this really happening?

He waits patiently until I manage to nod.

"It won't be for a while. She's being trained for the hunt. After that's over and the guests have left, I'll bring her back." He vaults onto the mare. There's magic in the way he moves.

I gather all my daring and ask, "What's her name?"

"Laila."

The word swims up through my memories . . . Manna in the village night, spinning tales. *Ah, our Sarkar, what a man! Once he decides he wants something, no one can stop him. Laila cost him sixty lakh rupaiyas . . .*

I'm struck at once by wonder and dismay. "Then you must be . . ."

"Ranjit Singh," he says. His eye crinkles in amusement at my expression.

I watch horse and rider moving as one as they set off. I can't stop staring even after they're out of sight. The foolish image I'd created of the Sarkar—towering, muscular, black-bearded, crown glittering with jewels—dissipates like mist in sunshine. This man possesses something more precious, a rare charisma. No wonder he united all of Punjab under him. If I were a soldier, I'd gladly follow him to my death.

I'm brought back to the present by Manna patting my head. "My smart girl!" he gushes. "How'd you know that was the Sarkar's horse?"

Wearily, I reply, "I didn't."

"Sure you didn't! You took a big chance with the gur, but it paid off. I think, like the horse, the Sarkar, too, has taken to you." He winks at me. "Why, your plan is better than mine!"

Disgust flares in me. He's assigning me his own crude motives, when all I'd wanted was for beauty to touch my life for a moment.

Manna looks me up and down assessingly. "I'll tell Jawahar to buy some sweet khoya for you. Let's get some curves on you. I'll buy you a pretty kameez to wear when the Sarkar comes back."

Now I understand Biji's fear. Manna will use me any way he can to get ahead. I'm caught in a quandary. I want the Sarkar to like me, but not in the disgusting, physical way Manna is hinting at.

Very well. I'll play Manna's game. The Sarkar, whose zenana must be filled with gorgeous, seductive women, may never visit me again. But his words have given me a fleeting power, and I intend to use it.

I plant my feet firmly on the mud of the yard. I fist my hands.

"I hate khoya. And I want to go to the market with Jawahar. I don't care about the kurta—get what you like. But I want books. And I want you to leave the door unlocked when you leave home, not pen me in like an animal."

Manna's face darkens. He raises his hand.

"If you hit me, I'll tell the Sarkar."

"The Sarkar would agree that it's a father's job to discipline impudent children," Manna growls. But he drops his arm. "One book—from the old-books stall. And if I hear from any of the trainers that they've seen you outside the yard, you'll be sorry, Sarkar or no Sarkar."

I watch from the doorway as he leaves with his usual swagger. But we both know that at least for the moment, I've won.

6

Shalimar

I'M TRYING TO LIGHT THE stubborn chulha so I can start dinner when Manna charges in. "Stop! You'll get an ember in your eye, and then it'll turn an ugly red."

I look up, surprised at his sudden concern.

"Get ready. Fast. Is there water in the bucket? Take a bath. You've already bathed? Take another one. Use all the water. Where's that sandalwood stick I bought for you? Make some paste. Rub it on yourself. Wear that new pink kameez. Quick. The Sarkar's going to take you riding."

I'm disbelieving, nervous, overjoyed. It's been a month since I saw the Sarkar. I'd been sure that I'd slid off his busy mind like a raindrop from a leaf.

"Use more sandalwood," Manna instructs. "This is our lucky day. Make the most of it!"

I've barely managed to pull on the kameez and gather my hair into a hasty braid when the Sarkar gallops up on Laila. Dressed in dazzling white, he looks stern and impeccable. I bow and stammer out a greeting. Then Laila nudges me and I'm surprised into smiling. I open my fist. She takes the lump of jaggery I had hidden there and nickers in pleasure. Now the Sarkar is smiling, too. It makes him look younger.

"Let's go!" he cries.

Manna rushes up to help me but the Sarkar orders him to get back to work. He tells me to put my foot over his stirruped one, climb on and seat myself in the front part of the saddle. Twice I slide off when I'm halfway up. I'm dreadfully embarrassed, but he says, bracingly, "You can do it." And I do.

We take the back way out of the qila, down a couple of narrow, oddly empty alleys. Soon we're in the countryside, galloping across fields. Laila goes faster that I'd imagined possible. I hadn't thought I'd be frightened, but I am. I clutch her mane; she tosses her head and snorts.

The Sarkar laughs. "She doesn't like that! Here, I'll hold you. You won't fall." His arm comes around my waist. My heart lurches, my face grows hot. I've never been so close to a man, and certainly never one so important. My braid unravels and the wind blows my hair into his face. I apologize and try to tie it up, but he says, "I don't mind. Just enjoy the ride. Move your body like I'm moving, in time with the horse."

I don't know how. I thud up and down like a sack.

"You're doing very well for your first ride. Relax. Think of the horse and yourself as a single body."

I close my eyes—and become aware of his grasp around my waist. I check, but there's nothing inappropriate in the way he is holding me. I relax and feel his heart beating against my back. *A single body.* And suddenly, we're all moving together: he, Laila, me. The Sarkar's chest is solid as a fortress wall. I've never felt so safe in my life.

I could have ridden forever. But he says, "Come, we've reached Shalimar."

We sit under a cloth-of-gold tent in the rose gardens, upon a carpet far more beautiful than the ones I'd longed to touch in Moti Bazaar. The fountains fill the garden with their silver whispers. The heady scent of roses makes me dizzy. Or am I dizzy because the Sarkar is looking into my eyes? Because every woman in Lahore would envy me right now?

Just before the Sarkar had arrived Manna had said, "Don't waste this opportunity. The family is depending on you." The entreaty in his eyes had frightened me more than any threat could have.

A huge array of food is artfully arranged in front of us. If only I could take some back for Jawahar. Saffron pulao, samosas, kebabs, bowls of glistening chhole, curried mutton, puffed-up bhaturas as large as my head. A silver basin filled with translucent white chunks. Ice, the Sarkar explains. Two flagons sit in the basin. One holds pomegranate juice. I ask if I can pour him some, but he points to the other one. "This is for me. Wine, with crushed pearls mixed into it. It makes a man stronger each time he drinks." Seeing my curiosity, he laughs. "Not for you. Not yet."

He picks up a fuzzy orange fruit, delicate and glowing, tears it open and hands me half. "An apricot. From Kabul."

Kabul. How far has this fruit journeyed to come to me! Farther than I'll ever travel, I think. Juice runs down my chin, dripping onto my new kurta. I flush and scrabble for a cloth to wipe it, but he doesn't seem to care. He chews heartily, wiping his mouth with the back of his hand.

"Do you like it?"

I want to say something intelligent and appreciative, but I can only nod.

"Did you enjoy riding Laila?"

"Yes!" In my enthusiasm, I forget my awkwardness. "I cannot believe how fast she can run!" *Or that I'm here with you at this banquet among the roses.* But I'm too shy to say that.

"She's a strong horse," he continues, "trained to carry warriors in full armor—not that I'll ever put her on a battlefield. Besides, you hardly weigh anything."

Does he think I'm too scrawny? Perhaps I should have eaten that khoya. I change the subject. "I was pleased that Laila remembered me."

"Horses are very intelligent—more than many humans I know. But anyone would remember a beautiful girl like you."

The compliment gladdens and worries me. I want the Sarkar to like me, but not in the way Manna wishes.

I change the topic, asking for Laila's story. He's happy to oblige. He'd heard from a traveling bard of the mare's beauty and speed. He sent a messenger to her owner, Sultan Yar Muhammad of Kabul, requesting the horse as tribute. Yar Muhammad sent him a beautiful horse, but the Sarkar, no fool, could tell it was not Laila. Enraged, he sent an army to Kabul. A bloody war was fought. Many died. Yar Muhammad was assassinated by his own people for endangering them over a horse. The Sarkar's army returned in triumph with Laila.

"The day she arrived in Lahore, I had the entire road from the Akbari Gate to the qila scrubbed so that no dirt would touch Laila's feet." He pauses, his eye on me. "Some say I was crazy to have gone to so much trouble for a horse. But I believe it was worth it to acquire the most beautiful—and now the most famous—horse in the world. What do you think?"

I know I should agree. But I can't stop thinking of all the Sikhs who died on that distant battlefield to satisfy a royal whim, their faces turned homeward as their eyes darkened.

I lower my head. "Laila is an empress among horses. Still, I feel sad that so many lives were sacrificed for her sake."

In my mind I hear Manna: *Stupid donkey. Can't you tell one small lie for the family's sake?* I'm good at lying. I've done it a hundred times to save Jawahar. But I don't want to deceive the Sarkar. If this means I have to pay a price, so be it.

I wait for his displeasure, but he's silent. When I look up, there's a strange expression on his face. "There aren't too many people who would have dared to disagree with me. You're brave. I like that. Come, let us walk in the garden."

He plucks a pink rose and hands it to me as we stroll. I put it in my hair. He describes the hunt: the beaters; the weapons; the dense, thorn-filled woods, dark even at midday. The British had stayed safely on their elephants and used their guns, while he, riding Laila, had led the party. He'd skewered a wild boar with his spear.

"But still they think they deserve to be masters of Hindustan."

His bitter tone pierces me. How dare the firang outlanders think they're better than my Sarkar?

He tells me story after story. His first battle was at the age of ten, when he went with his father to besiege Sahib Singh in Sodhran Fort.

"My father was badly injured. The wound festered. He was forced to return to Gujranwala. Lying on his pallet, he put a tika on my forehead, named me his heir and ordered me to lead our army. When Sahib's allies learned this, they hurried to attack us."

I imagine the boy he must have been: short, scrawny, squinting against the dust raised by the approaching army. Scared by the responsibility that had suddenly fallen on him. But when he gave orders, his voice was calm and decisive. By the time the dust settled, the enemy had been routed. Ranjit Singh rode at the head of his army, sword raised in victory.

"The last thing my father heard was that I'd won. When I reached home for his funeral, I saw the smile on his dead face. It made his absence easier to bear."

"Weren't you afraid?"

"Terrified," he confesses, matter-of-factly. "But once the battle began, something cold and sharp took over. There was no time for anything as useless as fear. What better way to die, in any case, than with my loyal men around me, all of us crying out 'Sat Sri Akal' with our last breaths?"

What better way, indeed, to live or to die?

"Was that when you lost"—I hesitate—"your eye?" I imagine

the thrust of a sword. Blood. The boy hero fighting on in spite of excruciating pain.

He laughs. "This? Oh no. I had the pox as a child. That's when this happened."

I've never met a man so comfortable with truth. Entranced, I forget to be polite. "Tell me more!"

He laughs and launches into other adventures. The time when he was out hunting alone and was ambushed by the traitor Hashmat Khan. He returned with Hashmat's head impaled on his spear. He was thirteen. Later, when he routed Shah Zaman's thirty-thousand-strong Afghan army with only five thousand men. And when he wrested Lahore from the corrupt Bhangi chiefs without firing a single shot.

He stops with a bemused laugh. "I'm not in the habit of talking about myself. But there's something about the way you listen—with your whole body—that makes me want to keep going . . ."

I'm not sure what he means. But I'm honored that he trusts me enough to tell me his stories. "One more, please."

He turns away, muttering a word that sounds like *foolishness*. He whistles and Laila comes galloping. He leaps onto her back.

"It's time I took you home, to your father." His voice is brusque.

I hide my disappointment and put my foot on the Sarkar's. I climb into the saddle on the first try. Elated, I wait for praise, but he seems preoccupied. Have I bored him? Behind us, the servants, invisible until now, are dismantling the golden tent, their eyes respectfully turned away from us. I feel for the rose I'd tucked in my hair, but it must have fallen while we were walking.

We ride to the qila in silence. I'm intensely aware of his arm around my waist, though it doesn't seem to mean much to him. What do I feel for this man who's as old as my father, yet so charismatic and fascinating? I only know that I don't want the ride to end. As before, we meet no one on the way. He must have given orders. He doesn't want anyone to see me with him. Is it for the sake of my reputation—or his own?

DISAPPOINTINGLY SOON, WE'RE BACK at the hut. A small movement at the window, behind the sacking. Manna. I dread his avid interrogation.

I slide off Laila, feeling oddly bereft.

"I hope you enjoyed yourself." The Sarkar's tone is that of a man who made an impetuous promise and is now done with it.

I know I should be equally formal. *I did, Sarkar. Meherbaani for your great kindness.* Instead I use every drop of audacity I possess to clutch the saddle. He might think I'm impudent. He might chastise me. But I have to do this. Not for Manna. For myself.

"May I see you again?"

He frowns. "To ride Laila?"

"No. Just to be with you."

I can't read his expression. Finally he says, "Then you shall."

AS I SERVE DINNER, Manna asks, "What did the two of you do?"

To tell him of my magical time with the Sarkar would ruin it. But Manna is waiting, hand paused halfway to his mouth. Jawahar, embarrassed, stares at the floor. "We rode. We ate. We walked around Shalimar. Then we came back."

"Don't mumble, girl! Did he say he'll come again?"

I hold on to the Sarkar's last words, their slender hope. I will not give them to Manna.

"Did he show interest in you? Did he kiss you? Did he—touch you?"

Disgust floods me. "No!"

He pushes his dinner away and gets to his feet. "You brainless goat! Why didn't you encourage him? Do I have to spell out everything? One chance we had of getting ahead in the world, and you wasted it."

He raises his arm. I force myself not to cower.

Jawahar, too, rises, his face flushed. Have I disappointed him as well?

"Leave her alone." He grabs Manna's shoulder. "You should be ashamed."

I notice, for the first time, that he's almost as tall as Manna. The muscles in his arm flex and ripple. He stares until Manna stomps out with a curse.

Jawahar turns to me. "I heard he lost a lot of money gambling. But it's not your job to save him from his stupidity. Certainly not by—" He breaks off. "Be patient, sister. I'm saving all my money. As soon as I have enough, I'll put you on the cart to Gujranwala."

His kindness makes me tear up. The irony is that I no longer want to go back to the village. But what I want is so outrageous that I can't bring myself to tell Jawahar.

I want the Sarkar to fall in love with me. Because he's powerful and charismatic and didn't take advantage of me though he could easily have done so. Because he tells the most fascinating stories.

And because, foolishly, I'm falling in love with him.

7

Scorpions

THREE WEEKS PASS. THE SARKAR neither comes nor sends any messages. My hopes sputter like a wick in an empty lamp. Days, I bear Manna's invective, the growing desperation in his eyes. Nights, I dream of the Sarkar's arm around my waist, his wine-scented breath. Soon, Jawahar will have enough money to send me back to Gujranwala.

Then, when I've gouged the thorn of expectation from my heart, the Sarkar appears. He rides a different horse this time, a tall, red-brown animal who ignores me superbly when I run out to admire it. The Sarkar looks tired. He tells me he's been preparing the troops, sixteen thousand cavalry, for a visit with the British. He met the governor-general, Bentinck himself, at Rupar by the Sutlej River.

He doesn't apologize. He is, after all, a king. I should be thankful that he even chose to explain. I sense he doesn't usually do so.

He describes the immense spread of the armies beside the Sutlej, greatest of our five rivers. The governor-general watching, stiff in his padded silk coat.

Did the gora laat recognize the greatness hidden inside my Sarkar's slender frame? Did he pay him due respect? I doubt it.

When I ask how it went, the Sarkar smiles mirthlessly. "My Khalsa army performed many complex maneuvers. Bentinck was impressed enough to remark that they put on a jolly good show."

"But your purpose was served, was it not? He saw how strong we are."

His eyebrows shoot up in surprise. "You're the first woman to understand this. My queens—even Mai Nakkain, the shrewdest—think I waste money entertaining the British because I love pomp and festivity. But you saw my true intent. Now the British will think many times before they try to cross into my territory."

"I'm glad your strategy was a success."

"For the moment. But the alliance I'd hoped for, a true partnership that might bring us peace . . . The British don't want that." He shakes his head sadly. "Still, I must keep playing the game. Tomorrow Bentinck arrives in Lahore. I am holding a banquet in his honor. I will give him many gifts. He will reciprocate, though with far fewer, because the British are tight-fisted. They came to this country as merchants. Their goal is to take from it everything they can. At the end of the visit, he will proclaim himself my lifelong friend—words that mean nothing."

I'd give anything to wipe the despondence off his face. Hatred for the goras glows like a hot coal inside me.

"The British have only one goal: to own all of Hindustan. They will not stop until it happens. But they won't get my Punjab—not while I'm alive." He lets out a long breath. "Enough of such depressing talk." Patting the horse's neck, he says, "This is Dildaar, very brave and steady. I want to take you for a ride on him. But could I have something to drink first?"

Luckily, I made some lassi earlier, churning the curds with black salt and crushed cumin the way we do in Gujranwala. I bring him a lota filled with the frothy liquid. He drinks it all.

"Ah! I haven't had lassi like this since I left my mother's home."

I can't stop smiling even after I climb on because the Sarkar says, "You did that well. I think you're a born horsewoman."

Dildaar gallops very fast, but with the Sarkar's arm around me, I'm confident. We leap over a wall of stones. I laugh out loud, and the Sarkar laughs with me. When the light turns soft, we dismount and walk along the edge of a cliff.

"Sorry, there's no banquet this time. I decided on this visit suddenly."

Daringly, I say, "I've cooked saag and roti. If you don't mind peasant fare, I'll give you dinner when we get back."

"I'd love that."

Below us rushes a great, galloping river. I stare at its roiling, mesmerizing waves.

"The Ravi," he says. "Beautiful and dangerous, like a headstrong woman. And like a woman, she drives me crazy sometimes. Once, I was returning from a campaign. We'd routed the Afghans after a long, dry fight in the desert. When I saw her foaming waters, and beyond it the walls of my beloved city, I couldn't bear to wait for a bridge. I rode my horse into the river, even though my men yelled warnings. I intended to swim across, but the Ravi, she had a different plan. She grabbed me and swept me under. The horse swam away, but I almost drowned! It took four of my ghorcharhas to drag me to safety. When they got me back to the qila—looking more like a drowned rat than a triumphant conqueror—Wazir Dhian Singh scolded me roundly for endangering Punjab with my foolish risk.

"Even now I remember how it felt, being tumbled head over heels by the dark, rushing water, my lungs burning. It was worse than facing a thousand armed horsemen."

I draw a shuddering breath. How is it that with this man, I feel his pain in my body?

"But it wouldn't have been such a bad way to die," he muses. "Better than being stuck in a stinking sickbed."

It takes me all my courage to touch his arm. "I'm glad you didn't die. Not only for the sake of Punjab, but for my sake, too."

He looks surprised. But after a moment he puts his hand over mine. He wears no rings except for one on his little finger, with a tiny red stone embedded in it. Jawahar, who has been asking around, told me that in durbar, too, he dresses simply and sits on a plain kursi, even when foreign dignitaries come to visit. The throne is reserved for the Guru Granth Sahib.

"I'm glad, too," the Sarkar says.

Tension hangs over us. His fingertips burn. I sway toward him.

He shakes his head as though clearing it of water. "Sun's getting low. Time to get you back."

ON THE RIDE HOME, I sit behind him, holding on tighter than I need to. I press my cheek against his back and breathe in his scent, sweat and wine and metal and a strong, wild fragrance which he explained was musk, his favorite perfume. Maybe he, too, doesn't want the ride to end because he clicks his tongue to slow Dildaar down. The stars are shining all across the night sky when we reach the hut.

Before I can ask if he has time to stop for dinner, Manna is at our side, oozing solicitousness.

"Greetings, Sarkar. I hope my daughter hasn't been boring you with silly girl-chatter. Come, beti, I'll help you down."

I tell him I can manage, but he pulls at me until I lose my balance and feel myself sliding off the horse. He grabs me and staggers back, both of us almost falling.

"Oof, hazoor, look at this girl! She's getting heavy. Too much for a poor old father like me. Take her off my hands, please! You're a strong man, janaab, you can handle her weight!"

Is that a wink? Is Manna winking at Maharaja Ranjit Singh? Where's Jawahar? I need him to come and drag Manna away before he says anything worse.

"She comes from sturdy village stock. Strong and energetic, if you know what I mean. A virgin, too. She'll keep you young for a long time."

I want to bury myself deep in the earth. *Waheguru, now the Sarkar will think we've been planning this together.* That I was trying to seduce him. I begin to walk away, my steps stiff with mortification, the night blurred by my tears. He'll never want to see me again.

The Sarkar's voice stops me, cracking like a whip.

"Have you no shame, Manna, talking about your own daughter as though she's a bazaar dancer?"

He must have made a gesture of dismissal because Manna slinks into the house. I start to follow him, but the Sarkar calls my name.

I can't bear to look at him now that everything's ruined. But he's the king. I must obey.

He leans down and wipes my tears with his thumb. His touch is gentle. Why does it make me weep further? I am a stupid goat, like Manna claims.

"Hush. Forget about your father. There's a banquet in the palace tomorrow. Remember, in Bentinck's honor. Would you like to come? We can't be together. You'll have to sit with the other women. But it'll be something fine for you to see."

My heart thuds so hard, surely he can hear it. Me, the dog trainer's daughter, at a royal banquet? Can such a thing be possible, especially after Manna's crassness? I manage to nod.

But here's a new problem: how does a girl tell a king she has nothing to wear?

He smiles. His beard shines, gossamer in the moonlight. "I'll inform Guddan. She's the kindest of my queens. She'll get you suitable clothes."

How does he know everything I'm thinking? Before I lose my courage, I press my lips to his hand.

For a moment, he's very silent. Then he says, "Go inside, Jindan. Step carefully. Sometimes scorpions come out at night, even inside the qila."

He waits, still as carved marble in the moonlight, until I shut the door.

8

Banquet

My feet ache from standing at the window all afternoon, watching the road. I feel stupid for having rushed through my cooking and cleaning. For having begged Jawahar to use his lunch break to buy me ritha pulp to wash my hair.

Jawahar, in whom I had confided last night after Manna slept, asked, “Are you doing this because of Manna?”

I said, “I know it’s foolish, but I’ve fallen in love.”

He frowned. “Careful, sister. Remember who he is—and who you are.”

When the shadows on our lane grow long, I throw myself on the floor, which is always dirty no matter how many times I sweep it. My pink kameez is ruined, but what does it matter? What folly to think I could attend a royal banquet. What folly to think I’d been more than just a brief diversion to the Sarkar. I’m angry for having been stupid enough to kiss his hand.

THE KNOCKING STARTLES ME. Is it Manna already? I can't bear to face him.

But no. It's a woman, stout and prosperous, her clothes respectably expensive but not too fine. I take it she's a serving woman to someone of importance. She looks me up and down and purses her lips. Then she opens a bundle and hands me a burkha made of fine black silk.

I slip it on. Through the dark netting, the world becomes a haze. I follow her past pillared gates and labyrinthine gardens until we arrive in a cool, marble chamber smelling of unknown flowers.

A young woman with beautiful hazel eyes lifts my veil. "Welcome. I am Guddan."

Rani Guddan is the kindest woman I've ever met. She dresses me in a maroon silk lehenga, which billows around my legs. "Look how well it fits you," she says with satisfaction. She herself is dressed in a sky-blue ghaghra-choli embroidered all over with diamonds. Her lips shine. Her glossy braid reaches past her hips. She moves in a cloud of sweet perfume, like a pari from heaven. Her maids help me with a matching stone-studded kurti with a deep neckline that makes me blush. They braid jewels into my hair, rub fragrant paste onto my face, darken my eyes with kohl. From her jewelry box, Guddan picks out earrings, bangles, a double-stranded chain. A maid holds up a mirror. I can't believe the graceful woman reflected there is me.

"What if I lose something?" I stammer.

"You'd better not, or you'll be sorry," snaps Aditi, the woman who brought me here. She's Guddan's chief attendant and fiercely protective of her princess, whom she accompanied to Lahore from the Kangra. Guddan is of royal birth. All the Sarkar's wives seem to be high-born, I've learned to my dismay.

Guddan pats my arm. "I know you'll be careful."

The maids place diaphanous veils over us, covering our faces in a shimmer of gold. "We must go now," Guddan says, "or all the good seats in the ladies' section will be taken. As it is, we'll have to sit toward the back. The front seats are reserved for the ranis from the most influential families, or for the king's current bedmates. I'm neither." She smiles wryly. "You'll have to crane your neck to see. It's a good thing that you're so tall. Watch out, though. Everyone will be dying of curiosity when they see you. The concubines will remain quiet, but the queens will ask all kinds of questions. Just smile and look shy. The Sarkar doesn't want people to know who you are. I'll say whatever needs to be said."

THE DIWAN-I-KHAS IS AN immense structure of arched marble pillars with a shining mosaic floor. Inside, musicians are tuning their instruments in preparation for the evening's festivities. We pass by it and go to a wide veranda where carpets have been laid down. A wall of elegant wooden friezes lines the front so that the Sarkar's women can watch without being seen. The guards standing at attention outside the entrance and the punkha bearers fanning the dampened rush curtains that hang on either side are all female. I hear whispers and giggles, the tinkling of bangles and anklets. But when I walk in behind Guddan, all sounds stop. I can feel the women's dagger glances. *Who is she? Is she important? Is she going to be a rival?*

"My cousin Jaya, visiting from back home," Guddan announces, her voice smooth as butter.

The real feast will begin later. Meanwhile, maids carry trays laden with chilled juices and platters heaped with nuts and raisins, offering them first to a woman who sits in the front row, surrounded by a fawning coterie. Her clothing, stiff with gold and pearls, is resplendent, though she herself is not beautiful and makes no pretence of it. She wears her wrinkles and her gray hair—atop which rests a large diadem—with confidence.

"Mai Nakkain," Guddan whispers. "Chief queen. Eldest among the wives. Mother of Prince Kharak, the heir. Her clan was a powerful ally of the Sarkar and helped him gain power in the early days, before he became maharaja. He's never forgotten it."

I have been carefully storing everything I learn about the Sarkar. I add this fact, too: he never forgets a friend. Does he remember his enemies equally well?

The maids proceed to serve a beautiful woman, dressed with deceptive simplicity in a silver-white kameez. Even I can tell that the soft material which glows and clings to her curves is expensive. She wears a single piece of jewelry, a large diamond tiara on her head. She sits apart from the other queens and does not speak. From time to time, she takes small sips from a goblet of wine.

"That's Gul Bahar Begum," whispers Guddan. "She has her own haveli in town and only comes to the banquets if there's going to be dancing. She always wears clothing to match the Sarkar's. She used to be a nautch girl, the best in the city. The Sarkar fell in love with her when he saw her dancing. He spent his days and nights with her and ordered her to dance only for him. They went for elephant rides together and played holi in the marketplace. The people were indulgent, for they loved their Sarkar. But then, they were already used to his infatuations."

My head whirls with the things I'm learning about the Sarkar's many women. All lovely, or high-born, with huge dowries. How could he possibly be interested in a dog trainer's daughter?

There's just one thing that might aid me. "Does he get infatuated often?"

Guddan laughs. "Oh yes! Have you heard of Moran the courtesan, reputed to be the most beautiful woman in north-west Hindustan? Soon after he became king, the Sarkar fell hard for her. When he declared that he wanted to marry her, his relatives and advisers were shocked and angry, what with her low birth and notorious occupation, and being a Muslim as well. Even his chief ally, his mother-in-law Sada Kaur, chided him. But our Sarkar refused to back down. He's very smart when it comes to warfare, but perhaps not so much when it comes to women. He married Moran against everyone's advice, not caring whom he alienated. After the wedding, he went to the Khalsa in the Golden Temple, bowed his head, and asked to be lashed one hundred times for his crime."

I wince, imagining the whip landing on the Sarkar's back. "Did they lash him?"

"No." Guddan smiles. "When they saw his humility, they relented. Besides, they knew he was the only hope for Punjab, the lone lion keeping the wolves away. And who knows, perhaps even the hearts of the Khalsa have a softness for a love story. With Gul Bahar, the Sarkar was wiser—and more powerful. He went to the Golden Temple ahead of time and got permission to marry her."

"And Moran? Is she here today?"

"No. For some years, things went well for her. But then—no one knows why—he banished her to Pathankot Fort. He can be ruthless when he wishes, our maharaja. There she remains to this day, poor lady."

I'm shocked to hear of the Sarkar's harshness, a side I haven't seen so far.

Guddan continues, "That's the fickle favor of kings. Even though Moran had been so beloved. Why, soon after their marriage the Sarkar issued a coin stamped with the image of a peacock in her honor. That's how crazy he was for her. He didn't do that even for himself. For his coronation, he minted a coin with Guru Nanak's face, saying that only he deserved such acclaim."

I tell Guddan that such humility is impressive. She nods.

"The kings before the Sarkar cared only about their own glory, and I'm afraid the ones after him will also—" Guddan breaks off abruptly, and I become aware of the silence around us.

"What are you afraid of, Guddan dear?" Mai Nakkain, who has turned to face us, asks. Her eyes glint steel. I remember that her son will be the next ruler of Punjab.

"Nothing, Mai," Guddan replies, politeness personified. "In our great Sarkar's realm, what can there be to fear?"

Mai Nakkain examines me through narrowed eyes. "You look nothing like our Guddan, girl. You're lighter skinned, and your nose is sharper. What kind of cousin are you?"

My heart pounds. I bow my head, pretending shyness.

"My second aunt's daughter, mother's side," Guddan says. "She takes after her father."

"Where in the Kangra are you from?" asks one of Mai Nakkain's coterie. "I lived there for many years."

Guddan opens her mouth, but Mai Nakkain stops her. "Is the girl a deaf-mute? Let her speak for herself."

All eyes are on me. Can they tell that I'm sweating? I know nothing about the Kangra except that it's famous for its apples.

There's a commotion at the entrance of the Diwan-i-Khas.

"Look," Guddan says with relief. "Here comes our Sarkar."

In spite of the throng, I pick him out right away in the distance. He is shorter than the looming figures of his guards and dressed simply in a pure white turban and tunic with an over-jacket of soft gold. Still, he exudes raw power. He wears a long necklace of pearls and an armband that flashes like fire in the light of the torches around him. The famed Koh-i-Noor! The bright clothing of the courtiers who accompany him looks garish next to his elegance.

Walking closest to him is a man dressed with equal simplicity. Mostly he nods as the Sarkar talks, but sometimes he speaks, and then it is the Sarkar who listens.

"That is Fakir Azizuddin," Guddan whispers. "The Sarkar's closest confidant and his ambassador. The Sarkar trusts him the most."

I'm surprised. "More than his Sikh chieftains?"

"The Sarkar doesn't care about a person's religion. Only his ability and commitment."

"I thought Dhian Singh was his favorite minister."

"Dhian is a favorite, yes. But Azizuddin is special because he doesn't want anything from the Sarkar. He's refused titles, gifts, lands . . . He lives simply, as a fakir should. The Sarkar admires that."

I watch Azizuddin with increased curiosity. How unusual, to want nothing. I can't imagine it. I'll remember this, though: the Sarkar trusts most those who don't want anything from him. I watch him lay an affectionate hand on the Fakir's arm.

Perhaps he loves them best, too.

The trumpeters play a rousing melody as the Sarkar takes his seat. When his courtiers approach him, he speaks with each one, laughing, or clapping a man affably on the shoulder. It's impossible not to love a man like that, even when you know he could end your life with a word.

The laat sahib, Bentinck, who must have been waiting in an annex, is announced. He walks into the hall with his men, all of them looking out of place in thick velvet coats, their cravats tight around their throats. I crane my neck to observe them. From what the Sarkar has said, I know he believes they are dangerous and untrustworthy. One would never know it, though, by looking at the Sarkar now. He rises graciously to greet the Englishman although he doesn't have to—it's clear who's in control in this durbar. He seats Bentinck next to him and gestures. Additional punkha-wallahs run up to fan the governor-general. Iced drinks are brought, cooled wine in tall silver pitchers. Platter after platter of food. The aroma of meat and pulao, kebabs and brinjal bharta assails me. I'm starving. In my anxiety, I haven't eaten all day. Bentinck, however, waves away most of the dishes. I bristle on behalf of the Sarkar; the British don't deserve his hospitality. If I get an opportunity, I'll tell him this.

The music grows louder. The dancers pirouette and leap, their ankle-bells resonating into the night. Gul Bahar watches with hungry eyes as the women swirl and turn, their long braids slicing the air. When the attendants offer her more wine, she sends them away brusquely. I notice her lips moving to the words of the songs, all of which she knows, and realize that Gul Bahar longs for her old life as a dancer!

How can someone lucky enough to be married to the Sarkar want anything else?

The women are being served dinner in order of importance. Mai Nakkain is first. Guddan ranks lower than several others, so she is served after some time. The attendant begins to walk off.

"Wait," Guddan calls, "what about my cousin?"

The woman bows apologetically. "I was given instructions. She is not to be served until the concubines have eaten."

"Why?" Guddan asks angrily. "Who?"

The woman lowers her eyes. "Your pardon, Rani ji. I only do as I am told."

"It's all right," I whisper to Guddan. I don't want her to get into trouble for my sake.

"Very well," Guddan tells the attendant. "Give me more kurma and pulao then. More parathas. More brinjals and meat. Fill my bowl to the top with kheer. Yes, woman, more!" She turns to me, a glint in her eye. "Come, sister, we will eat from the same thali today, as we did in childhood."

Here's something else for me to learn: how cleverly Guddan won over Mai—for clearly, she's the one behind this insult. I murmur my thanks and copy Guddan's movements carefully. I will not give Mai a chance to make a derogatory comment. I take tiny bites of meat and scoop the rice carefully so nothing falls on my beautiful skirt. But I'm so tense that everything tastes like ashes.

IN THE DIWAN-I-KHAS THE music swells to a crescendo. Dancers run in with curved swords and stage a mock battle, leaping and twirling until they are silken blurs slashed with lightning. The audience cries out in amazed delight. The governor-general stares. Even the moon holds its breath.

Then it is over and the Sarkar hands the girls pouches—filled with gold dust, Guddan whispers. I see their surprised jubilation as they bow to him. Guddan tells me that the women must wait until the maharaja and his guests have departed. I hope it'll take a long time. I can't bear for this magical evening to end.

Someone says, "So tell us, girl, before Guddan whisks you away, which part of the Kangra do you come from?"

It's the same woman as before. Next to her, Mai Nakkain leans on the biggest satin bolster and watches me. His lips are blood-red from the betel leaf she's been chewing. I'm shocked. To Sikhs, paan is forbidden, but clearly, the rules at court are different.

When Guddan attempts to intervene, Mai quells her with a glance.

I bow my head, pretending shyness. But my questioner persists. "Struck dumb suddenly, are you? Rani Sahiba, I don't believe this girl is from the Kangra—or even related to Guddan."

"Is that true, Guddan dear?" Mai asks. "Did you lie to me? I've been watching the two of you whispering and plotting all night. Have you brought this girl here, dressed up in your finery—oh yes, I recognized the clothes—hoping she'll catch the Sarkar's eye and he'll take a fancy to her? That you'll rise in his favor for procuring him a pretty virgin? Is that what your parents advised?"

I'm aghast. The other accusations are sordid enough, but to disparage one's family is the greatest insult of all. In Gujranwala, men would knife each other over such words; women would tear out each other's hair. Guddan's cheeks flame with humiliation, but she remains silent. She's determined to keep my secret.

I, too, should keep quiet, but temper uncoils inside me like a cobra.

"I'm here at the Sarkar's invitation," I say. My voice rises over the surprised silence of the assembly. "If you're so curious about me, instead of harassing Rani Guddan, who's only obeying the Sarkar, why don't you ask him directly?"

Guddan draws in a dismayed breath.

Mai sits up. "You dare speak to me like this? Who do you think you are? Here at the Sarkar's invitation, indeed." She claps for her attendants. "Tell the zenana guards to throw this lying harlot out of the qila and make sure she never comes back. Not that there'll be much left of her after a night on the streets of Lahore." She ignores Guddan's entreaties.

In a moment a group of women in soldier's uniforms marches in, their muscular bodies covered in studded leather. The hard-faced leader grabs at me, but running from irate farmers in Gujranwala has taught me certain skills. I have no chance against an entire cohort, but I can make it hard for them. I sprint to the back of the veranda, where the concubines huddle in shock. But one of them sticks out her leg and trips me. Two guards drag me before Mai.

Guddan cries, "Let her go! She's the Sarkar's guest. Truly she is!"

"And I'm Nur Jahan!" Mai scoffs. She slaps me so hard that my head spins. My cheek burns—a stone from her rings must have cut into my skin. "Take her to the women's lockup, Bhago," she instructs the chief guard. "Beat the truth out of her." Bhago grasps my arm in a vicious grip; I'm sure it will leave a bruise. I kick and curse as she drags me. I push away the terror of what will happen to me—and my family—if Mai learns who I am. I focus on one thing only: I will not give her the satisfaction of seeing me cry.

The guards haul me to the entrance. I feel the chilly night air. Bhago cuffs me so hard that my ears ring. "Just you wait until we get you to the qaidkhana," she hisses. "You'll never see daylight again."

I close my eyes. I've lost.

Suddenly, the clamor around me dies down, everyone around me grows deathly silent. Opening my eyes, I see that the guards have fallen to their knees. In front of me stands a figure in white, the great diamond on his armband shining like a beacon. Behind me, the queens—Mai Nakkain included—scramble to their feet, heads bent, palms joined. I hasten to do the same.

"What is happening here?" the Sarkar demands. His voice is low but clearly displeased.

Mai is the only one brave enough to speak. "We discovered an imposter, Sarkar. I was just having her removed. I think she's a spy. She wouldn't answer our questions."

"This woman is my guest, as I'm sure Guddan informed you." The Sarkar's tone is frigid. "How dare you treat her like this!"

Mai looks down. The guards melt away. I raise my grateful eyes to the Sarkar's face. There's anger in his knotted brow, but he touches the cut on my cheek gently.

"I apologize for the mistreatment you received in my home."

"It's nothing, my Sarkar," I say, "compared to the delights of this magical evening."

He smiles. "You enjoyed your first royal mehfil?"

"It's something I'll remember forever."

How provincial my accent sounds, so different from the sophisticated tones of Guddan and Mai. Embarrassed, I drop my eyes to his embroidered shoes.

He straightens my dupatta, which has been pulled askew in my struggles. His touch makes me tremble.

"This color suits you. I hope you will wear it often."

I don't know how to respond, so I dip my head in a deep bow. By the time I raise my head, he has moved on. He greets his harem courteously as though he hadn't been enraged a moment ago. He inquires after Mai's health, asks Gul Bahar what she thought of the dancers, and thanks Guddan for her help. He doesn't speak to me again. He doesn't have to. He has already saved me.

Once the Sarkar leaves, the queens whisper avidly among themselves. I sense that they're secretly pleased to see Mai discomfited.

Mai ignores us all as she sweeps out with her coterie. She must be infuriated, but her face reveals nothing. I have to admit that she's the epitome of regalness.

AT GUDDAN'S HAVELI, I pull on my salwar-kameez, the cheap cotton now abrasive on my skin. How quickly we learn the habits of luxury.

I'm shocked when Guddan makes Aditi pack the maroon lehenga-set for me. I protest, but she says, "You must have it. The Sarkar liked you in it. He certainly surprised us today. I've never known him to come to the women's area after a mehfil. But thank God he did!" She looks into my blushing face. "Don't read too much into his compliments. Sometimes he acts impulsively." I know she speaks out of kindness. She adds, "And remember this: whenever possible, don't fight openly with your enemy. Let them think they've won—and then strike when least expected."

It's sound advice, though perhaps too late for me. I doubt Mai will forget her humiliation, or forgive me for it.

9

Gurdwara

THE WEEK AFTER THE MEHFIL is filled with the scent of roses. Over and over, Manna asks me, with childlike excitement, to describe the moment when the Sarkar stood in front of me in the women's section.

"Tell me again what he said, how he admired your looks, how he saved you from the old queen's anger."

At first I don't mind. It's like reliving a moment out of a fairy tale. But as the days pass with no word from the Sarkar, I can't bear to speak of it.

I steel myself for Manna's curses. But he only taps his forehead and says, "What to do, dheeye, it's our naseeb. We were foolish to aim so high." His despondence makes me feel worse than if he'd flung something across the room.

Manna no longer spends his evenings carousing with the grooms. I don't know where he goes. He comes back very late and says he isn't hungry. Even with the dogs, he isn't his rambunctious self. Through the slats of the fence I see him sitting on the ground, his head in his hands, the animals milling around him.

"I've let the family down," I whisper at night to Jawahar.

"Don't be silly," he retorts, reaching across the dark floor to squeeze my hand. "Manna's worried because he lost a lot of money at cards. The other trainers have thrown him out of the group and given him a month to settle his debts. His problems aren't your fault."

He's right. Still, at odd moments, I find myself in tears. Is it because of Jawahar's kindness? Manna's shattered hopes? My own foolish longing?

Jawahar tries to find out where the Sarkar might be. The reports are conflicting. *He's meeting the British, who are drawing up a treaty that will allow them to navigate the rivers of Punjab. He's away at shikar, where he has killed six wild hogs. He's up north, fighting the Afghans with his faithful jarnail, Hari Singh Nalwa, by his side.*

But one thing is clear: he has no time, or no desire, to visit me.

TODAY MANNA SEEMS ODDLY cheerful. Perhaps he's weaseled his way back into the group and won some money. He tells me that he has invited a guest to dinner. I'm surprised. He's never done this before. He brings me fresh mutton and greens. Ghee to melt over the rotis.

"Cook properly, beti. It's important." He rummages through my clothes and tells me to wear the maroon lehenga. Looking at it makes me heartsick, but I obey, to make up for having disappointed him.

The guest, a merchant from a nearby town, is a portly man almost as old as Manna. He doesn't speak much, except to compliment my cooking and ask for seconds. After dinner, when the men go to the yard to talk, Jawahar creeps out and eavesdrops. Later, he tells me that Manna was negotiating my marriage.

I'm aghast. "With that man?"

"Yes. His wife died last year and he has two children who need looking after. He doesn't want a dowry. He'll take care of the wedding expenses. That's all I could hear."

I shudder. "I won't marry him! I can't."

"It's disgusting," Jawahar agrees. "Couldn't Manna find someone better than that old man?"

How do I tell my brother that since the mehfil, I find all men disgusting, young or old. All men except the Sarkar.

"I won't let him sell you off like this," Jawahar fumes. "I've saved enough money to send you to Gujranwala. Do you want to leave tomorrow? I'll ask Suleiman for time off and take you to the cart. Before Manna knows what's happening, you'll be halfway home."

I'm thankful for his support. But I say, "Let's wait a little."

He looks at me sadly. He knows the foolish hope I'm harboring.

THE NEXT NIGHT, MANNA tells me that I'll be getting married in ten days.

"It isn't what I wanted," he admits, a little shamefaced. "But it's the best chance we have. I'd hoped for better things when the Sarkar invited you to the mehfil. That didn't work out, though, did it? And your mother keeps sending me messages—Balbir's past twenty now, and the villagers are talking. I have to get her married, but I don't have the money. I'm no good at saving—you know that by now. And Balbir's not pretty enough for anyone to marry her without a dowry. This merchant, he's a generous man. He'll pay for this wedding and Balbir's, too. As soon as you're married, I'll look for a husband for her."

I'm sorry for Manna. And Balbir, too. But I refuse to sacrifice myself like this. The thought of being kissed by the merchant makes me nauseated. I can imagine only one man touching me.

I make my decision. As soon as Jawahar can arrange it, I'll run away to Gujranwala, where I hope Biji will protect me. I bow my head, weep a little so that Manna will not grow suspicious, then pretend to give in.

My Sarkar, where are you?

I'M FILLED, AT ONCE, with relief and sadness. Jawahar has arranged for me to leave for Gujranwala early tomorrow. In the morning, as soon as Manna goes to work, he'll take me to the Masti Darwaza and put me on the cart. I feel bad for my brother. Not only has he used up all his savings for my fare, he'll also have to face Manna's wrath once I'm gone.

"I don't mind, I'm happy to do it for you," Jawahar declares. "Besides"—he grins and flexes his biceps—"I can beat him in a fight."

"I'll remember this always," I say, hugging him.

PACKING FOR TOMORROW, I shake out the maroon lehenga—so out of place in this hovel—and I am overcome by anger. Why did the Sarkar invite me to the banquet? Why did he suggest that he found me beautiful when, clearly, I mean so little to him? Then I'm angry with myself. I'm the stupid one, to read so much into an invitation that was just an act of charity. Into words that were no more than courtly compliments. I fling the skirt across the room.

Footsteps outside. I thrust my bundle into the alcove, heart pounding. Has Manna discovered our plan?

But it's Jawahar, who has run all the way up from the bazaar. Panting, he cries, "The Sarkar is in town. He's praying in the Gurdwara Dehra Sahib, just outside the qila."

I don't even pause to comb my hair. Together, we race to the gurdwara while around us people stare and whisper.

"But why is the Sarkar praying in the middle of the day," I gasp, "when he should be in the durbar?"

Jawahar shrugs. "Who knows the motives of kings? Who dares question them?"

The gurdwara looms ahead, daunting in its white-and-gold splendor. I'm nervous, but I tell Jawahar to leave. Covering my head, I step into the dim coolness, steeling myself for looks and questions. But the great hall is empty.

Tears blur my vision. I stumble to the canopied platform where the Guru Granth Sahib is kept and fall to my knees. My last hope is gone. Escaping to Gujranwala will not solve my problem. Sooner or later, Manna will bring another man. And even if he's young and handsome, I'll hate him.

"What's wrong, beti?" The white-bearded granthi, whom I hadn't noticed, leans forward from his seat next to the holy book.

His kind voice makes me weep harder. "I came to find the Sarkar, but he's gone."

"Why do you need to see him?"

"Because I love him more than life itself." The words vibrate through the hall, surprising me. I hadn't planned to say this; I hadn't realized, until now, how true it is.

Perhaps the granthi senses my sincerity. "The Sarkar dismissed his men and went to the terrace. He wanted to spend time in silence."

I grasp at this thin thread of hope. "May I go there? I won't trouble him. I promise. If he doesn't want me, I'll leave at once."

An eternity passes. Then the granthi nods and points me to a narrow stairwell.

UPSTAIRS, MY EYES ARE blinded by the dazzle of sunlight on polished stone. I swivel, searching, but see no one. I slump down on the hot tiles. They burn through my thin kurta.

Waheguru, I'm too late.

Then I catch a movement by the far balustrade, the flutter of a white kurta against white walls. The Sarkar stands still, looking out at the city as though he's never seen it before. I want to run to him, but I force myself to walk slowly, the way one should in a house of prayer. He's dressed even more simply than usual. The plainest of turbans, a cotton kurta. His beard is uncombed. There is such sadness in his bearing that if he weren't the king, I'd have thrown my arms around him.

I've made no sound, but he swings around, kirpan in hand. He may be a ruler now, but he was a warrior first.

"Jindan!" he says sharply. "What are you doing here?"

Had I been naive to hope he would be pleased to see me? If nothing else, I'll leave with dignity.

"I came to say goodbye. I'm sorry if I disturbed your prayers."

If he says goodbye, it will be the end of my hopes.

But he says, "Today my soul is too burdened with guilt to pray. I was asking forgiveness of the woman whose death day it is. Had it not been for her, I wouldn't be king. She died of a broken heart because of me."

"Your wife, Sarkar?"

"My mother-in-law."

I wait. Silence is a persuasive tool.

Eventually he says, "Her name was Sada Kaur. Her daughter Mehtab was my first wife—an unhappy political alliance. I never loved Mehtab, but Sada grew closer to me than my own mother. She saw something in me that no one else did. She convinced me that I was destined to do great things, that I could unite the Sikhs into a powerful force. What a warrior she was! What a strategist! She knew that the one who controls Lahore controls Punjab. She negotiated on my behalf and rode by my side into this city. Because of her, the people opened the gates. We conquered Lahore with almost no bloodshed."

For a moment I forget my troubles. "A woman warrior!"

"Yes. She was one in a lakh. But as the years passed she wanted more power; she wanted to make decisions about the kingdom. She wanted me to grant jagirs to Mehtab's children. She chided me for my unwise marriages. Which man likes such things? I told her to retire and hand over the governing of her estates to her grandchildren. She became angry. My spies discovered that she was plotting with the British. So I invited her to Lahore, and when she came, trusting me, I imprisoned her."

This is a different side of the Sarkar I'm seeing.

"She fell ill—from the shock of betrayal, I think. And then she died."

I blurt out, "That was a harsh end."

The Sarkar lowers himself heavily onto a bench. "She requested, over and over, that I visit her, but I refused. Everyone thought I was ruthless—would you not agree?"

I kneel and take his hand. I long to comfort him, but I will not lie. My heart aches for Sada. Finally I say, "Your action was ruthless, but you did it for the good of Punjab. You couldn't allow Sada Kaur to ally herself with the British. That would have destroyed everything you'd fought so hard for. And after she was imprisoned, you couldn't go to her because you loved her too much. Face-to-face, she might have persuaded you, against your better judgment, to do what she wanted."

He's taken aback. "You're wise beyond your years. How did you know what was in my mind? Even my ministers didn't understand. They thought I just wanted more power."

I know because I love you. But I can't bring myself to say it.

He raises me up to sit beside him. Together, we look out over Lahore's roofs, gray and muted now under a thick canopy of rain clouds.

The Sarkar says, "Karma circles back, sooner or later. I know that. And this is just one of the many dark things I've done. I don't care if I suffer. But I pray to Waheguru: Don't make Punjab pay for my sins."

There's something ominous about his words. But before I can say, *Waheguru protect you*, he moves on. "Enough of the past. Did you say you came to bid me goodbye?" His tone is polite, unconcerned.

I must try one last time. "Yes. I couldn't bear to leave without seeing you."

"Where are you going?"

"Back to the village. I'm running away." Everything spills out of me. Manna's plan. Last week's hated suitor.

There's faint amusement in his eye. "And what kind of suitor would you like, young Jindan? Tall and muscular and handsome? One of my ghorcharhas, maybe? Shall I arrange that?"

Anger makes me forget discretion. "You joke with me? You think I'm a child? The merchant isn't a bad man. Many would have accepted him. But my heart has been ruined. It wants you. Only you."

For a moment, his single eye blazes. Is it annoyance, or surprise, or some other emotion?

I've come so far, I might as well go all the way. "Keep me with you," I plead. "I'm not well-born, like your queens. I know you can't marry me. But I could be one of your concubines. I could—"

"Stop!" he orders. Now, clearly, there's displeasure on his face.

My heart sinks.

"Didn't your father say you were only sixteen?"

When I draw myself up to my full height, I'm almost as tall as the Sarkar. "Age doesn't depend solely on how many years one has lived on this earth."

"I'm too old for you," he states flatly.

It's a strange thing to say to a concubine.

"I don't think so. And even if you are, I don't care. I love you."

I've humiliated myself completely now. But had I left without telling him this, I would have regretted it all my life.

He tilts up my chin. What is he looking for? Finally he says, "Go home, Jindan Kaur. I'll send my counselor Fakir Azizuddin—he's good at such things—to inform your father that I'm sending you to Gujranwala tomorrow, with a royal escort. I'll bring you back after two years."

Why would he do this for a concubine?

I start to protest, but he says, "Hush." He slips his ring, the plain band with its small red stone, off his little finger. The finger is crooked, as though it was broken and allowed to heal heedlessly. It fills me with tenderness. *My Sarkar, I will take care of you.*

The ring is too loose for me, but I tell him I'll wrap a string around it and keep it safe.

His lips are warm on my hand. His beard is like strands of silk, as soft as I'd imagined, though more tickly. "You had better! It's a blood ruby all the way from Kabul, sent as a tribute. But more than that, it's your betrothal ring."

My mouth falls open.

Laughing out loud, he declares, "Yes. Standing here in Gurdwara Dehra Sahib, I promise that in two years, I, Ranjit Singh, will marry you—if I'm still alive."

Marry?

I'm filled with incredulous joy. Then the rest of the sentence hits me. "Don't say that! Of course you'll be alive. I'll pray every day for your well-being."

He pulls me close. His lips are firm against mine. My entire body tingles with this, my first kiss.

"It just might work." He smiles. "After all, you are a very persuasive girl."

II

Bride

1835–1839

10

Sword

All day I stride back and forth between house and yard in a swelter of impatience, opening the outer door to see if anyone has arrived from Lahore, then kicking it shut when I see the alley empty as a dried-up river. It's my eighteenth birthday, the day I've been longing for, but it seems no one outside these four walls remembers it.

The morning had started well. Biji woke me with a blessing and a pink phulkari dupatta that she'd embroidered in secret. She didn't say anything—Biji was superstitious that way—but I knew she'd made it for my wedding. The expensive silk-work spilled over my lap, gleaming. A good omen, surely. But it's night now, and no one has come. Not even a courier bearing a gift from the Sarkar, as on my last birthday, or a letter from Fakir Azizuddin, whom the Sarkar has put in charge of me.

The Fakir's silence, particularly, hurts me. Over these two long years, he's been more of a father to me than Manna ever was. He writes every month, letters I wait for hungrily, keeping me informed of court news and zenana intrigues. He includes messages from the Sarkar who, astonishingly, has never learned to read or write. The

Fakir sends money, too, in my name. Thanks to the Sarkar's generosity and my careful management, we no longer worry about food or clothing. Balbir is married to a soldier from a nearby village. We've even purchased our home from our cranky landlord and added on a small room. I've done all this quietly, because I sense the Sarkar doesn't want people to know about our relationship.

None of this would have been possible without the Fakir's involvement, because small matters slip easily from the minds of kings busy with the fate of nations. That's why I'm distressed—and worried—by his unusual silence.

"I'm not hungry," I say at dinner, although Biji has cooked shahi paneer, my favorite. "I'm going to sleep."

But even in bed I toss about. At least I have my own room now. Else Biji would wake up and I'd have to dodge questions to which I have no answers. Her face was shrunken with anxiety earlier. I knew what we were both thinking: *It's not uncommon for a man to forget promises of marriage, especially when he is a king and the girl, low-born.*

For comfort, I grasp my betrothal ring, which I wear on a chain concealed under my kurta so that no one will see it. It brings back that day on the gurdwara terrace when I told the Sarkar I love him. It brings back his silken kiss.

THE EVENING OF MY betrothal, the Sarkar had sent the Fakir to talk to Manna.

How worried I'd been when the Fakir arrived, severe in a dark shawl, with intent eyes that took in everything, and asked Manna to step into the yard. He was not a man to suffer fools. Would he go back and say, *Sarkar, I advise you to have nothing to do with this family*? But then Manna returned, striding like a lord, puffed up with jubilation.

"My little girl to be a queen! I never expected less! But the Fakir is thirsty. He asks you to take him water. Hurry!"

Out in the yard, the Fakir took a small sip from the lota I'd brought. He wasn't thirsty, but he had a lot of questions. At first I was nervous, but he had an easy way about him and I found myself telling him about the things I loved: storms, jalebis, books, Laila. I told him how angry I'd felt when the Sarkar described the men who'd tried to kill him.

The Fakir turned his head sharply. "The Sarkar told you this?"

"Yes. And about Sada Kaur. Her story made me sad. For her—and for him."

"He talked to you about Sada Kaur?"

I nodded, startled by the incredulity in his voice.

"He never mentions her," the Fakir said. "Not even to me. But tell me, why were you angry with his enemies?"

"Because I love him." I was surprised at how easily I could admit this to the Fakir, without embarrassment. "But also because they couldn't see that he was the only one holding Punjab together. They were ready to destroy the whole kingdom with their selfishness. That's why he imprisoned Sada Kaur, too. She no longer wanted what was best for Punjab."

The Fakir's hooded eyes glinted. "All his life the Sarkar has been searching for a woman who will understand him, who will love Punjab as fiercely as he does. Someone with spirit. But also beautiful, because he's a man who craves beauty. He married many times but was always disappointed. Maybe he's finally found her."

"But I'm not high-born like the queens who brought him wealth and armies. I'm not educated in the ways of the court."

"Birth is a poor second to character. You're smart, loyal, honest, a good listener. And you have two years before you become queen. I'll send you newspapers and books. I'll teach you a code tomorrow, before you leave. Using it, I'll inform you of what's going on at court. By the time the Sarkar marries you,

you'll know enough to survive. The rest you'll learn directly from him."

Before leaving, the Fakir said, "The betrothal must be kept a secret—mostly for reasons related to your safety. I've already impressed the importance of this on your father."

"I expect he didn't like that!" How Manna would hate being unable to boast about becoming the king's father-in-law!

We smiled at each other, fellow conspirators.

Over the next two years, the Fakir became my trusted guide. He sent me books and maps, taught me the history of Punjab and its clans, and kept me informed of court intrigues and the growing threat of the British. He encouraged me to question and evaluate situations for myself. Most importantly, he sent me the gruff but heartfelt letters that the Sarkar dictated to him, and gave him my shy messages of love.

Why had he sent nothing today?

LONG PAST MIDNIGHT THERE'S a banging at the door. I wake, startled, and light a lamp. Peering through the midwinter fog, I recognize Manna and Jawahar. What are they doing here? Manna looks about the same as before, only a little grayer in the beard. But Jawahar, whom I haven't seen all year, is taller than Manna, broad-chested and muscled from his work at the smithy. I rush to him, wanting him to whirl me around as he used to, but his face is sullen. Is he angry? Why? With whom?

Their cart was late in leaving Lahore, Manna explains grumpily over a meal of leftover roti and sabzi. He adds that an escort of soldiers will arrive in the morning. They'll bring a granthi—and the Sarkar's sword.

"A sword?" I ask.

"The Sarkar can't be here because of state matters. You're to be married to his sword as soon as it arrives."

"So fast?" Biji cries. "Jindan doesn't have proper clothes. And how can we invite guests at such short notice?"

"No guests," Manna says. "Sarkar's orders. Jindan will leave for Lahore right after the ceremony." His body slumps with dejection. Poor Manna. For two years, every time he visited, that's all he talked about: how he'd invite the entire village, even his enemies—especially his enemies—to the wedding and hold a feast that people would remember for years.

I'm disappointed, too. I don't care about wedding festivities. But I'd hoped to see in the Sarkar's eyes that special look I remembered from the gurdwara rooftop. I'd hoped to place my hand in his and follow him around the Guru Granth Sahib as we recited our vows of love.

Still, what's important is that the Sarkar is keeping his promise. That tomorrow night we'll be together after our long separation. There will be time enough then to look into his eyes. I imagine the night, what else it might hold . . . My face grows hot and I turn away so no one else will notice.

But why is Jawahar upset? It can't be because of the lack of festivities. He never cared for such things.

I put my hand on his arm. "Veer, will you go back to Lahore with me? Maybe stay with me in the qila for a few days before you go back to work? I'd dearly love your company."

Jawahar pulls away, a vein pulsing in his jaw.

It's Manna who explains. The Sarkar has ordered them to return to Gujranwala. He'll give them enough money to start a business, or buy a kheti and become farmers. But he cannot have the people of Lahore pointing to them in the smithy or the dog runs, whispering that these are the Sarkar's new in-laws.

I finally understand Jawahar's resentment. He loves his work at Suleiman's, his friends. Recently, he was promoted to overseer. And now he's being forced to give it all up for me.

I try to apologize, but there's no time. Soldiers are already clamoring at the door. The Guru Granth Sahib, wrapped in silk, is carried into the courtyard under a golden canopy, and behind it a long ceremonial sword in a jeweled sheath. The granthi arrives. I was hoping he'd be the kind old man from the Gurdwara Dehra Sahib, but this is a stranger.

"What'll I feed all these men?" Biji cries, wringing her hands. "It's bad luck if people go hungry at a wedding."

A familiar figure strides up through the fog. Dark turban, somber shawl, calm eyes that miss nothing.

"Fakir ji," I cry, delighted. "You're here!"

"I wouldn't miss your wedding unless I were on my deathbed," he says with a smile. He informs Biji that a cart will arrive soon with enough food for everyone. She only needs to get the bride ready.

I'm caught in a whirlwind. A hurried bath, clothes pulled on somehow. Biji dabs me with sandalwood paste, takes a couple of bangles from her arms and slides them over my wrists. She drapes the phulkari dupatta over my head. A ragi begins to sing a shabad.

I find myself sitting in front of the Guru Granth Sahib, the sword on a cushion next to me. After prayers have been chanted, it is tied to my dupatta. The sword is heavy, but I carry it proudly around the holy book while the ragi sings the Lavan, describing how the souls of the bride and groom have merged into one.

When the ceremony ends, I find myself standing next to Jawahar.

"Don't worry, veer," I whisper. "I'll talk to the Sarkar. Maybe there will be a position at court—"

"Really?" Suddenly his face is that of the boy I loved, excited and hopeful. "You'll do that for me? You won't forget your veer, now that you're so important?" He touches my arm with his calloused hand, an uncertain gesture, because I'm a queen now and he, a commoner. It sends a pang through me.

I'd like to hug him, but my hands are occupied with the sword. I can't set it down until the granthi instructs me.

Forget? After all that you've done for me? Why, I wouldn't even be marrying the Sarkar if you hadn't taken me to the gurdwara—

But there's no chance to tell him this. The food cart has arrived and is being unloaded. Manna strides up and down, shouting unnecessary instructions. The Fakir congratulates me, addressing me as Rani Jindan, which sounds so unreal that I have to work hard to keep from laughing. His eyes twinkle; he knows what I'm thinking. The captain of the soldiers informs us that we must start soon—we have a long way to go. Biji insists that I must eat something. The ragi is singing one last shabad. *Pooree asa jee mansa mere Raam. All my hopes have been fulfilled.* His voice, surprisingly beautiful, pierces me.

My old life is ending.

"I promise," I whisper to Jawahar, and then Biji draws me away.

11

Zenana

THE JOURNEY BEGINS WELL. I travel in a covered carriage with the Fakir riding beside me, regaling me with court news. Then a horseman gallops up with a message.

The Fakir frowns. "I have to go. The Sarkar needs me."

Don't leave me alone, I want to beg. But his first duty is to his king. As is mine. I try to keep my voice from quavering. "He isn't in Lahore?"

"No. He went to Ferozepur for a funeral. That's why he couldn't come to Gujranwala. He was supposed to return to Lahore today. Now he's been delayed."

Anxiety at being left alone makes me petulant. "Who's this person, so special that the king would rather attend his funeral than his own wedding? And now he won't even be at the qila when I arrive!"

"The Sarkar was very sorry he couldn't be there in person for the wedding, but he did it this way because he thought you'd prefer not to wait any longer," the Fakir explains patiently. "Lachman Kaur, the woman who died, was special indeed. She governed Ferozepur, a highly strategic town on the border, for many years, and was his staunch supporter. He had to be present at the funeral to honor her. Also to stave off the British, who have been trying to take control of the town. You'll be safe with Gurbaksh, chief of the troop. He'll take you to the zenana. The Sarkar will return when it is possible."

I understand his unspoken message. *This is the life of a queen. You'll always be second to Punjab. Get used to it.*

"At least Rani Guddan will be there," I say, remembering the beautiful queen's kindness to me at the banquet. I'd longed to contact her, but the Sarkar had told me to wait.

The Fakir looks unhappy. "Guddan's mother is deathly ill. The queen has gone to the Kangra to be with her."

I'll be completely on my own when I get to the qila.

The Fakir makes a sign and the soldiers back away. My palms grow clammy. What is it that requires such privacy?

"I was going to save this for later," he says. "I didn't want to ruin your wedding night. But news flies across the qila, changing shape as it goes. I'd rather you hear it from me than from malicious fools. A few months ago, the Sarkar had an accident. He'd had a long day in durbar, mediating between two warring misls. Upon returning to his chambers, he collapsed. He could not move or speak. Luckily, I was there. I had his guards surround him instantly so no one saw what happened. They carried him to his bed. The physician said our Sarkar had had a stroke."

As the Fakir explains what a stroke is, my own dazed brain, too, seems paralysed.

"We managed to keep it from the citizens and the Khalsa army. There may have been riots otherwise. Jackals in the shadows baring fangs. Only Mai Nakkain and her closest attendants ministered to him. I worried and prayed daily. But the Sarkar has great willpower. In a few weeks, against the advice of his vaids, he was back in court, though he spoke less than before and, thankfully, drank less, too.

"I tell you this because he'll be spending most of his leisure hours with you, at least for a while. Don't let him drink too much. Don't argue. And don't let him overexert himself in trying to please you."

My face heats up as I realize what the Fakir is referring to. But I appreciate his frankness. I'm not sure, however, that I have the power to influence our stubborn king.

He smiles as though he knows my doubts. "Love is your greatest weapon."

I have a hundred questions. A thousand worries. But the Fakir salutes me and is gone.

I WAIT IN THE carriage in the dark outside the qila while Gurbaksh bangs on the closed gates, yelling for the sentry to open up. We're late because one of the carriage wheels came off and Gurbaksh had to find a blacksmith. The jeweled sword is heavy in my lap, but I don't want to set it down. It comforts me amid the commotion.

"I can't open the gate without permission from higher up," the sentry says. "I'll lose my job."

"I have the Sarkar's new queen with me," Gurbaksh yells. "You want her to sleep out here tonight? When the Sarkar hears about that, you'll lose more than just your job."

Tired and hungry, I've had enough. I adjust my veil carefully, step out, and hold up the sword. The precious stones on the scabbard glitter in torchlight. The sentry's expression changes.

"I am Rani Jindan," I declare authoritatively. "I am sure the Sarkar will reward you for opening the pedestrian door to let me in. Gurbaksh will walk me to my haveli. You may keep my trunk until tomorrow."

Perhaps it's my show of confidence. Perhaps it's the sword. The sentry bows. The door creaks open. Gurbaksh offers to take the sword and the small bundle Biji has given me. But I choose to carry the sword myself, though it's heavy and I must pause often to catch my breath as we climb the steep stairs.

We walk across the grounds of the sleeping palace. Night makes everything look different from my memories. The silvered turrets are cold and forbidding, and the fountains, filled with broken moonlight. Loneliness twists my heart.

But then, hasn't loneliness been my companion these last two years?

Suddenly, a figure detaches itself from the darkness and blocks our path with an upraised sword and a harsh command to halt. An armed woman. She's followed by others. The zenana guards! One grabs my arm with steely fingers. A second presses her blade against Gurbaksh's throat.

For a man to be in this part of the palace at this hour of night, I remember Manna saying, is a crime punishable by death.

The chief guard glares at Gurbaksh. "What are you up to, creeping through the dark?"

Shock has struck Gurbaksh dumb. The woman holding the dagger says, "He's clearly guilty. Shall I—"

I must stop her! "Let him go," I cry.

The chief guard turns to me. "Who are you? His accomplice?"

I remember, all of a sudden, where I've seen her—in the women's pavilion, when Mai Nakkain ordered her to throw me into the dungeon. A name swims up through my murky memories.

"Bhago Kaur," I say, "I am Rani Jindan, the maharaja's new wife. I was married this morning to his sword." I raise the sword. The guards step back, murmuring. "This man was ordered by the Sarkar to bring me from my parents' home to the palace." I force steel into my voice, though all I feel is fear. "Surely you were informed that I would be arriving today!"

Things happen rapidly after that. Gurbaksh is escorted out of the qila. Bhago bangs on the door of a long, low building, muttering under her breath, until an old woman with a flickering lamp opens it and leads me to a small, damp, windowless room. Inside, the bed is hard and narrow, the bedclothes musty, the floor filthy. I step over black pellets of mouse droppings. Mismatched furniture—an almirah, a discolored mirror, a footstool—lines the walls, as though the room was used for storage. In a corner, atop a chest, sit a covered dish and a pitcher of water, along with an unlit lamp.

"Are you sure this is my room?" I ask, incredulous. "For Rani Jindan?"

"It is your room. I was given orders." The woman points at the dish. "Your dinner."

Ranting will do no good. I'll have to try a different tactic. I take a coin from my pouch and hold it out. "Thank you for your help so late at night."

The woman looks taken aback, as much at the courtesy as at the baksheesh. Her hand darts out and grabs the coin. She says, "Toilets are at the end of the corridor." She uses her lamp to light mine. Then she whispers, "Maybe you shouldn't eat the food."

My heart skips a beat. "Why not?"

The woman doesn't meet my eyes. "It's been sitting out a while. May have spoiled."

"That is sound advice."

"You can drink the water, though." She hobbles to the door.

I enquire, casually, "Who assigned me this room?"

"In the zenana, Mai Nakkain makes all decisions."

Left alone, I examine the door. The latch is flimsy—one good kick would break it in two. I sit on the bed, my mind in a whirl. Could the food be poisoned? Was that what the old woman hinted at? Surely Mai Nakkain wouldn't dare to kill the Sarkar's new bride?

Yes, she would.

So many problems. The Sarkar's ill health. My promise to Jawahar. And now, Mai's enmity. How will I solve them?

I open my bundle. Biji had packed a few laddus for me. I'd taken them mostly to please her, certain I wouldn't need them. Now I eat them all, then take a cautious sip of the water. It tastes fine. My throat is dry, but I only allow myself two mouthfuls. I don't want to go searching for the toilet.

I feel more optimistic after having eaten. Tomorrow I'll send word to the Sarkar. He'll sort everything out.

Footsteps shuffle along the corridor, then stop. Is someone outside my room? I set the dish of food on the ground and push the heavy chest against the door. I decide to leave the lamp burning. Then I lie down on the bed, covering my head with a sheet in case rodents decide to visit.

Waheguru, send me someone who can help me . . .

In the middle of my prayer, exhaustion drags me into oblivion.

In the morning when I wake, my dinner is scattered on the floor. My rodent room-mates seem to have enjoyed their feast.

THREE DAYS HAVE PASSED since I arrived. I gave the old woman a note for the Sarkar, along with more coins from my dwindling store. But I've heard nothing from him. She insists that she delivered it to one of his attendants, but she could be lying. Each day, my worries increase. Has the Sarkar been delayed further? Is he ill? Has he forgotten me?

At noon I take my place again on the worn carpet of the dining room beside the forgotten ranis and concubines and feel their hostile stares. Not knowing whom to trust, I've kept to myself, but they've interpreted my caution as haughtiness. I hear their whispers: *Who does she think she is, this peasant? Too good to talk to us because she has a pretty face?*

The morning after my arrival, an attendant had brought a heaped thali of delicacies to my room, stating that as a new queen, I need not eat with the lesser members of the zenana. But I declined. The food in the dining hall is cheap and indifferently cooked, but at least it's safe. We eat peasant fare: roti, dal, saag. We've had mutton only once. Whoever's in charge of the budget—possibly Mai—keeps a tight hold on the purse strings.

How I'd fantasized, these last two years, about a queen's luxurious lifestyle!

We've just begun eating when there's a commotion at the door, a voice raised in irritation. The women scramble to their feet and stand with lowered eyes. I'm not sure what's happening, but I figure it's wise to follow suit. Then I recognize the steely tones and discreetly pull my veil over my face, hoping to go unnoticed. But Mai Nakkain's heavy footsteps stop in front of me.

Of course. I'm the reason she's here.

"Here you are." Mai's voice is deceptively mild. "I was wondering why you weren't in your room. That's where you're supposed to take your meals as a new queen. But how would you know the ways of royalty, seeing as you're the daughter of a kennel-keeper?"

I keep my face impassive. I won't give her the satisfaction of seeing me upset.

"Let's take a look at you," she says.

An attendant yanks the veil off my head, a gesture so insulting that several women gasp in dismay. I use all my self-control to remain silent, my head bowed. Mai is powerful enough to make me disappear before I even get to see the Sarkar. She could claim I never arrived at the qila. She could bribe or threaten the soldiers who brought me and have them say there was an accident on the road. No one in the zenana would speak up against Mai, not for me. If only Guddan were here! But she isn't. I must rely on my own wits.

I feel Mai's eyes raking me. I'm glad that I oiled my hair and tied it back in an unattractive bun this morning. And that all the ornaments the Sarkar gifted me are in a pouch tucked into the waistband of my salwar.

"All your scheming finally paid off, didn't it? But don't think you'll entice the Sarkar for more than a few weeks. That isn't how things work with him."

I venture a glance at the old queen. The years haven't been kind to her. Her hairline has receded; there are bags under her eyes.

"Once he tires of your plump lips and soft curves, he'll be after other conquests. You'll never see his bed again. You'll never get to speak to him except when he thinks it necessary."

For a moment, I hear the sorrow in her voice. Is she remembering the moment when the Sarkar lost interest in her? I feel an unexpected pang of pity.

As though she senses it, Mai says harshly, "Make the most of your brief glory. Maybe you'll be able to wheedle enough trinkets out of the Sarkar for a few years of comfort after he packs you off to that godforsaken village of yours."

If you really believe I'll be gone, why are you afraid of me? Because that's what I glimpse beneath the hatred. Fear. *Did it make you poison my food?*

One day I'll confront her. But today Mai Nakkain walks away in a victorious jangle of jewelry.

THREE MORE DAYS PASS without any news. Mai's taunts echo in my head. Is the Sarkar off chasing another woman, more intelligent, more beautiful, and—most importantly—from a family better suited for a royal alliance? Is it my fate to rot, forgotten, in the bowels of the zenana?

I battle my insidious doubts with exercise. A year ago, the Fakir had sent me a treatise on how physical movement and deep breathing calmed the mind. The parchment contained pictures of yogis in intricate poses. I practise these in my room, dodging the excess furniture. I want to stroll around the qila, like the other ranis, but Bhago refuses permission. There's no one to appeal to, so I pace up and down the dank corridors like a caged animal.

Dusk, when the women are allowed on the terrace of the zenana, is for me the most poignant time. I look down at the lights of Lahore, filling my lungs with the vibrant, frenzied sounds of the city. If only

Jawahar were here, I'd escape to his room and he'd help me find the Sarkar. The thought makes me feel more alone.

I send another message—with a different maid this time. No answer. The woman can't tell me if the Sarkar is back in Lahore.

At night I read from my Granth Sahib. *Why are you so afraid, O mind? The birds fly hundreds of miles, leaving their young ones behind. Who feeds them, and who teaches them to feed themselves? Have you ever thought of this?* The message fails to comfort me. In the middle of reading, my lamp flickers and goes out—because the maids (no doubt by instruction) don't fill it properly.

Waheguru, I've flown even further—from a dog trainer's hovel to a royal palace where I'm no better than a prisoner. Only you can help me now.

12

Sheesh Mahal

Another week passes. At dinner, the women titter because the Sarkar hasn't sent me the platter of nuts and dried fruit with which even the commonest of guests are welcomed. Back in my room, which smells increasingly as though something has died in here, I'm too disheartened to pray.

Suddenly someone throws open my door without knocking, startling me. It's Bhago, scowling. "The Sarkar wants to see you in one hour."

Delirious with excitement, I rummage through my trunk. There's little to wear. The trunk had arrived in my room with the lock broken, my best clothes missing. The maids who carried it in shrugged in response to my questions.

"It was like this when we went to get it," one said, while the other hid a smile. "Maybe you should ask Bhago Kaur what happened."

They cared nothing for my rage. Everyone knew Mai Nakkain hated me. Anything could be done to me. I didn't bother to question Bhago. I knew I'd get neither answer nor apology. But I promised myself that I would remember.

Fortunately my maroon lehenga, the one Guddan gave me, is still here. Will the Sarkar remember that he'd admired me in it? The bodice, which had been loose before, fits snugly over my breasts. I darken my eyes and pinch my cheeks to add color. If only I had some sandalwood oil. At least my hair cooperates, falling in a glossy braid down my back.

Bhago returns early, hoping to catch me off guard, but I'd expected this and am ready.

"Let's go," I say brightly. "You don't want to keep the Sarkar waiting, do you?" I grip the Sarkar's sword, hidden carefully under my bedclothes all this time, with both my hands to stop them from trembling.

THE NIGHT IS DARK, the moon covered by clouds. I hurry to keep up with Bhago, who strides ahead, holding the lantern away from me so that I can't see where I'm stepping. She'd love for me to fall on the uneven cobblestones, to tear my dupatta, arrive streaked with mud and disgrace. But I won't give her the satisfaction. Finally we reach a wall, shimmering from top to bottom, as if in a magical tale. Bhago whistles, and a woman steps out from behind the wall.

"Welcome," she says with a smile—the first I've seen since I arrived at the qila—and bows. "I am one of the Sarkar's attendants. He's waiting for you."

Relief and longing wash over me. But first I must take care of another matter. I turn to Bhago. "I will be sure to inform the Sarkar of your service to me."

The guard's eyes widen—in fear, I'd like to think. Let her imagine what I'm planning. Let her worry. The constellations are shifting. My star is finally rising.

"Take me to my husband," I tell the attendant.

Tiny, glittering mirrors cover the walls around me, lamplight reflected in them a thousandfold. I realize I'm inside the Sheesh Mahal, built by Emperor Shah Jahan centuries ago. We climb the stairs and enter a large chamber with friezed windows. Sheer curtains flutter in the night breeze. Roses in silver vases. A vast bed covered in rose petals. The attendant disappears.

Leaning on a cushion, splendid in white, there he is. Finally. Maharaja Ranjit Singh. King of this entire land. My feet refuse to move. I can't remember the proper etiquette for greeting him. But then he smiles and holds out his arms. I lay down the sword, run to him and kneel. He looks older. The circles under his eyes wrench me. Can he sense my love? Because I'll never be able to tell him how I feel.

"Don't cry, my heart," he says. "Come, sit by me. I'm sorry to have kept you waiting so long. There was a difficult situation in Ferozepur I had to take care of. I only returned to Lahore today."

He wipes my face with a soft kerchief. His tenderness makes me weep harder. Now I'll look ugly, with puffy eyes.

As though he has heard my thoughts, the Sarkar cups my face in his hands. "You've grown more beautiful since the last time I saw you! I did not think it possible."

Which woman can resist smiling after that?

We sit cross-legged on the bed, eating from a gold platter piled with snacks: mithai, dates, cashews, apples. Of course, he thinks I've had a good dinner. I try to take small, ladylike bites. It's hard, though. The food is tastier than anything I've had since I arrived in Lahore, and I'm so hungry. But I don't want to seem greedy.

On a crystal dish there are dark-brown squares covered in gold foil. Chocolates from across the ocean, he explains, a gift from one of his French jarnails. He places one in my mouth. I grimace at the bittersweet taste. He laughs. "You'll get used to it, maybe even crave it after a while." There's a hot light in his eye. I guess he's alluding to other pleasures as well. He pours a goblet of wine, a deep jeweled red, drinks some and offers me the rest. "You're old enough now." The heavy sweetness makes me queasy, but he clearly likes it. He drinks another gobletful, then pulls me to him. I find myself stiffening. All I know of marriage nights are Biji's embarrassed, cautionary whispers. *Watch out for . . . Men don't like . . . It'll hurt . . . Be sure not to complain . . . Women don't really enjoy . . . Hopefully a baby . . .* I remember, too, the Fakir's cautions. *Don't let him overexert himself.*

But the Sarkar is gentle and unhurried. He kisses me, murmuring all the love words I've longed to hear. When he takes off his kurta, his arms and chest are full of scars. What a fearless warrior he must have been. I run my hand over his body and find myself growing strangely aroused.

He smiles as though he knows everything I'm feeling. Untying my bodice deftly, he positions me under him. He touches me in ways that make my body come alive. He's done this many times before. The thought fills me with jealousy but also triumph because it's me he's with now. The lamps around the bed flicker in the night breeze. The crushed rose petals give up their sweetness. I forget the Fakir and Biji. I bring my breast to his mouth and feel him grow hard. Instinctively, I raise my hips, bracing for the sharp, piercing pain that I've been warned to expect. But there's nothing. Only him thrusting over and over, his breath harsh. Finally he rolls off me with a muffled curse and I know I've failed.

I cover my face. Is this the end of my dreams?

He embraces me gently. "It's not your fault. I'm an old man. It doesn't happen for me every time. Less and less nowadays, in fact. Let's not worry about it." He kisses my shoulder and wraps me in a silken sheet. "Come, let us enjoy the night breeze. It's what I love best about sleeping in the Sheesh Mahal." With the Sarkar's arm around my waist, I look down at the slumbering city, mysterious and newly beautiful. The Sarkar points out monuments, tells me their history. "That tower, the eight-sided one, is the Musamman Burj. It's the first place in Lahore I remember seeing. The Afghans had taken the city and looted the countryside; things were looking grim for our people. The Sarbat Khalsa elected me to fight them. I guess no one else wanted the job! I was only eighteen then. I rode up to the Burj and challenged Shah Zaman to fight with me, one on one."

I shiver in delight at my king's recklessness. "That was very brave."

He laughs. "It was youthful stupidity! He could have had one of his archers shoot me down! But he didn't. Perhaps he was amused by my foolhardiness. Or perhaps the Gurus were with me. We barricaded the city until he ran out of money to pay his army. That's really what it comes down to in battle. Whether you can keep the troops happy. Shah Zaman fled to Kabul. My ghorcharhas and I chased him all the way from the Jhelum to the Sindhu. After that, the citizens asked me to take over Lahore."

"Tell me that story."

"Another time. Now we should sleep. Do you want more chocolate?"

I shake my head. "But I could eat another laddu."

"My sweet Punjabi kudi," he says, chuckling. "I like laddus better, too." We break a large laddu and feed each other the pieces. I lick the sugar from his fingers and suddenly we're kissing again, falling back into bed, pulling the sheets off each other's bodies. This time everything works. He presses his face against my neck and cries out as he comes inside me. I hold him, flushed with elation. Later, when we lie spooned against each other, he covers me with a quilt light as a cloud and asks, *Did you enjoy?* I say yes because this is all I know.

As I'm drifting into sleep, he murmurs, "What can I present you with, my Jind, my life, for giving me so much joy? Gold bangles? A seven-stranded pearl necklace? A palace? I'll give you all of them, if you like."

I remember Mai Nakkain's coarse laughter. *Maybe you'll be able to wheedle enough trinkets out of him to live in comfort when he sends you back to your godforsaken village.*

I'm never going to be avaricious like that.

The Sarkar continues, "I owe you a wedding present, too. You can tell me what you want tomorrow night, if you can't think of it right now."

His words pierce me with joy. He wants me again! That is gift enough.

Then I remember. "I need a maid. Someone smart and trustworthy."

The Sarkar stares into the night, silent for so long that I fear I've displeased him. Was it inappropriate to ask him to solve my domestic problems?

Then he says, "Practical. I like that about you. And I believe I know just the right person!"

13

Transformations

BEFORE I ENTER THE HALL for my midday meal, I cover myself with a thick shawl to hide the pearl necklace the Sarkar gave me, from around his own neck, when I left him this morning. I don't want the women to see it and poison my life with their envy. But they're already jealous; news travels through the zenana as rapidly as mosquito fever in the rainy season. Resentful whispers fill the room as I take my seat, scowling so that no one will dare to ask me questions. I try to eat, but after last night's magical feast, I can't stand the coarse roti and congealed dal. I sit there worrying. How can I be sure the Sarkar wants me again? What if he was just being kind?

Returning from the dining hall sweaty, annoyed and hungry, I see that the door to my room, which I'd latched carefully behind me, is ajar. I can hear someone moving around inside, muttering. Probably stealing the few things I have left.

I fling the door open. A woman stands there—short, dark, wiry, not much older than me.

"How dare you come into my room!" I shout.

A grin splits open her pockmarked face; her teeth are startlingly white. "Pardon, my queen. My name's Mangla. The Sarkar has sent me to take care of you. I thought I'd get an early start. You just make yourself comfortable on your bed, and watch."

I sit down, bemused. Mangla bustles about the room. She has caught hold of a maid—one of the two who brought my broken trunk—and is making her clean.

"What about under the bed? Who do you think is going to do that? Your mother-in-law?" Mangla makes a disgusted face at the balls of hair and dust that emerge and stomps with satisfaction on the cockroaches that scurry out. "Something here stinks, and you're not stopping until we find it." She makes the maid drag the almirah forward and discovers a dead mouse. "I knew it!" she says, triumphant.

I stare in fascinated horror as the maid removes the carcass. I'm sure the mouse died after eating my dinner the first night. Someone *had* poisoned my food, then. I start to tremble.

Mangla has stripped the bed and thrown the sheets on the floor. "What are these rags doing here? Get my lady new bedclothes, and I mean *new*. Tell the zenana housekeeper that these are the Sarkar's orders. Send her to me if she refuses. Pour more oil in that lamp, for heaven's sake. You're acting as though it's your dowry you're pouring away. No, don't touch the pitcher, kambakht! I'll fetch the queen's drinking water myself. And her food, too. Be thankful I'm not reporting you to the Sarkar for how badly you've all behaved toward his favorite rani."

She shoos the cowed maid from the room, then turns to me. "Why, even the Sarkar's dogs are treated better."

I stiffen. Is this a dig at my ancestry?

Mangla gives me a hard, but not unsympathetic, look. "I said that purposely, my queen. I know about your family. Everyone does. People will try to shame you for it. You must be prepared for their comments. You must carry yourself proudly. And why not! After all, if a princess marries a king, there's nothing special about that. But you—when people look at you, you *want* them to think, she was a dog trainer's daughter and still the Sarkar chose her, she must be really something! But for that to work, *you* have to behave like the queen you are."

I never thought of it this way, but she's right.

There's a scar above Mangla's right eyebrow. A drunken father lashing out? An angry employer? It brings me strange comfort. If Mangla has made it this far, surely I can overcome my challenges, especially with her by my side.

When she asks me what has happened since I arrived in Lahore, all my woes tumble out: the pilfered trunk, the flimsy latch, the footsteps at night, Mai's insults, Bhago's hostility, this prison cell of a room, the tasteless meals, the hatred of the other ranis and, worst of all, an entire week of fearing that the Sarkar had forgotten me.

Mangla doesn't waste time sympathizing. In her raspy, matter-of-fact voice, she tells me, "But the Sarkar *didn't* forget you. Keep your mind on that until I get back."

She returns carrying a large platter. Uncovering it, I find stacks of pooris, steaming-hot rice, dal, vegetables, mutton curry, curds, pickles and laddus. Mangla watches with satisfaction as I devour everything.

"Sorry it took me so long," she says. "There was a lot to do, and people weren't cooperative until I threatened them. I've found you a better room in the Khilwat Khana, where you should have been put in the first place. They'll get it ready by tomorrow. Till then, I'll bring you food and water. You needn't go to the dining hall again. I must run more errands now, but don't you worry." She holds up a sturdy iron lock. "Just lock the door behind me."

I grasp Mangla's hands. "You're the best companion I could have wished for."

She looks touched; I sense that not many people have paid her compliments. "Rest now," she responds in a gentler tone. "You have to look good. The Sarkar wants you to spend the night with him again. I'm going to buy you some proper clothes." I scrabble worriedly in my waistband for coins, but Mangla holds up a fat silken purse. "Our

Sarkar thinks of everything. How do you think I managed to get you that room in the Khilwat Khana? Wasn't because of my pretty face!"

Just before Mangla leaves, I tell her my suspicions about my poisoned meal that killed the mouse. I fear that she'll think me fanciful, but she looks grim. "I'm glad you told me. I'll take extra precautions. No harm will come to you, not while I'm around."

I lock the door behind Mangla and, for the first time since I came here, fall into a deep, relaxed sleep. Mangla's words echo in my brain. "The Sarkar said, Mangla, take special care of my Jindan. She has the makings of a great rani."

Did Mangla really say this, or am I dreaming it? No matter.

My Sarkar, I'll make you proud.

MY LIFE HAS TURNED into a fairy tale. Every night I sleep with the Sarkar in the Sheesh Mahal and wake in his arms. The sex is uneven, but I've learned not to be anxious, mostly because he's good-humored about it. Am I disappointed with the pleasures of the marital bed? I push that question away. My husband enjoys my company and loves me. And I love him. Isn't that enough? An additional coup: I've cajoled the Sarkar into drinking less. At dinner, when I replace wine with juice or water, he grumbles but submits to me.

I particularly enjoy conversing with him late into the night, learning what's happening in the kingdom.

"I'm impressed by your curiosity and intelligence," he says. "None of my other queens care about what goes on outside the qila."

Sometimes when he meets with a courtier in the Sheesh Mahal, he lets me wait in a back room and listen. Later, we discuss the visit. Over time, I learn many things, especially the growing threat of the British.

Today, Suchet Singh, Wazir Dhian Singh's younger brother, brings news that the British have taken over Coorg. "They deposed Vira Raja," he fumes, "because he was tired of their interference and rose up against them. What gives them the right? They did the same thing to Mysore a few years back. And to Bahawalpur, not so far from us."

Tall, muscular, dressed in a red kurta, Suchet Singh burns with rage like the sun. The maharaja, though not particularly handsome himself, likes having good-looking men around him. I admire the confidence that enables him to do that.

The Sarkar puts a hand on Suchet's shoulder. "It happens because we let them. We Hindustanis don't know how to unite, not even when we know the outsider is dangerous." His voice is unusually sad, and I feel my own throat constrict. "That's what happened to the Marathas—one of the greatest empires of Hindustan. You're too young, but I remember receiving the news—I was busy with the siege of Multan then. The British used their spies to learn each Maratha leader's weakness. They negotiated with some of them, then attacked the others. One by one, the firangs defeated them all. The poor Peshwa didn't stand a chance. We can't allow them to do this to Punjab. Promise me this." He fixes his eye on Suchet until the younger man puts his hand over his heart and bows. Behind the curtain, I, too, make my own silent promise.

On his wall, my husband keeps a map of Hindustan where he has marked, in red, the kingdoms taken over by the British. Every time I look, the crimson blotches have crept closer to Punjab.

"Soon it'll all become red," he says.

I protest. "You're too smart and too strong to be tricked by any firang."

"It will not be in my lifetime, but I fear it might be in yours."

I notice what hero worship had blinded me to until now: my husband is worn out from constantly guarding Punjab from her enemies. How many more years will I have him with me?

The longing for a child rises in my heart. Something of my beloved's that will live on after him. Something that will give me a reason to keep living.

THE SARKAR LIKES TELLING me about the important men in his court. Afterward, he tests me, making a game of it. Each time I answer correctly, he tosses a coin into the air for me to catch.

And so I learn about the three Hindu brothers: Suchet, Gulab, and Dhian Singh Dogra, who rose from nothing to become the most powerful men at court, and the rulers of Jammu. How they are envied and hated by the Sikh sardars, the Sandhawalias and the Attariwalas.

"I can't blame them," the Sarkar admits. "They helped me win my early battles, riding by my side, risking their lives. They gave their sisters and daughters to me in marriage and strengthened my clan. For that, I'll always be grateful. But the Sikhs are no good at strategy. I need warriors, yes, but I need statesmen more, to stave off wars. My country suffers too much when there is fighting."

Another day he says, "When I'm gone, Dhian will help you. But the man I trust more is Hari Singh Nalwa, the leader of our Khalsa army. You haven't seen him because he's always at the outposts, guarding Punjab's borders. If you send word, he'll come to your aid. Remember also the Rana of Nepal. Our soldiers fought side by side. He swore to help me if ever the need arose. But his kingdom is distant, across many mountains. You'll not need to go that far."

I must look distressed, for he changes the topic. "Let's see what you know about the foreigners."

I've seen a few of the firangs from afar; the rest I have only heard about. But I've been practising. I count them on my fingers. "The American Harlan, who served you well but then tried to cheat you; the French Allard, the jarnail you love like a brother; the Italian Avitabile, who fights like a cornered tiger; Dr. Honigberger, whose gentle cures you trust; Dr. McGregor, whom you trust less, though his electric treatments fascinate you. And finally, the British politicians: Burnes, Bradford, Wade, Fane, and that wily fox, Bentinck."

He nods, then questions me further. "What must you remember about the British?"

"They should be treated with hospitality but cannot be trusted. They are men of honor, but only where other Englishmen are concerned. Their aim is to cause dissension among the chieftains of a kingdom. Each time you learn to deal with one, he returns to England and others come, their heads filled with new schemes."

Pleased, he tosses me a gold coin. "You've understood the firangs better than most."

"Thank Waheguru, I'll never have to deal with them."

"I pray for that, too. But why am I teaching you all this?"

I have no answer. When the Sarkar dies, Kharak Singh, his son by Mai Nakkain, will be king. I'm certain that he'll banish me, immediately and forever, to Gujranwala.

Why then do I feel that this knowledge is crucial?

THE SARKAR'S RELATIONSHIP WITH his family is even more complicated than with his court. He has many wives and several sons, only some of whom he has acknowledged as his. His heir, Prince Kharak, lives in Lahore, as does Kharak's son, Naunihal, though they have their own havelis. I see them sometimes when they visit the Sarkar in the Sheesh Mahal.

Kharak was once a fine warrior, but now he has gained weight and moves lumberingly. The dark circles under his eyes, Mangla tells me, are a sign of his opium habit. On the rare occasions when we are in the same room, he watches me with suspicious sideways glances. I'm not surprised. Mai is sure to have poisoned him against me. Do mother and son discuss me after his visits—what I wore, what I said, whether the Sarkar showed me affection?

Naunihal, the Sarkar's favorite grandson, is the opposite of his glum father: handsome, slim, and so full of energy that he can barely sit still. I like Naunihal. He is just a little younger than me and jokes with me freely. He listens intently to his grandfather and discusses policy with more intelligence than courtiers twice his age. An excellent warrior, he is hugely popular with the army.

"If only I could name Naunihal my successor!" the Sarkar tells me. But he can't. So he has made Kharak his heir but includes Naunihal in his decision-making.

Sadly, Kharak and Naunihal don't get along. Each time they visit the Sarkar together—upon his insistence—I notice the warning signs. When Kharak misses an important political point the Sarkar has made, I see the the barely hidden contempt on Naunihal's face. After they leave, the Sarkar stands by the window, staring silently at Lahore. I put my arms around him, wishing I could take on his troubles. But when he asks, *Do you think they'll be able to rule together successfully?* I remain silent. I will not lie to him.

I'VE FAILED TO DO the one thing that Jawahar asked of me. In letter after letter, he writes, *Dear Sister, when are you inviting me back to Lahore? I'm suffocating here among these ignorant peasants.*

So, after a night of successful sex, when the Sarkar is about to fasten a string of rubies around my neck, I hold back his hand.

"I have enough jewels."

He looks astonished and amused. "I never thought I'd hear a woman say this! What can I give you, then? More servants?"

"No. Mangla is all I need."

"A haveli of your own? There's space in the corner of the qila—I could build a mansion to your liking—"

I'm tempted. A house of my own. Something I'd never believed possible. But I shake my head.

"I would like something for my brother. Jawahar misses Lahore and hates being back in Gujranwala. He isn't interested in the business our father has started. They fight whenever they work together. I hear from my mother that he's getting into bad company. Could you find him something at court, even something small?"

The Sarkar's face is stern. "I love you, Jindan. But it is my strict policy to not allow the relatives of my wives to live in Lahore unless it is their ancestral home. And I never show them favoritism at court. Too many complications would arise from that. All across Punjab, I'm known for only rewarding men who deserve it. That is a big part of my power—and a major reason for my courtiers' loyalty. I cannot veer from it, not even for you."

His words are a wall of iron. I could beat my head against it all my life, but it would be useless. As a queen, I can see he is right. His impartiality is what makes the durbar of the Lion of Punjab exceptional among courts which crawl with sycophants. As a wife, though, I'm hurt and angry at being turned down. What, then, is the worth of all his love words?

In my room, I weep as I realize that I'll never be able to invite my family—for me, that means Biji and Jawahar—to share my good fortune. Biji will be sad, but she'll understand. Jawahar, however, will be enraged. I imagine him spiraling down into drunkenness and depression. I can't bear to be the cause of that.

I write, *Patience, my brother. I'm trying. I don't have enough influence yet. But I'll bring you here soon.*

Once the letter is on its way, I feel guilty. The Sarkar will never change his mind. I should have told Jawahar the truth. Then he might have tried to make a successful life for himself elsewhere.

NOW THAT I'M THE Sarkar's favorite queen, I'm showered with gifts. Ranis wish to become part of my entourage; wives of courtiers want me to intercede on behalf of their husbands. I accept everything graciously but promise nothing.

"Why, you're a born queen!" Mangla laughs.

More surreptitious gifts are left outside my door at night. Silks. Silver anklets. Rose attar from Persia. Attempts at verse are attached to some. *O moon of mine, if I were invited to go to Paradise without you, I would refuse, for would not Paradise then be a prison?*

"There should be laws," I tell Mangla, "to punish men who write such bad poetry."

The most handsome of my admirers is a young water-carrier for the zenana named Gulloo. He stands below my window every morning, silent and worshipful.

"He told me he'll give me a month's pay to meet you face-to-face for even one moment," Mangla informs me, sighing romantically. "To touch your hand, he'll give me a year's pay. Not that I'd ever accept it. But it's quite charming, how drunk he is with love."

Gulloo sends me a glossy mynah that he's taught to say my name. He hires musicians to stand on the street beneath my window and sing of Heer and Ranjha, the thwarted lovers. I suspect Mangla told him that it's my favorite song.

Mangla whispers, "Shall I arrange a meeting? When he comes to fill our cistern? No one would think anything of it. He's in and out of the havelis all the time . . ." Her eyes are sympathetic. She knows my love life has its shortcomings.

I'm shocked at Mangla's suggestion and, I must admit, tempted. Not by Gulloo's good looks, but because it's thrilling to be the center of someone's world. The Sarkar loves me, but I'll never wield this kind of power over him. Then I shake off my folly.

"You should know better than to even think of such things," I say sternly. "Tell Gulloo to stop his idiocy. It'll bring me nothing but trouble. And it could get him killed. From now on, if any man sends me a gift, throw it away. Publicly."

Mangla bows, abashed.

I don't ever want the Sarkar to doubt me. Not just because I love him, but because of a greater desire. I want a baby—a child whose parentage no one will ever question.

Does my heart twist when Mangla carries away the singing mynah? When a procession of handsome ghorcharhas passes beneath my window, do I stand there a moment longer than necessary, wondering who among them dreamed of me last night? *Forgive me, Waheguru.* Adoration is a powerful intoxicant.

THE ONLY PEOPLE WHOSE visits I await hungrily are the Fakir and Guddan. He is the father I'd always longed for, and she my dearest friend, my sister. He brings me valuable political information; she guides me through the quicksand of zenana protocol. What could be better gifts?

For a while after I came to Lahore, I didn't see the Fakir. When he finally appeared at my door, he looked old and frail. Bursting into tears, I threw my arms around his neck.

"Why did you take this long? I was alone, and everyone was so cruel."

"Hush, my child. I couldn't help it. The Sarkar sent me to warn the Afghan king, Dost Mohammed, to cease encroaching upon our territory. In response, flouting all protocol, Mohammed threw me into his dungeon!"

I'm horrified. "You could have died!"

"Everyone dies sometime," he replies mildly.

The Fakir discusses the latest problems at court with me. Encouraged by the British, the Amirs of the North-West had attacked the Punjabi settlements along the Sindhu. When our troops drove them back, the British took the Amirs' side and warned the Sarkar to return their territories. Otherwise they would be obliged to battle us.

"I've never seen the court so divided and angry," the Fakir says. "Most of the ministers clamored to go to war against the British for violating their non-interference treaty and for trying to cut away our outlying territories."

"But that's just what the British want!" I cry. "It'll give them the excuse to attack us with full force."

He's pleased at my insight. "Our Sarkar—though he was incensed, too—saw that. He chose not to fall into their trap. But the young sardars were unhappy. Some even whispered that the Sarkar was growing too old for battle." He moves to another topic. "The British threat is still distant; you have one right here. Mai Nakkain is livid with jealousy at your prominence."

A shiver goes through me. I haven't told the Fakir about the dead mouse. It would worry him, and he has enough troubles. Besides, Mai can't harm me now. "She wouldn't dare to do anything," I declare, "when I'm under the Sarkar's protection."

"Don't underestimate her," the Fakir warns. "She's a devious one."

GUDDAN HAS APOLOGIZED MANY times for not being in Lahore to assist me when I first arrived. Her informants must have told her how badly I was treated by Mai. I tell her I understand. Her mother was deathly ill. It was Guddan's duty to be by her side.

"Yes," Guddan admits. "My mother has been depending on me more and more since my sister Banso died." Her eyes darken with sorrow. "You remind me of her."

Perhaps that's why she lavishes me with gifts. Today she drapes a pearl-studded dupatta around my shoulders. "Wear it when you go to the Sarkar."

"Don't you mind?"

"That you're sleeping with him? I would, if it was one of those high-nosed ranis. But you're like my sister." She stares into the distance. "Let me tell you Banso's story."

Guddan and her younger sister were given by their father Sansar Chand to the Sarkar in marriage—a political union, as so many royal marriages are. Guddan understood this, but Banso did not. She fell in love with the Sarkar. For a while, all was well. He lavished attention upon her because she was a great beauty. Then he grew busy with other things—hunts, banquets, war campaigns, visits to the Golden Temple. He was a king, after all. And yes, new women came into his life.

"I tried my best to make Banso understand that this was a rani's life. The Sarkar would never be hers alone. But Banso couldn't bear it. She was found dead one morning, her face black. She'd swallowed poison."

I realize that Guddan has shared with me this painful story out of love. It's a warning. *He may grow tired of you, too. Be prepared.*

That night I lie sleepless beside the Sarkar. Surely I'm more than a pretty face to him. Doesn't he talk to me about things he can't tell anyone else? Am I not the only one of his queens who understands his dreams for Punjab?

But what if I'm wrong? If a new woman came into his life, what would I do?

I'd be heartbroken, certainly, but I wouldn't kill myself over it. I might kill the other woman, though, if I got a chance.

Why, I'm more like Mai Nakkain than I thought!

14

Wedding

NAUNIHAL IS GETTING MARRIED!

From the royal family to the commoners, we're all delighted because we love the affable and generous Naunihal, the hope of Punjab. Didn't he rout Dost Mohammed? Hasn't he spoken out boldly against British plots? And now he's going to exchange garlands with the daughter of the Attariwalas, one of our most powerful clans.

"I'll invite every person in Lahore to a feast," the Sarkar tells me. "I'll give newly minted silver coins to all who line the streets when the bridal procession returns home. I'll make it an event no one will forget."

As grandmother of the groom, Mai Nakkain's stature has grown greater than ever before. Her sense of the dignities due to her has grown along with it.

Guddan says, "She insists upon seeing the gifts each queen is giving to Naunihal. Only those which she approves of will be sent with the baraat to the wedding. Her poor, bullied daughter-in-law, Chand Kaur, isn't even allowed to choose the clothes she'll wear to welcome her son and his new wife to the qila."

As is custom, only men will accompany the Sarkar, Kharak, and Naunihal to the wedding. The party will be made up of the chief sardars and court dignitaries, two hundred of them, and the entire royal cavalry. Prince Sher Singh, the Sarkar's supposed son by his first wife, Mehtab, has recently patched up his relationship with his father. He will escort the firang guests, including the British commander-in-chief—mostly because he speaks some English and cuts a fine figure on the very expensive stallions he possesses.

"He's handsome, tall, black-bearded, and usually dresses in a brocade sherwani," the Fakir tells me. "He loves jewelry, particularly emeralds, and foreign perfumes, which the Sarkar's French jarnails are happy to supply him with—at a premium, of course."

"Did the Sarkar look like him when he was young?" I ask. Sometimes, when we make love, I close my eyes and imagine my husband in his twenties, wishing I'd met him then.

The Fakir laughs. "Not at all. That's why there's gossip about who Sher's real father might be, though the Sarkar has—for the good of the land—now accepted him as his son. Our Sarkar, Allah bless him, never cared about his appearance. He was too busy uniting Punjab. Even in the durbar, he's the most simply dressed."

Sher's new importance does not delight Kharak, but the Sarkar has spoken firmly to all his sons, even the docile ones like Kashmira and Peshaura, and extracted from them a promise to be on their best behavior. There must be no hint of animosity among them, especially in front of the foreigners.

MAI HAS ORGANIZED SEVERAL lavish feasts to which she has invited wives of the nobility and her favorites from the zenana. They will participate in many ceremonies: the turmeric bath for the groom, the mehendi hand-painting, the sending of sagan gifts to the bride, the singing of bawdy wedding songs. She has hired the best dancers, musicians, and cooks. The guests will be seated—and given gifts—according to what Mai considers their importance.

I'm the only queen who hasn't been invited.

"It's for the best," I say with a dry laugh to Guddan when I visit her. "Mai would have put me in the last row and given me the paltriest gift. At least I won't have to deal with that insult, with two hundred amused women watching to see what I'll do about it."

"You won't miss much," Guddan assures me. "The entertainment is second-rate, and you won't have to put up with Mai droning on and on about her renowned family." But I know she's lying in an effort to make me feel better.

As I'm leaving, she says, "Maybe you should talk to the Sarkar. I'm sure he doesn't know what Mai is doing."

"No," I respond. However much I hate Mai, I refuse to be a talebearer. Besides, I know that the Sarkar, who hasn't been able to spend time with me in weeks, has a lot on his mind. The Fakir told me that he's been busy collecting tributes from landowners and digging deep into his own coffers for the wedding expenses. He's recalled troops from all over Punjab for security—and for show, if one were to be honest. They will accompany the bridal party. His enemies are taking advantage of this. Trouble is brewing along the north-west border. Hari Singh Nalwa must miss the wedding and take care of it.

The Fakir added, "The Sarkar also has to make each important guest feel he's being shown enough respect. The clan heads are quick to take offense and start fights, especially after the wine has been flowing. My job is to keep them calm. Especially as the British will be watching for weaknesses to exploit later."

"Why do we even invite the British?" I asked angrily. "They don't respect the Sarkar. I remember the letters your spies had once stolen. They described him as a withered old fox and his court as a den of debauchery. The Sarkar knows it, too."

"He knows everything. But it's not good for Punjab to be their outright enemy—and the Sarkar's first thought is always what is good for Punjab. You should know that by now. The British have signed documents claiming friendship. It's important that we treat them accordingly."

I made an obstinate face. I refused to trust the British.

No. I'm not going to add to my husband's troubles by complaining about Mai. I love him too much for that.

BUT SOMEONE MUST HAVE said something, or perhaps the Sarkar is more aware of zenana politics than I realize, because soon after I return from Guddan's, he calls me to the Sheesh Mahal. I dress with care, applying to my eyes a sparkly surma from Persia that Mangla bought for me from Chor Bazaar. The seller claimed that it had magical powers. The Sarkar will be seeing a lot of beautiful women at the wedding events—including dancing girls who will be gifted to him; I could do with some help.

Perhaps there's truth to what the vendor said, because as soon as I arrive, the Sarkar kisses me hungrily, fumbling with the tassels of my choli. He doesn't wait until after dinner, as is usual, to make love. Instead of leading me to the bed, he takes me on the carpet. I don't mind. His urgency is flattering. I entwine my legs around him, and when we climax together—a rare event—I focus all my will on my womb. *Waheguru, I beg you.*

Afterward, we watch the lights of Lahore, which I find as beautiful as ever. He nuzzles my neck. "Ah, how I've missed you. Once this wedding is over, let's go away to one of my forest lodges, just you and I and Laila. Would you like that?"

The intimacy of being alone with him. Of riding together on Laila as though the world had no end.

"I'd love that above all things," I whisper.

"We'll ride through the woods and eat under the trees—like before we were married. But only better, because I won't have to hold myself back and return you untouched to your father. Do you know how hard that was for me? How much willpower I had to exert?"

Had he really felt that way? I'd had no idea. "I only remember how distant and powerful you seemed, despite your kindness. I didn't dare hope that you'd remember me afterward, and certainly not that you'd ever love me."

He holds me close. "And now look at us, together forever, Waheguru ji di kripa. But tell me, are you enjoying all the wedding excitement?"

It's the perfect opportunity to complain about Mai.

I say, "Yes indeed. It's an event that people will talk about for generations. How happy I am for Naunihal. He's a fine young man, and he loves you so."

The Sarkar looks at me with his piercing eye, but he only says, "Naunihal is fond of you, too. Once, he said that of all my wives, you have the noblest heart. He's right. Now, let me tell you what I'm planning for the baraat procession."

I lie with my head nestled in the hollow of his shoulder and listen contentedly. First the Sarkar will go to the Harmandir Sahib in Amritsar, the gurdwara he decorated with gold, to seek blessings. Then the bridal party will start for Attari. There will be one hundred elephants in the procession; the Sarkar and Fane, the British commander-in-chief, will ride on the first one. Six hundred of our best riders will follow them. Dhian Singh will lead the horsemen, along with his handsome son, Hira, whom the Sarkar loves dearly. Dhian and Hira have ordered matching gold-studded saddle sets for the occasion.

The Sarkar laughs. "They know how to celebrate a wedding, these Dogra kings!"

The Sarkar hasn't forgotten the common people either. He will give a gold mohur—silver is too paltry—to all those who line the procession roads. Thousands from all over Punjab are traveling to Lahore for this occasion. The Sarkar has set up camps to house and feed them. Almost the entire army has been recalled to the capital to provide security.

"It's good for the British to know the extent of our power and wealth, and the love my people have for me." His smile glints like a knife. Then he adds, mischievously, "Fane and his company will stay on afterward to participate in Holi. I'll douse the firangs with color and show them what a real festival looks like!"

His laughter is infectious and I find myself joining in.

"Fane has asked to see my cannons and some of our battle formations. I have agreed," he mentions casually.

"Is that a good idea?" I ask uneasily. "He'll know your strength, but you will not know his. And when they see the magnificence of the wedding, will the British not grow jealous? Will it not make them long to take over Punjab?"

"I believe they'll see that we would be a formidable enemy—and a good ally. Besides, why should I allow anyone to stop me from celebrating my favorite pota's wedding as grandly as I want? It might be the last family celebration that I'll live to see."

I drop my arguments and throw my arms around him. "Waheguru protect you! You'll see many celebrations by His grace. Maybe even the birth of Naunihal's child. You're right. Why should the firangs affect the way our royal wedding is celebrated? They aren't that important."

But I can't help feeling that he's making a grievous error.

Next morning I visit the gurdwara to pray for the Sarkar and the success of the wedding. A voice inside me whispers, *Wouldn't it be nice if something that Mai Nakkain has planned—just one small thing—goes wrong?* But I quash that unworthy thought and recite the Japji Sahib twice as a penance.

I've barely returned to my rooms when someone knocks loudly. I'm surprised. Zenana protocol dictates that guests only visit later in the day, and never without sending word ahead.

"Mai Nakkain's special maid has brought you something," Mangla reports.

The woman hands me a pair of heavy scrolls with gold lettering. They are invitations to the two most important wedding events that the women may attend: the send-off for the groom tomorrow, and the welcoming of the bride in a week. I hide my astonishment and incline my head—regally, I hope—to accept.

She says, "All the ranis are wearing the same colors: dark blue for the send-off, and pink for the welcoming. Please dress accordingly."

After she leaves, Mangla does a dance of delight. "The Sarkar must have ordered Mai to include you. I bet her mouth is bitter with ashes. What a victory for us! I'm going to look through your clothes to find you a suitable blue outfit—there isn't time to have anything made. But we'll have the tailor stitch you something special in pink."

I'm delighted that the Sarkar cared enough to go to all this trouble for me. I'm even more delighted that Mai Nakkain's nose is out of joint. I can't help gloating a little as I recount the incident to Guddan when I visit her in the afternoon.

Guddan claps gleefully. "Serves the old witch right for being so mean to you! But what do you have here?"

"I'm planning to wear this for Naunihal's send-off. I wanted to show it to you."

There's a strange look on Guddan's face as she holds up the blue ghaghra-choli. "How did you decide on this color?"

"Mai's maid told me to wear the same color as the other queens." Suddenly, I understand. "The queens aren't wearing blue, are they?"

"No. We'll be dressed in marigold. Blue is for the concubines."

I'm furious. "Mai planned to humiliate me in front of the entire zenana. Even though she'd been forced to invite me, had I gone dressed like a concubine, she would have won. If it weren't for you, that's what would have happened."

Guddan finds me a marigold salwar-kameez. With a gold dupatta, my pearls, and a diamond nose-ring she loans me, it looks sufficiently festive. The correct color for the queens at the welcoming ceremony is emerald green. My tailor promises to make me a fine ghaghra-choli for that event.

I send Mangla over to Mai with the blue outfit, to ask if she thinks the shade is acceptable.

"Mai said it was just right," Mangla reports. "She looks forward to seeing you wear it tomorrow."

"For once she was telling the truth!" I say.

The Sarkar will be busy with guests tonight. I will not get to see him. I redden my lips and kiss a sheet of paper on which I've sprinkled attar of rose and send it to him through Mangla. He sends back a message: *I will keep it close to my heart.*

The next morning I stand triumphantly beside the other queens as they throw flowers on Naunihal and wish the party good luck. The look on Mai Nakkain's face when she sees me dressed in marigold is something I am going to remember for a long time. But what I will remember forever is how, when our eyes met during the ceremony, the Sarkar tapped the chest-pocket of his kurta—it must be where he put my letter—and touched his fingers to his lips.

15

The Royal Game

THE WEDDING FESTIVITIES WENT OFF as perfectly as the Sarkar had wanted. Life in the qila is finally back to normal. I'm grateful for this, as the Sarkar summons me again at night. The celebrations took a lot out of him, though he refuses to admit it. But he allows me to rub his aching back with the herbal oil that Dr. Honigberger has concocted.

We spend most of our nights talking, which is fine by me. I've decided that I don't care much for sex, all that straining and sweating, the burning later between the thighs. But I never refuse the Sarkar if he wants to make love to me. I want my baby—though as the days pass my hopes grow dim.

Currently, the Sarkar's favorite topic is Naunihal's wedding. He describes to me the processions, the food, the extravagant gifts, the all-night fireworks, the wrestling competitions between the bride's side and the groom's, the jewels and ceremonial outfits worn by the bride and groom and their parties.

But one day I find him in bed, a white sheet covering him from head to toe as though he were a corpse. My heart gives a frightened jolt. Only after much cajoling do I discover that his beloved general, Nalwa, has passed away.

"It's my fault," the Sarkar mumbles. "I left him to guard the north-west border with insufficient troops because I wanted to show off my army at the wedding. Nalwa was so loyal, he didn't complain. But the Afghans found out and attacked him. He was mortally wounded. If he had retreated to a city, he might have received the right medical care and lived. But he didn't do that because then the Afghans would have taken our fort. Even from his deathbed, he strategized with his second in command, making him wear his headgear and lead the soldiers in the Nalwa formation he was famous for creating. Our army routed the Afghans, but I have lost my right arm."

I suffer with him. I worry, too. By now the British must have ferreted out the news of Nalwa's death. What might they be planning? I remember how the Sarkar had assured me that Nalwa would come to my aid if I ever needed it, and I feel even more bereft.

Later, the Sarkar says, "That's another thing I appreciate about you. You know when to be silent."

One day, the Sarkar tells me about his other weddings. He remembers his marriage ceremony with Mai Nakkain vividly, though he was barely eighteen. The horseback procession, the musicians with their dholaks, and the smoking torches planted by the roadside were all paid for by the bride's brother, because their clan was richer than the Sarkar's. The Nakkai chief must have seen something in the young Ranjit, however, to give him his sister in marriage. Later, he became one of the Sarkar's staunchest allies.

"She was a sweet girl," the Sarkar recalls. "Maybe not the prettiest, but slender and gentle-voiced. And always looking out for my comfort."

I realize from his tone that he'd fallen hard in love with Mai. I push down the jealousy bubbling up inside. The Sarkar is a kind man; if he realizes he's upsetting me, he'll stop. I don't want that. I want him to be able to tell me whatever he wants. Besides, it's important to learn as much as I can about the Sarkar's world. Knowledge is power.

"Her name used to be Raj—but that was my mother's name, so we changed it. She didn't mind. *Whatever pleases you, ji*, she'd say. She used to be very compliant, though you wouldn't guess that by looking at her now! She was a welcome change from my first wife.

"That first one, Mehtab, she fought with me all the time. Teeth, nails, throwing whatever was at hand. I can't blame her, though. How can you love the man whose father killed yours, and to whom you were then handed over as part of a treaty? Our wedding was a joyless affair—I don't think we even had a feast. We were both relieved when she went back to her home town. But her mother, Sada Kaur—you remember me telling you about her?—was a remarkable woman. I acknowledged Mehtab's son, Sher Singh, as my own only for her sake."

How can I ever forget Sada Kaur, on whose death day the Sarkar promised to marry me?

"What a warrior!" he continues. "One time, our troops were exhausted and ready to give up. She said to them, *Give me your clothes and take my women's wear. You stay home. I'll take your place on the battlefield.* She shamed them into fighting harder than ever, and we won. She's the reason I became king."

He changes subjects suddenly, as he often does. "But tell me about my wedding to you. It's the only one where I wasn't present!"

I tell him about the simple hurried ceremony in the yard of my parents' home in Gujranwala: no guests, no wedding dress, no feast. The only music was the shabads sung by the ragi. The end of my dupatta was tied to a piece of steel instead of the groom's scarf.

The Sarkar looks sad, so I'm quick to add, "I didn't mind. I was so happy that I was going to see you again. That I was finally your wife. I hugged your sword all the way to the qila."

He kisses my forehead. "I love that you aren't greedy and grasping like most other queens. Well, my dearest, you aren't my first wife, but I promise you this: you will be my last. The one who has filled my heart totally."

I'm light-headed with surprise and delight. I'd resigned myself to the fact that the Sarkar would eventually move on to a new woman. I'd never dreamed he would make a declaration like this.

The Sarkar continues, "I'll make up for the simplicity of your wedding by building you a beautiful haveli, right here in the qila, known by your name. I'll give it to you for a special occasion."

I start to say that his love is all I want, but the Sarkar is pulling me down on top of him. I give myself to his eager lips, his ardent hands. Afterward, I fall into a dreamless slumber. The Sarkar, who is restless in bed, often tells me that he envies me my ability to sleep so soundly.

THIS MORNING, THOUGH, I'M jerked out of sleep. A terrible nausea rises in me. I push off the Sarkar's arm and run to the chamber pot in the alcove, not even waiting to grab a sheet to wrap around my nakedness. But I'm too late. I throw up on the beautiful marble floor inlaid with precious stones. Mortified, I apologize. I can't understand what happened. I have a cast-iron stomach, thanks to all those green guavas from my childhood. Besides, the Sarkar is fine, and we ate the same things.

The Sarkar doesn't seem to be listening. There's a strange light in his eye. Mangla runs in, having heard the commotion. She helps me clean up and get dressed. When I emerge from the water closet, the Sarkar is still sitting on the bed, staring at me. Have I disgusted him?

"Don't you have to get ready?" I ask, trying to distract him. "Isn't that Belgian jarnail coming today to meet with you? The one who's going to teach the troops some new—"

He interrupts me. "Come here." When I stand in front of him, he touches my breasts. I wince. Additionally, I'm surprised because the Sarkar is always very proper in front of the servants.

"Did that hurt?"

"They're really sensitive." Then it sinks in, along with the realization that I've missed my monthly blood. I have to sit down. *Waheguru, could it be—?*

Mangla asks, "Shall I call the vaid?" Excitement throbs in her voice.

The Sarkar nods. "I have to leave for court now, but bring me the news at once. And don't tell anyone."

He kisses me and holds me carefully, as though I am made of spun sugar.

IN SPITE OF THE Sarkar's precautions, within a week everyone in the qila knows that I'm pregnant. How can they not? Two guards stand outside my room in the Khilwat Khana day and night. Each morning, the vaid checks on my progress. My meals are prepared by the Sarkar's own cook and tested for poison by the royal taster. Once this is done, Mangla carries the dishes to my rooms; no one else is allowed to touch them. I wish I could view these proceedings. Mangla has described to me how scared the taster looks every day, and how he'd doubled up after a meal, once, clutching his stomach. But it had only been an attack of gas.

"It isn't fair," I complain. "I'm the reason for all this drama, and I'm missing out on all of it. Ever since the pregnancy, I feel like a prisoner."

Mangla has no sympathy for my griping. "It isn't fit behavior for a queen-mother-to-be," she says, a sentence she's taken to using at every opportunity. "We are taking precautions only because we don't want anyone harming you, either physically or through the evil eye. The whole zenana is burning with jealousy right now. Especially since the Sarkar started the royal builder on the foundation of your haveli."

"The one I'm not allowed to go and see?"

"For your own good. Construction sites are dangerous."

Mangla isn't exaggerating about the evil eye. Strange objects make their way into my rooms—and even into the Sheesh Mahal, who knows how. Tiny wooden babies with heads lopped off. A broken mirror. A strangled mouse. Cloth dolls with bulging stomachs, their legs soaked in what looks like blood. The Sarkar scoffs at such things, but Mangla takes them seriously, and tosses them into a fire. She buys nazar-beads with bright, bulging eyes and hangs them from every door. She waves red chillies around my head and burns them, even though the pungent smoke makes us cough.

"I didn't know you were so superstitious!" I tease, though secretly I'm touched by her caring.

She retorts, "I'm not taking any chances with our baby."

Our baby. Warmth thrills through me. He'll have two mothers to watch over him, as well as a father who is the most powerful maharaja in all of Hindustan. Yes, I'm sure the child is going to be a boy, though the Sarkar, who doesn't have daughters, is hoping for a girl.

Since my pregnancy, the ranis jostle with each other to send me more gifts than before. Mangla is routinely bribed by people who want to know what I would like. Food? Clothing? Jewelry? Baby items? A pet monkey?

Mangla grimaces. We both suspect that these same women are secretly sending me the bad-luck items, too. "People have discovered a new love for you, now that you are going to be the mother of a royal child."

I send everyone the same message. *My health does not permit visitors. Instead of gifts, I request prayers and alms in gurdwaras and temples.*

"You should have taken everything," says a disappointed Mangla. "I would have sold them for you in Chor Bazaar!"

But the Fakir declares, "You have behaved with dignity and wisdom." He brings me treatises about the upbringing of princes, and we spend many happy hours debating matters of discipline and education.

Guddan glows as though she herself were pregnant. She has embroidered a mountain of tiny quilts, and is making even more. "Babies piss a lot," she informs me. "Especially boys." She, too, has decided I'm having a son. "Whenever you get tired of his crying, just send him over to me."

I smile. The child will have three mothers. When my Guru Granth falls open on a page that declares *Even the mightiest of kings will depart the world empty-handed*, I shrug away the omen. My son is going to be lucky. His hands will never be empty.

THESE DAYS, I'M CONSTANTLY hungry. I crave cauliflower pickle; I've already gone through two jars. I'm concerned that I'm putting on weight, but the Sarkar insists he likes my new curviness.

"Like a real woman," he says, his hand lingering on my hip.

I pretend anger. "Wasn't I a real woman before?"

He laughs and gives me a careful hug.

The Sarkar has stopped having sex with me ever since he learned about the pregnancy. I feared he would go to another rani. I had been ready to recommend Guddan. But he hasn't shown any desire to do so. We lie in our bed, side by side. He holds my hand or strokes my belly. Sometimes he talks to the baby.

One night he comes directly from a banquet, the Koh-i-Noor sparkling on his arm. I am already in bed. He places the stone on my belly.

"I can't give this child a kingdom," he says, "but I will bequeath him this jewel. There is no other diamond in the world like it."

I should be grateful. He has just given my child a magnificent gift. But even as I murmur my thanks, I can't help shivering. The Fakir has told me the bloody tale of the Koh-i-Noor, for whose sake son turned on father and brother on brother. The Mughal emperor Shah Jahan had it placed in the apex of his peacock throne; his son Aurangzeb wrested the throne from him and imprisoned him for life. The Mughals were attacked by Nadir Shah of Persia, who looted the city and took the Koh-i-Noor. Within a decade, his vast kingdom collapsed and he was assassinated. The stone then passed to the Afghan king Shah Shuja. Overthrown, he fled to the Sarkar, begging for refuge. In return for protection, the Sarkar demanded the Koh-i-Noor. Thus it came to Punjab.

True, it hasn't harmed the Sarkar yet. Perhaps it's waiting for a less powerful owner. I don't want my son to be that person.

"I'll make sure this child is brought up differently from me—or even his brothers," the Sarkar promises. "I was too busy fighting wars to learn my letters, but I'll educate him the way a prince should be. As the youngest, he will not have to worry about ruling the kingdom. But perhaps he'll help Kharak . . . No, by then surely Naunihal will be king. Perhaps he'll help Naunihal frame better laws for the good of the people." He smiles. "Perhaps he'll write poems to immortalize his father."

Inside me, the baby kicks as though in agreement.

A DEEP SLEEP DESCENDS on me each afternoon. Today it brings a dream of Biji, who appears aged and hollow-cheeked. Guiltily, I realize she has slipped from my mind in the last few months. She's weeping. *I'll never get to see you again. Or meet my grandchild. I'll never get to feed him motichoor laddus. Remember how you used to love them?*

I protest. *I prefer jalebis. Have you forgotten?*

A familiar voice wrenches my heart. *What's the use of speaking to her, Biji?* Behind my mother stands Jawahar. His eyes are red-rimmed, from tears or alcohol. *It's she who has forgotten us. Forgotten her promises. Why, she doesn't even answer my letters.*

More guilt assails me. I'd put Jawahar's last letter into my almirah without opening it.

I hear other voices, one angry, the other placating.

"How dare you stand in my way, you pockmarked daughter of a prostitute?"

"Please, Maharani ji, you can't come in. The Sarkar has ordered that no one should disturb Rani Jindan's rest."

"I'm not *no one*. I'll have you buried alive in a hole filled with thorns before tomorrow's sunrise. Guards, remove her from my path!"

"Guards, if you do, you know the Sarkar will hear of this."

Even buried in the bog of sleep, I recognize the voices. I force myself out of bed and stumble to the door. It's as I feared. Mai Nakkain stands at the entrance, red-faced with rage, while Mangla blocks the doorway with outstretched arms. Beyond them, the guards dither, slack-mouthed with confusion.

"Mangla," I speak sternly. "What's this? You should have welcomed our honored guest at once, and woken me." I bow to Mai with joined palms. "Respected Maharani, my humblest apologies for my maid's misbehavior. I'll deal with her appropriately. Please enter my humble abode."

Quick as a whiplash, Mangla understands the game. She bends low, *Forgive, forgive*, and backs out. I hear her shouting. *Bring the special sandalwood kursi for the Senior Maharani. Bring silk cushions for her feet, mango sharbat, mithai.*

Mai is taken aback by my politeness, but not for long. "So. You managed to get yourself pregnant. I wonder who the father is. Is it that brainless pretty boy Gulloo Mushki, who used to stand mooning outside your window? Did you let him in one night?"

Angry responses fill my mouth. Then inside me the baby kicks nervously, and I don't want to fight Mai anymore. I just want a peaceful life for my child.

"Maharani," I say, "you know that isn't true. If you had the smallest evidence of my infidelity, you'd have already taken it to the Sarkar. If the Sarkar learns that you came here to upset me, he will be most displeased." I wait for the words to sink in. "But he will not hear of it from me."

Mai watches me, curiosity battling with hatred on her face.

"I'm no competition to you, Mai ji, nor do I wish to be. You are the Sarkar's chief consort, mother of the king-to-be, grandmother of the king to follow. You are the first woman the Sarkar loved. I can never measure up to that. I only wish to live quietly with my child."

There's a strange look in her eyes. Is she relieved that she need not battle with me? Has the reminder that she was the Sarkar's first love softened her?

"It is true that the eagle does not bother to swoop down upon a sparrow," she says at last.

I bow in agreement.

Mai Nakkain deigns to rest her large posterior on the sandalwood chair the maids have carried in. She claps her hands and four women—they must have been waiting in the passageway—carry in a silver tray heaped with sweetmeats. In the center is a jewelry box holding two elephant-headed gold bangles. I offer fulsome thanks as I slip the bangles onto my wrists. They're ugly but hefty and must have cost a great deal.

My maids bring presents for Mai: Sweets. A phulkari dupatta. A silver box to hold betel nuts. Mai daintily picks up a jalebi. She motions to her own gift tray, urging me, too, to take a sweet. She waits, eyes narrowed, to see what I'll do.

To refuse would be a great insult. It would make Mai Nakkain my enemy forever. Against all caution, I bite into an almond burfi. I can feel Mangla cringing behind the door. I force myself to swallow. I wait for the burn of poison. Will Mangla be able to run to the vaid in time?

But there's nothing.

"It's delicious," I manage to say.

Mai bares her teeth in a smile. She knew what I'd been thinking.

She'd enjoyed my moment of terror. "This jalebi is not too bad." She rises to indicate the visit is over. "You must send your maid over with the recipe."

I, too, rise and, noticing that I'm taller than the old queen, slouch a little. "It will be my pleasure."

Later, Mangla says, "Now I'm no longer worried for you. You've learned to play the royal game!"

WHEN I DESCRIBE THE incident to the Fakir with elation, he cautions, "You did well, but don't grow too confident. The royal game has many levels. This is only the first. Let me give you an example."

He tells me that Auckland, the new governor-general, had sent a delegation to our court. After days of being hosted lavishly, the leader presented Auckland's demands, barely disguised as a request. The British wished to oust Dost Mohammed of Kabul and restore the throne to Shah Shuja—and they wanted us to help.

"They want to use our army to establish a puppet king in Kabul who will obey them," the Fakir says. "In return, they have promised us undying friendship."

"Undying friendship! How many treaties have the British broken, in just this decade, all across Hindustan?"

"That's what Dhian said. He said we should turn them down. He pointed out that the British want to gamble with the lives of our men for their benefit. They don't respect us. His spies had heard them refer insultingly to the Sarkar as the one-eyed gray mouse."

I'm livid. "I hope the Sarkar agreed with Dhian."

"He was angry, but he listened to me when I advised him to help the British."

"But why!"

"Punjab must stay involved in the coup, for our own sakes. Shuja needs to know that it's the Khalsa army that has put him on the throne. This way, we'll have an ally on our western border, not just a puppet of the British."

I'm impressed by the Fakir's grasp of strategy.

"But Dhian is angry with me," he adds. "I'm afraid I've made a lifelong foe."

If even the Fakir, with all his wisdom, can make such bitter enemies, what chance do I have?

"This game is too complicated. I don't want to play it anymore. I just want to be a good wife and mother. Cherish the Sarkar. Give my baby a happy childhood."

The Fakir says, "Your kismet has already spoken. You are not only a wife and mother, but a queen as well. And a queen who is a mother must play the royal game more skillfully because she has more to lose."

16

Birth

THIS IS THE HAPPIEST DAY *of my life.*

I've thought this before. When I went for my first ride with the Sarkar. When he slipped his betrothal ring onto my finger. When we were reunited in the Sheesh Mahal. But seeing the crumpled red flower that is my son's face, I know I was mistaken. This, *today*, is the happiest day of my life.

The dai places him in my arms and shows me how to guide his mouth to my nipple. He latches on powerfully, causing me to wince. But the joy that shoots through me is pure and perfect. When Guddan, who held my hand from the moment the pains started, asks if it hurts, I shake my head.

"I didn't think it was possible to love someone so instantly. I'd throw myself between this child and death any time."

Guddan's eyes well up with emotion, but Mangla spits on the ground. "Don't say such bad-luck things! Why would you ever need to do something like that? This baby will have lots of other people to throw themselves between him and death. Like soldiers. Besides, he's not the heir, far from it. He won't be in any danger." Still, she ties an amulet around his arm with black thread.

There's a commotion outside. The Sarkar has dismissed the

durbar early and come to the birthing pavilion to meet his son. Mangla bows and is rewarded with a fistful of gold mohurs. I hold out the baby.

As he clasps the bundle to his chest, I marvel at his expression. I thought I knew the Sarkar in his most tender moments, but I was wrong.

He says, “I thank Waheguru for this gift, which I never thought to receive again in my lifetime.” Tears glimmer in his good eye. He places a gold chain around the baby’s neck. “I promise to be present for this child as I never could be for my other sons.” He hands the baby back to me, then holds out a large gilded key.

“For your new palace. It was completed last week, but I told Mangla to keep it a secret. It’ll be known as Haveli Mai Jindan, since you are a mother now.”

Haveli Mai Jindan. The dog trainer’s daughter—with a mansion inside the Badshahi Qila named after her?

“There’ll be plenty of room in the haveli for our son to run around,” the Sarkar says. “But we can’t keep calling him *our son*! I’ve chosen a name for him. He will be known as Dalip, after the Sant of Thanesar. I hope that he will be wise like him and emanate peace, that he will never accept injustice. Do you like it?”

“It’s beautiful,” I murmur. But I’m in a turmoil. Has the Sarkar overlooked the fact that the word means *king*? My son will never be king. Is it not cruel, then, to name him thus? Or is it some premonition that has influenced the Sarkar’s choice?

I must consult an astrologer and learn what Dalip’s future holds.

The Sarkar leaves reluctantly. There is much to do. News of the birth must be announced in durbar and city. Beggars must be given alms. Donations of gratitude must be sent to gurdwaras—and temples and mosques also, for the maharaja respects all houses of

God. Invitations, accompanied by gifts, must be sent to the heads of the important misls, requesting them to come and bless the prince. Festivities must be planned, with fireworks, singers, dancers, and banquets.

"It is a pity," the Sarkar says, "that women cannot attend such events. I would have liked to enjoy them with you by my side, my beautiful. Without the magic you worked, there would be no celebration."

"No magic, just Waheguru's grace," I say. I take on an admonishing tone that I feel entitled to now that I'm a queen mother. "Don't celebrate too much! You have to wake up clearheaded in the mornings to greet your son."

I insist on moving to my haveli right away. The dai wants me to rest in the birthing pavilion, but I'm feverish with impatience. Our small procession wends its way across the courtyard: I am assisted by Mangla and Guddan; the grumbling dai follows with Dalip; guards shield us with umbrellas; servants bring up the rear with bundles of baby things.

My new home renders me speechless with joy. Its red-stone facade is warm and welcoming. There are two stories, a covered veranda, and floor-length friezed windows because the Sarkar knows I love looking out. It isn't overly ornate, like Mai's palatial chambers. I would have felt uncomfortable surrounded by walls inlaid with jewels and intricate mosaic floors. The Sarkar, ever perceptive, had known that.

"Do you like it?" Guddan asks, concerned. "It's rather plain—"

I consider telling her about the mud hut I grew up in, but there are some things Rani Guddan, descendant of kings, will never understand, no matter how fond she is of me.

"It's perfect," I say. I unlock the door and step in.

THE ENTIRE CITY, MANGLA informs me, is filled with jubilation. Overnight, I've become the people's darling. They love my romantic tale of rags to riches. People claim that I'm more gorgeous than Shah Jahan's Mumtaz. That the Sarkar has built me a palace to rival the Taj Mahal. Firecrackers shatter the night every few moments. I'm afraid it will disturb Dalip, but he sleeps soundly. When awake, he doesn't cry but fixes his large black eyes, fringed with thick lashes, on my face. I refuse to believe the dai when she says newborn babies can't focus.

VISITORS BEGIN TO ARRIVE the very next day. Fortunately, Mangla has already fixed up the formal baithak with cushioned kursis and elegant carpets and arranged for sweetmeats and drinks. By the Sarkar's orders, only the most important members of the royal family are allowed to see me. Still, it takes all my willpower to get my aching body out of bed and into suitably ceremonial—and thus hot and itchy—clothing.

The first to come is Mai Nakkain. There's been an uneasy truce between us ever since she visited my rooms. She examines the sleeping baby and remarks that he looks like me. She's insinuating that he doesn't look like the Sarkar, but I thank her, pretending not to understand. There's nothing Mai can do in this regard. This morning in durbar the Sarkar announced the birth of his beloved son Prince Dalip Singh, thus acknowledging him as his offspring. Mai has to satisfy herself with making snide remarks about the haveli: "Quite pretty, my dear—but really, this cheap red stone? And is that *brick* on the floor? What on earth was the Sarkar thinking!"

KHARAK'S WIFE, CHAND KAUR, leans over Dalip's cradle. She has come to visit, along with Naunihal and his new bride, Sahib Kaur, whom he affectionately calls Bibi. "Look at that pretty smile!"

I suspect it's a grimace caused by gas, but I accept the compliment graciously. Chand is a quiet woman who keeps out of other people's business—an admirable quality in a zenana.

"My little uncle!" Naunihal laughs. "When he's older, I'll teach him to ride. Gift him his first stallion. Take him hunting. The Sukerchakia misl is known for its fine horsemen. He's got to keep up the reputation!"

Naunihal, considered a grandson to all the Sarkar's wives, has free access to the zenana. But he rarely visits any of the queens, so I'm flattered.

"By Waheguru's grace, soon you'll have a little one yourself," I say, smiling at Bibi, who stands shyly behind Naunihal, very much in love.

"Well, if not, it won't be for lack of trying!" Naunihal laughs as Bibi draws her dupatta over her blushing face.

"The things you say!" Chand chides. But she smiles indulgently, as do I.

"Everyone likes to see young love," I tell Mangla later.

Mangla says, "I'm happy that Chand and her daughter-in-law get along. She hasn't had much joy in her life. Mai Nakkain has always ordered her around. And Kharak has many addictions. I've even heard that he likes men."

Before I can express my shock, a maid runs in with a message. The Sarkar is on his way, accompanied by Dhian Singh. I'm surprised. I hardly know the wazir. Why is my husband bringing him here today?

Mangla has barely managed to arrange a gold-embroidered veil over my head when the Sarkar and the wazir arrive. Dhian holds a box wrapped in white silk. Is it a present for Dalip? When he unwraps it, I see it is the Holy Gita.

The Sarkar informs me: "I am appointing Dhian to be Dalip's guardian. Should I die, he will protect you both."

Fear grips my throat. Why is the Sarkar speaking of death?

Dhian touches the Gita to his forehead. “I swear to fulfill this sacred responsibility.”

Perhaps Dalip senses my nervousness, for he begins to cry. The Sarkar picks him up and calms him, then hands him to the wazir. I’m startled, and from the look on his face, so is Dhian. But he stands taller, clasping Dalip close, and vows, “I will serve the queen and the prince until my last breath, my Sarkar. You need not worry about them.”

“I thank you, my friend.” The Sarkar places a hand on Dhian’s shoulder, and adoration brightens the wazir’s eyes. What magic does my beloved possess to arouse such devotion?

“I will announce this in the durbar,” the Sarkar says. “Everyone should know what a powerful protector Dalip has.”

Why does he look so relieved? Is he unwell? Tomorrow I’ll interrogate the royal vaids about the Sarkar’s health. I’ll put him on a strict diet and force him to rest more. *Your son needs you to be around for a long time*, I’ll tell him, shamelessly wielding the blackmail of love.

LATE AT NIGHT, UNDER the cover of darkness, my last visitor arrives, a man who, Mangla claims, is Lahore’s best astrologer. He has created Dalip’s star chart. It took him all day because he checked it many times.

“Are you sure the dai recorded the time accurately?” he asks.

“Absolutely,” Mangla replies. “There are two pendulum clocks kept in the birthing pavilion for this purpose. The dai and I both noted the time. Why do you ask?”

The astrologer looks unhappy. “According to the time of his birth, the prince is born under Pisces and Pisces, a most unfortunate combination. He will lose all that is dear to him. Father, mother, wife, possessions. Even his spiritual direction. He will wander far from home. He will be surrounded by enemies—and worse, be tricked into believing they are his friends. I have noted down all the details I could ascertain, and given you the probable dates of events."

"Enough!" I should never have asked for Dalip's horoscope. I snatch the heavy roll of parchment from the man. "I order you, under pain of death, never speak of this to anyone."

The astrologer stammers his assent.

I gesture to Mangla, who gives the man a bag of gold coins and ushers him out. I hear her say menacingly, "Keep your word. Remember, I know where you live."

With shaking hands, I light the brazier and throw in the horoscope, watching until the parchment is reduced to ashes. *Waheguru, please let my child's bad luck burn away with it.*

Later I regret my impulsiveness. I shouldn't have acted so hastily. I should have read everything carefully and pondered it. That way, I could have anticipated my son's misfortunes and averted them.

17

Dejection

I HAVE WHAT EVERY WOMAN CRAVES: a handsome and healthy baby, my own haveli, ample wealth, loyal servants, and a doting husband who is, additionally, a great king. Why, then, does my chest feel weighed down by sorrow when I wake?

The Sarkar tries to divert me with entertainment. He sends for the best dancers and singers to perform in my haveli. He encourages me to call whomever I like to these events. I invite Guddan and the Fakir, Dhian and his handsome brother Suchet, Naunihal and his shy wife, and Naunihal's closest friends, Udham and Hira Singh, sons of the Dogra brothers. When Kharak is away on expeditions, I invite Chand, too. She is most appreciative. I like Chand. If Kharak didn't make me so uneasy, I would have made friends with her. I sit beside the Sarkar at these events, sharing the same silken cushions. I eat from his golden dishes and am feted by my guests.

Why then is foreboding my companion all evening, like the drone of a tanpura?

"Will you cook for me, my Jind?" the Sarkar asks sometimes in an attempt to distract me. I hurry into the kitchen and move the cook aside and make him khichri or alu parathas, as I'd dreamed of doing when I was a dog trainer's daughter. I serve him myself, as though he were a simple farmer and I, his wife. We eat on the terrace, the lights of Lahore spread out before us like a carpet of stars. Afterward, Mangla brings Dalip so the Sarkar can hold him.

Why, watching them, am I overcome by dread?

The dai calls it the birthing sadness. She gives me bitter concoctions, which I force down my throat. Mangla scours the city to bring me taabizes from holy men. I wear them obediently. Nothing helps.

I try to engage myself in the affairs of state, which the Sarkar shares more and more with me nowadays. There is much turbulence in the durbar. He is debating whether to send an army to help the British, as they have requested, against the Afghans at Herat. Many at court are against it, especially since Dost Mohammed has already drawn back. Dhian Singh asks, *Why should we cut short the lives of our brave men so that the British can claim one more victory and create one more principality?* Kharak and Naunihal have taken opposite sides on this issue—Naunihal is for war, and Kharak against—and this has split the court even further.

I lie sleepless at night, worrying. If things are so bad now, what will happen once the Sarkar is gone?

I instruct Mangla to cut down on our expenses. "Send more of my allowance to my account in the toshakhana."

Mangla agrees, but she also advises me to keep some money and jewelry hidden in the haveli, just in case. She doesn't elaborate, which makes me worry even more.

TONIGHT, WHEN THE SARKAR tells me that he is going to Ferozepur to meet with Governor-General Auckland, I burst into tears.

"Please don't go. I have a bad feeling about this trip. You aren't well enough."

Some weeks ago, he had another stroke. Though minor, it weakened him significantly. Nowadays, when he goes on horseback to inspect his troops, as he insists on doing, he has to be lifted into the saddle. This is done secretly in the stables, but news travels, especially within the zenana where everyone's fortunes are tied to the king's.

The Sarkar is taken aback; so far I've hidden the worst of my depression from him. He kisses me and says he cannot cancel this meeting. "It is too important for Punjab. I promise I'll eat and drink only what the vaid recommends. I'll even instruct the servers to fill my goblet with red grape juice instead of wine, just for your sake." He'll be back soon, he assures me, with Auckland and his party. He'll arrange a special banquet where he'll hire a magician Naunihal has discovered, a man who can do vanishing tricks. "You'll have a special seat in the zenana section, second only to Mai Nakkain, so that you can enjoy all the spectacles."

When I continue sobbing, he suggests, helplessly, "Perhaps you are missing your mother. At times like this, I believe a woman needs a mother's care. Would you like her to visit?"

Surprise stops my tears. The Sarkar never allows his wives' relatives to come to Lahore unless they are his military allies. He has, in the past, turned down every request I've made for Jawahar to visit. Only last week, letters arrived from Gujranwala: Biji asking plaintively if I might send her a portrait of Dalip since she will probably never meet him. I wept for an hour after reading it. I couldn't bear to even open Jawahar's letter.

Perhaps the Sarkar is right, I think with a glimmer of hope. Perhaps being with my family, from whom I've been separated so long, will heal me. I'm touched that he's willing to make this exception for me.

"I would love that," I say. "But my mother has never been outside Gujranwala, and she would be uncomfortable traveling with soldiers. May my brother bring her?"

The Sarkar is not pleased, but he says, "I'll indulge you this one time, as a gift for having made me a father. They must leave before I return—in ten days. And they must remain inside the qila and speak only to your household."

I'm troubled. Though Biji will not mind these restrictions, Jawahar is certain to feel offended. But I have no choice. I send a letter with a trusted courier, and receive an immediate reply: Biji and Jawahar will arrive the day after the Sarkar leaves.

Excitedly planning for their visit, I pay little attention when the Sarkar develops a cough. No need to worry, I tell myself. The vaids and Dr. Honigberger will travel with him. I'm distracted by other details: where my guests will sleep, what to serve at each meal. I decide to put Biji in the room next to mine, and Jawahar upstairs, where he can watch the comings and goings at the Diwan-i-Khas.

I tell Mangla, "Instruct the bawarchi to make biriyani with cardamom and oranges, lamb cooked in poppy-seed paste, and chickens stuffed with ground meat and cinnamon. They've never eaten Mughlai dishes like that. I'll cook a few things myself, too, to show Biji that I haven't forgotten what she taught."

"Too bad that the Sarkar has decreed that they can't go into the city," Mangla says sympathetically. "To come all the way to Lahore and not be able to enjoy the bazaars and the special sights! Ah well. You can take them around the qila gardens in the evenings. The roses are blooming, and the Sarkar has bought all those new white peacocks."

The days speed by, and suddenly it's time for the Sarkar to leave. I meet him at the entrance of the Sheesh Mahal to say goodbye. The Sarkar sits erect in his palanquin, dressed in an embroidered kurta, the Koh-i-Noor shining on his arm. He holds my hand, his grip firm but too warm. Does he have a fever? *I should have urged Honigberger to give him a strengthening potion*, I think guiltily. The palanquin, thickly padded to keep his leg comfortable, is lifted and placed on an elephant.

In the past, whenever the Sarkar has left Lahore, I have prayed fervently for his well-being, but today I'm distracted. Even as I wave goodbye, I'm making plans to send Biji and Jawahar to the hamams so they can soak in a scented bath for the first time in their lives. Ten days are too short for all I want to do with my family, for them. If only the Sarkar would stay away a little longer!

I'M NAPPING IN MY bedroom, a sleeping Dalip tucked into the crook of my neck, when Mangla wakes me. "Your guest is here."

"You mean my guests?"

"There's only one."

A man stands in the entry. Large, bulky, sweat-stained, with bags under his eyes. For a moment I don't recognize my brother.

Jawahar is wearing a new green kurta, overly bright, cheaply shiny. He must have bought it for his visit, thinking it to be very fine. Once, I would have agreed. But living with the Sarkar's understated elegance has made me finicky. He stands biting his lip, unsure of how to greet me now that I'm queen. My heart aches, realizing the chasm that has grown between us. I hand Dalip to Mangla and throw myself into Jawahar's arms. And then we're laughing and weeping, both speaking at the same time.

"Veer! It's been so long."

"My little sister, a queen and a mother! How beautiful you look. And you must be the amazing Mangla." He flashes a smile at her. "Jindan has written much about you."

Mangla does a low kurnish to Jawahar, as though to royalty. "And she has said much about you, janaab."

I'm surprised to see her blushing.

"But where's Biji?" I ask.

Jawahar explains. Two days ago, Manna and Biji both developed a high fever. Jawahar didn't want to disappoint me, and he longed to see his nephew, so he sent word to Balbir to come and take care of them, while he traveled to Lahore alone. "I hope you don't mind," he says apologetically.

I feel disappointed and guilty—I'll never be able to help Biji the way Balbir does. But I push it aside and take Jawahar's arm. "I'm delighted you came."

Jawahar turns to Dalip. "My nephew!" he cries with a booming laugh, taking him from Mangla. Dalip's lip trembles; he's going to cry. Jawahar lifts the baby high above his head. It looks terribly dangerous. I'm about to snatch Dalip back when he gurgles with laughter.

"See, he loves his uncle already!" Jawahar says. "Arre puttar, we're going to be great friends. We'll have so much fun together!"

My heart expands, even though what Jawahar proclaims with such certainty can't happen. The Sarkar would never allow it. I'm suddenly angry: because of him, Dalip will never experience his uncle's affection.

I change the topic. "Come, veer, and see your bedroom."

Jawahar says, "After that, can we go around the qila? I want to visit all the special buildings, especially the Sheesh Mahal. Manna always said he'd take us there, but he never did."

It would be most unwise. Though the Sarkar is away, durbar is held regularly and the qila is crowded with courtiers and attendants. They will notice me—and my companion. Questions will be asked. Answers whispered. Word will travel until it reaches Mai Nakkain, as it always does. She'll make sure to taunt me. *I'm told your brother, the kennel keeper's son, is visiting you. I heard about his fine outfit and his courtly accent . . .*

Yet how can I deny Jawahar's very first request?

Mangla hurries forward, saving the day. "Our rani can't go out when there are so many people around. That isn't how things are done in the palace. But I could take you around. I'll make sure no one notices us." Almost as an afterthought, she adds, "With our rani's permission, of course."

"Certainly." I send her a grateful glance, but Mangla's attention is totally focused on Jawahar.

My pragmatic maid is infatuated with my brother! I'm not sure I like this unexpected development. Where earlier Mangla used to hover around Dalip all day, accusing his nursemaid of carelessness, now she finishes her tasks quickly and asks if she might take Jawahar around the qila. They're gone for hours. I suspect they're going into the city. But I'm reluctant to confront them, to have them lie to me.

Before Jawahar arrived, Mangla slept on the floor of my bedroom, next to Dalip's cot, although I'd given her a room of her own.

"I sleep better here because I know you're both safe," she insisted.

But recently she asked if she might sleep in her own room. I agreed. How could I not? I'm sure, though, that she's spending her nights with Jawahar, and this makes me jealous. It's not as though they are neglecting me. Mangla makes sure the household runs as efficiently as ever. Jawahar spends plenty of time playing with Dalip and reminiscing about our childhood. Still, I feel abandoned.

Jawahar has been with me for a week. Soon he'll be returning to Gujranwala. I look forward to his departure with a mix of relief and guilt.

This morning, I receive an invitation, a beautiful ivory parchment wrapped in red silk. Prince Naunihal has arranged a small mehfil for close friends and family tomorrow evening. He would be most honored if his respected grandmother, Rani Jindan, would grace his humble abode for the occasion.

I sway between surprise—it's the first time Naunihal has invited me—and amused chagrin at being called a grandmother! I ask the messenger what the occasion is.

"Our dear Naunihal ji needs no occasion." The woman smiles indulgently. "He loves to enjoy life—just like our Sarkar."

At the bottom of the invitation a line has been added, extending a warm welcome to the rani's honorable brother.

How does Naunihal know about Jawahar? Could Mangla have spoken to someone?

Just then, Jawahar walks in—with suspicious timeliness—and asks what I'm looking at.

I consider lying; then I'm annoyed. Why should I lie? I'm a queen.

I tell him, ending with, "But I'm not going."

"What a beautiful invitation! May I look?"

To refuse feels churlish in the face of my brother's childlike eagerness.

"Why, Naunihal has invited me as well. You didn't tell me that! A mehfil would be so much fun. Why can't we go?"

"The Sarkar wouldn't like it."

"But Naunihal is his favorite grandson. He's been to your mehfils. Isn't it natural for you to go to his?"

I explain that Naunihal doesn't live inside the qila. Jawahar points out that I go outside for other things—to the gurdwara, to feed the poor, to the women's bazaar.

"It's the first time he's inviting you. Will he not feel slighted if you refuse? He might even think that, as a queen mother, you believe you are too important to accept his invitation."

Jawahar's arguments, neatly piled one upon another, surprise me. He's always been swift and strong—my protector—but never particularly sharp, especially with social intricacies. Did Mangla teach him what to say? His accent, too, has changed. It sounds more Lahori. Has Mangla been coaching him?

In the end I agree, mostly because of the plaintive desire in his eyes. He'll be going back soon to Gujranwala, never to return. Let him have a taste of court life. Naunihal's home is probably as safe a place as any. I'm a little curious myself to see how the Sarkar's beloved grandson lives.

I summon my tailor and use some of my savings to order a maroon silk kurta-pajama embroidered with gold thread for Jawahar. I have to pay extra to get it by tomorrow. But when I see how reverently Jawahar touches the outfit, I'm glad I did it.

18

Mehfil

We travel to Naunihal's haveli in two palanquins. Mine is covered; I can only see things through tiny peepholes. Why must women always remain hidden from the world? Jawahar leans out of his, commenting on the fancy houses we're passing. He should have ridden a horse, like the other noblemen. But I don't trust his skills, and don't want him ending up in a ditch.

We're followed by two guards and a maid—not Mangla. I knew she wanted to come. I suspected she'd arranged the invitation somehow. I ordered her to stay back, claiming I couldn't trust anyone else with Dalip. This wasn't untrue. But the real reason is that I am displeased with her.

Naunihal's mansion, large and imposing, is in excellent taste. Its entrance, decorated with friezes and intricate stone inlays, reminds me of the Sheesh Mahal. Clearly, Naunihal has modeled his home on the Sarkar's favorite building. I imagine his wife standing on the beautiful covered balcony, enjoying the spectacles of the street. For a moment, I wish I, too, lived in the heart of the city instead of sequestered inside the fort. Then I chide myself. I'm the Sarkar's queen, the qila is where I belong.

"We'll watch a few dances, eat a little, and leave," I tell Jawahar.

"When I send a message, say your goodbyes. Be careful. If Naunihal's parties are anything like his grandfather's, wine will flow generously. Stay away from it." I pause until he nods. I know, from Biji's letters, that Jawahar loves his drink. "Converse with the other guests as little as possible. In fact, it's best if you don't talk at all."

"Yes, bhainji," Jawahar jokes, making a face. True, I'm behaving like a fussy older sister. But who else will warn Jawahar about the dangers of courtly life?

We're greeted at the great carved door by retainers. I'm led up a winding staircase to the women's area, a beautiful balcony covered by elegant wooden screens where the women can enjoy the mehfil in privacy. I'm warmly greeted by Chand and Bibi, joint hostesses for the evening. They're very finely attired, and I'm glad that I wore my golden silk ghaghra. I find a corner seat near the edge of the balcony so I can keep an eye on Jawahar. I'm pleased to see him sitting quietly in the back. The other guests—young and fashionably dressed—clap each other on the shoulder, laughing loudly at jokes. They ignore Jawahar.

For a moment I feel bad for him. But it's for the best.

A group of women have noticed me. They rush up and, bowing deferentially, ask about Dalip's health. Embarrassed by the commotion, I try to quieten them. But it's too late. A woman sitting in the best seat up front turns to look. It's Mai Nakkain. I'm forced to walk up and pay my respects. I brace myself for a sarcastic remark, but Mai merely smiles. "I'm delighted you came," she says.

The show begins; a group of accomplished musicians play the shehnai and drums. The singer who, Naunihal announces, has traveled all the way from Delhi, begins a ghazal by Mirza Ghalib, *Ye na thi hamari kismat—It was not my destiny to be united with the beloved.* It's a favorite of the Sarkar's. As its haunting notes fill the hall, I feel a pang of guilt. The Sarkar would be angry if he knew I was here—and that I'd brought Jawahar.

Waheguru, I'll make it up by being the best wife once he returns.

Now the singer launches into a spirited complaint to a sweetheart.

You are the only thing in the world worth looking at. Why do you hide your face in a veil? Naunihal raises his goblet toward the balcony in a salute, and the women tease the blushing Bibi. I'm happy to see that Naunihal and his wife love each other dearly; it's rare in political marriages. I hope my Dalip will find someone he loves. I'll host a splendid engagement banquet for him at the beautiful Naulakha pavilion. Regal in a silk sherwani, Dalip will enter the hall side by side with his father while I shower rose petals on the two men I love the most . . .

I'm shaken out of my reverie by Chand, who clasps my hands warmly. "I'm so glad you came! I've often wanted to invite you, but I was afraid of Mai. She seems to have mellowed with age, though. It was she who told Naunihal to invite you and your brother. Please, have something."

An attendant brings a tray with drinks. The silver goblets hold juice; the gold, wine. I choose juice. Mai's personal attendant hands her a jeweled goblet. Mai points to the men's area, and the attendant bows and leaves. The old queen catches my eye and smiles again.

Perhaps Chand is right. Perhaps Mai has put aside her enmity since nothing more can be gained by it.

A GROUP OF DANCERS dressed in provocatively cut pishwases have entered the courtyard. Someone whispers that they are from the notorious Hira Mandi district. The men give them a raucous welcome. This is a different kind of mehfil from the Sarkar's decorous ones! A storm of gossip rises around me as the women argue which dancers get paid the highest and have the most lovers.

I notice Mai's attendant in the men's area. She goes to Jawahar, who has been drinking juice, and offers him a large gold goblet. What is Mai up to?

I must warn Jawahar not to accept the drink. But I can't enter the men's area. I look for my maid, but she's off somewhere, gossiping. I regret not bringing Mangla. She would have known just what to do.

Jawahar shakes his head, but the attendant points to the women's area. He grins, accepts the goblet, raises it toward the balcony, and drinks. She must have told him that I sent the wine. Of course he believed her, poor Jawahar who knows nothing about royal games.

The wine must be delicious. Jawahar takes a large swig. The attendant refills his goblet.

My palms grow sweaty. I find Chand and say that I must leave—it is time to nurse Dalip. But she begs me to stay until dinner is served. It would be churlish to refuse, so I sit down reluctantly.

Another dance begins. The attendant keeps refilling Jawahar's goblet. Jawahar is clapping loudly now, swaying to the beat. As the music grows frenzied, the dancers dare the men to join them. The noblemen decline, laughing, but Jawahar gets up and attempts to follow the dancers' steps. The men jeer and point. I watch in horror as my brother grabs a dancer by the waist. She twists away. He lunges at her, getting in the way of the other dancers, breaking up their routine.

Naunihal's friends yell, "Who is this kambakht? How did he get in here? Get rid of him!"

Naunihal gestures to a servant, who tries to guide Jawahar back to his seat. But Jawahar pushes the servant so hard that the man lands on the floor. The dancers back away, bumping into each other. The musicians falter and stop. Naunihal claps his hands angrily. Two guards appear and drag Jawahar toward the door. He protests loudly all the way. *How dare you do this to me! Don't you know who I am? I'm the Sarkar's brother-in-law. His saala.*

"Throw the saala out on the street!" one of the courtiers sneers.

I rush to the staircase, mumbling something about feeling ill to a surprised Chand. Busy with organizing dinner, she hasn't seen what happened below. I find my maid chatting at the foot of the stairs and grab her by the shoulders.

"Fetch my guards. Run, you idiot! We've already lost precious time thanks to your gossiping. Tell them to meet me at the entrance. Then go find our palanquins."

I wait, wrapped in my veil, praying that none of the guests will see me. When the guards arrive, I order them to take custody of Jawahar from Naunihal's men and put him in his palanquin. "Force him if you need to. Tell the palanquin bearers to go as fast as they can. I'll pay double."

All the way back, Jawahar complains loudly. *Rani Jindan, my sweet but cruel sister, pulled me away from the party just when I was having fun.* I'm mortified to see passersby pointing to our palanquins. Even the qila gatekeepers snicker behind their mustaches.

MANGLA OPENS THE HAVELI door, smiling. She must have been waiting there for us to return. "How did it go, my queen? Did—"

Her words die away when she sees Jawahar being helped in by my guards. He's in a most affectionate mood, trying to hug everyone within arm's reach. There's no point in speaking to him tonight.

"Put him in bed and keep him there until he falls asleep," I order the guards.

I tell Mangla about the fiasco at Naunihal's. "I was a bigger fool than Jawahar. I walked right into Mai Nakkain's trap. But how did she know about him?"

Mangla wrings her hands, distraught. "I was careful not to mention him to anyone. I should have been more suspicious of that invitation. I know better than most that the qila is infested with spies. But I was so happy that Jawahar ji would get to enjoy some court life before leaving that I didn't think." She throws herself at my feet. "I've failed you. And I've failed the Sarkar, who trusted me to watch over you. I don't deserve to continue in your service. I'll leave tomorrow," she sobs.

She looks so miserable that my anger fades. "What is this foolish talk? I can't do without you. You know that. Especially now . . . Mai is sure to tell the Sarkar everything that happened tonight, exaggerating it to the fullest. He'll be enraged. I need your help. I have to think of some way to calm him down—"

Mangla kisses my hand. "Thank you, my queen, for giving me another chance. We'll find a solution. And Mai Nakkain will suffer. I promise you that."

EARLY NEXT MORNING, I shake Jawahar awake. I'm no longer furious with him. If anything, I feel sympathy as he rubs his forehead, grimacing. But I hide it and tell him that he needs to leave for Gujranwala at once. Jawahar looks abashed. He tries to defend himself, but I say sternly, "You've done me great harm. I know you didn't mean to; you were tricked. Nevertheless, you created a shameful scene at the mehfil—and I'll have to pay the price."

"I'm sorry." Jawahar hangs his head. "I was stupid. I was drunk. You know I'd never hurt you on purpose. Of all the people in my life, I love you the most."

I know this. It made my decision even harder. "I, too, made some stupid choices. No sense looking back now. You must promise me that you will never speak to anyone about last evening. No bragging to your friends or even Manna and Biji about your evening at Prince Naunihal's."

Jawahar mumbles assent, then begs, "Can I please stay until Dalip wakes up? I want to play with him one last time!"

I harden my heart. "No. Mai Nakkain might decide to stop by to gloat. And the ministers will begin arriving at the Diwan-i-Khas soon. You need to leave before that."

As he climbs into the palanquin, Jawahar looks at me entreatingly. He's hoping I'll change my mind. But I can't. I stare ahead, stone-faced. Only after the palanquin turns the corner do I weep. "This is all my poor brother will remember of his visit—how harsh I was to him. I'll probably never see him again."

"Never is a big word," Mangla says. "Who can tell what the future holds? For now, our little prince needs to be fed. After that, we'll decide how to handle the Sarkar."

This is the one ray of light amid the gathering storm clouds: now that Jawahar has gone, Mangla is back to being her pragmatic self.

19

Illness

THE SARKAR'S RETURN HAS BEEN delayed. No one seems to know why. But finally, tonight, he's supposed to arrive. I pace the bedchamber in the Sheesh Mahal with great trepidation. I paid a hefty bribe to the attendants to let me in; queens are not supposed to enter the Sarkar's quarters unless he sends for them. Mangla waits outside, hidden in a corner, in case he throws me out.

I've dressed with care in a new pink salwar-kameez, a shade which flatters my complexion, and lavishly applied my most expensive rose attar. I've put together a large platter of the Sarkar's favorite snacks and arranged for a flagon of his preferred Kashmiri wine. And mangoes, the Sarkar's favorite fruit. The mangoes were particularly difficult to get because it isn't the season. The Sarkar will be touched, I hope, by my efforts. Still, my heart thuds unevenly as I wait. He's a perceptive man. It's not easy to fool him.

My plan is to greet the Sarkar with a passionate kiss, telling him that I couldn't bear to be away from him for another night. It isn't a complete lie, I *have* missed him, especially these last few days as I wandered around the haveli with regret as my only companion. But a deeper truth is that I'm terrified. What if he's not in the mood for company? What if Mai Nakkain has already informed him of my misdeeds? I've seen how angry the Sarkar can get, though that wrath hasn't been turned on me. Not yet.

If all goes well, we'll share the meal and make love—successfully, I hope. Afterward, when he's in a mellow mood, I'll confess what happened at Naunihal's and ask for forgiveness.

If my plan fails—I'm not sure what I'll do then.

A SERIES OF THUMPING sounds make me back into a corner. Something bulky is being transported up the stairs amid much shouting. A foreign voice—Honigberger's—breaks through the hullaballoo, ordering people to be careful. The doors are flung open and bearers carry in a pallet on which the Sarkar is stretched out, eyes closed and face so pale that for a moment I'm sure he's dead. He's followed by several grim-faced men who crowd the chamber: courtiers, his ghorcharhas, the vaid with his attendants, and Dhian Singh.

Ignoring propriety and the astonished stares of the men, I rush to the Sarkar's side. I watch fearfully as he is transferred to his bed and the attendants massage his limbs. Honigberger answers my questions in his broken Punjabi. The Sarkar had another stroke, brought on by the strain of too many daytime meetings and too much feasting at night. "Dr. McGregor and I begged him to rest, but you know how stubborn His Majesty is."

I sink down by the Sarkar's bed and hold his hand. I'm overcome with guilt as I remember how, when he was leaving, I'd wished for him to stay away longer. My wicked wish has come true.

Dhian sighs as he watches the Sarkar's still form. "I had best send word to Mai Nakkain to come and look after—"

"No," I interrupt. If Mai gets here, she'll make sure I'm kept away from the Sarkar until she has poisoned his mind completely. In desperation, I push back my veil and fix my gaze on Dhian, putting all the charm I can muster up into an entreating smile. "Wazir ji, please let me tend to him. I'll make sure he rests properly and eats what he should. When he's better, I'll bring Dalip over. You know how much the Sarkar loves to spend time with his son. I'm sure it will speed up his recovery."

Dhian hesitates. "We'll try it for a day. Two at most. If he isn't better by then, I must summon Mai. She has much experience in taking care of him."

Hugely relieved, I thank Dhian, then ask the physicians for instructions, carefully repeating everything they say.

"The globules need to be placed under the Sarkar's tongue every four hours. The right side of his body is to be massaged every hour with medicated almond oil, especially the arm, which he isn't able to move. I'll hold this aromatic vial near his nose so he can breathe its healing vapors. If he wakes up, I'll give him barley water by the spoonful."

Dhian fixes his shrewd eyes on my face. "And do not bring up any matters that might anger him in any way."

I offer him an innocent look. "Of course not."

I send Mangla—she bullied her way past the soldiers—to wake the royal cook, who will prepare the barley water, and the royal taster, for especially under conditions such as this, one must be careful of plots. I send the exhausted physicians downstairs to sleep, tell the assistants to wait in the alcove until they are needed, and request Dhian to go home. I promise to summon them if anything changes. At first Dhian refuses, but finally he agrees with a weary sigh.

"Do you think our Sarkar will be better tomorrow?" I ask the physicians.

The vaid says it is possible. But Honigberger's long German face is heavy with pessimism. "A quick recovery from a stroke like this would require a miracle."

SILENCE DESCENDS UPON THE room once everyone has gone. Mangla settles herself by the door. I hold the Sarkar's hand, which feels cold and slack, like a dead man's. My eyes fall on the covered thali which I'd readied for an evening of love. How worried I'd been that the Sarkar would be angry and punish me. But this is far worse. I have to bite my lip to keep from weeping.

Pull yourself together, I chide myself. *Focus on him, not yourself.* I call to him gently but he doesn't respond. When I kiss his cheek, its coldness penetrates my body, too. The moon sinks low. Mangla replenishes the lamps. The attendants massage the Sarkar and leave. I tuck medicinal globules under his tongue. Not even a groan passes the Sarkar's lips. I've run out of prayers. When I place a finger in front of his nostrils, I can scarcely feel a breath.

Impetuously, I slip into bed with the Sarkar and hold him close. "Come back. I need you. Dalip needs you. Punjab needs you. You can't die. Not yet." I whisper the words over and over until exhaustion drags me down into sleep.

I wake with a guilty start to find the window bright with sunlight. I must have turned in the night, for I'm facing away from the Sarkar, and toward Mangla, who sits cross-legged by the bed. She smiles and points. I angle my head and see that at some point, the Sarkar, too, had moved, turning toward me, and placing his good arm around me in a loose embrace. He's breathing normally, even snoring a bit.

I should get up and fix my attire. It isn't proper for the physicians to see me like this. But I don't want to disturb the Sarkar. So I lie there, his warm body curved against mine. When the physicians arrive and marvel at his improvement, I smile at them without embarrassment. It's the smile of a queen, but more so the smile of a woman in love who knows she's loved back.

WORD HAS TRAVELED TO Mai Nakkain, who has spies everywhere. She storms the Sheesh Mahal with her attendants and a train of vaids just as I'm giving the Sarkar his barley water. She insists that Honigberger and the royal physician hand over his care to her vaids immediately. She ignores their entreaties that the Sarkar should not be disturbed, nor his medications changed in this fragile condition.

"Haven't my vaids and I brought him through all his illnesses?" she demands. "I know better than all of you what he needs."

I can sense the Sarkar getting agitated. I try to calm her down. "Please, Mai, can we talk outside? All this commotion isn't good for him."

She turns on me. "You little upstart, pretending to be such a devoted wife! I know all your tricks. You hurried here last night, hoping to seduce the Sarkar before he punished you. Too bad he wasn't well enough to throw you out. But I'll do it for him." She calls for her guards.

My mouth is dry with dismay; I force myself to speak with a confidence I don't feel. "Most respected queen, you are disturbing the Sarkar. My presence has done him some good—his physicians will attest to that. The wazir has tasked me with taking care of him, so if you disagree, you must talk to him."

I steel myself for battle. She isn't going to give in easily. What will I do if she orders her guards to drag me away, as she did at that long-ago mehfil?

Then the Sarkar moves his hand slowly to clasp mine. He fixes his eye on Mai Nakkain and shakes his head. And, just like that, Mai is defeated.

THE DAYS GROW COLDER. The shalmali trees shed their crimson blossoms. I massage the Sarkar's limbs myself. I feed him his meals one spoon at a time. If the Sarkar is restless at night, I stay up to keep him company. Sometimes, even though I'm not musically talented, I sing to distract him until he falls asleep. In the morning he jokes that my voice was so off-key that he was forced to escape into the land of dreams.

Dalip, too, is a help. Guddan has taken over his care, thank Waheguru, but Mangla still brings him to me several times a day for his feedings. Afterward, I lay him beside his father. The Sarkar watches as he kicks and babbles to himself. When Dalip grabs his finger, a slow smile breaks over the Sarkar's face.

Finally, the day comes when the Sarkar sits up and eats by himself. He walks to the balcony, wrapped in a shawl. The entire durbar, gathered in the courtyard below, sends up a jubilant cheer. Dhian has been conferring with him regularly. But when I ask if I might invite the Fakir, Dhian refuses.

"I don't want to expose the Sarkar to too many people for fear of infection," he declares.

I can see his plan—to reduce the Fakir's influence over the Sarkar—but when I write to the Fakir about it, he sends me a warning: *Don't bring me up again. Dhian's star is rising. Don't antagonize him. Focus, instead, on your own problem.*

On the day the Sarkar starts planning his return to court, I tell him about the fiasco at Naunihal's mehfil.

"I am very sorry that I disobeyed you. I'll accept whatever punishment you give me. I only ask that you don't send me away until you're stronger. Let me take care of you for a little longer."

I expect fury, but after an unbearable stretch of silence, he says, "I knew this already. Mai sent me word that same night."

The crafty old hag. She'd beaten me again.

The Sarkar continues in the slow, slurred way that is his new manner of speaking. "I expected you to be smarter. Not get taken in by tricks."

I bow my head, more ashamed than if he had railed at me.

"Many will dangle shiny bait in front of you," he says. "For Dalip's sake, you must learn to recognize it. You must learn to think about consequences. You must protect him, because—"

I interrupt him. "Waheguru bless you! I won't need to. You'll be around for a long time to take care of us."

But I see the knowing look in his eye, melancholy as morning mist. It says, *Let us not pretend.*

"I promise you," I say. "I will protect our son."

20

Decision

THE YEAR BEGINS AUSPICIOUSLY. THE Sarkar celebrates Baisakhi by leading a ceremonial procession to the gurdwara. He cannot ride a horse, but he sits regally atop his favorite elephant as he throws fistfuls of sweetmeats and coins into the huge, cheering crowd. Only his closest attendants and I know that he has to take to his bed, exhausted, afterward. But his will is like iron. The next morning he is in the durbar, as usual.

Ever since his illness, my husband craves my company. I spend every night in the Sheesh Mahal, though sex is no longer a possibility. He leans on me as he walks in the rose garden. When he goes to the stables to visit Laila, I accompany him in his palanquin. He submits to my dictates—no alcohol, no late nights, and a light vegetarian diet. Each day he looks stronger.

Then Governor-General Auckland—maliciously, I'm certain of it—sends another delegation to Punjab. The visitors want to see the Golden Temple.

The Golden Temple is the Sarkar's weakness. He loves it more than any other holy place. Nine years ago, he overlaid the entire sanctum with gold. Since then, he has delighted in showing it off to guests. He ignores my entreaties and personally takes the delegation to Amritsar. There he has another stroke.

When they bring him back this time, his condition is far worse. I hide my fears and nurse him day and night until I'm so weary that Mangla begins to worry about my health. He doesn't get better. He lies unmoving, drifting in and out of consciousness. Much of the time he doesn't recognize me. Dhian sends messengers to the heads of the clans, asking them to come to Lahore. Then he informs me that the Sarkar must be moved to the Musamman Burj, at the edge of the qila. "He needs to be in a larger, more public building. Many people will come to pay their respects to him."

My heart twists. He means *their last respects.*

"I must be with him." I throw back my veil, shocking him. "Wazir ji, you know the Sarkar needs me. Is some outdated custom more important than that?" I glare until he agrees.

Perhaps the Sarkar senses that his end is near. In the Musamman Burj, he draws on his meager strength to whisper urgent instructions to Dhian. From time to time, he looks for me. I can always tell if he's thirsty, or if the sheet that covers him feels too heavy, or if he just wants me to hold his hand. Occasionally he will mouth Dalip's name and I will run outside to where Mangla is waiting and fetch him. He's ten months old now and can walk a few steps before he loses his balance and lands on the floor. A small smile tugs at the corner of the Sarkar's lips. Once or twice, his eye fills with tears. I wipe them away quickly. He wouldn't want his courtiers to see the Lion of Punjab weeping like an ordinary father.

In spite of all my care, the Sarkar takes a turn for the worse. His breath comes in shallow gasps now. In his conscious moments, he orders his treasurer to donate large amounts of wealth, including the Koh-i-Noor, to the Jagannath temple at Puri, known for its miracles. Perhaps he believes it will save his life. Dhian and the treasurer mouth assurances, but they don't obey him.

I realize then that they have no hope of his survival.

TONIGHT THE QUEENS WERE allowed to come to the Musamman Burj to pray for the Sarkar—a bad sign. Afterward, Dhian sent us away so that the Sarkar could use the last of his strength to put the tika of kinghood on his son Kharak's forehead in the presence of the courtiers. Everyone has accepted that his death is inevitable, but I refuse to join them in that treachery. All night I stand at my window, praying to Sant Jhingar Shah, protector of the qila, to save my beloved's life. But I find myself forgetting the familiar lines, repeating the same words over and over. I know then that I've failed.

In the morning when I hear the wails from the women's quarters spreading across the qila like ink on white silk, I'm devastated but unsurprised. In the other room Dalip starts to cry—unusual howls of distress as though he has sensed the fear spiraling around us. I try to nurse him, but I'm too tense and the milk refuses to come. He cries louder.

What will happen to us now, child?

I GO TO GUDDAN'S haveli, looking for her. My best friend, my sister. She'll tell me what to do. She'll protect Dalip and me. But she's not here. Her maids tell me she's in the zenana.

I hurry there and find the queens, young and old, milling around, side by side with the concubines and slaves. Death has leveled us all. Some of the women weep and tear at their hair and clothing. Others whisper, their heads close, already trying to form alliances that might help them survive.

Guddan sits apart, an oddly serene smile on her beautiful face. It frightens me.

"Sister," I ask, "why are you smiling?"

She doesn't answer. It's as though she hasn't heard me.

The minutes move slowly, like tar. Finally Dhian sends word: we may pay our last respects to the Sarkar. Mai Nakkain arrives from her haveli and takes her place at the head of the line. I clasp Guddan's hand as we walk barefoot across the courtyard. The sun has leapt high above the curved roof of the Naulakha pavilion. After last night's storm, the sky is blue as lapis. It's going to be a splendid day.

The Sarkar's body lies on the floor of the Burj, diminished by death. It has been washed and dressed in white. There is a great commotion around him. Because he respected all religions, Brahmins chant from the Gita and maulvis offer salat-al-Janazah. An old man, a ragi, is singing, his voice quavering, *With their death already preordained, mortals come into this world.* With a shock, I recognize him as the man who chanted at my wedding. He tells us to sprinkle Ganga water on the Sarkar's feet. Some of the women throw themselves on the ground, keening, but I don't. The Sarkar would have found such behavior distasteful.

I know I should look carefully at the Sarkar's body, imprint its features upon my memory. But my mind balks at the idea. This shrunken corpse is not my beloved husband. I close my eyes and see, instead, the man in shining white who lifted me onto Laila's back and swept me into a magical world.

All too soon, Dhian asks us to leave. Many courtiers, chieftains, and ministers of neighboring kingdoms are waiting to pay their respects. Even some of the British Residents from the principalities have arrived with gifts to be placed on the pyre.

"Can we attend the funeral?" one of the queens whispers to Mai Nakkain.

Mai shakes her head sadly. When she speaks, her voice is cracked and raw. "The queens may only watch the procession from the zenana balconies."

Among us, only Mai has nothing to fear. As the mother of the new king, she'll be even more powerful than before. But she's been weeping—far more than custom dictates. Looking at her swollen eyes, I realize that she'd truly loved the Sarkar.

Trained to submit to custom, the queens begin to follow Mai out. Suddenly Guddan steps out of line, lifts her veil and faces Dhian. I'm shocked, but Dhian gives her a sad, knowing look.

In a clear voice she says, "Wazir ji, I wish to exercise my divine right to become a sati, to burn with the Sarkar on his pyre." Her face shines with an other-worldly light. She takes Dhian's hand—a huge taboo, for a married woman to touch another man—and asks him to be loyal to the new king and to Punjab.

"I promise, devi," says Dhian.

I'm startled to hear him refer to Guddan as *goddess*. He stares at her face, her terrible beauty, as though mesmerized. Three other queens and seven concubines step forward and stand next to Guddan. Inspired—or is it hypnotized—by her, they, too, want to become satis.

Am I the only one who thinks this is horrifying?

Dhian whispers to attendants to make the appropriate arrangements. The Brahmins praise the women with loud prayers, louder when the women give them their jewelry. I feel as though they're staring at me now, expectation in their eyes.

I shudder. I must stop Guddan from committing this awful act. I can't lose both my husband and my dearest friend on the same day.

I'VE BEEN BEGGING GUDDAN for an hour.

"Please, sister, don't do this. Give alms to the poor, instead, for the Sarkar's soul."

Guddan smiles calmly. "Money is a dead thing. I'm offering God my living body. In return he'll bless the Sarkar and me, so that our souls will never be parted. Don't try to stop me. I decided this a long time ago. It is the custom of my father's house, and not such a terrible thing."

She answers all my objections patiently.

"I'm not being brave. Just the opposite. Do you know how hard life is for a widow? Even—or maybe especially—for those who were queens? We'll be powerless—shunned, perhaps even murdered, so that our valuables can be confiscated by the treasury. But as a sati, I'll follow my husband to heaven, while on earth, a temple will be built in my name."

The maids dress Guddan in her flame-colored wedding ghaghra, arranging the dupatta over her breasts, making sure everything is perfect. She waves away her veil. Satis are goddesses. They no longer need to be protected from the gaze of mortal men.

"But the pain!" I cry.

"I've bought the opium already. I'll feel almost nothing."

My head spins from exhaustion. Could she be right?

Guddan's lovely eyes shine as she kisses me goodbye. I can sense her thoughts. *Come with me, dearest sister. We'll be together with our king. Peaceful, joyful, protected.*

I'm shocked by how tempted I am.

Inside me, a voice, like the jinns found in stories, whispers, *Guddan is right. The future's going to be tumultuous. Kharak isn't strong enough to hold together his father's empire. He'll think of the Sarkar's other sons as threats to be eliminated, Dalip no less than the others. But if you became a sati, if you gave Mangla all your money and jewelry, she could take Dalip somewhere far away. She'd be as good a mother to him as you, and far more canny. He'd be forgotten. He'd be safe.*

The voice continues, more enticing now. *And you'll be remembered. Not as a kennel keeper's daughter but as a heroine. A worthy, loving consort of the Sarkar. The only Sikh queen who loved him enough to die on his pyre. A goddess.*

Fame: it's a drug more potent than opium.

WALKING BACK TO MY haveli, I feel like I'm floating through a deep, peaceful underwater cavern.

"Why did you take so long?" Mangla sounds scared. "The other queens returned to their chambers hours ago." She sets Dalip on the floor so that he'll crawl to me. I pick him up automatically. He kicks his feet in excitement, laughing. He does not know his life has changed.

I close my eyes. "I'm going to join Guddan as a sati. You must help me."

"No!" Mangla cries. "You're a Sikh, not a Hindu like Guddan. Why should you do this terrible thing? You don't see Mai Nakkain planning to kill herself, do you? Think of what will happen to Dalip if you die."

"You'll take care of him."

"How? Even if I try to hide him somewhere, without a patron to protect us, they'll find us for sure. They'll kill him before the year is out. Is that what you want for your baby?"

The cavern is calm, devoid of problems. No duties, no worries, no gut-twisting grief. I want to remain here. But someone keeps patting my face. A babble of baby sounds breaks into my refuge.

I hear another voice, too. Gritty, gruff, displeased. *Surely I've taught you better than to run away from problems! If it's fame you crave, instead of killing yourself, why not live in a way that people will remember?*

The Sarkar's.

It's hard to emerge from the cavern once you're deep within. But the Sarkar's voice pulls at me. *You must be both father and mother to our son. Didn't you promise me that?* He does not relent until I take a shuddering breath, open my eyes, and find Dalip chewing my hair. His sloping forehead is his father's. His tip-tilted nose is mine. He is watching me as though there are no other faces in the world.

What spell had brought me so close to abandoning my baby? To forgetting my vow to the Sarkar? To letting go of the teachings of my faith? *O Nanak, some burn themselves along with their dead husbands . . . But if they really loved them, they would endure the pain alive.*

I hold Dalip hungrily, burying my face in his neck. *I'll live for you, my heart. I'll protect you with the last drop of my blood. If I have to, I'll kill for you.* He squeals in delight; he likes this game.

But here's another truth that I've just discovered, crouching in the shadow of the first. One I can never say aloud because it feels like a betrayal of the Sarkar.

For my own sake, too, I want to live. I've barely touched the world. There's so much out there to see and feel and taste. I'm greedy for it. I'll take the bitter with the sweet. I'll endure the pain.

21

Departure

MANGLA COMES RUNNING. "THE SARKAR's funeral procession will pass by our haveli soon. Please, my queen, remain inside. Rani Guddan is walking behind the Sarkar's bier. Even people who don't know her are weeping as they watch. You will not be able to bear it."

But I thrust Dalip at Mangla and rush to the terrace. I must say goodbye to my beloved. And beg forgiveness of my dearest friend for abandoning her.

The procession is huge. Even leaning out over the parapet, I cannot see the end of it. In the front are musicians and ragis. Then come the Sarkar's adored ghorcharhas, though today they're on foot, dressed in mourning white like all the noblemen. The Sarkar's bier follows, a sandalwood ship with gold fittings and cheerful silk flags.

The Sarkar would have found the spectacle wonderfully entertaining. He was like a child where such things were concerned. I search for his body, half buried under piles of shawls and flowers. How frail it looks, now that his gigantic spirit has abandoned it. *Go in peace, my love, to your next kingdom.*

My eyes are drawn to the women following the bier, a clump of color fierce as the flames they've decided to embrace. Dressed in shades of red, they toss coins and jewelry into the crowd lining the road. The people bow to them, shouting, "Devis, your sacrifice will bless Punjab."

Tears blind me, but I manage to locate Guddan at the head of the women. I'd intended to send her off with a brave prayer. But when I see her slight form, stumbling a little because of the opium she has taken, I beat my fists on the parapet, shouting, "Guddan! Don't do this terrible thing to yourself, don't leave me all alone!" It's no use. She cannot hear my cries, and even if she did, she cannot change her mind now. Still, I shout until I collapse, my throat raw, on the burning tiles. The drums drown out my voice. The procession continues. Long after Mangla forces me downstairs, telling me I can't afford the indulgence of falling apart, I'll hear those drums beating inside my head.

IN THE DARKNESS OF evening, the Fakir comes to see me, unannounced, wrapped in a cheap blanket like a beggar. His countenance is harried, his face dark with exhaustion. He refuses refreshments. He's observing a mourning fast. Ignoring etiquette, he holds me as I weep. His eyes, too, grow wet. "Beti, I had to see you, but I'll have to leave in a few minutes. It will harm you if certain people learn of my visit."

"Who? Why? You've always come to see me. The Sarkar himself approved—"

"Everything is different now. Don't you see that? The Sarkar put Dhian in charge of you—and rightly so. Dhian will be angry if he knew that we have met. I'll be in touch whenever I can, but opportunities will be rare. You'll have to rely on your own wits."

His words worry me. "Rely on my wits for what?"

"Turbulence is coming. People will be watching Kharak. His half brother Sher, the British, and even the Afghans—they will all want to swoop in at the first sign of weakness . . ."

"What have I to do with them?"

"Nothing, if things go the way the Sarkar planned when he named Kharak his heir and trained Naunihal to follow him. But don't forget—Dalip is a prince. Just that fact puts him in danger. Keep your eyes open. Be quick and clever." He sighs. "I must leave now."

"Wait, please!" I feel incapable of making any decisions, let alone quick and clever ones. "Tell me what to watch for . . . What to do—"

"When danger arises, you'll recognize it. I have full faith in you." With that, he melts into the darkness.

SLEEPLESS IN BED, I can't stop thinking about the funeral. Mangla has told me a few details she gleaned from the other servants; I imagine the rest.

The pyre is tall, the sandalwood logs arranged like steps. Men carry the Sarkar's body to the top and cover him with flowers. Guddan takes Kharak's hand and Dhian's, and joins them. She makes them promise to work together for the Sarkar's sake. Then she ascends the pyre and places the Sarkar's head on her lap. Her face is fearless. The other ranis and concubines, dizzy from the opium, have to be helped up. Together with Naunihal, a weeping Kharak sets the pyre ablaze, their enmity forgotten in the moment. Dhian beats his forehead against the ground until it is streaked with blood. He tries to throw himself onto the pyre, but the courtiers hold on to him. The sandalwood cannot mask the smell of burning flesh.

All of a sudden, a cloud appears in the sky. Rain falls on the pyre for a few moments. *Punjab herself is weeping*, people whisper. When the blaze is at its highest, two white birds swoop down—who knows from where—and dive into the flames.

As the Fakir was leaving, I asked him if the part about the birds was true. He nodded.

"Is it a good omen, or a bad one?"

He didn't know.

IN THE MORNING I remember the Fakir's advice to be prepared and send a guard to the toshakhana to collect two hundred gold coins from my account. I want some extra money on hand. To my surprise, he returns with nothing.

He says, "The munshi told me that upon orders of Maharaja Kharak Singh, all accounts have been frozen. They will be available after the coronation."

My temper rises. "That'll happen only after the Sarkar's ashes are taken to the Ganga. It'll take ten days, maybe more. How will I run my household until then?"

"I am sorry, Rani Sahiba."

I control my anger. "It's not your fault."

"There's another thing. Your guards have been recalled. Our supervisor said we're needed at the gates. We must leave right away."

I can't believe my ears. "Are you saying my haveli will be left unguarded? Dalip and I won't have any protection?"

The man lowers his gaze, silent. Within the hour, the guards are gone.

I wipe away angry tears and give Mangla some of the money I'd kept in the haveli. "Go and buy food. Buy extra, in case there are shortages later."

But Mangla is worried about more than food. She sleuths around the qila and finds out that not all guards have been removed, nor all accounts restricted. "Only the ones belonging to people Mai Nakkain doesn't like."

The turbulent times the Fakir warned me about have arrived. And it's only the beginning.

I grasp Mangla's hand. "I need you to do something difficult for me."

THE NIGHT IS COVERED in rain clouds. The watchman announces the midnight hour. I pace through the haveli, my hopes dwindling.

"You must rest," Mangla says. "You're wearing yourself out. I'll wake you if anyone comes." But I'm too nervous to sleep.

Suddenly, there are three knocks, the planned signal. Mangla rushes to open the door. Two men stand outside, shrouded in shawls. One seems to be a soldier. I catch the glint of a pistol tucked in his waistband. The other is Dhian Singh.

I draw on everything I know about the royal game. I greet Dhian formally and accept his condolences, but my nerves are on edge. Should things go ill, I've instructed Mangla to escape from the back with the sleeping Dalip and make for the Fakir's haveli. For myself, I've slipped a dagger into the folds of my pishwas.

"You asked me to meet you secretly. You said it's an emergency," the minister says in clipped tones. He looks exhausted. I can see crusted blood on his forehead from where he'd struck it on the ground to grieve his king's passing. It gives me a little hope.

"Wazir ji," I say, "my guards have been removed."

He doesn't look surprised. He knew. He knew but did nothing.

I continue. I have no choice. "This haveli is no longer safe for Dalip and me. I invoke your aid because the Sarkar put us in your care."

Dhian paces, considering. I hold my breath.

Finally he says, "I will fulfill my oath to God and my king. I will look after you." Even as relief courses through me, he adds, "But I cannot keep you safe here. Too many factions in Lahore are vying for Kharak's favor. One of them might decide that the way to get it is by harming you and our young prince. You've made some powerful enemies on your own, too! I must remove you and Dalip right away. I'll send you to our kingdom in the Kangra Hills, where my brothers rule. You'll be protected there. I cannot keep you in my qila in Jammu. As Kharak's wazir, I must obey him if he orders me to turn you in. I'll hide you in the mountain fortress belonging to my younger brother, Suchet. No one will look for you there. If you agree, you must leave within the hour."

My head whirls. Dhian is asking me to leave behind everything I know, everyone I trust. To go to a place so remote I've barely heard of it. I'd be safe from Kharak there, but I'd be totally under Dhian's control. That would be dangerous in its own way. I want to consult the Fakir about this enormous decision, but Dhian taps his foot impatiently.

"May I have a couple of hours to pack?" I ask. I want to get word to the Fakir and hear back from him.

"One hour only. Even that is risky. Someone may have seen me coming here. Pack only your valuables and what Dalip will need for the journey."

"My money and jewelry are in the toshakhana. I wasn't allowed to withdraw anything." I decide not to tell Dhian about my small cache.

"Don't worry about money. Suchet will make sure you have the necessities. He'll provide you with servants as well."

I tense. "I want Mangla to come with me."

"It would be better if she remained in the haveli and pretended that you're still living here—"

Though it's unforgivably rude, I interrupt him. "Mangla is like my family. I can't leave her behind."

It's true. Besides, she's the one person who can be my eyes and ears in a strange palace. I need that; I don't trust Dhian completely. He's helping me, but he's also helping himself. Having Dalip in his control is, for him, a powerful secret weapon, to be pulled out at the right time. But I have no one else to turn to.

"Very well." Dhian's voice is displeased. "You may take her along."

I thank him profusely. Dhian lets out a breath. Why, he, too, was tense! My decision was important for him as well.

Dhian gives instructions. A carriage will be outside in an hour. His companion will be with the driver. We must get in quickly. The gatekeepers at the western entrance will let the carriage through. A small group of Dhian's soldiers will escort us through the city, and outside Lahore, a larger troop will take us to Suchet's fortress.

He ends, "You must not tell anyone where you are going. That is the only way I can keep you safe."

I HADN'T THOUGHT I could gather up all that we needed in an hour, but it's strangely easy. When one has to leave behind almost everything, it hardly matters what one takes. I bundle up my jewelry and money, along with a miniature portrait of the Sarkar, and let the efficient Mangla decide the rest. Illogically, I wish I could say goodbye to Laila and give her a piece of gur. I consider sending a letter to Jawahar so he'll know I am safe, but decide against it. However, there is one thing I must do. Disobeying Dhian, I pen a brief note to the Fakir, using our code. At least one person I truly trust needs to know where I'm disappearing to.

Mangla is already dressed for travel in a dark salwar-kameez. I catch a glint, at her neck, of the thick gold chain I'd gifted her when Dalip was born—her most treasured possession.

"You'd better remove that for now," I tell her, "and deliver this note to the Fakir quickly."

Mangla says, "I'm sorry, my queen. I must complete a very important task before we leave. Please don't ask what it is. I'll make sure the housemaid delivers your letter."

I'm curious and concerned. What could be so important? What if Mangla can't return in time? But I trust her, so I assent.

THE SOUND OF HOOVES is so loud in the still night that I'm terrified the qila guards will come running. But there's no one. Dhian must have bribed people well. From the carriage window, I give my haveli—the only home that's been truly mine—one last regretful glance. The Sarkar had built it for me with so much love.

"Will I ever live here again?"

It's a rhetorical question, but Mangla responds with a bald monosyllable. "No."

"Why do you say that?" Disappointment sharpens my voice and Dalip whimpers in his sleep.

"When you return," Mangla says confidently, "it'll be as queen regent, to rule on behalf of our Dalip until he's old enough. You'll live in the Sheesh Mahal, as would befit your new rank."

Her words fill me with misgiving. "Let's not have any talk of Dalip becoming king. There are many people between him and the throne. Kharak, Naunihal, Sher Singh. They'd all have to die. The Sarkar wouldn't want that, and neither do I. The upheaval would be terrible for Punjab. Besides, the life of a king isn't easy. Plotting, politics, endless battles for power . . . I don't wish that on my little boy."

"He'll be king." Mangla speaks with certainty. "It's in his horoscope."

"How do you know about his horoscope?" I ask, astonished. "I burned it right away."

"I questioned the astrologer." Mangla lifts her chin stubbornly. I notice that she's no longer wearing the gold chain and I'm glad she's put it away. "Dalip will be king. I feel it in my bones."

I drop the matter, though I wonder if Mangla's certainty has anything to do with her secret errand.

We exit Lahore via the Masti Darwaza. The city is shrouded in fog. Still, I recognize the stone ramparts from the day Jawahar and I arrived with Manna. How enormous they'd seemed to my child-eyes. How impressed I'd been with the yellow-coated soldiers on the ramparts. Tonight, too, the ramparts are overrun with soldiers. The city is on alert because the Lion is dead and jackals may come sniffing.

Goodbye, Lahore, city of my dreams, city that transformed me in ways I'd never have imagined. How naive I'd been when I first came to you. I fear my heart is harder today, but I hope my eyes are sharper and my will stronger. Otherwise, how will I safeguard my son?

III

Queen

1840–1849

22

Jammu

"FASTER, TOOFANI!" I BEND LOW over the mare's neck and speak into her ear. She gallops faster over the fields that extend from the forest to the fortress. The four horsemen accompanying me struggle to keep up. I grin fiercely. She's no Laila, but she makes my exile bearable. When I ride, the rushing wind blows away my pent-up worries, my sadness for all that I've lost, my fear that life is passing me by.

The horsemen have been appointed by the commander of the fortress to watch over me. Wherever I go—for a ride, an excursion in the carriage with two-year-old Dalip, a visit to the tiny gurdwara—they're always there. They make me feel more like a prisoner than the precious guest that the commander insists I am.

At first, things were better. Suchet Singh, my host, had greeted me kindly and tried to make me feel at home. He often invited me to dinner, where he reminisced about the Sarkar, whom he had hero-worshipped. But soon enough there was gossip, as there inevitably is when a woman is young and husbandless. Word reached Dhian's ears. He summoned his brother to Lahore, claiming he needed his help. It was not totally untrue. Dhian, whom people now call "the kingmaker," has his hands full balancing the increasingly tumultuous relationship between Kharak and Naunihal.

I'm grateful to Dhian for giving Dalip and me refuge, but he makes me uncomfortable. I fear he plans to use us for his own benefit. But I don't complain, not even to Mangla, without whose bracing presence I would have gone mad by now. Sanctuary, I know, has its price.

There are compensations in the sleepy hills of Jammu. I've had a year to focus on the simple pleasures of motherhood: seeing Dalip learn to walk and then run, teaching him songs, playing hide-and-seek in the dim corridors of the fortress wing allotted to us. Like his father, Dalip loves animals, so I've bought him a pony on which he's led around the compound. But he prefers to be taken up on Toofani with me. *Faster, Biji*, he'll say. He's fearless like his father and has the same ability to inspire love. The servants ply him with goodies, Mangla spoils him shamelessly, and even my stone-faced guards break into smiles when he greets them. He loves being read to. Children's books are hard to find here, so I read to him from mine: romances, a history of Punjab, the Gutka. He curls up in my lap, watching me with unwavering eyes, though surely he's too young to understand.

Mangla says, "He just loves to hear your voice."

Yes, I'm grateful—in the daytime.

But at night in my sleep, I reach across the bed for the Sarkar and, encountering emptiness, feel his absence like the edge of a knife.

Who can I blame for that except my own foolish heart?

Reluctantly, I turn Toofani toward the fortress. I must return by sundown. It's one of the rules. Dalip, too, will be looking for me, waiting at the window. At times I worry that he's too attached to me.

Today, though, it's not Dalip who rushes up to me but Mangla. When I see her face, I know a letter has come. I don't get letters from family. I wasn't permitted to tell them where I was going. The thought of Biji and Jawahar worrying about me fills me with sadness, but there's nothing I can do.

The only letters I get are from the Fakir. Rare, brief, written in code and unsigned, they are secretly delivered to Mangla by people disguised as peddlers or beggars. Though I long for them, the news they carry is always disturbing. I have only a few hours to respond; after that, the letter-bearer disappears.

The first letter had come three months after I reached Jammu, when I'd given up hope of hearing from the Fakir. He wrote that Mai Nakkain had passed away, strangely and suddenly. There were whispers about poison or perhaps witchcraft.

My initial response was a mean joy. She had hated me from the moment we met. Over and over she had schemed to harm me, even when I was at my most vulnerable. She had felt no pity for my fatherless infant. Who knows what she would have done to us if Dhian hadn't whisked us away?

Then I was ashamed of my ill will toward the dead and prayed for forgiveness.

"Do you know how it happened?" I asked Mangla. She'd made friends in the qila here and often found out things from them.

"No," Mangla replied. "I'm shocked to hear of it. It's too bad that Mai passed away just when she was enjoying being queen mother."

She looked so innocent that I grew suspicious. I thought back to the night we'd left Lahore, the mysterious errand she refused to tell me about. Could it have had anything to do with this?

It struck me that I hadn't seen Mangla wear her gold necklace since then.

"Where's the necklace I gave you?"

Mangla lowered her head. "I lost it during the journey, my queen. I'm very sorry. I didn't want to tell you because you had many troubles of your own."

I didn't believe it. I considered prizing the truth out of her. Then I recalled what the Sarkar once told me. *A ruler should gather as much information as possible. But sometimes it is better to remain ignorant.* I let the matter go, but it struck me that here was a woman ready to kill for those she loved. It gave me a strange kind of comfort. On Dalip's birthday, I gifted Mangla one of my own necklaces, of greater value than the missing one.

I hurry inside now, waving away the maid who offers me the Kashmiri salt chai I've grown to love. Mangla locks the door. I open the letter, which is longer than usual. Mangla is already lighting the brazier in which we'll burn it.

Since I last wrote to you about the fighting between Kharak and Naunihal for control over the affairs of the state, a terrible thing has happened, and the repercussions are shaking the throne. Naunihal was running the court well. He had the blessings of Dhian, whom he made wazir, and the powerful Sandhawalia clan. But the Afghans attacked, and Naunihal had to lead the army to the border. Without our great commander Nalwa, there was no one else.

Kharak's intimate friend, Chet Singh Bajwa, made use of this opportunity to incite the king to regain control of the durbar. He created much trouble between the two factions and, on Naunihal's return, gravely insulted Dhian in open court.

That night Dhian, his brothers, the Sandhawalias, and Naunihal entered the chamber where Chet was sleeping and slaughtered him. Kharak was there, too, and witnessed the murder. Crazed with grief, he cursed his own son. He is now ill and imprisoned in the palace.

But it seems the curse is bearing fruit already. Naunihal and Dhian have fallen out. The prince insulted Dhian and took from him control of the lucrative salt-mines. Dhian retaliated by resigning. I myself have been pushed aside for refusing to support Naunihal in this action. Punjab is now being ruled by a nineteen-year-old hothead. The Sarkar's other son Sher is watching. The British armies are gathering just beyond our borders.

They say the spirits of the dead look down at the living. If so, it would tear open the Sarkar's heart to see his kingdom in such disarray.

Dhian will leave for Jammu soon. Should he ask anything of you, be cautious in your answer.

Dhian arrives in Jammu with much gold, many soldiers, and his pretty young wife, Rani Pathani. He sends me a message: *At your convenience, I would like to pay my respects to Shahzada Dalip.*

I dip into my dwindling savings—despite his promise, Dhian has not given me much spending money—and send Mangla over with a platter of sweets and shawls, and silver anklets for Pathani. I write: *It is always an honor to meet with Wazir ji. Even more so if Rani Pathani accompanies him. How, then, can any time be inconvenient?*

Mangla says, "The wazir smiled when he read your note. You know that crooked grin of his, like he's seen all the tricks of the world already. 'Your rani is very eloquent,' he said. I replied, 'Her words rise from her heart. She is most appreciative of the refuge you have provided her.' I could tell he was pleased. He tossed me a rupee—silver, not gold. They're stingy, these Dogras, except when it benefits them to be generous. He said, 'You are quite eloquent yourself. Tell her I will come tomorrow morning, but alone.'"

I nod. "He's coming to discuss matters of state. I need to dress appropriately."

Mangla rummages through the few things we brought from Lahore and finds me a silk salwar-kameez in widow's white. She pulls back my hair into a neat bun. I wear my pearls, a gift from the Sarkar. In the mirror, my face is severely beautiful, a face to be taken seriously. I think I will wear white from now on.

I dress Dalip in red. He looks good in it. Besides, it forms a dramatic contrast to my attire.

When Dhian comes, I send away all the servants except Mangla and personally serve him. As he takes the plate of mithai I have offered, his fingers brush against mine. It strikes me that I've just touched the hand of a murderer—a murderer who is in control of our destiny. The Sarkar, too, had killed people. But there's a difference between meeting an opponent on a battlefield and attacking a sleeping man. I'm careful to suppress my shudder, but I can't help pulling Dalip closer.

"I have brought you and the prince a gift from Lahore," Dhian says. He looks very fine in his silk sherwani; there is an increased sense of power about him, even though he has resigned his wazirship. He claps and a soldier carries in a pair of white peacocks, their beaks trussed. Tears spring to my eyes. The Sarkar loved to watch them strut through the qila gardens, and feed them with his own hands.

Released, the peacocks ruffle their feathers in displeasure and rush at the guard, pecking until he retreats. Dhian gives Dalip some corn kernels and instructs him to throw them on the floor for the birds. But Dalip holds out his cupped hands. The birds advance on him. With his tail feathers fanned out behind him, the male is as tall as my son. I tense, ready to drag Dalip out of the way of those sharp beaks and claws, but he's smiling. *Come, birdie.* The peacocks dip their graceful necks and take the corn gently from his hands, making soft sounds in their throats.

"Why, he is a true shahzada!" a surprised Dhian remarks. He narrows his eyes, considering new possibilities. Before leaving, he says, "Should I be recalled to Lahore, I would like you and the prince to move back there. My position is stronger now, and I can remind the right people that here is another son of our Sarkar, brave and wise and calm like him. I will send for you when the time is right."

I offer profuse thanks, then take a deep breath. I'm venturing into dangerous waters, but I need to know something. "How is our other shahzada, Naunihal, doing? He must be facing many troubles without you to guide him."

Dhian speaks mildly, but his eyes flash. "I am sure the shahzada is doing well. He has many other counselors."

Later I tell Mangla, "He hates Naunihal! I don't want to get caught in the middle of whatever Dhian is plotting."

But I know I'll have to do what he wants. I can't afford to anger him as Naunihal has done.

Sure enough, Naunihal is unable to manage the intricacies of administering a kingdom. He's forced to send his best friend Udham, Dhian's nephew, with apologies and gifts, requesting the wazir to return to Lahore. Dhian agrees magnanimously. His purpose is served: all at court know that he's the true power behind the throne. The Fakir writes: *He is stronger than ever before, and more dangerous.*

My clever Mangla has ingratiated herself with the qila commander's wife, doing her hair and make-up for special occasions, exclaiming that she looks as elegant as any of the ranis of Lahore. Soon she becomes the woman's trusted confidant. Thus I learn that Naunihal's wife, Bibi, is pregnant. A delighted Chand has gone to the Golden Temple to offer prayers. I'm happy for them both. I learn also of Kharak's death—no surprise, as his health had steadily grown worse. Naunihal—perhaps out of guilt—is planning a grand funeral.

"A huge honor guard will accompany the body to the pyre outside the qila's Roshni Darwaza," Mangla reports. "The cannons will fire one hundred times. Dhian has offered to provide all the soldiers—"

I cut her off. I can't bear to listen to the details of a royal funeral. The last one, which wrenched away my beloved husband as well as my best friend, looms over me still.

I'm playing with Dalip and his toy soldiers when Mangla comes running. From her face I can see it's serious. I send Dalip off with a servant. A good boy, he doesn't protest.

"Naunihal is dead," Mangla whispers.

Shocked, I sink onto the nearest kursi.

"Dhian sent a message to the commander," Mangla continues.

"A portion of the Roshni Darwaza collapsed on Naunihal as he was returning to the qila after the funeral. He fell down unconscious. Udham was walking by his side. He died right there. Naunihal was taken into the qila; he died three days later."

My thoughts are in a whirl. Naunihal's cheerful face rises in my mind. Bibi's shy smile. The Sarkar's proud expression as he watched his grandson performing maneuvers with the ghorcharhas. It was his dream that Naunihal would rule Punjab. *My Naunihal will be a greater king than me*, he used to say.

Soon I receive a note from Dhian. I break the heavy red seal and unfurl the parchment, but I already know what it will say.

You must bring Prince Dalip back to Lahore at once.

Outside my window, the mountains are hoary with snow. When I first came here, I hated how they towered in the gloom, and longed for Lahore. Now I wish I could remain in their safe shadow.

WE FINISH PACKING OUR few belongings by evening. Our contingent must leave at dawn so that we can make it safely to the next town before nightfall. But late at night, Mangla wakes to a man scratching at her window. He brings a letter from the Fakir.

> *The gateway did not collapse by chance. Naunihal was only slightly injured when Dhian Singh had him carried into the Hazuri Bagh and shut the gates on all who would follow. Lahore will be in turmoil and particularly dangerous for potential heirs to the throne. Stay away.*

I pace the bedroom for hours and finally come up with a plan. Mangla sneaks into the kitchen and finds some garlic. She places the cloves in the sleeping Dalip's armpits and holds his arms steady. By the morning, he has a fever. I send for the doctor.

"Please inform the commander that we cannot travel until my son is better," I say.

When he protests that the fever is slight and will probably pass soon, Mangla holds up a purse.

The doctor bows. "Indeed, travel is out of the question. The shahzada must not exert himself for at least a week."

"Perhaps longer," I say. The doctor agrees.

In this way, ten days pass.

THE COMMANDER SUMMONS ME to the inner courtyard for an urgent matter. A man has been captured. My mouth grows dry. What if they've caught one of the Fakir's messengers? But Mangla shakes her head.

The man is dark and whiplash-thin, with sunken, blazing eyes. His face is bloody from a beating; his nose looks broken. The commander says he was hiding in the stables, under the hay in Toofani's stall, where I go almost every day. He was carrying a knife. No one knows how he got past the guards.

"I fear his plan was to kill you when you went to Toofani. We tried to make him confess who hired him. But look—"

He gestures and a soldier forces the man's mouth open. To my horror, I see that he has no tongue. Someone cut it off a while back, leaving only a stump, so that he'd never be able to betray his employer. I look away from the gaping emptiness.

"He's illiterate, so we can't make him write a name," the commander says. "There's nothing to do except execute him. But I cannot guarantee your continued safety here."

The soldiers drag away the would-be assassin, who does not protest or struggle.

"Who would want to kill me?" I cry.

"I don't know," the commander responds. "But we must leave

for Lahore right away. The wazir will be angry if you stay on here after this."

I hear a gunshot, a guttural groan, followed by a heavy thump. My hands begin to shake. It sinks in: I could have been murdered by now.

"We'll be ready in the morning," I say, defeated.

OUR SIMPLE CARRIAGE MAKES its way down to the plains accompanied by a few soldiers. People don't give the small procession a second glance. They probably think a local landowner is making a trip to the city. They have no idea that the carriage holds the Sarkar's youngest son, whom fate has pushed two steps closer to the throne.

The rocking motion of the carriage soon puts Dalip, whom I'm carrying, to sleep.

"Lay him down on the seat," Mangla says. "He's getting big. Your arms will start aching."

She has made a nest of quilts for him, but I shake my head. It comforts me to hold him. Mangla, too, dozes off, but I continue to sit stiffly upright. I can't forget the assassin, the black absence where his tongue should have been. Who could have sent him? Who wants me dead? Who knew that I was here?

23

Chand

Back in Lahore, we move into a small, elegant haveli on a quiet side street. It has a spacious compound filled with beautiful old siris trees with dense foliage and large hanging pods that Dalip loves to play with. A tall brick wall topped with spikes surrounds the property so that no one can look in. Armed guards stand, day and night, at the iron gate.

The house is decorated with ornate carved furniture piled high with silk pillows. Plush carpets cover the floors. Exquisite miniature paintings hang in the baithak, scenes of hunts or of lovers taking their ease on a terrace. Dinner is served on silver plates. I'm responsible for none of this. Everything here—the decorations, the soldiers, the servants—belongs to Dhian. The only thing I did was choose this house from among the three havelis that he offered me. I picked it because it was the smallest. I didn't wish to be more beholden to Dhian than absolutely necessary.

Dhian, who lives in a grand palace himself, was disappointed. "The prince deserves a finer home than this."

"This house is perfect, Raja ji. Dalip will have space to run around. That's all he needs."

"At least he will be secure here," Dhian said. He'd been livid upon hearing about the would-be assassin and had fined the commander a month's pay. He told me, "See? This is why I want you to be in Lahore, where I have more men to protect you."

By the time we moved into this house, barracks had been constructed in the fields behind the property and filled with guards.

I'm grateful that we are safe. But it occurs to me that being safe is not very different from being imprisoned.

THE FIRST THING I wanted to do upon arriving in Lahore was visit the Fakir. Mangla had told me that he'd been ill. I wanted to make sure he was taking care of himself. And to consult with him about certain things that were too dangerous to commit to paper.

So far, the visit has not happened. Dhian refuses to allow it. Nor has he permitted the Fakir to come. If fact, no one except Dhian's family enters the haveli. He claims it is for reasons of safety. *I cannot protect you if you go all over the city, Rani ji. Princes have many enemies, even if they are still far from the throne.*

Still—a small word, yet compact as a bullet.

I bristle under his control—but silently. I must remain in his good graces.

THE ONE PERSON I manage to visit is Chand, Naunihal's mother, now queen regent of Punjab.

Dhian objects to this, too, but I silence him by insisting that the Sarkar would have wanted me to do it. "Chand Kaur is queen regent," I add. "Don't you think, if she'd wanted to harm me, she'd have done so already?"

My heart twists as the palanquin enters the qila. Memories are stamped on every building. The zenana where I was almost poisoned to death on my first night as a bride. The birthing pavilion where I became a mother. Mai Jindan Haveli, the Sarkar's gift of love to me.

The palanquin stops in front of the Sheesh Mahal. How many nights did I spend in the arms of a man who shone brighter than the Koh-i-Noor, who told me stories more enchanting than the ones in *Heer-Ranjha*, who knew me better than anyone in the world! I almost can't bear to enter. But I must. Chand has chosen this as her residence and lives here with Bibi.

I'm taken aback by the regal woman I find. Chand had always been quiet and retiring, but her husband's and son's deaths, which might have broken another woman, have transformed her into a queen. When I'm ushered in, she is discussing a new tax with a group of courtiers. Her courteous but firm tones as she suggests a change to the firman amaze me. All this is done from behind a silk curtain, for Chand is a strict observer of purdah. When the courtiers leave, she speaks graciously to me, but I can tell she's wondering whether I'm trustworthy or a spy of Dhian's.

When the heavily pregnant Bibi comes into the room, though, all sternness falls away from Chand. She smiles and embraces the younger woman, asking what she has eaten since morning. She makes Bibi sit beside her on the royal kursi. "Has my grandson been kicking you very hard?" she inquires. Bibi leans unselfconsciously against Chand as though she were her daughter, and Chand rubs her back. The gesture hits me hard—Guddan used to do this for me when I was pregnant. Ah, gone now.

I see that, after Naunihal's death, Bibi has become Chand's reason for living. For the sake of Bibi, who is delicate and pliant as a lotus stem, Chand has made herself strong.

After I offer condolences, after Bibi weeps and Chand consoles her, the queen invites me to stay for lunch. Perhaps because I'm no longer involved in the royal game, she feels we can be friends. I'm happy to accept.

Chand apologizes for the meal's blandness. Bibi gets heartburn easily nowadays. "For myself, I don't care what I eat. In fact, there's not much I care about anymore." She makes a sweeping gesture that encompasses the qila, the city, maybe even all of Punjab. "All these trappings of luxury. The royal title they've given me: Malika Mukaddas. Empress." She shrugs dismissively. "I only moved into the qila because it's safer for Bibi here. For her sake, for the sake of the baby, I invited my clansmen, the Sandhawalias, to Lahore and asked for their protection. I didn't want to do it. They're difficult to get along with, and they detest Dhian. To balance that, I've made Gulab—Dhian's older brother, the only man in Hindustan as wily as him—my chief counsellor."

My head spins just to think of this intricate maneuvering.

"Did you know," Chand continues, "Sher Singh wanted to marry me. Many at court pressured me to do it, pointing out that it was a respectable option for a Sikh widow to marry her husband's half brother. It would have made my position more secure. But I said no. Can you guess why?"

I think hard. It can't be because of Chand's loyalty to Kharak, the opium addict with a propensity for male lovers. Finally I ask, "Does Sher have a son from a previous marriage?"

"You're a smart woman. He does. After Sher, he would become king. Naunihal's child would be disinherited. I can't do that to Bibi."

I look at Chand with undisguised admiration. "You've weighed so many things. I couldn't have managed it."

"Yes, you could," Chand says firmly. "Do you know why? Because you're a mother."

As I'm leaving, she grasps my hand. "May I ask you for a kindness? If anything happens to me, will you help Bibi? She's so innocent. I worry about her. Promise me on the Guru Granth . . ."

It's doubtful that I, Dhian's virtual prisoner, will have the resources to help anyone, but I promise.

I PASS MY DAYS playing with three-year-old Dalip, reading to him, teaching him prayers and songs. But I can sense the storm clouds gathering. The *Punjab Akhbar*, carefully wording its news so it will not anger Chand, writes: *Sher Singh has retired to his estates in Batala. The Malika Mukaddas has paid him one lakh rupees a year for giving up his claim to the throne. She has also generously offered to adopt Dhian Singh's son, Hira.*

Mangla, who still has friends in the qila, tells me that matters have grown more fraught between Dhian and the Sandhawalias. Last week they barred him from entering the Sheesh Mahal to meet with Chand. The irate wazir is threatening to return to Jammu.

"I hope he doesn't order us to follow him to that backwater again," Mangla says. "Maybe you can persuade Rani Pathani to stay on in Lahore, and we can remain with her."

Over the last few months, Pathani and I have become friends—mostly because of her persistence. She visits me regularly. At first, I suspected that Dhian had asked her to spy on us, but Pathani is incapable of such guile. She adores playing with Dalip, tucking up her fine silk kurtas to chase him as he flees from her, screaming in delight. If at all she asks questions, they're about my adventures in the zenana, which fascinate her. She loves to dress up, taking a childlike pleasure in pretty things, and often urges me to come over when the merchants stop at her home with their latest wares.

Finally I ask, "Even if I had the money, what would a widow like me do with such fine clothes?"

Aghast, Pathani claps a hand over her mouth. "Forgive me! I didn't think. Wazir ji says my tongue runs faster than my brain."

The artless Pathani tells me the secret of her marital success. "I know when Wazir ji wants to talk, and when he needs quiet. I massage his forehead with almond oil when he comes home with a headache. I know what kinds of food suit him. People would never think it, but Wazir ji has a delicate stomach . . ."

I hide a smile as she goes on. So Dhian likes being pampered by his young wife. And why not? After spending all day with schemers and flatterers, he has every reason to value her simple affection.

PATHANI INVITES ME TO a family dinner at her mansion, though palace would be a more accurate word. Armed guards line the walls. Fountains sparkle in the light of numerous torches. The gardens are bursting with roses. I'm surprised to see white peacocks roosting in the trees. Dhian has filled his home with things the Sarkar had loved. Is it because he believes he deserves the same things?

The dining table is marble, the carpets Persian, the platters inlaid with ruby flowers, and the goblets solid gold. But the food is simple: rice, lentils, lightly cooked vegetables. Pathani mixes a glass of buttermilk for Dhian, and he smiles, tenderness transforming his usually impassive face. Pathani is loving to his son Hira as well, putting another chapati on his plate, scolding him for staying out too late the previous night. "I'll never have a child of my own because Wazir ji— I'm sure you understand," she has confided. "So I think of Hira as my son."

Pathani teases Hira about getting married. "Your friends are a bad influence. A pretty wife will settle you down. Shall I look for a suitable girl?"

Hira teases her back. "But what if she turns out to have finer jewels than you?"

"Impossible!" Pathani says. "Your father would never let that happen."

Hira and Dhian grow sentimental as they reminisce about the Sarkar. How generous he had been, treating Hira no different from Naunihal. He had let the boy call him *Bapuji* and allowed him to sleep in the Sheesh Mahal and ride his favorite horse. On Hira's birthday the Sarkar sent over as many gold mohurs as he gave to Naunihal on his. But he was strict, too, making sure the boys were trained by the toughest master swordsmen. After practice, he would examine their bruises with satisfaction. *You must both become great warriors*, he had insisted.

"There will never be another man like the lionheart," Dhian ends, his voice breaking.

I'm glad my veil hides my own brimming eyes. If only Dalip had a few memories like the ones Hira treasures. No matter. I'll tell him everything he needs to know.

"I'll always be loyal to the Sarkar's blood," Dhian proclaims. But when, at the end of the evening, I ask again if I might visit the Fakir, he refuses.

I MAKE MY WAY by palanquin to the Gurdwara Dehra Sahib, escorted as usual by six of Dhian's soldiers. The gurdwara is the only place Dhian cannot object to my visiting—especially since today is the Sarkar's death day. I've told him that I'm going to give gifts to the poor in the Sarkar's honor; it will take some time.

I have another reason for visiting the gurdwara, but only Mangla, who made the arrangements, knows about it.

I pass by Naunihal's haveli, locked up now. How diminished it looks with its windows covered and a great iron lock hanging from the front door. It fills me with sorrow. I wonder again if Dhian had been involved in his strange death. It's something Mangla and I discuss late at night, after the servants so kindly provided to me by Dhian have gone to bed.

At the gurdwara, I order the guards to wait outside. I offer a quick prayer and give the granthi alms for the poor. Then I hurry to the terrace. I have only an hour. As I climb the stairs, I am assailed by bittersweet memories. Here the Sarkar promised to marry me. Here I insisted, with youthful hubris, that my prayers would keep him safe.

A stooped figure in gray sits on a bench. I run to him.

"My dear child," the Fakir says. He holds out an uncertain arm in my direction, his eyes opaque and unfocused. He's blind! A boy waits near him, to help him get around. The Fakir sends him away with some money. "Go and eat. Come back in one hour."

I want to tell him how happy I am to see him, how much I miss the Sarkar, how frightened I am about Dalip's future. But there isn't enough time. Yet when he clasps my hands, I know he understands.

"How thin you've grown," I say.

"That's the way of life, my dear. Better men than I have passed away. It will be my turn before long." I protest, but he stops me. "We must use our time well today. I don't know if we shall meet again. Dhian is pushing me to retire. Soon I'll have to give in. I'm of no help to Chand anyway; she listens only to her clansmen. And with my vision gone, I will not be able to write to you."

I listen with every fiber of my body.

"The alliance between Chand and Dhian is breaking. Dhian has approached Sher Singh secretly, inviting him to take over Lahore."

I'm shocked. "But isn't Gulab on Chand's side? Would Dhian go against his own flesh and blood?"

"The only side the Dogra brothers are on is their own. The Sarkar had the power and charisma to bind them to him. No one else does. It's possible that Dhian and Gulab have planned this together, so that no matter who is the ruler of Punjab, the wazir will be a Dogra."

I remember Sher. A lover of expensive horses, exotic perfumes, foreign liquor, and pretty women. A brave warrior, handsome and charming. But would he make a good king?

"Doesn't Chand have strong allies?"

"Her clan supports her, but the Khalsa army doesn't. They want a ruler who can lead them in war, not a woman behind purdah. She sends them orders through Ajit Sandhawalia, and they resent that. Sher has made overtures to them, promising a raise."

"What must I do?"

"For now, nothing. Be aware. Don't attract attention. Don't be too friendly with anyone, not even Dhian's family."

"Why do you say that?"

The Fakir shrugs. "Just a feeling."

I ask the question that has been weighing on me. "Was Dhian involved in Naunihal's death?"

The Fakir stares unseeing into the distance. "The collapse of the gate may have been an accident. After all, Dhian's own nephew, Udham, died under it. But what happened after Naunihal was carried inside, no one knows. I wish you'd stayed in Jammu."

"I couldn't." I describe the assassin, the silent black hole of his mouth. I wait for the Fakir to express shock, but he asks, "Who do you suppose sent him? Who knew that you were there?"

"You. Dhian. Suchet."

The Fakir cocks his head, listening with the acute ears of the blind. "The boy is returning. Think fast. Who had the most to gain if you returned to Lahore?"

"Dhian," I say without hesitation. "I'm under his eye all the time." The truth strikes me hard. "*He* sent the assassin. To scare me into returning."

"Why would he want that?"

"To protect us better?" I see from the Fakir's faint smile that it's the wrong answer. "To use us?"

He nods.

"I won't let him!"

He says, "A wise person allows herself to be used when it suits her purpose. She pretends weakness, then waits for the right moment to take control."

It's time to leave. From the edge of the stairs, I look back at him, tapping uncertainly on the ground with his cane, his lips moving in silent prayer. How severe and majestic he'd been the first time I saw him, outside Manna's hovel. He'd taken me under his wing and taught me everything I knew about being a queen.

Father, will I ever see you again?

24

The Stillborn

I BRING DALIP TO THE ROYAL Samadhi which holds the Sarkar's ashes, the portion that wasn't poured into the Ganga. He doesn't understand, but I hope that somewhere inside him a memory will remain. *My mother took me by the hand and said, Bow to this lotus urn. Inside are the remains of your father, the greatest king Punjab has ever seen. He didn't leave you a kingdom, but your inheritance is more valuable: his courage, his generosity, his razor-sharp intelligence, his love of life and laughter.*

The mausoleum, grand and ornate, with its great fluted dome in white and gold, sits on an elevated platform so it can be seen from afar. Built between the Badshahi Mosque and the Gurdwara Dehra Singh, with statues of Hindu gods and goddesses carved into its massive front door, it reminds people that the Sarkar respected every religion. But to my dismay, the interior is unfinished, the walls and ceilings bare. Construction halted with Kharak's death, and Chand hasn't continued it. Perhaps she's short of money. I hear rumors that the army isn't being paid regularly.

You deserve better, my Sarkar. If I had the power, I'd make this interior unforgettably beautiful.

There are eleven smaller urns as well, representing the satis. One has Guddan's name on it. I touch it gently, though it doesn't really contain her remains. All the women's ashes got mixed up after the funeral. The queens are lucky that their names, at least, are recorded; no one remembers the concubines.

Stepping out, I see a huge crowd gathered around the Samadhi. Word must have traveled. People chant, *Long live Maharani Jindan. Waheguru bless our little shahzada.* I make Dalip wave. The cheers grow louder. My escort has to call for reinforcements in order to take us home safely. I fear Dhian will be upset, but he smiles complacently.

"It's good the people love their prince. I will send you my best carriage so you can take him on rides through the city." He pats Dalip's head and gifts him a gold coin.

Mangla, who isn't fond of Dhian, says, "I wonder why he suddenly wants you in the public eye."

I, too, wonder. But I plan to make the most of it, to show Dalip my favorite spots: the Zam-Zammeh cannon, the Anarkali Bazaar, the Gurdwara Lal Khoohi where Guru Arjan Dev became a martyr.

"Jawahar took me to those places when I was a girl. It's one of my happiest memories."

"Jawahar ji is such a good brother!" Mangla says warmly.

I can tell she hasn't forgotten him.

I'M JERKED AWAKE BY a great, terrifying roar, like a river in flood. A distressed Mangla informs me that Sher Singh has invaded Lahore. The Khalsa army has joined his soldiers. This morning, Dhian went over to him with his own forces.

The Fakir was right. The Dogras are loyal only to themselves.

Mangla says, "They've entered the city. There's no one to stop them. They plan to attack the qila. They're shouting, "Sher Singh for king. Dhian Singh for wazir. Death to Chand Kaur.""

I wring my hands. "I must help Chand—or at least save Bibi. I promised on the Guru Granth."

"It's impossible!"

There's a loud knocking at our front door. I grab my veil and run downstairs. It's the captain of our guards.

"There's looting in the markets," he says. "People are being killed. Rani Pathani wants you to hurry to her house with the shahzada. It'll be safer there. She has many soldiers to guard her. I can take you right now."

A tremendous explosion rends the air, making me flinch.

"Cannons," the captain explains. "Sher Singh has opened fire on the qila."

The servants gather around me, terrified. Several maids are sobbing. If I leave with the guards, their lives will be in grave danger.

I think hard. Then I lift my veil. The captain looks shocked. The action signifies that I consider him my family. I ask him his name.

"I am Avtar."

"Avtar, I cannot abandon my household. The looters will kill them. I trust you to protect us."

He takes a deep breath and bows. "I will do it, my queen—or die in the process."

"If the looters come down this street, be sure to inform them that this house belongs to Sher Singh's wazir. That should deter them."

After he leaves, Mangla says, "That was heroic! But was it wise?"

"I need to stay, in case Chand sends Bibi here," I reply. "Besides, Dhian must have arranged for our safety. Dalip is too valuable to him."

Fortunately, I am right. Soon an armed company joins the guards outside my gates.

The explosions continue. Some come from the qila. Chand is fighting back. A burning smell fills the air. The cries of dying men echo across the city. Avtar sends updates: things are going badly for Chand; more soldiers have defected; her own men are refusing her access to the gunpowder stores; snipers have climbed the minarets of the Badshahi Mosque and are firing into the qila. I cannot sleep. I keep imagining Bibi's screaming face. In the morning, Avtar tells me that Chand has surrendered.

Pathani comes by to check on us. She holds Dalip close and scolds me. "All night I worried about you—and also about Wazir ji and Hira. But Hira stopped by this morning and gave me good news. He knows how anxious I get. Wazir ji took care of everything. He and Gulab ji have managed to find a compromise. Sher will take over the qila. Chand and Bibi will move back to Naunihal's haveli. If Bibi gives birth to a son, he'll become the next king, and Sher and Chand will be co-regents for him. Maybe they'll even marry each other, now that those contentious Sandhawalias who gave Chand such bad advice have been banished. Wouldn't that be romantic!"

DHIAN REFUSES TO ALLOW me to visit Chand, claiming it will anger Sher Singh. I'm only able to send her messages. *How are you faring? Is Bibi well? Does she have a good midwife for the birthing? It must be getting close now. Can I send you anything?* When no replies come, I grow increasingly worried and ask Mangla to see what she can find out. She reports that Naunihal's haveli is surrounded by heavily armed soldiers. She doesn't think they are Chand's men.

Is Chand a prisoner, then, in her own house?

I entreat Dhian to let Bibi, at least, visit me. "It'll do her good to get out of that haveli filled with sad memories."

He says, "Bibi Kaur is not in good health. The vaids have put her on bed rest. We cannot risk her losing the baby."

"I don't believe a word that man says," I fume to Mangla.

But perhaps Dhian was telling the truth. A couple of weeks later, I hear that Bibi gave birth to a stillborn and died from too much bleeding. The child was a boy, the heir Chand had so hoped for.

I'm devastated. "I failed Bibi. Her dai must not have been experienced. I should have insisted on sending one of the Sarkar's vaids to her."

Mangla says, "I doubt that Dhian would have allowed it. But what's worse is that now Chand is accusing Dhian of paying the midwife to kill both mother and baby."

I have to stop the grief-crazed Chand from saying such dangerous things! Only one person can help. I beg Pathani to come with me to visit Chand.

"She's all alone in the world now. Can you imagine how she must be feeling? Please persuade the wazir."

Softhearted Pathani agrees. If Dhian doesn't consent easily, she'll use her most powerful weapon. "Wazir ji hates it if I cry."

She sends a message the next day. *We may visit Chand tomorrow for one hour.*

NAUNIHAL'S HAVELI IS GUARDED by two dozen heavily armed men. But they bow respectfully to Pathani and hold open the massive carved doors.

"Our orders are to remain outside," their leader says. "But one of Mai Chand's maids will take you to her."

There's something I must know. "Are you here on Sher Singh's orders?"

The leader stands tall and proud. "We only take orders from Raja-e-Rajgan Dhian Singh."

The dank, dark foyer smells of mildew. I almost don't recognize it as the grand entrance where I'd been welcomed to Naunihal's mehfil. When we announce ourselves, no maids respond. Something is wrong. Where is Chand?

We walk through the haveli in search of someone. The baithak where Naunihal would have greeted important guests. The dining area where they would have feasted. The furniture is shrouded.

Cobwebs hang from the ceiling. The kitchen looks abandoned. My heartbeat quickens with hope. Has Chand managed to escape, somehow, from Lahore?

Then I see it in the bathing area: a body, naked, slumped on the floor, neck twisted. Chand. The white marble is discolored by the congealed blood from her forehead. She must have fallen hard—the skull is cracked. Almost as if it were bashed in.

Pathani starts to scream.

I fist my hands to control the shaking. "Stop that!" I say sharply. "Fetch the captain of the guards."

Before the guards arrive, I wrap Chand in the largest towels I can find. Malika Mukaddas, I've failed you in every other way, but at least I can save you from this indignity. No man should see a queen in her nakedness.

Informed of Chand's murder, Dhian goes into a fury. He vows to find her maids, who were clearly bribed to murder her. He sends his men to search the countryside.

Mangla brings me the news in a couple of days. "They found all four maids hiding inside a brothel in Hira Mandi."

"That was quick." But I'm not surprised. When Dhian puts his mind to it, things happen. "What did they say? Did they confess?"

"They weren't given a chance. Dhian cut out their tongues and put them to death."

My shocked eyes fly to Mangla's face. We're both wondering if their tongues were cut out so that they couldn't identify the man who had hired them. We're remembering the assassin in Jammu.

"Whose tongue was cut out, Biji?" Dalip, who has run in, asks.

"It's just a story," I say, kissing him.

We must be more careful about what we say around him. A precocious child, he picks up far more than others his age. I want to preserve his innocence for as long as I can. The world will take it from him soon enough.

SHER SINGH, WHO HAD gone to pray at Guru Nanak's shrine in Batala, cuts his visit short and returns to Lahore. Avtar tells me that Sher denounced Chand's murder in the durbar as cruel and shocking. On the day of the funeral, he follows the bodies of Chand and Bibi barefoot to the burning grounds, dressed in mourning clothes. Is he sincere? I cannot tell. Many courtiers—none of whom had helped Chand in her need—accompany him. Behind the nobles come their wives, and finally the servants who had served Chand when she was queen. She must have been a kind mistress, for they have nothing to gain by being here. Dhian, looking suitably solemn, offers an eloquent eulogy about the many virtues of the two women. The tenderhearted Pathani is overcome by tears. Following her example, some of the other noblewomen also weep—the hypocrites—but I remain stone-faced. My sorrow is lodged in a deeper place.

The funeral is barely over when Sher walks across to greet me. I'm taken aback. Veiled and hidden among so many women, I hadn't thought he would know who I am.

"I've heard much about you, Rani Jindan," he says. "The Sarkar spoke most highly of your intelligence—and your beauty. I'm glad you have returned to Lahore. I wish to invite you—and my young brother Dalip—to the qila so I may know you better. I will send a carriage for you soon."

The gleam in his eyes makes me wary. What does he want of us?

I bow, and speak calmly. "My deepest thanks, maharaja." No one would guess how hard my heart is hammering as I say the first thing that comes to my mind. "Dalip would be most excited to meet his big brother who is such a magnificent king and warrior. However, we are about to embark on a journey that cannot be put off."

He frowns. "What is so important that you would turn down the king's invitation?"

I cast about frantically for a suitable response. Everyone around us has turned from the pyres to watch our exchange. Live intrigue is so much more interesting than the tragedy of the dead.

I hear the Sarkar's voice. *Of all places, this is the one I love best. Had I not been a king, I would have happily spent my days singing Waheguru's praises here.* I take a deep breath. "I vowed to take Dalip to Amritsar to the Golden Temple to give thanks when he turned four."

"Ah, the Golden Temple," Sher says in a disgruntled voice. "A most auspicious place. Very well. I will defer the pleasure of your company until you return."

I'VE BARELY CHANGED MY clothes when Dhian comes to see me. I'm surprised because I know he still has many funeral duties.

He wastes no time in pleasantries. "I saw Sher talking to you. What does he want? What did you say?"

When I tell him, he shakes his head. "This worries me on several levels. Sher has a bad reputation where beautiful women are concerned. And Dalip is, after all, a rival for the throne."

"Dalip's barely four!" I protest, but I recall Naunihal's dead baby and know that youth is no protection.

"You were smart to mention a holy vow. He cannot argue against that. You must leave right away."

"The Golden Temple might well inspire a widow to bring up her son in its auspicious shadow, might it not?"

"Indeed, it might," Dhian replies. "I will speak to Sher about the importance of supporting such a devout decision."

We smile at each other. For once, we are in agreement.

25

Amritsar

For someone who wishes to live incognito, Amritsar, though smaller than Lahore, is perfect. So many pilgrims visit the city that people pay no attention to a quiet widow who rents an old haveli on the outskirts, with high walls and no neighbors to wonder about the armed guards who patrol the compound. Mangla and I have concocted a fake past for me, involving a husband who died from cholera and cruel in-laws who forced me to leave home with my infant. But to my disappointment, there has been no occasion to use it.

My quiet life helps me focus on Dalip's education. I hire tutors to teach him sword fighting, wrestling, and riding. I teach him his letters myself, sending to Lahore for books and fine parchment paper to write on.

Every evening, we visit the Golden Temple, and after prayers, we admire the magnificent dome, dazzling in the setting sun.

"Your father built that dome," I tell Dalip. "He covered the entire upper temple with gold. He was a great king. He loved his country and his God above all else—and so should you."

Dalip throws his arms around me. "But Biji, I love you the most."

I hug him back, but I worry that I'm not teaching him his royal responsibilities.

Mangla says, "There'll be plenty of time for that. Right now, your job is to keep him safe. Thank God Sher has been too busy enjoying himself to order you back to Lahore. Now there's a man whom no one taught about royal responsibilities! He's more interested in watching dancing girls than watching over his people. No wonder he's having problems!"

Avtar, who visits us secretly, has been keeping us informed of Sher's troubles. I appreciate the risks he takes for my sake and seat him in my living room, as I would an honored guest. He tells us that, soon after he was crowned, Sher discovered that someone had stolen most of the gold that had been in the treasury when Chand became queen. People whispered that they had seen Gulab's soldiers leaving the qila at night with covered carts, but no one dared accuse him openly. Sher was unable to pay the army what he had promised them. In retaliation, the soldiers rioted. Many of the Sarkar's loyal European officers were killed. The rest went over to the British. The soldiers have now elected their own officials, the panches, to head them.

Avtar says, "The panches are excellent soldiers, but they've never led a regiment in battle. They know nothing of strategy. If there really is a war—and there might be, because the British have gathered a big force in Ludhiana, they won't know what to do."

I'm filled with sorrow. The mighty fighting force that the Sarkar brought together with such care is in disarray. Who, then, will stop the British if they decide to pounce on Punjab?

Before he leaves, Avtar hands me a crumpled letter. "My deepest apologies, my queen. I almost forgot this. So many turmoils nowadays—I am not myself. It came to the qila. One of my friends who works there brought it to me."

It is from Jawahar.

Sister, are you safe? I haven't heard from you since our maharaja passed away. I hear that there have been several kings in Lahore since that time. Many battles. This worries me. I wrote to you many times, asking you to come and live with me in Gujranwala. Manna and Biji passed away last year from a sudden fever. I wrote to you of that, too. Perhaps you did not get the letters. I miss them—even our bad-tempered father—now that I'm alone. I don't even know if you are alive. I send blessings to my little nephew and wish I could see him again.

My eyes grow wet as I read the uneven, effortful lettering. I write back:

Dearest veer, Dalip and I are well. Due to political matters outside my control, I was removed from Lahore and not allowed to inform you of my whereabouts. I did not receive your letters until this one. I am truly sorry to hear of our parents' passing and to learn that you are all alone. I am in Amritsar now. Please come and visit me. This time you may stay as long as you like.

Jawahar, when he arrives, looks older, thinner, quieter. He, too, had almost died from the fever. Filled with compunction, I feed him his favorite dishes and take him sightseeing. I watch fondly as he plays with Dalip. Remembering his penchant for fine clothes, I get several kurta sets made for him, even though there is little opportunity for him to show them off. And when at night Mangla goes missing, I sigh, but not unhappily.

Waheguru, my time for loving has passed. But let my brother be happy.

Two unexpected visitors arrive today. When Mangla announces their names, I know I'll have to draw upon everything I've learned about the royal game.

"Ajit and Lehna Sandhawalia? Chand's kinsmen? Didn't Ajit escape into exile while Lehna was imprisoned?"

"Clearly their fortunes have changed," Mangla says. "Their horses are among the finest I've seen, and they're accompanied by a large armed troop. What can they want with you?"

"We'll soon find out."

I dissuade Jawahar, who wants to accompany me, hide my trepidation behind a white pearl-edged veil, and sweep—superbly, I hope—into the formal baithak where the Sandhawalias have been seated.

I don't have to wait long. As soon as the formalities of greetings are over, the rugged and muscular Ajit, with his curling black beard and flashing glance, gets down to business. He requests me to swear on the Guru Granth that I will keep this meeting a secret. Once I have agreed, he tells me that the Sandhawalias are deeply unhappy with the wastrel Sher. They would like Dalip to replace him as king.

"You could be queen regent until Dalip reaches adulthood. The Sarkar often told me how sharp you were, how much you love Punjab."

My heart pounds. I had guessed that this might be the reason for the Sandhawalias' visit, but hearing it spoken so plainly fills me with a confused mix of excitement and fear. If their plan works, would it be better for my son, or worse?

His uncle Lehna, with his hooded hawk eyes and gaunt cheeks, adds, "You were a true friend to Chand in her darkest hour. If you hadn't found her body, instead of being given a royal funeral, she would have been thrown into a well somewhere."

I think of the laughing Naunihal, gone in his prime, of Bibi and her dead infant, of Chand with her battered head. I hide my shaking hands in the folds of my ghaghra and tell them I'm honored by their offer.

"But how can it work?" I ask. "Dalip is just a child, and I have no experience in ruling a durbar. Besides, I'm the daughter of a dog trainer."

"That'll be your strength," Ajit says. "You'll be the outsider, impartial in your decisions. The courtiers will respect that. The soldiers, who are commoners, will embrace you as their own. And Dalip's innocence will draw the citizens to him."

"What about Dhian? He might not agree. He has helped me in my time of trouble. I cannot turn on him."

Hatred twists Lehna's lined face. But it's gone so quickly that perhaps I imagined it. "Don't worry. All Dhian cares about is being wazir. It doesn't matter to him who becomes the king, as long as they don't try to curb his power."

Ajit adds, "We'll take care of him. Only return to Lahore soon and be ready for great changes. At the right time, we'll get in touch with you."

One more thing troubles me. I must bring it up, though it might anger them. "I need your assurance that you will not harm Sher Singh. No matter what, he's still the Sarkar's son."

Lehna's eyes flash. "Blood leads to blood—"

"Don't worry," Ajit interrupts. "We know how to persuade Sher. If he's offered a rich enough jagir and allowed to keep his royal horses and hunting dogs and his collection of foreign wines, he'll happily hand over the throne." His tone is harsh. "We had such hopes when he pardoned us and welcomed us back to court. But all he cares for is drinking, hunting, and hosting banquets. He's destroying everything our beloved Sarkar built."

His last words hit me hard. I capitulate.

The exhilarated Sandhawalias wish to meet Dalip before they

leave. When I bring him out, I'm taken aback to see tears in the eyes of the two hardened warriors. They gift him gold chains from around their necks, kiss his hands reverently, and call him their dearest prince. I'm even more stunned to see how naturally Dalip accepts this adulation.

"When I first met your father, he wasn't much older than you," Lehna says.

"You knew my father?" Dalip asks excitedly. "Will you tell me stories about him?"

"I certainly will," Lehna says as he picks Dalip up.

"Look, the shahzada has already won Uncle Lehna's heart," Ajit says to me. "He'll do the same with his subjects. Return quickly to Lahore. But don't tell Dhian about us. Make him believe that you are the one who wants to return."

I agree. Dhian would be most displeased if he knew I'd met with the Sandhawalias. Or that they planned a future for Dalip in which they envisioned playing a central role.

I'VE LEARNED FROM THE past, so I send no requests to Dhian. Instead, I write to Pathani, addressing her as *sister* and telling her that Dalip isn't getting a proper princely education in Amritsar. I add—perhaps disingenuously—that I miss her.

I hear back almost immediately.

> *My dearest sister Jindan, I have arranged for your return to civilization! Wazir ji acted difficult at first, even though I told him how like a sister you are to me. But when I threatened to undertake an extended visit to my father's home, he agreed! You need not worry about Sher anymore. He has a new wife named Dakno Kaur. She is very beautiful, though not as much as you. Also,*

his son Pratap has now been proclaimed Kanwar, so our darling Dalip is no threat to him. I can hardly wait for you to come back. I have much court gossip to share and of course we must go shopping because all your clothes I am certain are wholly out of date. What fun it will be . . .

26

Sher Singh

My only regret as I prepare to return to Dhian's haveli is that I have to send Jawahar back to Gujranwala against his will. I try to explain that I'm entering uncertain times, but he's offended.

"I'm not a child that you need to watch over. Maybe I can even help you."

I have to speak honestly. "You can't. You don't know the intricacies of survival at court. I barely know them myself. People might try to get at me—or Dalip. They'll search for the weakest link."

"And that's me?"

He doesn't speak to me for the rest of the visit, though I promise to bring him back as soon as possible.

"I feel so guilty," I say to Mangla after he leaves. "But it would be easy for my enemies to manipulate Jawahar."

I wait for her to reassure me as she usually does. But she stands silent, refusing to meet my eyes.

EVER SINCE I ADDRESSED her as a sister, Pathani's behavior toward me has changed. Like a sister, she comes over uninvited and scolds me freely if she thinks I'm not taking care of myself or Dalip. She showers embarrassingly expensive gifts upon us, invites me to every event she hosts, and pouts if I don't attend. And like a sister, she often annoys me. But I can tell she loves us genuinely, so I put up with her affectionate bullying with good grace.

Sher's fortunes have changed for the better. The Khalsa army, led by one of his new generals, has won a great victory at Ladakh. Sher has signed a truce with Dost Mohammed. His marriage to Dakno seems to have calmed him down. He attends durbar regularly and does not throw as many wild banquets. The Sandhawalias no longer seem keen on deposing him. With a mix of relief and regret, I conclude that they have no further need of Dalip and me.

I now focus on getting Dalip a royal education. I hire several tutors, all of whom tell me how intelligent he is. He reads fluently, memorizes passages from the Guru Granth, and solves mathematical problems meant for older children. He is good at wrestling and sword fighting. But his favorite activity is riding. Like his father, he is a born horseman.

One day Dhian stops by with a message: the Sandhawalias wish to meet me. "They were friends of the Sarkar and would like to pay their respects to you and meet his son. They've somehow found favor with Sher, so they might be good allies for you."

"I will do as you say," I reply in docile tones. Inside, I wonder what they are planning.

Ajit and Lehna arrive the following week with Dhian. They speak at length of old campaigns where they'd fought beside the Sarkar until a bored Dhian excuses himself to attend durbar. Once he leaves, the Sandhawalias ask to see Dalip. I take them to the courtyard where he's dueling with his teacher. He drops his sword and runs up, crying, "Uncle Lehna!"

Lehna is touched by Dalip's warmth. "I have a gift for you, puttar," he says.

The next morning he brings over a beautiful black Arabian pony that must have cost a great deal. Dalip loves the horse and names him Veer. Several times a week, Lehna takes him for a ride in the maidan. I'm happy to allow it. I'm quite sure the Sandhawalias have given up on their plans for Dalip. But my fatherless boy needs as many well-wishers as possible.

THIS MORNING I WAKE to find two messages. One is from Pathani. Dakno Kaur has given birth to a baby boy. I am surprised to feel a pinprick of disappointment—now Dalip will be even farther from the throne—and tell Mangla to send a tray of sweets up to the qila with my good wishes. The other message is from Lehna. He regrets that he cannot ride with Dalip today. Something important has come up. Dalip is disappointed, so I promise to take him to Jagmohan's toyshop, which he loves. I ask Avtar to accompany us, along with a few guards.

We've barely entered the shop when armed men push their way in, overpower Avtar, and press a sword against his throat. Terrified, I thrust Dalip behind me. Has someone ordered our assassination?

But no. The leader identifies himself as a Sandhawalia soldier. Ajit Singh wants me to return to the haveli immediately, he says. Dangerous things are about to happen. "We've been ordered to escort you home."

The man standing over Avtar raises his sword, ready to bring it down. Avtar stares stoically ahead.

"Stop!" I shout, pressing forward though I'm dizzy with dread. "What are you doing?"

"Our orders are to kill all of Dhian's soldiers."

"But Avtar isn't Dhian's soldier!" I cry, though this isn't quite true. "He's my faithful retainer. Free him now! If you disobey me, I will make sure the Sandhawalias hear of it."

Faced by my fierceness, the leader releases Avtar. I insist on him riding in my carriage; I don't trust the Sandhawalia mercenaries. The terrified coachman sets off at a rattling pace. As the carriage turns, I see my other guards lying in a pool of blood. I stifle the scream rising in my throat. Avtar quickly pulls down the curtain so that Dalip will not notice anything. I hear the boom of cannons. Are the Sandhawalias attacking the qila?

When we reach home, the Sandhawalia soldier instructs me to stay inside. His men clang the main gate shut and position themselves outside, rifles at the ready. My guards have disappeared. Thank God Avtar is still with us. But even as he bolts the haveli door, Mangla pulls me to the back of the house, toward the servants' rooms.

"Sher Singh is dead," she whispers.

A hand of ice squeezes my heart. "How do you know this?"

Mangla opens the door to a servant's room. A figure shrinks against the wall, a woman in a cheap cotton salwar-kameez, swathed in a veil. It is Pathani, dressed in her maid's clothes, her hair in disarray, her arms and neck bare. She must have taken off all her jewelry—the pieces she was so proud of—so that she would not be recognized. Shivering and weeping, she tells me what has happened.

Last night the festivities to celebrate the new prince's birth had gone on until late, so Sher decided to cancel durbar today. The Sandhawalias invited him to the Gardens of Shah Bilawal to watch a wrestling match and inspect their troops. Ajit Singh had said he had a special gift for the maharaja, a rare double-barreled gun from Calcutta. They had invited Dhian, too, but he did not care for wrestling and promised to join them later. After his morning meal with Pathani, he set off for the gardens with a small escort.

Pathani says, "A little later, I heard my maid screaming. I rushed to the door to find one of Wazir ji's ghorcharhas collapsed on the ground, bleeding heavily. He told me that the Sandhawalias had met Wazir ji on the way. Ajit Singh shot him and ordered his men to hack him to pieces. Most of the other guards were killed. But he'd been determined to come and warn me. The Sandhawalia soldiers were on their way, to burn down the house and probably kill me, too. I tried to help the ghorcharha but he made me leave. You were the only one I could think of . . ."

Pathani rocks back and forth, holding her head in her hands. I'm too shocked to console her. How can Dhian Singh, so canny and powerful, be dead?

There is a commotion outside. Someone bangs on the haveli door. Mangla runs to look. When she returns, her face is pinched with fear.

"Ajit and Lehna have come, with many soldiers. They insist on seeing you."

I step toward the door. I have no choice.

Pathani grabs my hand. Her eyes blaze. "Are you part of their conspiracy? Is this why you made me persuade Wazir ji to bring you back?"

Guilt twinges through me because there's a tiny kernel of truth in Pathani's accusations. But I say, truthfully enough, "I'm as shocked as you. I had no idea what the Sandhawalias were planning. I'm their prisoner in this house. But I swear to you, they will get to you only over my dead body."

In the baithak, Ajit and Lehna sit triumphantly on the best velvet chairs in their bloodstained clothing. They have ordered the servants to bring them food and drink as though they are the masters of this house. I hide my fury at that, but when they tell me that they have made my son into a king, I cannot control myself.

"You promised me that you wouldn't harm Sher or Dhian. You lied! I want no part of this."

Lehna bares his teeth in a feral grin. "Did you really believe we'd let our kinswoman's murderers go free? Chand is avenged now, the Sandhawalia clan can stand tall again, and your son will rule Punjab. Everyone wins. Why are you complaining?"

Ajit says, "We tried to get Sher out of the way peacefully. But he was too stubborn. We've already announced throughout the city that Dalip will be the new maharaja. You have only one choice. You can be the regent"—his hand moves toward the hilt of his sword—"or Dalip can become an orphan whom the Sandhawalias will adopt out of love for the Sarkar. Once Dalip gets over his shock, he'll be happy enough—he already loves Uncle Lehna, who will become the next wazir."

I've been beaten at the royal game, at least for the moment.

"I'll go along with your plan," I say, careful to keep the hatred out of my voice. Inside, I add, *But I will not forget.*

THE SANDHAWALIAS WANT DALIP and me to move into the qila tonight. Their troops, garrisoned there, can protect us better.

I beg them to let me remain here until the funerals are over. "Please—I can't bear to be there with the dead bodies," I entreat. The truth is that once I leave the haveli, Pathani's life will be in graver danger. Thankfully, Ajit and Lehna are distracted by soldiers who inform them that they've killed most of Dhian's troops. But they haven't located Suchet, Hira, or Pathani. They must have fled.

The Sandhawalias berate the men for failing at this simple task. They order the soldiers to guard my haveli, inform me that I must move to the qila in the morning, and depart. Thank Waheguru that they did not insist on seeing Dalip. I couldn't have borne it if Lehna had embraced him.

I'M WOKEN FROM THE dark sleep of exhaustion by Mangla, who hushes me and leads me to the back entry, where a figure stands wrapped in a shawl. In the dark he looks so much like Dhian that an illogical hope surges in me. Perhaps the wazir escaped somehow? But no, it is Hira, clothes torn, face bloody. He tells me that the Sandhawalias had Dhian's body chopped to pieces and thrown in a ditch. Hira has been hiding all day. When it became dark, he managed to climb over my back wall and find Avtar.

"I didn't know if you'd joined the traitors, but I had nowhere else to turn. Do you know where Mai Pathani went? Our house is burned rubble, the servants dead. I'm terrified for Mai. She has never had to take care of herself." He wipes his eyes with his torn sleeve, and I realize that he loves Pathani as though she were his own mother.

I take him to her.

He kneels by the bed, stroking her hair. "I'm so thankful you are safe."

Pathani sits up, dry-eyed and composed. "I've decided to become a sati."

"No, Pathani!" I cry, horrified. "No!"

Is this my fate, over and over, to have my dearest friend—for I see now that Pathani has indeed become that—kill herself on her husband's pyre? I grasp her hands, begging her to change her mind, but both Pathani and Hira ignore me.

"First, however, I want revenge," Pathani says. "Bring me the heads of the traitors. I want them placed at your father's feet on the funeral pyre."

Hira stands up tall, his face pale, determined. "You shall have it, Mai. Uncle Suchet and I have already gathered our Dogra troops. We've met with the Khalsa army in the cantonments, telling them what happened. Ajit offered a fancy double-barreled gun to Sher Singh as a gift, and when the king reached for it, the traitor shot him in the chest. They even killed his little boy, Pratap. Ajit and Lehna stuck the heads of father and son on spears and rode through the city. The Khalsa army is shocked by such brazen treachery and disrespect. It has promised to fight on our side. Of course, it didn't hurt that we have promised them a hefty bonus if we win!" He laughs mirthlessly.

"You've done well," Pathani says. "Your father would be proud. I have one more request. Jindan saved my life today at great risk to herself. When all this is over, I want you to seat Dalip on the throne, make her queen regent, and guide her as wazir."

Hira bows, agreeing, and Pathani finally smiles.

THE PYRES HAVE BEEN stacked high with sandalwood logs and readied for lighting. I stand in front of them. Though I long to be elsewhere, I must honor the dead—and those about to die. It is the least I can do for Dhian, who, in spite of his machinations, had protected Dalip and me in our need. And for Pathani, who is now climbing onto her husband's pyre with unsteady steps. I made sure she was given a hefty dose of opium and held her hand as she walked behind Dhian's bier.

Hira fulfilled his promise. He led the Khalsa army to the qila in the dark of midnight and fired the cannons. They breached the walls and stormed the fort, shouting, "Death to the king-killers." The unprepared Sandhawalias were quickly overwhelmed. Ajit and Lehna were captured and their heads severed. Hira placed them at the feet of his father, whose limbs had been recovered from the ditch and sewn together.

Beside Dhian's pyre stands that of Sher Singh, and next to it, a smaller one for his son Pratap. I cannot even look in that direction.

Hira will perform the ritual for all the deceased. He lights the pyres of the king and the prince first. When he approaches Dhian's pyre, I turn away. I can't bear the horror of watching Pathani burn. I hope it will be over for her soon, and that the effect of the opium will last until the end. I clap my hands over my ears in case it doesn't. In spite of that, I hear Hira's broken voice. "Mai, I don't know how to live without Father's guidance and your love. I pray it will not be long before I join you both."

The fire hisses and crackles. Even from where I'm standing, I can feel its greedy heat. All around me, people applaud Hira's filial devotion, but I'm stricken with fear. What made Hira utter such unlucky words? For Dalip's sake, I hope they will not come true.

TWO DAYS AFTER THE funeral, Hira moves Dalip and me into the Sheesh Mahal. It is awash with memories, sweet and bitter. I can feel the presence of so many departed souls: the Sarkar, Kharak, Chand and Bibi, Sher, the Sandhawalias for one triumphant night. I ask to stay in Jindan Haveli, but Hira points out that it is not appropriate for the new king.

My little boy is no longer just mine. He belongs to the people and must behave in appropriate ways. I try to explain to Dalip that he is a king now, but though he nods obediently, wanting as always to please me, he doesn't understand. Right now, he's playing with the courtiers' sons in the garden, while just a short distance away, workers are scrubbing bloodstains off the stones.

Hira and I argue about the coronation. He insists Dalip must be declared king—with himself as wazir—as soon as possible. "The throne of Punjab cannot sit empty. The Sarkar has two other sons, Peshaura and Kashmira. If we don't forestall them now, while we have the support of the Khalsa army, they'll stake their claims."

He's right, but I want an auspicious day for the ascension, especially because of Dalip's unlucky horoscope. But there are no suitable dates until several months later.

Finally, we reach a compromise. Hira and I will present Dalip in the durbar where he will sit on a temporary throne. The work of the court will continue uninterrupted. The coronation ceremony can occur when I want.

"I'll handle everything," Hira says. "Don't worry!"

His complacent tone, however, makes me do just that. It tells me he would like to confine me to the zenana and Dalip to the schoolroom and be the real ruler of Punjab. I refuse to allow it. But to succeed against Hira, I need strong, trustworthy allies.

I write to the Fakir, begging him to return to court and be my chief adviser. And I write to Jawahar that Dalip needs his uncle. Remembering our tense parting, I add, *Come soon, veer. What fun we'll have!*

Avtar sets off with the letters, promising to travel as fast as possible. The Fakir lives far from the capital—and from Jawahar. It'll take several days for their replies to reach me. Still, whenever I hear a knock, I wonder if Avtar has returned.

IN THE INTERIM THERE are many things to keep me busy. Each day, clan leaders come to the durbar to pay their respects to their young maharaja. Hira offers to escort Dalip there, but I insist on accompanying my son. I know I must claim my place in the durbar right away, or it'll be too late. So I dress dramatically: all in white—salwar, kameez, veil, the Sarkar's own pearls that he gifted me. I know the assembly will recognize them. I stand tall behind Dalip's temporary throne. I'm breaking tradition; women, if at all they come to court, should be a shadow behind a screen. Even Chand Kaur, Malika Mukaddas, did that. But I need to show everyone that Dalip is not alone.

I've taught my son how to address visitors. When he thanks them in his artless child-voice, his guests respond warmly. Youth and innocence have a special strength, and I plan to use it. I follow up with my own thanks, telling the men how much the Sarkar would appreciate their support of his son. I create an impression not of power—it's not yet the time for that—but of a mother's gratitude.

Still I can sense Hira reassessing me, realizing I am more than the pretty widow who was Pathani's friend. He doesn't like it.

Nor does he like that I've hired my own guards with Avtar's help. Led by my trusty retainer, they stand outside the Sheesh Mahal, and accompany me wherever I go. Hira would be a lot more upset if he knew that Avtar has also hand-picked a cadre of spies, a couple of whom have been placed in the wazir's household!

Hira is further annoyed when I visit the toshakhana and go over the inventory, but he can't deny that it's my right as regent. I discover that the treasury holds only a fraction of what it contained in the Sarkar's day.

"What happened?" I ask angrily. "When I visited the vaults with the Sarkar, they were filled with gold coins. Now they're empty."

The treasurer stammers that he was appointed recently. Lal Singh, his predecessor, might know. I contact Lal, a handsome, well-spoken man I'd noticed already in court. Impressed by his abilities, Dhian had rewarded him highly, giving him the title of Raja. Lal is direct with me: many cartloads of treasure went missing the night Chand was defeated. It would be dangerous to us both if he names anyone. I don't need him to. I've heard the whispers: Gulab's men took them to Jammu. His treachery infuriates me, but as Hira's uncle, he's untouchable for now.

Lal points out that Sher's lavish lifestyle also contributed to the problem. He spent freely but paid little attention to whether revenues were coming in. Lal gives me good advice: cut down unnecessary expenses, and check the records to make sure the clans are paying their tributes on time. He writes me a list of those who have often conveniently forgotten to do so.

I thank him warmly. At night before I fall asleep, his handsome face floats in my mind. His honest eyes. He will make a fine ally.

I'VE JUST PUT DALIP to sleep with a bedtime story, a task I love and always make time for, when Mangla tells me that Avtar has returned. He's dusty and exhausted, having ridden hard all day to bring me a letter. I thank him warmly, tell him to rest, and eagerly open it. It's written in code, the handwriting firm. My heart leaps. Perhaps the Fakir has made a miraculous recovery?

> *My dearest queen, my daughter,*
>
> *My younger brother Nuruddin, who knows the code, is writing this, for I am unable even to lift my head from the pillow. I am heartbroken that I cannot be in court to guide you, but it is time for me to leave this earth. I have full faith in your intelligence and courage. Rely on yourself. Do not trust too quickly. Remember Sada? Be like her. Look to the Khalsa soldiers. They will be your protectors. Beware of the Dogras—*

Below is an apology from Nuruddin: *Due to breathing difficulties, the Fakir was unable to dictate anything else.*

My eyes fill with tears. I'd so hoped that my Fakir, my loving guide, my shield, would be with me. Instead, he is dying.

Avtar, I notice, is still standing by the door.

I wipe my eyes, embarrassed. "Do you have a letter from Jawahar, or a message?"

He shakes his head.

"Is Jawahar not well?"

"He is in excellent health."

I'm surprised at Jawahar's silence, and additionally disappointed. Tears overwhelm me again. I turn away, not wanting Avtar to see.

Suddenly a figure, face covered with a shawl, rushes into the room, grabs me and whirls me around. Shocked, I flail out, then realize it's Jawahar.

"Fooled you!" he cries. He throws off the shawl and laughs uproariously. I, too, begin to laugh. He hugs me tightly. Over his shoulder, I see Mangla and Avtar smiling.

"Conspirators!" I retort.

But I feel happier than in a long time. All through my childhood, Jawahar protected me. My own blood, he'll never let me down.

I say, "Thank you, my veer. Now that you're here, everything will be better."

27

Coronation

THE CORONATION WILL BE HELD in a few weeks, on a suitably auspicious date. There's much to be done. I want to hold the ceremony in the Diwan-i-Aam, the biggest hall in the qila. The mosaic floor must be polished, the kursis scrubbed clean, coronation outfits stitched for Dalip and me—and Jawahar, too, because I've insisted that he be a part of the ceremony. Gold-embossed invitations are being sent to the heads of clans and the neighboring kings, though they are, in truth, vassals of the British.

Hira offers to handle the details, but I'm afraid to let him take control, afraid that it'll lead to other power shifts. So I insist on signing the invitations.

"Of course, you must sign them, too," I offer.

Trained by his canny father, Hira hides his annoyance. "Your signature is sufficient, Rani ji. Thank you for doing this. It will free me up to take care of more important court business."

The tension between us grows each day. A pity; we would have done well as allies. What angers me most is his animosity toward Jawahar. When I request a seat for Jawahar at court as the maharaja's uncle, Hira acts as though I have asked for the moon.

At the heart of our problems is Pandit Jalla, a sour-faced Brahmin who has suddenly appeared at court as Hira's chief adviser. Jalla opposes whatever I want. From Avtar I learn that he used to be Hira's tutor, banished from Lahore by Dhian because he wielded too much influence over the young boy. Jalla must have stayed in touch with Hira secretly, because he was back in the city immediately after Dhian's death.

A NOBLEMAN WHO OWNED a large estate near Kasur has died without an heir, and there's a heated argument in court about who should be awarded his jagir. I speak up for his widow, who has asked that she be allowed to handle things. I point out that her brother, head of a powerful clan, has promised to help her. Our consent will make him our staunch ally. Several senior courtiers agree, but Jalla wants to give the estate to a Hindu nobleman. Hira sides with Jalla, and as wazir, he has the final say. But I hear several people muttering about a conspiracy by Hindus to take over the kingdom.

I return to the Sheesh Mahal, fuming. "Hira follows Jalla blindly even when experienced courtiers offer better counsel. It's causing a dangerous split in durbar between the Hindus and Sikhs, which the Sarkar worked so hard to prevent!"

"I hate that Jalla," Jawahar—my dear, loyal brother—says. "I've seen him watching you with his beady eyes, like a snake getting ready to strike."

I sigh. "Jalla wants to be the real power behind the throne. He wants to control Dalip like he controls Hira. He can't do that as long as I'm here. That's why he's turning Hira against me."

"We must get rid of that man. Find an assassin—"

"Things aren't so simple!" I interrupt sharply. "You mustn't do anything rash."

"You're too cautious," Jawahar grumbles. "I wish you'd let me handle the problem." But I insist until he gives me his word.

That night, I lie sleepless. Jawahar worries me, and not only because he's hotheaded, and ready to plan murders. He regularly charges expensive outfits and jewels to my account even after I've told him I must reduce expenses, as Lal advised. In durbar he's quick to take offence when courtiers ignore him. He wants me to organize a banquet, with dancers and fireworks. *You've become the queen regent. Shouldn't we be celebrating?* I explain that it would be unseemly to celebrate so soon after so many horrifying deaths. But it concerns me that he cannot see that on his own.

Is it my fault, for writing, so facetiously, *What fun we'll have*?

An added thorn is that he's sleeping with Mangla again. Mangla is discreet, but Jawahar is not. He often makes sexual jokes or grabs at her when she passes by. It makes me uncomfortable, especially when he behaves so in front of Dalip, who loves Uncle Jawahar and has started copying his mannerisms.

Perhaps the Sarkar was right in enforcing the policy of never allowing relatives in court.

I push away that treacherous thought. Jawahar is my only brother. Of course he should be here, by our side.

I focus instead on the Fakir's last words. What did he mean when he advised me to be like Sada Kaur? I think all night. When dawn brightens my window, a plan comes to me. I stop Hira as he is leaving durbar and request him to invite the Khalsa army to meet their new maharaja.

"Dalip can perform a ceremonial inspection and give them a gift."

"Now?" Hira says. "We have a thousand things to do before the coronation!"

I make my voice soft and sweet, like Pathani's. "It'll raise the troops' morale and increase their loyalty. Surely you want that."

I don't know if it's my argument or my tone, but Hira gives in. "Have Avtar bring Dalip to the Akbari Gate next Monday. I shall take him to the parade grounds."

ON THE MORNING OF the inspection, Dalip rides to the gate with Avtar. Jawahar and I follow. How could Hira think I'd allow this crucial meeting to happen without my presence?

Riding the black Arabian that Lehna had gifted him, Dalip asks, "Is Uncle Lehna going to join us, too?"

His innocent question robs me of words. I shake my head. "No."

"Why not, Biji?"

Jawahar comes to my rescue. "Uncle Lehna had to go somewhere, but I am here. Come, let us race to the edge of the field!"

I hold my breath as they gallop off. I've made Jawahar practise riding every day this week, and Avtar has found him the mildest horse in the stables so that he will not have any embarrassing mishaps. But I see now that he's a competent horseman.

Every time I think I know Jawahar, he surprises me.

I'm thankful that I haven't lost my own riding skills, although I haven't had a chance to be on a horse since we left Jammu. I'm riding a spirited bay, a beautiful animal—but not the one I long for. When I moved to the qila after the funerals, the first thing I did was send Avtar to the stables to find Laila. I planned to visit her the same day. I even had a lump of gur ready. But Laila was gone. Someone must have stolen her during the confusion of the attacks.

We reach the parade grounds, where several nobles await. I know my unexpected presence in this male arena is going to astonish them. I'll deal with that problem in a bit. Right now, the soldiers take up my attention. They fill the huge field, a vast ocean of red-and-yellow uniforms. And this is only a small part of Punjab's forces. Other battalions are stationed at the borders: Tibet, Kabul, and most importantly, at the Sutlej, across from the British garrisons. I've always known how large our army is; the Sarkar had often described it lovingly. Still, facing all these soldiers, I feel my palms grow clammy. Will they—like Hira—be shocked to see me, even though I'm appropriately veiled? Will they disapprove?

The first attack comes, unsurprisingly, from Jalla. "With all due respect, Rani ji, *what* are you doing here?" he demands, shrill with indignation. "It is inappropriate! The royal women of the court of Lahore are expected to remain in purdah."

I rein in my anger and speak loudly, so that all the courtiers will hear. "As regent, it is my duty to be here with my son. Besides, have you forgotten that it was a woman, Sada Kaur, mother-in-law of the Sarkar, who rode with him into Lahore and helped him take his place as maharaja?"

I don't waste any more time on Jalla. I gesture to Avtar, who hands me a speaking trumpet. The entire assembly is now staring at me. I urge my horse forward until I'm directly in front of the troops. I grip the trumpet with trembling fingers, but my voice—thank Waheguru—comes out clear and strong.

"Khalsa ji," I begin, because this is how the Sarkar liked to address his army, "my son and I honor you and thank you for your service to the throne. We depend upon your valor to protect us and our beloved Punjab. Please bless Dalip as he gets ready for his coronation. To show his appreciation, he will distribute to every soldier here a Nanakshahi coin after observing your maneuvers."

The soldiers are silent, their faces inscrutable. Have I failed? I can feel the satisfaction emanating from Jalla. No matter what, I must carry my plan through. I beckon Dalip forward. He sits tall on his horse—as tall as a five-year-old can be—and raises his arm in a regal gesture. I am astonished at his poise in front of this huge assembly. He is indeed his father's son.

The soldiers burst into loud cheers. "Waheguru bless our maharaja!" And then, astonishingly, "Jai Rani Jindan!"

After the maneuvers have been brilliantly executed, Avtar's men bring sacks of silver coins for Dalip to touch before they're given to the panches to distribute. The soldiers applaud again. My heart is light as I leave the grounds. The army now feels a connection of the heart to Dalip—and perhaps to me as well.

"That was very impressive, Rani." Jalla's malicious tones break into my thoughts. "But where did those coins come from? Are you bankrupting an already depleted treasury to make your grand gesture?"

My face grows hot at his insolence. I'd conferred carefully with the treasurer in planning this event. I'd taken some money from the toshakhana, but most of it was from my allowance and Dalip's. But I'm not going to explain anything to Jalla.

Instead I say, "Pandit, surely a man as educated in propriety as you knows that the regent only answers to the wazir. Should Hira see it fit to question me at a more appropriate time, I will give him my answer."

I gallop ahead, fuming. Jalla has ruined the moment. I say nothing to Jawahar—I don't want to incite him further—but I tell Mangla, "Jalla has to go."

Mangla nods. "For that you'll need a powerful ally."

"I may have found one," I say.

THE DAY OF THE coronation dawns bright. Mangla dresses Dalip in red silk. Jawahar is resplendent in a new emerald kurta. I wear my usual white. Mangla and Jawahar protest that it's too simple, but I know what I'm doing. I've created a persona. In the bazaars, people whisper in awe about the young queen in white, faithful, beautiful and tragic, her only ornament a string of her husband's pearls.

In the Diwan-i-Khas, Dalip does everything the way I've taught him, bowing solemnly to the Granth Sahib and accepting the red tilak of kingship smeared on his forehead by the priests. But when I attach the glittering kalgi of white feathers and diamonds to his turban, his face breaks into his little-boy grin.

"Did I do well? Are you proud of me?"

"You did everything perfectly, my chand." I can't stop my tears. He wipes them away.

The courtiers, generals and clan-heads swear fealty to Dalip, giving him expensive gifts that pile up on either side of the throne. In the line, I notice the treasurer from our main toshakhana at Gobindgarh Fort. He carries a gold box. When he opens it, I see that he's brought Dalip the Koh-i-Noor. He ties it to the maharaja's arm. My heart is wrenched as I remember the Sarkar telling me that he wanted Dalip to have the diamond. At the same time, I want to snatch the unlucky diamond away from my son. But I can't have the courtiers thinking that I'm a superstitious fool. I'm forced to let him wear it.

To my relief, the ceremony concludes smoothly. Cannons are fired to inform citizens that Lahore has a new maharaja. Musicians start up in the garden and dancing girls begin their leaps and pirouettes. Servants carry a feast of many courses across the courtyard. The aroma of biriyani and rogan josh fills the air.

Suddenly the sun disappears behind dark clouds, a freezing wind starts up, and the qila is pelted with hailstones. Gusts blow the stones right into the Diwan-i-Khas. Entertainers run for shelter; guests scurry about, trying to keep their finery dry; servers are forced back to the kitchen.

The festivities I had planned so carefully are ruined.

I stare at the sky in dismay. In all my life, I've only seen hail twice, and those stones were tiny. These are as big as my fist. Is this an omen? Looking at the dark faces around me, I can see that many are thinking the same thing. The astrologer's words echo in my head: *His stars are most unfortunate. He will gain everything and then lose it all.*

THE HAIL THAT RUINED Dalip's coronation feast ravaged all of Punjab, blighting crops and causing thousands to starve. I send grain from the royal stores to the villages. I have the durbar charge the nobles a storm levy and send the collected money to gurdwaras and temples so the hungry can be fed. Still, people murmur that Dalip has brought them bad luck. Courtiers make flimsy excuses to keep their children away from my son. When Dalip asks me where his friends went, I have no answer.

Other troubles are brewing, too. I learn about them in durbar, where I remain all day after Dalip goes back to the Sheesh Mahal for his lessons. The courtiers are uncomfortable at first, but after some time they get used to my presence. Yesterday two spies were caught in Lahore. Upon interrogation, they confessed that they were here to lure some of our European officers to the British side. Attar Singh Sandhawalia, Ajit and Lehna's kinsman, to whom the British had given asylum, had planned the operation. He wanted the firangs to start a war against Punjab, and they, always willing, had brought more than two hundred guns and several regiments to Ferozepur. We also discover that it was the British who had incited Ajit and Lehna to kill Sher.

The spies have been put to death, the officers involved are being held for questioning, and now the council must decide what our next steps should be. Some suggest waiting for the British to make the first move. Others want to pressure the British agent in Lahore to make the firangs pull back. The jarnails want to go on the offensive. Hira believes we should ready our army along our border. But the border stretches for hundreds of miles. Where should the soldiers focus? Voices and tempers rise as people argue about it.

A memory resurfaces: the Sarkar unfurling a map on our bed, pointing to Ferozepur, explaining why he hadn't been able to come to Gujranwala to marry me. He'd been negotiating with the British. He had to give them Ferozepur, but he told me that if the British ever tried to attack Punjab from there, he had the perfect defense.

I frown, trying hard to remember. "We must send our troops to garrison Kasur on our border," I say loudly, trying to be heard over the din. "It's close to Ferozepur but not visible from there. And flood the moat at Phillaur Fort. It is what the Sarkar would have done."

Everyone stares at me. I feel myself flushing. Jalla tries to jeer, but Hira says, "An excellent solution! It seems that the Sarkar is speaking through you." He sends out orders. Within a few days the British pull back.

The courtiers treat me with new respect, seeking my opinion about complicated political situations. I offer suggestions, relying on whatever the Sarkar taught me. Sometimes I even come up with my own solutions. Jalla is infuriated by my growing popularity; that pleases me even more.

JAWAHAR HASN'T BEEN A success at court despite my best efforts. He doesn't know enough about durbar affairs to comment on them intelligently and, unlike me, has no desire to learn. He believes he should be accorded special privileges as the maharaja's uncle, and feels slighted when this doesn't happen. Most of the courtiers ignore Jawahar, but Jalla goes out of his way to bait him. Today he reprimands Jawahar for occupying the seat of a senior nobleman. It's an innocent mistake on Jawahar's part, but when he tries to explain, Jalla cuts him off rudely, telling the court, "What else can we expect from someone like him?"

Jawahar interprets this as a dig at his family origins and demands that Jalla take back his words. When Jalla pays no heed to him, he asks me to order the pandit to apologize. I'm caught in a dilemma. Jawahar has a right to his anger; Jalla's words have offended me, too. But this is exactly what Jalla wants so that he can accuse me of favoring family. I try to pacify Jawahar, but he stalks out even as I'm speaking.

That night at dinner, we have a loud argument in front of Dalip. Jawahar, who has been drinking, berates me for allowing Jalla to get away with insulting our family. I tell him that durbar is no place to resolve personal disputes. He accuses me of being ashamed of him.

In my anger I blurt out, "Now I see why the Sarkar never allowed his wives' families to come to court. All you've done is cause trouble and cost me money."

Jawahar flinches as though slapped. Then he walks out.

We make up after a few days. I offer Jawahar my haveli as amends. He accepts gladly, especially as I give Mangla the evenings off to spend with him. Some weeks later I hear from Avtar that Jawahar has made new friends and often invites them to dinners at which Mangla presides. I'm happy for him. But I'm also lonely. All this time, struggling to survive and keep Dalip safe, I pushed away my own needs and overlooked the deep emptiness in my heart. Now I'm forced to admit the truth: I'm parched for love.

Several courtiers would be glad to help me quench this thirst. Chief among them is the handsome Lal Singh. In the midst of important political discussions, I feel the heat from his ardent eyes. When Jalla attacks me, he is the first to rush to my defense. He longs to court me, but we both know that, as queen, I'm the one who must make the first move. I daydream about it sometimes. But I can't afford to get tangled up in a romance. My position as regent—and Dalip's fate—depends on my reputation as the Sarkar's faithful widow.

28

Love and Hate

Power and Jalla's bad advice have gone to Hira's head. I try to counsel him, but he will not listen. He has had a falling-out with Suchet Singh, his uncle. When Dhian was murdered and Hira's own life was in danger, Suchet and his troops fought staunchly by his side. But after Jalla dug his claws into him, Hira turned his back on Suchet. Now Suchet complains bitterly and publicly about his nephew's ingratitude.

I say, "Suchet saved your life, Hira. All he wants is some respect. Give him that and he'll be your strongest ally."

Instead, on Jalla's advice, Hira offers Suchet the governorship of Peshawar, a city so distant and unimportant that Suchet sees it as an insult.

The princes Kashmira and Peshaura are also giving Hira trouble, stirring up unrest in the north. They insist that, as children of the Sarkar, they deserve more lands than what the durbar has awarded them.

"Let them have a jagir or two," I suggest. "It'll satisfy them, and they'll stay away from Lahore. It's worth the price."

But Jalla bristles at this. "Are you telling Wazir ji to give in to the demands of those callow youths? Do you want the citizens to think he's a weakling?"

Hira asks his oldest uncle, Gulab, to rout the princes. The wily Dogra is delighted to do so. Having defeated the princes, he takes their lands. Kashmira and Peshaura travel across the country, complaining to all who will listen—and there are many—of how the Dogras dispossessed them.

Public opinion turns against Hira. When I point this out in durbar, he is affronted. In retaliation, he picks a quarrel with Jawahar and, claiming that he made treasonous threats, has him thrown in prison. Jawahar is kept in chains until I'm able to persuade the nobles that he is completely loyal.

It's the last straw. I tell Jawahar, Mangla, and Avtar, "I'll no longer help Hira. Let him drown in his own folly."

Thus, when Suchet comes to Lahore to challenge his nephew, I don't point out to Hira that Suchet, who has only brought forty-five soldiers with him, doesn't intend to fight him. I don't try to persuade him to make up with his uncle.

Hira incites the Khalsa army to attack Suchet. Suchet and his small band die fighting so valiantly that our soldiers are filled with remorse. They blame Hira for involving them in his private feud. Hira gets into further trouble with the army when, to placate them, he promises to become a Sikh but then procrastinates.

I watch the events unfold with grim satisfaction. Then I visit the cantonment with Dalip and Jawahar and speak flatteringly to the panches. "You are the Khalsa, warriors of integrity, who are following in the footsteps of the Gurus—but perhaps only a Sikh can recognize that. You are the greatest fighting force in all of Hindustan, yet you were used shamefully by the wazir on the advice of that crooked Jalla." I have Dalip and Jawahar ride through the cantonment, handing out coins. "You are the best defenders of your little maharaja," I tell the soldiers. "Jawahar and I thank you from our hearts." The army cheers so loudly that I'm afraid they'll be heard all the way to the qila.

I have a plan, though it must remain a secret for now, from everyone, including Jawahar. But even as I craft it patiently, something I never planned on happens.

WHEN DID THINGS BEGIN to change between Lal Singh and myself? I'm mortified because I behave like an infatuated teenager when he is around—and I can't seem to stop. I blush when he praises my suggestions in court; his commonest courtesies make my heart race. How did this dangerous situation come about, in spite of my vow never to be so foolish? I fight my feelings as best as I can. I return, unopened, the gifts Lal sends me on festive days even though I accept other people's offerings. In durbar, I wear my heaviest veils in order to hide my expression. When Lal addresses me, I answer curtly and turn from him. So that he will cease to be a daily temptation, I discuss with ministers the possibility of sending him to a distant post. But my behavior only draws more attention to me. Courtiers raise their eyebrows at my uncalled-for harshness. Even Jawahar, not the most observant of men, wonders why I am so rude to Lal. And the shrewd Jalla watches me like a cobra about to strike.

Lal grows increasingly concerned by my brusqueness. He finally inquires if he may speak with me in private. Saying no would be the wise thing to do. But I give in to temptation and tell him to come to the Sheesh Mahal.

"Rani Sahiba," he begins when we are alone, "I have offended you, though I don't know how. Please tell me what I've done wrong."

I cannot think of what to say, so I remain quiet.

Lal takes my silence for disapproval. He kneels in front of me. "I'm your staunchest admirer. I've never seen a woman with such determination and intelligence. I'll do whatever you want to prove my loyalty. Please don't be vexed with me—it is causing me great unhappiness. And please don't banish me from the court."

I should speak to him as a queen to her subject, reassuring him that he is not to blame, and send him away. But something wild inside makes me throw back my veil and look into Lal's eyes. This is the first time I've knowingly enticed a man. With the Sarkar, I was too innocent, too much in awe. When I hear Lal gasp, I feel powerful—and a little wicked.

"Indeed you have done great wrong, Lal Singh," I utter softly. When he looks distressed, I add, "You have stolen my heart."

For a moment he is shocked. Then exhilaration transforms his face. "In that case, my queen, I must give you mine in reparation."

I hold out my hand. It trembles a little. He comes to me wordlessly. His hand, when he holds mine, is trembling, too. His lips sear my skin. I am both elated and terrified at once.

He says, thickly, "You are more beautiful than I imagined, all those nights when I lay sleepless. Now I can die a happy—"

I stop his words with kisses, though I plan to ask him to repeat them later.

Waheguru, can something so sweet be a sin? If it is, I'm willing to pay the price. I only ask one thing: don't let my Dalip suffer for this.

Days and nights merge into each other, milk and honey, the intimate smell of love. I float through them as though under a spell. I feel fully alive only when Lal comes, wearing the cloak of darkness, to my bed. I've confided in Mangla and she, loyal as always, has made the arrangements for his visits. I sense that she has told Jawahar about these developments. He has said nothing, but he has not visited me lately. And the upright Avtar, whose help we need to ensure Lal's safe passage to and from the Sheesh Mahal, has stopped meeting with me; instead, he sends information through Mangla.

I cannot let this continue. I ask the three of them to meet me.

All my life I've been taught that it is shameful for women to talk of desire, but I force myself to be frank. "I value your love and loyalty more than my pride, so I will speak my mind. I've been a widow since I was twenty-one. The years stretched ahead of me, empty as a desert. Then, miraculously, I found love again. But I cannot marry Lal. If I do, I must give up being regent. I cannot abandon Dalip like that. But should I be sentenced to loneliness just because I wish to protect my son? Many of the nobles have several wives—and mistresses, too. Their liaisons are accepted. Am I a sinner just because I'm a woman? I love only one man, but society will denounce me if it finds out.

"You three are my closest, my kin, the ones I trust the most. I hope I can continue depending on you."

Jawahar and Avtar promise their support, though they glance away, clearly uncomfortable. But Mangla nods, looking at me with shining eyes that understand.

AS THOUGH TO BALANCE my joy, the world sends me one trouble after another. The first concerns Jawahar. His banquets are getting wilder. Wine flows freely in Jindan Haveli. Opium makes regular appearances. The dancing girls remain through the night to please his guests. All of this exacts a cost—on his health and his purse. Avtar reports that he visits the moneylenders in Hira Mandi. I caution Jawahar, but I am unable to be as forceful as in the past. What if he accuses me in return? There are fewer banquets for a while, but soon there are just as many as before, only wilder.

The second is my own fault. I'm losing my standing—for which I fought so hard—in the durbar. Although I continue to attend court, I'm often tardy and fatigued from my late nights. Where before I gathered information ahead of time and spoke energetically on issues, now I sit daydreaming about my lover. The nobles are disappointed at first, then they revert to ignoring me. Only Jalla watches both me and Lal, who is similarly distracted.

The durbar is facing many troubles. A new, fiercer governor-general has come to Hindustan—Hardinge, whom we call "tunda laat" because he lost an arm in battle. Jalla insists that he's planning to attack Punjab, and that Hira must dispatch the army to the Sutlej. I point out it's unlikely that Hardinge will undertake such a major enterprise so soon after his new appointment. Several courtiers side with me. But when Jalla shouts me down, I shrug and let Hira do as he pleases. My supporters feel abandoned. The troops are sent to the border. Much money that we cannot afford is spent on unnecessary military posturing.

To complicate matters further, Attar Singh re-enters Punjab and joins the camp of a respected holy man, Baba Bir Singh. Kashmira and Peshaura, too, take refuge there. Bir Singh wishes to bring about a reconciliation between them and the durbar, but Hira will have none of it. He wants to send the Khalsa army to attack them. I recommend a diplomatic solution, but when Hira insists on teaching the rebels a lesson, I don't have the stamina to argue. Hira attacks the camp; the peaceful Bir Singh dies, his thigh shattered by a cannonball; the populace denounces the Khalsa army as killers of a guru; the soldiers are demoralized and angrier than ever. I am torn between sadness at the unnecessary violence and a mean joy at Hira's troubles. I should take advantage of this situation somehow, but enthralled by love, I let it slip by.

My biggest challenge is Dalip. Before Lal and I became lovers, I spent all my spare time with my son. But now I'm distracted. I smile and nod when Dalip tells me about his day, but now that he is older—almost eight—he is not so easily fooled. He can sense my mind is elsewhere. *You didn't hear anything*, he accuses me. In the evening, ignoring his protests, I unclasp his arms from around my neck and hand him to Mangla. When he cries, I feel guilty, but not enough to stay—because Lal is waiting in my bedchamber, where I will dress up in the beautiful, brightly colored silks I've begun to wear for him. With Lal, I'm transformed into a different woman, wild and uninhibited, telling him what pleases me in a way I'd never dared with the Sarkar. Our conversations afterward are just as magical. We share with each other things we've hidden all our lives. My childhood of poverty and hunger; my education that was cut short by male misbehavior; my father's plots to use me for his advancement. Lal's own youth in a provincial family determined to stifle his ambitions; his escape to Lahore, where he clawed his way up the ranks, enduring abuse, until he caught Dhian's eye. We talk until the nightwatchman's cry warns us that the dawn is near and Lal must slip away.

Dalip responds to my neglect by throwing tantrums—something he has never done before. Remorse keeps me from disciplining him. I indulge his every whim, buying him more toys, horses, an expensive falcon. When he refuses to study, I tell his tutors to let him be. When his favorite cat has kittens, he insists that the cannons in the qila be fired, as they are for state occasions. I swallow my pride and request Hira to do this; he agrees with a taunting smile.

Thus I float in my dream of love, skirting disaster.

A FAMILIAR NAUSEA JERKS me awake before sunrise. I rush to the toilet, where I empty myself, retching. I know this feeling all too well. Dizzy with shock, I sink down to the soiled floor. How can this be? I've been religiously taking the bitter concoctions, guaranteed to prevent pregnancy, which Mangla bought from a renowned herbalist.

A weeping Mangla apologizes over and over, threatening to kill the herbalist. I have to put aside my own distress to calm her down. "It's not your fault. Just my bad luck. But now you must find a dai, trustworthy and discreet, to perform the abortion."

Mangla weeps even more; abortions are dangerous. We both know stories of women who died from them, or were crippled. But what alternative do I have?

"Marry me!" Lal declares that night, when I tell him my plan. "We'll go to a city where no one knows us. I have enough money for us to live a simple, carefree life—you, me, our baby."

For a moment I allow myself to imagine such a future. How idyllic it seems. How impossible.

"What would happen to Dalip without me here?"

"Jawahar would look after Dalip. He loves him like his own son. Hira, too, would take care of him because it would be to his advantage."

"Jawahar's an innocent himself, and Hira too easily swayed by Jalla."

"Think of the little one inside you," Lal pleads, stroking my belly. "Isn't he or she your child, too? And more helplessly dependent on you than Dalip?"

I turn my face so he will not see my tears. I use my regal voice. "Please leave me. I am unwell."

After he leaves, I send him a message through Avtar. *The queen wishes you to stay away until informed otherwise.* I cannot have him weakening my resolve.

Later that night Dalip's nurse knocks at the door. "The maharaja has a fever. He's crying for you."

Everything is happening at once. I drag my exhausted body to Dalip's bedside. I make him drink the fever medicine. I lay wet cloths on his burning forehead. He clutches my hand. *Biji, stay with me.* I rub his back until he dozes. I want to stay—at least until the vaid comes—but I must get some rest if I'm to attend durbar in the morning. And I *must* attend. No one must guess what's wrong with me. I leave Mangla in charge. Behind me, I can hear Dalip starting to cry again. *I don't want you. I want Biji.* Guilt squeezes my heart, but I force myself to walk away.

THE BEDROOM IS SWELTERING. A pot of water boils on a large brazier. The dai throws her instruments in there. Tight-lipped and nervous, she doesn't inspire confidence, but Mangla informs me that she's trustworthy and good at keeping secrets. It was hard to find someone willing to perform the abortion. Most dais were terrified of what might happen to them if I died. The dai has given me opium for the pain. Already my mind is wandering. A shadow on the wall looks like the Sarkar's silhouette, glaring with displeasure.

"I'm sorry," I whisper. "I was so lonely."

Two maids, sworn to silence, hold me down. The dai inserts something long and sharp inside me. I feel a scraping and a fiery pain. It'll hurt worse when the opium wears off. No matter. There's always more opium. I'm drifting into a haze. By the time I wake, I hope it'll all be over. Just before I lose consciousness, I hear voices raised in consternation. Mangla's, then the dai's. Running feet. The door banging shut. The Sarkar's face looms over me, frowning. Then everything is gone.

THE PAIN IS FAR worse than what I'd imagined. I'm unable to move my limbs. I struggle in terror until I realize that I've been tied down. Mangla, who looks like she hasn't left my bedside in days, gives me a drink that dulls the pain somewhat. She tells me three days have passed. After the abortion, I'd bled so much that everyone was terrified I would die. Finally, she'd been forced to go to a retired royal vaid, a man who had served the Sarkar.

"Does everyone know?" I croak.

Mangla shakes her head. "The vaid has a good heart. He promised to keep your secret. The many gold coins I offered him—but only if he healed you—may have helped, too. Also, I swore on my mother's soul that if he betrayed us, I'd kill him and his family."

When the vaid comes, I recognize him as one of the Sarkar's

physicians from his last days. He chides me gently for not having called him in the first place. "Believe me, I've seen everything you can imagine in the zenana. You did a very dangerous thing. Your womb was punctured. You almost died. You must remain in bed for a week and take the medicines I've prescribed."

I tell him that I have to appear in court.

"Out of the question," he says. "But don't worry. I've already informed the wazir that you have a high fever. He believes me—there's a great deal of illness right now in Lahore. Even our little maharaja had a fever—the court-appointed vaid is keeping an eye on him."

Concerned about Dalip, I ask Mangla to bring him to me. He looks thinner, weaker. He struggles out of her arms, stumbles to my bed and hugs me. His hands are hot, his eyes feverish.

"Biji, I had scary dreams. I called you, but you didn't come. Please let me sleep with you."

"Of course, my dearest," I say. He falls asleep soon, but then he mutters and flails about. I put a pillow between us to make sure he doesn't hurt me. In the morning, there are pustules on his face.

"He has chechak," his maid cries, backing away.

Mangla comes running. "We must separate him from you. I hope to God that you had the pox when you were a child."

I can't remember. Dalip refuses to be taken away and weeps heart-rendingly. Finally I say, "Bring another bed. Let him stay here. I don't care what happens."

Mangla and two maids, who have had the pox, nurse Dalip. I put aside my pain and sit by his side, holding his hand. He's attended by the court vaid and the old physician, whom I've now hired. Their faces look grim. Dalip's throat is full of blisters. His fever spikes. He grows delirious. We cover his body with wet cloths in an effort to bring down his temperature.

The Sarkar's words from years ago echo in my ears. *Karma circles back to you.*

I killed one child. Is that why death is reaching for the other one?

I pray as I've never prayed before. *Waheguru, punish me but spare this boy.*

It takes two weeks for Dalip's pustules to burst and the itchy skin to start healing. The day he sits up and eats a simple meal, I feel light-headed with joy. Or is something else making me dizzy? The next day, I have a raging fever, then a rash, then blisters. I grow delirious. My throat is swollen. I can barely drink water. As if in a dream, I glimpse the worried faces of the vaids and Mangla. Once I see Jawahar, weeping in the doorway. Or is that Hira, his nostrils stuffed with cotton wool to keep away the illness?

When people have lost all hope, the fever recedes. I open my eyes.

"Where's Dalip?" I ask.

Mangla kisses my hand, weeping, and tells me he's recovering well. Jawahar has taken him to his haveli and bought him a pet monkey to keep him entertained.

I sit up with difficulty and ask for a mirror. Mangla tries to dissuade me, but I insist. I look as ugly as I'd feared: face gaunt, eyes dull, cheeks pockmarked. Mangla insists that she will find me special oils to massage away scars, but I'm strangely calm. If losing my looks is the payment for my sins, so be it.

Mangla informs me that Hira had, indeed, come to check on my condition.

"He was concerned?" A little of my long-forgotten warmth for him awakens in my heart.

"Not really." She looks distressed. "Many bad things are happening in the durbar, my queen. Perhaps you should gain a little more strength before I—"

"Tell me!"

She starts with state matters. Gulab and Hira have become sworn enemies. Gulab took over all of the dead Suchet's estates and didn't pay any revenues. When Jalla sent threats, the Dogra taunted him by putting up gallows in Jammu and announcing that they were for him. An outraged Hira sent the army to capture him, but the crafty Gulab submitted without a fight. He won the soldiers over with many gifts, and turned them against Hira. Hira's maneuver came to nothing, except that he now holds Gulab's son Sohan hostage here in Lahore."

This is an interesting development: perhaps I can use it at some point for Dalip's benefit. But it doesn't account for Mangla's distress.

"Tell me the real issue."

She speaks haltingly. "Jalla must have an informant somewhere in our household. He has accused you openly in the court of having an abortion. He said that an immoral woman like you cannot be the regent of Punjab. The court is considering his proposal that you be removed and Dalip be put in Hira's care."

Faint with shock and rage, I have to lie down again. Mangla apologizes profusely, but I thank her. "I needed to know this. Send for Jawahar and Avtar. We must fight back."

After much debate, I decide to pay a surprise visit to the court the next morning with the two vaids, who will testify that I had the pox. My three advisers beg me not to do this; I'm too weak and might have a relapse. The vaids say the same thing when I send them word. But I am determined.

Dressed in stark white, my hair in a tight knot that makes me look even more haggard, and covered by a thick veil, I walk to court, leaning on Jawahar. We're followed by the physicians. I'm pleased by the shock on the courtiers' faces, even Jalla's, when I enter. His informants don't know everything, then! Halfway to my seat, I falter and have to hold on to Jawahar. It isn't play-acting; I'm weaker than I thought. For a moment, everything goes black. But I exert all my willpower and make it to my kursi.

Waheguru, punish me at another time. But please help me now.

Before Jalla or Hira can say anything, I begin. My voice quavers with weakness and anxiety, but I push on. "Respected durbar, my character has been wrongfully blackened by certain personages who wish to exile me from court. I've risen from my sickbed and come here today, against the vaids' orders, to tell you the truth and seek justice. Dalip and I were both deathly ill from the pox. It is only by Waheguru's grace that we are alive."

I turn to Hira. "You know this. You visited the Sheesh Mahal when I was delirious. Tell the court—"

Hira looks away. "I saw the queen in bed, but I was kept afar by her attendants. I cannot vouch for her statement."

Hira, I'll remember this!

I force down my fury. "These two royal physicians who attended us through our illness will support me."

The vaids corroborate my story, giving vivid details of our illness and its dangers. Most of the nobles listen with horrified sympathy, but Jalla jumps to his feet. "Physicians can be bribed. You cannot trust the queen! She is most conniving. The child was sick with the pox, I admit that. But she was bedridden for the most shameful of reasons."

The courtiers murmur, confused. Some look suspicious. No one speaks up for me. I'm paying the price for having allowed my hard-earned position in the durbar to slide. There is only one final desperate act I can think of. I rise unsteadily to my feet. My hands shake. As everyone stares, I pull off my veil.

There's a collective gasp as I turn my pox-ravaged face to the courtiers. Except for Lal, who looks down at his hands, no one has seen me uncovered before. A part of me shrivels under their avid gaze, but I force myself to not turn away. I say nothing. I don't need to. After a few moments, a cacophony of outraged voices berates Jalla. As I'm helped back to my rooms by Jawahar and the physicians, I allow myself a bitter smile. The destruction of my beauty has served some purpose, after all.

Lying in bed in a stupor of exhaustion, I think of the power of that flimsy cloth, the veil. It helped me win a crucial battle today. I must learn how to use this unique weapon to its fullest.

I START ATTENDING COURT in short spurts. I'm fatigued afterward and lie for hours in bed, but the nobles are listening to me again. I spend as much time with Dalip as I can and I'm gratified to see his bad habits falling away. I meet with Avtar regularly and keep myself informed of the goings-on in Punjab. Thus I know that letters go back and forth between Gulab and the British; the army panches and Hira are at loggerheads; Hira plans to curb the army by reducing its size; Peshaura, who had taken refuge with the British, is planning to return to Punjab with their blessing to stir up trouble.

Lal sends message after message begging to see me. It takes all my willpower to not reply. As penitence, I vow that on the next Sankrant I will visit Gurdwara Dehra Sahib and give generously to the poor in gratitude for our recovery. The royal cooks prepare trays of sweetmeats. Mangla buys a hundred shawls from the Kabuli traders. I requisition twenty bags of silver coins from the treasury.

On Sankrant morning, I make my way on foot, as a devout Sikh should, across the qila to the Alamgiri Gate. Servants bearing trays and bundles follow me. Avtar accompanies me with a handful of guards—a mere formality as the gurdwara is just outside the qila. Several of the courtiers' wives join our procession, for somehow word has spread. Outside the gate, a crowd awaits. When they see me, they cheer exuberantly.

But someone else is also waiting: Jalla, with a large contingent of armed men. He blocks my path. "Rani Jindan, what are you taking out of the qila?"

How dare he question me! But I don't want to fight him now, so I respond politely. "I'm going to the gurdwara to give thanks and give alms."

"Indeed, you have much to be thankful for." Jalla's sneer leaves no doubt as to what he's implying. "But you cannot give away the wealth of the durbar like this, without the court's permission. You may take the sweets and shawls, but I must return the coins to the treasury."

I'm taken aback by his audacity. "By what authority do you do this?"

He bares his teeth in a grin. "By the authority vested in me by Raja Hira Singh."

I am shaking with anger. Over the years, I've seen the amount kings toss away on hunts and banquets and courtesans. Compared to that, twenty bags of silver is nothing. Every time Hira has sent our army to fight his kinsmen, it has cost a thousand times more than my simple offering. But I refuse to demean myself by arguing with Jalla, especially in front of the citizens.

"I will reimburse the treasury from my personal allowance," I say. "Move out of my path so that I may go to the gurdwara."

Jalla allows me to pass, but first he counts every bag of money. The crowd whispers angrily. Someone calls *Shame!* Others take up the cry. Jalla, unmoved, takes his time. Finally I'm allowed to proceed.

I force myself to maintain my composure. At the gurdwara, I distribute gifts and accept the granthi's blessing. But inside I'm seething. My peaceful pilgrimage has been ruined by Jalla. As I bow in front of the Guru Granth, I pledge to make him—and Hira—suffer for it.

The next day I send Avtar to the cantonment with a secret message: Rani Jindan and Maharaja Dalip wish to pay their respects to the Khalsa army.

DALIP, JAWAHAR, AND I leave the qila in an unmarked carriage and are welcomed by the panches. I find myself shivering. I'm about to make the riskiest move of my life. If it works, it'll destroy Hira and Jalla's power. If not, it'll destroy me.

I waste no time on niceties. I tell the chiefs that I've come to request them to right a great wrong. I describe how Jalla tried to stop me from giving alms at the gurdwara. My voice quivers with emotion. I don't try to control it. I want the chiefs to feel my outrage, to share it.

"Jalla has humiliated me before," I end. "He slandered me in the durbar. He tried to separate my son from me and banish me from court. I overlooked these attacks for the good of the kingdom. But this time he insulted my holy vow. He demeaned our Sikh religion in full view of the populace. Should we allow this slight to go unpunished?"

I see the incensed faces of the chiefs and push forward. "Jalla is so swollen with pride that he believes he can get away with anything. He acts as though Hira and he are the real rulers of Punjab, and Maharaja Dalip Singh, a nobody. Khalsa ji, only you have the power to remedy this situation."

"Hira and Jalla have treated us badly, too," a panch says. "Hira sends us here and there to fight his personal battles as though we're his servants."

Others join in angrily.

He lies to us.

He cuts our pay.

He fired five hundred of our brothers this week, just because he felt like it.

It's all that crooked Jalla's doing.

"Shameful," I say, "to abuse the Sarkar's great army in this manner. If I were in power, I'd never do that."

The panches come to a quick decision: "We'll teach Hira and Jalla a lesson they'll never forget." They advise us to remain in the cantonment, where we'll be safe while they mobilize the army. They agree when I request to meet with the soldiers.

I borrow a horse and a speaking trumpet. I'm still so weak that I have to be helped into the saddle. But when I meet the army, I sit straight and tall, the way the Sarkar did even in his final days. I'm heartened by the applause. When it quietens, I speak simply. "My son and I thank you for being our champions. If by Waheguru's grace I come to power, I will not forget you." In one swift move, I toss away my veil. "You are my own family. I'm entrusting you with my honor and my life. Why then should I hide my face from you?"

The cheers are deafening. I think they'll never stop.

"Victory to Mai Jindan, Mother of the Khalsa and our true ruler. We will not fail you."

INFORMATION TRICKLES TO US as we wait anxiously in the cantonment. The army has besieged the qila. The panches have ordered Hira to give up the post of wazir. They'll let him leave Lahore safely if he hands over Jalla, who must be punished for his insolence to the queen. Hira asks if he might meet with their leaders to discuss these terms. The panches agree.

"Hira will never give up Jalla," I tell Jawahar. "He must be planning something."

Sure enough, Hira manages to get word to his uncle Gulab, who puts aside their enmity to dispatch his Dogra regiments to help his nephew. Perhaps he does it because his son Sohan is a hostage in Lahore. Hira and Jalla attempt to escape under cover of darkness, taking Sohan with them. They also steal several cartloads of treasure—just as the shrewd Gulab had done when he had abandoned Chand.

The enraged Khalsa army chases them.

We fret all day, waiting.

"Hira and his party are probably halfway to Jammu by now," Jawahar says, sighing.

"Never mind," I say. "All I want is to be rid of them."

At dusk, Avtar brings us news. The Khalsa army caught up with Hira before he could reach Jammu. A bloody battle took place. Hira, Jalla, and Sohan were killed. Their heads, impaled on spears, are being paraded through the streets of Lahore.

Jawahar leaps up, ecstatic. "Serves them right! Now, sister, you can be a proper queen, with the power to do whatever you want."

But I'm deeply troubled. Much as I'd hated Hira and Jalla, I hadn't wanted the army to slaughter them. And Sohan, poor young man, was an innocent victim. I'm shocked at the army's brutal ways. Surely, Gulab will seek vengeance for the deaths of his son and nephew.

The Khalsa army is a powerful beast. Now that I've unleashed it, will I be able to control it?

29

Jawahar

I RETURN IN TRIUMPH TO THE qila the next day, accompanied by the cheering ghorcharhas. The citizens lining the roads take up the cry: *Long live Mai Jindan! Long live Maharaja Dalip!* The following day, I dress for durbar in my usual white, but I no longer cover my face. I know I am beautiful. My skin is almost back to normal, thanks to Mangla's poultices. Dalip walks by my side. Jawahar follows close behind. The courtiers, many of whom had chafed under Jalla's tyranny, welcome me enthusiastically. When I sit in the Sarkar's seat with Dalip on my lap, they call me "Mother of the Sikhs' and give me a standing ovation.

In my first days, I assure the court that I will live by the Sarkar's principles, rewarding loyalty and ability. Sikhs, Hindus, and Muslims will be treated equally. I award high posts to experienced courtiers from different faiths: Diwan Dina Nath, Fakir Nuruddin, and Attar Singh Kalianwala. In only one respect am I adamant: Jawahar must be the wazir.

Although he has no experience, I'm confident that I can teach my brother whatever he needs to learn. I know he'll be completely loyal, and more importantly, I want someone who loves me to share my glory.

However, the courtiers and panches oppose me, and even the astute Avtar suggests that I reconsider, which troubles me. The panches are troublingly partial to Prince Peshaura—perhaps because he's charismatic, brave, and excels in fighting and hunting, like the Sarkar did. They suggest that I invite him back from exile and make him wazir.

I'll never do that. Peshaura's presence at court will be deeply dangerous to Dalip. Once he's here, it would be easy for him to persuade the army that he'd be a better king for Punjab than a seven-year-old. So I cajole the panches, using all my charm and giving the soldiers a pay increase, until they agree to try out my plan. I send a secret message to Peshaura: *Stay away and be safe.* I offer him money and a jagir and am relieved when he accepts.

I warn Jawahar that we must both be on our best behavior. The gruesome deaths of the Attariwalas and Hira have shown me that the Khalsa army can transform quickly from an ally into a deadly enemy. And that they hold their rulers to high moral standards. Thus, when Jawahar goes to Hira's mansion and seizes his wealth—gold coins worth many lakhs—I make him turn it over to the toshakhana in full view of the nobles. We use it partly for charity and partly to strengthen Punjab's outlying forts, and I ensure the news reaches the army as well as the common people. I make sure that Hira, Sohan, and even Jalla are given honorable funerals. I grant Gulab immunity to attend the last rites and when he comes, I treat him respectfully. I offer him my condolences and tell him that I had not wanted these deaths. But he doesn't believe me. Even as he thanks me, I can see hatred glittering in his eyes. I've made an enemy for life. After Gulab returns to Jammu, I tell Avtar to have our spies watch him.

Each week, I meet secretly with Avtar, Jawahar, and Mangla to discuss the state of the kingdom. My two main concerns are the British and Peshaura.

The British have grown increasingly aggressive. Messages go back and forth between them and Gulab and Peshaura. They have strengthened Ferozepur with additional soldiers and artillery and, more worrisome, a fleet of flat-bottomed boats that might quickly be put together to form a pontoon bridge for an army to cross the Sutlej. Their new agent in Ludhiana, Broadfoot, is rude and aggressive. The durbar is humiliated when he fires at our judge, Lal Singh Adalti, whom we'd sent to our own territory on the other side of the river on court business. I send an official complaint to Hardinge, but I remind my durbar of the Sarkar's philosophy: *Don't start a war against the British. No good has ever come of it to any Hindustani ruler.*

For the moment, they listen to me.

LAL AND I HAVE become lovers again. I hadn't planned it, but late one night he came unannounced into the Sheesh Mahal and told me that he couldn't live without me.

"If you will not take me back," he cried, kneeling at my feet and covering my hands with kisses, "then banish me, or better still, execute me. That will be better than seeing you every day in court, so near and yet so distant."

I couldn't resist him. Perhaps I didn't try. I asked myself: *What's the worst that can happen? Due to the botched abortion, I cannot get pregnant again. Don't I deserve a little happiness?* We continue to be discreet, meeting clandestinely, and I'm vigilant in durbar, treating him no different from the other noblemen. But Avtar informs me that news has traveled.

The panches visit me and speak in their frank way.

"Mai Jindan, we realize that you were widowed at a very young age. It is difficult for anyone, man or woman, to live out their lives alone. That is why our religion encourages remarriage. Our Sarkar himself married several widows and gave them his protection. We would support your marriage to an appropriate Sikh chieftain."

"Only to a Sikh?"

They understand what I'm asking. Displeasure darkens their faces.

"We have called you Mai. We have put you on the throne as Mother of the Khalsa. You may only marry a Sikh."

I promise to consider it, but in my heart I know I cannot share my bed with anyone other than Lal.

I'm angered, too. What gives the army the right to control my personal life?

JAWAHAR'S NEW POSITION HAS gone to his head. He is hosting banquet after banquet in his haveli. I hear about alcohol, opium, and a fawning coterie that encourages his excesses. He no longer attends my briefings with Avtar, and often keeps Mangla away, too. Bleary-eyed and muddle-headed in court, he usually sits silent, or says foolish things. If any courtiers question him, he grows sullen. When I admonish him—and I only do so in private—he loses his temper.

"You think I'm wasting time and money," he rages, "but I'm making powerful allies. You'll see when the time comes."

His remarks worry me. Have I made a mistake in appointing him wazir?

THE COURT IS ABUZZ with Peshaura's latest exploit. He entered Punjab secretly, with just seven companions, and managed to seize Attock Fort. The soldiers there have accepted him as overlord, as have the local people. Even my courtiers admire his bold maneuver. Several grizzled commanders say that he's a true son of the Sarkar. I can see what they're thinking: Peshaura would be a strong ruler. I fume inwardly, but I suggest that we parley with Peshaura and learn what his intentions are.

When Jawahar rises, I tense, but he's remarkably calm and

clear. He insists that we cannot encourage insurgence. It will set a dangerous precedent. He points out that Peshaura is a British sympathizer. They gave him sanctuary and brainwashed him in the process. Perhaps he is planning to invite them into Punjab. Hasn't he already negotiated with the Barakzais, asking for arms and soldiers and offering them Peshawar in return?

Impressed—and surprised—by his cogent arguments, I rush to support him. "We must capture Peshaura and bring him to Lahore. At that point, the durbar in its wisdom can decide what is to be done."

The court agrees. Jawahar asks for a commander to lead the expedition. Two of his close friends, Chattar Singh and Fateh Khan, volunteer. A large contingent of soldiers goes off to Attock. We wait, but I'm not too worried. Our army will easily overpower Peshaura's ragtag forces.

DALIP COMES RUNNING. "BIJI, Biji, see the lights."

I look out of the window of the Sheesh Mahal. The qila walls are lined with glimmering lamps. Fireworks explode above us in the night sky. I stare in astonishment. There's no festival today. Why are we celebrating?

"Who arranged for this?"

"Uncle Jawahar. Aren't they pretty, Biji?"

I hurry outside. There's my brother, in the middle of the rose garden, instructing servants to set up more lamps.

"Peshaura is dead!" he shouts in triumph.

I can smell the wine on his breath.

"Fool!" I cry. "No matter how pleased we might be at the turn of events, we can't celebrate the death of one of the Sarkar's sons."

"Turn of events!" He doubles over, laughing. "It didn't happen by chance. I arranged it!"

Shock silences me.

"I planned it all, with Chattar and Fateh. They told him they didn't want to fight him, that they would bring him to the durbar as a respected guest. Peshaura fell for it. The army, too, thought it was a great idea—the fools! On the way back, Chattar and Fateh asked Peshaura if he wanted to go boar hunting with them. We knew he loved things like that. They got him off on his own, and that was the end of it! Now Dalip is safe."

"Idiot!" I cry. "You've endangered us all. What do you think the panches will do when they find out?" I send Jawahar with a few servants to his haveli to sober up. And I order the lamps to be put out and the fireworks to be stopped. But I fear it's too late. People all over Lahore will have seen us celebrating. Soon they'll know why.

I send for Avtar and Mangla to see how the situation might be salvaged. But before we have time to strategize, a soldier arrives with a message from the panches, signed with their holy seal, the Akal Sahai, which cannot be denied.

Turn over the murderer Jawahar to us.

EARLY IN THE MORNING, Jawahar, Dalip, Mangla, and I dress in plain white to signify our repentance and ride out on two elephants loaded with gold and silver. We're alone. None of the courtiers dared take our side against the army. I cannot blame them. Jawahar is clearly guilty. Still, he is my blood; I cannot abandon him. In spite of my misgivings, I've allowed him to put Dalip on his elephant, hoping that my son's innocent presence will keep Jawahar safe from the wrath of the panches. Sitting behind me, the usually calm Mangla is silent and stiff with tension. This makes me additionally afraid.

I've brought my speaking trumpet, hoping that I can bribe the army into sparing my brother, but the soldiers lined up at the qila gate give me no opportunity. They surround our elephants and forcefully escort us to their camp in Mian Mir, where the stone-faced panches are waiting. I offer them our deepest apologies and a huge increase in pay—twelve rupees per month—for every soldier. I present to them all the riches I've brought and beg them to forgive Jawahar. I even promise to banish him from the durbar. But as I'm speaking, soldiers gallop up to our elephants. They remove Dalip from Jawahar's arms, force Mangla and me to dismount, and escort the three of us to a tent. Behind me, I can hear Jawahar calling desperately. *Jindan, Jindan, sister, help me!* I struggle with my guards, trying to run back to him, but they are too strong. As I watch in horror, a ghorcharha rides up to Jawahar with an upraised sword and plunges it into him. Other soldiers join in. Mangla has the foresight to clap her hand over Dalip's eyes, but I see the blood pouring from Jawahar's body as they stab him over and over. His white kurta, the elephant's howdah, the earth—all is red. I can't bear to look anymore. I fall to the ground. I hear a woman shrieking and realize it's me. My cries are drowned out by the jubilant soldiers who yell that justice is done.

All night long I lie on the ground, weeping. In the morning I wipe my tears and ask the panches for my brother's body so that I may give it a proper funeral. At first, they refuse.

"Peshaura's body was chopped into pieces and thrown into a river," one of them says. "We should do the same to Jawahar."

I stand silent. I will not beg. Nor will I weep. Finally the panches take pity on me and send Jawahar's corpse back to the qila.

With Mangla's help, I prepare the body for cremation. A small pyre is built outside the Masti Darwaza. It is a simple funeral: no processions or music, no heaped sandalwood, no ragis singing. A line of armed soldiers keep watch, their expressions stern. Just a handful of courtiers are brave enough to attend the ceremony, and among them, only Lal dares to step forward and stand by my side. A lone granthi offers prayers. The flames flicker hesitantly.

My dearest brother, I promise to avenge you, if it's the last thing I do.

THE COURTIERS HAD NEVER been particularly fond of Jawahar, but they're surprisingly sympathetic toward my loss. Perhaps it's because they are beginning to realize how dangerous the army has become. The durbar rules the kingdom, but the panches rule us. Tomorrow, they could decide to put any one of us to the sword, and who would stop them? The courtiers agree with me (though only in secret) that we must curb the power of the soldiers and teach them a lesson. But we're unable to come up with a plan. Meanwhile, I make use of their sympathies to insist that Lal should become the new wazir. I point out that he is an experienced statesman, trusted by Dhian. They agree reluctantly. Only one man, Sardar Tej Singh, a relative newcomer at court whom Lal has befriended, is enthusiastic.

Over the next few months, I behave as though I've put Jawahar's murder behind me. I invite the brigades to perform their maneuvers outside the qila gates. I have Dalip give them gifts. I accept their accolades as Mother of the Khalsa. When the panches ask me again to marry a Sikh chieftain, I act willing and ask them to give me some suitable names. Beneath my smile, my vow of revenge burns like a fire covered with ashes.

Lal is my one solace. He holds me as I weep into the night, or watches me helplessly as I pace up and down. He's the only person I can talk to about Jawahar, because Mangla—otherwise so strong—still dissolves into tears if I bring up his name. Lal listens patiently as I describe how Jawahar risked beatings to steal food for our family. How he took me foraging for guavas, how he listened patiently to my dreams. How he was my only protector against Manna, how he'd saved his first salary to buy me red jutis.

Lal has agreed to support me in my plan to humiliate the army, but he's honest enough to point out its dangers. "The only way to break their pride is to pitch them into a battle where they'll suffer casualties. But weakening them will also weaken Punjab."

"Are you with me or against me?" I ask, fuming, because I know he is right.

"I'm always with you, my love," he says, sighing. "Even when it's against my better judgment."

Lal spends more time with me nowadays, entire evenings when we dine or listen to music before we go off to my chamber. I've introduced him to Dalip, and perhaps because he misses Uncle Jawahar, my son has taken to him. Lal shows him how to make his lattoo spin, how to play danda goli. Sometimes they wrestle. He wants to take Dalip hunting, and laughs when I tell him Dalip is too young. He says I'm being overprotective. Perhaps he's right. Since Jawahar's death, I cannot bear to let my child out of my sight.

Tonight, as we play chess—at which I am better than Lal—Avtar arrives with news. It must be bad because he's hesitant to speak. Or perhaps it's because Lal is with me. When I order him to speak freely, he reports, with some embarrassment, that the English laat has come up with a new ploy to weaken my power. He has bribed some of my own countrymen to go around the countryside blackening my name, gossiping about the many lovers I've had for years, some even while the Sarkar was alive. Among them, Gulloo the water carrier, Suchet in whose home in Jammu I lived, and now Lal. The British call me the Messalina of the Punjab, after a promiscuous queen of their culture. Gulab Singh is an ally in this plot.

I'm stunned by the lies, but also by the Englishmen's presumption of superiority. How dare these outsiders, these looters, judge me? I'm particularly incensed at the ungrateful Gulab, to whom I'd extended amnesty so that he could collect the ashes of his dead kin.

I've done nothing wrong—nothing except follow my heart. But the world is cruel to women who love. Even the pure and beautiful Heer was poisoned by her own kin only because of her passion for Ranjha.

"They besmirch my name because I'm a woman," I fume.

"It's the way of the world, dearest," Lal says. "That's why I keep begging you to marry me."

The practical Mangla says, "What you need is a way to demonstrate to the public your devotion to God, your son—and your husband, even after his death."

She's right. Once I calm down, I come up with a plan: I'll finish the construction of the Sarkar's Samadhi as I'd vowed long ago. Then I'll go to Amritsar with Dalip and the courtiers, to pay my respects at the Golden Temple.

And meanwhile I'll spend every moment thinking of a way to make the British pay for their heinous, underhanded attack on me.

A FEW DAYS AFTER the Samadhi is completed, I walk into the durbar to find the courtiers in an uproar. Our spy from the Sutlej border has brought troubling information. The British are marching to Ferozepur. They're only forty miles from Lahore and they have trebled their store of guns.

"Hardinge himself will be arriving in the cantonment soon," Diwan Dina Nath announces. "They've put together the flat-bottomed boats they brought earlier and created a pontoon bridge. Now tell me, why would they do that unless they intend to attack us?"

Our spy has managed to obtain copies of letters being sent between Englishmen in high places. One reads, *We shall cross the Sutlej, sooner or later.*

The peaceful Nuruddin says, "But we have a treaty with them."

I believe the British are merely posturing, but they've created an opportunity for me. "Have the British been known to uphold their treaties?"

Tej Singh leaps up. "They have not!" He recites a litany of kingdoms—Coorg, Mysore, the Maratha Empire—where the British violated previous treaties and struck while the kings were trustingly oblivious. I'm impressed by his knowledge, passion—and ambition. I will keep him in mind as I strategize further.

"Is that what we want to happen to Punjab?" I ask.

A deafening roar drowns out the voices of the few moderate courtiers. "We do not! Let us teach these treacherous firangs a lesson they will remember."

"We must plan carefully," I caution. I recommend a visit to the Golden Temple to seek Waheguru's blessings. Then we'll meet at the Sarkar's Samadhi with the army panches and make our final decision about war. Everyone agrees. My plan is now in motion. The British are in for an unpleasant surprise.

"And if, in the process, the Khalsa army suffers," I say to Lal that night, "so be it. In the future they'll think twice before they try to control Rani Jindan."

THANKS TO MY EFFORTS, the Sarkar's Samadhi, neglected for so long, is now as grand as any palace in the qila. Its domes gleam white and gold in the evening light as we file in solemnly. Inside, the walls are inlaid with precious stones. The marble urn holding my husband's ashes shines, newly polished. The courtiers and panches sit down side by side, their differences forgotten, while Dina Nath lists the latest perfidies of the British. They are demanding tributes from our territories, including our sacred city, Anandpur. When we asked the British agent to explain this behavior, he threatened to sever diplomatic relationships. Clearly, war is coming. Are we to wait until the British march on Lahore?

The assembly agrees unanimously that we must make preparations. We will not fire the first shot, but our soldiers will cross the Sutlej and move into our territories on the other side of the river. As is customary, the wazir will lead the army, along with a commander of his choice. Lal proposes Tej Singh as his fellow commander. To support Lal, I agree enthusiastically, so the panches accept him. The assembly approaches the urn one by one, vowing loyalty. When we emerge from the Samadhi and announce our decision, the air is rent with cheers. Hundreds of soldiers, waiting outside, cry, "We will protect our Punjab with the last drop of our blood!"

I find myself weeping. Partly it's the gravity of the moment, and partly guilt. It would have been safer to amass our troops on this side of the Sutlej. If indeed the British crossed the river to launch an offensive—which was unlikely—we would have been in a better position to fight back—and completely in the right. If I'd spoken up strongly, suggesting this, the assembly might have listened. But I allowed battle hysteria to take hold of the panches. Now it's too late.

How many men will die because of my hatred of the British, and my desire to avenge myself on the army? I remember the girl from a long time ago, who told the Sarkar that it saddened her to think of Sikh soldiers dying, their faces turned toward their homes. How far I've traveled from her!

THE INITIAL BATTLE PLANS are complete. Within a week the army will be sent to four strategic points: Rupar, Ludhiana, Harike, and Ferozepur. Busy with preparations, Lal hasn't had time to visit me for the last few days, so when he arrives tonight, we kiss hungrily. I want to know every detail. How does it feel? Is he excited? Impatient? Anxious? Calm and clear-sighted, like the Sarkar used to be? I want to experience, through him, the warrior's life that will never be mine.

But he holds me by the hand and says, urgently, "Come away with me." My face must show my shock, because he continues quickly, in his most persuasive tones, "We can leave secretly tomorrow night. We'll take Dalip with us—and Mangla, if you wish. I have enough money to take care of you. We can live anonymously, peacefully, far from battles and constant plotting. Dalip is too young to care. We can give him a happy childhood, a safe and comfortable life. Please don't say no. This is our last opportunity to be a true family."

I'm deeply tempted by the life Lal is offering me. It's a chance to bring Dalip up far from the ugly intrigues of the court. I can see myself married to Lal, managing a small, prosperous household in a quiet town by a lake. In the evenings, when he returned from work, we would sit in our courtyard, drinking lassi and sharing the details of our day. Most importantly, we wouldn't have to hide our love. As the thought occurs to me, I realize how much I've hated being secretive, how, deep inside, I've worried that soon Dalip will grow older and despise me for it.

But I can't do it. For better or worse, I am Rani Jindan, mother of Maharaja Dalip Singh, Mother of the Khalsa. That is my identity and my fate.

In my agitation, I lash out. "How can you even think of deserting your soldiers, who are depending on you?"

At once I know that is the wrong thing to say. Lal has just offered to give up everything he's worked so hard for, including his reputation, for me. He's even willing to be known as a deserter and a coward. I should have expressed my gratitude and explained how painfully torn I am between responsibility and passion. But it's too late.

"Love makes us foolish," he says coldly. "You should know—your love for your dead brother is pushing us into an unnecessary war against an enemy that is stronger, more cunning, and far superior to us in strategy." He takes a deep breath and holds me by the shoulders. "If I'm not there to lead the army, the panches might reconsider this dangerous move."

I'm troubled by Lal's opinion of the British, but I've made up my mind. I push away his hands and say, "I cannot deprive Dalip of his birthright—his throne—for the sake of my own happiness. And I cannot abandon my army on the eve of battle."

"Have you considered that Dalip may not have a throne left at the end of this—and you may not have an army?"

There's an expression on Lal's face that I cannot read. Might it be resignation? He bows with stiff formality and leaves. I make no attempt to stop him. For now, we've exhausted the possibility of words. I have good hope, though, that things will be better when he returns, buoyed up by victory.

We don't see each other privately again. Three days later, he leads the Khalsa army to war.

30

Treachery

THE DURBAR IS A SKELETON of its former self. Many courtiers have joined the army and left for the front, along with their troops. Sham Singh Attariwala, Gulab Gupta, Mubarak Ali, Hira Singh Topee—I miss their gallant presence. Nevertheless, we are not alone. The fields outside the qila are filled with citizens. Together, we wait eagerly for reports from the battlefront.

The news is heartening. Lal has crossed the Sutlej safely. The British are nowhere to be seen. He has entrenched his soldiers in the village of Pheru Shahr, in a good location, with seven drinking wells. Tej is marching toward Ferozepur, as planned. Lal takes a smaller force on reconnaissance, to find out where the British are hiding. He comes upon a very large company near Mudki. There's a great battle. Our men fight valiantly. Many British are killed. Finally, our soldiers fall back, but they've frightened the British so much that their commander sends to Delhi for reinforcements.

But deep at night, Mangla wakes me. Avtar is here, his expression so bleak that I'm sure Lal has been killed. No, it's worse. One of our best spies intercepted a messenger that Lal sent to Captain Nicholson at Ferozepur. Threatened with death for himself and his clan, the messenger showed our spy the message and, on his way back, the reply.

Lal wrote, *I have crossed the Sutlej with the Sikh army. You know of my friendship with the British. I will do as you say.*

In his reply, Nicholson instructed him not to attack Ferozepur, as it was not yet well-defended, but to take a small force and march, instead, toward the main British army, led by the experienced veteran, Gough. That was the army our forces came upon, as though by chance, at Mudki.

Avtar tells me more: at Mudki, even against the larger British army, we were doing well. Our snipers were particularly effective in taking out enemy targets. But in the middle of the battle, Lal deserted his men and retreated to Pheru Shahr, leaving them leaderless.

"He's the reason we lost that fight," Avtar says through clenched teeth.

I am stunned. Clearly, Lal's relationship with the British had started a while back. How is it that I hadn't sensed anything? Had my infatuation blinded me so completely to his real nature? Or did he decide to betray Punjab only after I refused to go away with him? Was this his way of punishing me?

Sleep eludes me the rest of the night. I try to imagine what the Sarkar would do, but it's no use. No one would have dared betray him like this. Toward dawn, heartsore, I lie down with Dalip. He snuggles against me sleepily. "I'm sorry," I whisper into his hair. "I've endangered your throne with my blindness. Will you hate me for this some day?"

In the morning I announce my findings to the shocked court. We send a decree, signed with the royal seal, to Lal, with a company of experienced soldiers. Their orders are to bring him back—by force if necessary. *We know of your treachery. Turn the army over to Tej and return to Lahore immediately.*

Our soldiers do not return. A few days later Avtar brings more bad news. Tej, too, is part of Lal's conspiracy. He was supposed to storm Ferozepur and defeat General Littler's army, but he allowed the firang soldiers to escape and join the larger British force.

I'm devastated by this additional treachery, but the army, Waheguru bless them, doesn't let us down. When the British assault the Punjab camp at Pheru Shahr, the men fight into the dead of night. The British suffer huge casualties and have to fall back. Victory seems imminent, especially when Tej arrives with reinforcements. Then, inexplicably, Tej and Lal retreat, leaving their gallant soldiers without any direction, flailing in confusion. The British use this opportunity to fall upon the Sikhs, capture their artillery and kill many men. Our soldiers continue to fight, but their supplies run low.

O my dear Khalsa army, what have I done to you!

There's only one choice: I advise the durbar to call upon Gulab for the tribute he still owes us. He agrees to help, to send his Dogra troops with food and ammunition for our troops. We feel briefly hopeful. But Gulab's soldiers never show up. Defeat follows upon defeat, treachery on treachery. I flinch when I see messengers coming from the front.

TODAY, THOUGH, IT'S NOT messengers but a delegation of panches that rides up, uniforms torn and filthy, faces streaked with mud and blood. Durbar has been dismissed, so they come to the Diwan-i-Aam and call for Dalip and me.

"We're laying down our lives for you," they shout. "We demand to see you."

I must meet with them. It's the least I can do, after having sent them to their destruction.

Dalip is frightened, but I tell him that he has to be strong like his father, the great Sarkar. With trembling hands, I seat him on the royal kursi—how small he looks on it—and stand behind a screen.

The leader tells me how the army's positions have been betrayed over and over by Lal and Tej, how they've been ordered to retreat when they were winning. They've eaten nothing in the last few days except raw carrots because Gulab has sent neither soldiers nor supplies. "The men are demoralized and starving," he ends. "You must help us."

I struggle to hold in tears. *My Sarkar, to what straits have I reduced your proud army!* Even in my wildest rages, I'd never wanted this. I want to express my sympathy, but I know that will only make matters worse.

My desperate mind flails around, finally seizing on a story the Sarkar had told me about Sada Kaur. I steel myself and pull off my under-petticoat and throw it out over the screen. I shout, "Give me your clothes and take mine. You remain in the palace and rest. I'll ride to battle in your stead and die as a true Khalsa soldier should."

There's a moment of terrifying silence. Will they, in their fury, attack me—or worse, my innocent Dalip?

Then someone cries, "We will fight! Who cares about death, if it brings glory? We'll gladly give up our lives for our king, our Punjab, and our Mai!"

I come forward and thank them for their loyalty. I give them the best meal the palace cooks can put together. I order attendants to fill up carts with all the food in the qila and send it with the panches to the front. As they ride away, blessing me, I know I've sent them to their doom.

Most of our messengers have been killed by now, so Avtar himself brings the news to the court: the war is over.

When he finishes describing the final battle of the Khalsa army, there are tears in every eye. But soon afterward, several courtiers scurry off. I know they've gone to make their own deals with the British, who will be arriving in Lahore soon. As for me, I send for

Dalip. I sit on the throne one last time, holding him in my lap, and ask Avtar to tell us again how bravely our men fought at Sobraon for their king and their motherland.

"Our troops found themselves trapped between the flooded Sutlej and the British army," Avtar says. "They fired until they ran out of artillery. Only one pontoon bridge remained for them to return to the base camp. Midway through the battle, the coward Tej decided to flee. He tried to persuade his fellow sardars to do the same, but they refused. Tej deserted his soldiers shamefully, escaped across the bridge, and destroyed it. Then Sham Singh Attariwala dressed in white and told his groom, 'Go back and give my family this message: Sham Singh will not be coming home.' He swore on the Granth to fight to the death. His fellow generals—Gulab Gupta, Topee, Mubarak Ali, Nawaz, Kishan Singh—stood by him staunchly, battling the firangs until they fell on the field. Not a single soldier surrendered. Even the British generals were forced to admire their bravery. Ah, the Sarkar would have been proud indeed to see how courageously his precious Khalsa army fought, in spite of their generals' treachery, at Sobraon."

THE VICTORIOUS BRITISH ARE determined to humiliate us. They insist that Dalip should go with his entire court to the village of Lulliani to present the governor-general with the keys to Gobindgarh and Lahore. I'm barred from accompanying them. Dalip looks so small and scared on his elephant that I beg Nuruddin, the only courtier I trust, to ride with him. I don't rest until he's escorted back to the fort by the British cavalry. I'm thankful to see my son safe, but furious that the British make it appear as though they are magnanimously restoring his kingdom to him.

Later I learn from Avtar how shamefully the courtiers allowed our Punjab to be dismembered. The British took our best lands between the Sutlej and the Beas and demanded the impossible amount of one and a half crore rupees as war indemnity. When we could not pay that amount, they took Hazara and Kashmir, which they then sold to Gulab Singh. Thus, the treacherous Gulab became the king of Jammu and Kashmir and kept all of Suchet's wealth, which should have been surrendered to the durbar. Lal and Tej were also handsomely rewarded for their treason, retaining the posts of wazir and commander-in-chief. I'm further incensed when I learn how our courtiers—bootlickers, all of them—brought in our greatest treasures from Gobindgarh to display for Hardinge. How the Sarkar's Koh-i-Noor—my son's inheritance—was passed around carelessly among the joking firang generals as though it were a bauble.

What breaks my heart, though, are the punishments meted out to our army. Large numbers of the Khalsa are disbanded and the rest ordered to move across the Ravi. Many are confined in the Shahdara camp. Sikh soldiers are forbidden to enter Lahore. Homeless and starving, the Sarkar's beloved ghorcharhas roam the countryside. In their place, at great cost to us, a British garrison has been posted in the city and British soldiers strut along our qila walls.

"Why did we give in so quickly to the firangs?" I fume. "I advised the durbar to delay negotiations and call back our armies from Raiban, Peshawar, and Multan. We would have then had more soldiers than Hardinge. But our cowardly courtiers only care to feather their own nests."

"Hush, Mai," Avtar cautions. "The British—or their curs—have spies everywhere. You, especially, are being watched. Please be careful. Things could get worse."

I promise to be discreet for Dalip's sake, but my blood boils when I see the British agent, Lawrence, strolling around the fortress as though he owns it. Nowadays I'm regent in name only; I have been confined to the zenana and am no longer allowed in the Diwan-i-Aam. All state decisions are made by a pliant council set up by the British. They don't dare to do anything that might displease

Hardinge. My only hope is that at the end of the year, when the British garrison leaves us—according to the treaty—to govern ourselves, my situation will improve. Meanwhile, when I'm asked to attend a public programme, I remain silent and veiled. These insidious firangs will never see my face.

But when I come across Lal in the qila courtyard, I cannot control myself. I spit on him and say, "I'm deeply ashamed that I ever loved a traitor like you. May you be cursed by the riches your British masters have tossed to you, wealth soaked in the blood of the Khalsa." He tries to visit me in the Sheesh Mahal, but I give strict instructions to turn him away.

Perhaps my words shame Lal, because he finds an ally—Sheikh Imamuddin of Kashmir—and incites him to rebel against the British. But it is too late. The British vanquish Imamuddin easily, Lal's role in the conspiracy is exposed, and he is exiled from Punjab. Avtar tells me that he has moved to distant Dehra Dun; perhaps he has finally found the quiet life he had dreamed of for both of us.

AT THE END OF the year, I learn to my dismay that the durbar is planning to request the British garrison to remain. I insist on speaking to the courtiers, entreating them to reconsider.

"Don't hand over our motherland to the firangs. Don't become their vassals. Our brave soldiers will come back if we call on them. They'll re-form the Khalsa army and protect Punjab—as they've always done. I'm willing to be the liaison between you and them."

But, greedy for the jagirs and titles the British have secretly promised them, the courtiers sign the Treaty of Bhairowal behind my back. Lawrence becomes both Resident and governor of Punjab, more powerful than the entire council. The British garrison stays on and is paid twenty-two lakh rupees a year. Dalip becomes a ward of the British government—as though he were an orphan. And I?

I'm pensioned off with a pittance and confined even more strictly to the zenana.

In my fury, I forget my promise to Avtar. I send secret messages to the citizens of Lahore, telling them how wrongly I, the Mother of the Khalsa, am being treated. I urge them to resist the firangs; it is our land, not theirs. My messages are whispered into many ears. They ignite my people. There are uprisings in various places. British soldiers, if found alone, are attacked. One day, a few of them beat some cows for getting in their way. As retribution, they're stoned by a crowd. Lawrence punishes the attackers, hanging one of them publicly. More people turn against him.

Among the rebels is a man named Prema, who was stripped of his possessions by Gulab Dogra. Prema contacts me through one of my clerks. *I'm willing to kill the traitor Tej Singh, along with Lawrence*, he says. *I want you to be queen again*. I dig deep into my dwindling purse and send him money. He plans carefully, but is discovered at the last moment. Even under torture, he refuses to give the British my name. Still, they blame me.

Avtar is now under constant surveillance as well. His visits grow rare, but with Mangla's help he recruits and trains a group of brave women to be his agents. I'm given passwords by which I'll know them. Disguised as hairdressers and tailors, cooks and cleaners, they move about easily. I send one of them to Mulraj, the governor of Multan. I've heard that he is an honest man and hates the British. I entreat him to start a rebellion. I promise him many supporters. But he does not respond.

As I seethe with frustration, another blow falls. The British have decided to make Tej the raja of Sialkot. According to tradition, however, he can only be given this position if the maharaja puts a holy tilak on his forehead.

At last, here's something I can do. I tell Dalip, "Remember the massacre at Sobraon? This traitor, Tej, was responsible for it, and for our ultimate defeat. Because of him, you've lost half your kingdom. You must not reward him. Do not put the tilak on his forehead, no matter who asks you. You are the maharaja, most powerful in the eyes of Waheguru. No one can force you to do wrong."

Dalip, bless him, looks at me unblinkingly and nods as though he were much older than his nine years.

When Tej kneels in front of him in the durbar, Dalip refuses to honor him with the tika. When the other nobles cajole him, he crosses his arms determinedly and stares ahead. From behind the screen, I glow with pride at my son's courage. In the zenana, Mangla and I hug him and tell him he's a true son of the Sarkar. We make sure the citizens of Lahore learn of Tej's humiliation.

Only Avtar looks concerned. "I wish you hadn't made Dalip do that, my queen. You've embarrassed both Tej and Lawrence in public. They will not rest until they get their revenge."

I pout. "You're always worrying! Can't you just let me enjoy my moment of triumph?"

ON A SUNNY AUGUST day, Lawrence invites Dalip, along with a group of courtiers, on an excursion to the Shalimar Gardens, where a flock of rare parrots has made its appearance. Dalip loves parrots, and he has had few amusements lately—when he's not attending durbar, he remains in the zenana with me. So I send him off with my blessings and strict instructions to stay out of the sun because the heat gives him a headache.

Hardly has Dalip's carriage left the qila when Lawrence sends me a message through a clerk. Due to my harmful influence over the maharaja, the governor-general has decided that I am to be separated from Dalip. Additionally, my allowance has been cut down to one-third of the amount promised me earlier. Before I can recover from the shock, women guards—strangers whom Lawrence must have employed for this purpose—pull me from the zenana and force me into a windowless carriage. My maids are dismissed. Mangla is instructed to pack me only a few outfits and the handful of jewels I have in my rooms. An icy numbness descends on me. I know Lawrence will not listen to my pleas to remain in Lahore, or my promises of non-interference in the future, so I don't waste energy on them. I make only one request: I wish to bid Dalip goodbye before I'm parted from him. The clerk returns, shamefaced, to report Lawrence's refusal.

Just before the carriage doors are slammed shut, Mangla throws herself down in front of the horses. I hear her cry, "I will not leave! Send me with my queen, wherever you're taking her—even to death." I hear soldiers shouting abuses as they drag her away. The carriage rattles along the bustling streets of Lahore, filled with my loving subjects. I bang on the carriage doors and shout for help, but no one hears me. People go about their daily lives, placidly ignorant of what the British are doing to their queen. When we finally come to a halt, I discover that I am a prisoner in Sheikhupura Qila.

Sheikhupura, a gloomy, decrepit Mughal fortress, is only a few hours from Lahore. But it might well have been at the other end of Hindustan, because I receive no news of the city, nor does anyone come to see me. It is possible that no one knows, that the British have kept this disgraceful act of separating mother and child secret. Surely my people would rise up against them if they discovered it. Or would they? Perhaps the British have crushed their spirit too thoroughly.

For months, I pace the halls of Sheikhupura, muttering to myself like a madwoman because there's no one here I can share my distress with. I've never been separated from Dalip before this. I'm too distressed to eat. I lose so much weight that my reflection in the tiny sliver of a mirror provided to me looks like a skeleton. If I am so desperate, how much worse must my son be feeling? He's prone to nightmares. Whenever he had one in the past, Mangla and I were always there to comfort him. How is he managing now?

And Mangla, my helper, friend, and confidant during these years, the practical one who kept me moored to earth, who cautioned me out of my follies—*where are you now? I see in my mind, over and over, the soldiers dragging you away. Your only fault was to be faithful to me. It fills me with guilt and despair to imagine what the British have done to you.*

If only I had listened to Avtar when he had advised me not to incite Dalip to refuse the orders of the British. But I let my hot-headedness get the better of me.

Lawrence has withheld even my reduced allowance, in a bid to increase my helplessness. But I bribe a guard with one of my bangles and send a letter to Dalip, along with a few laddus—his favorite sweet. I am careful to keep the note innocuous. *I am well but unable to come to you; I pray for you; be brave and study well. I miss you, my heart.* I don't hear back.

I write to Lawrence, too, berating him for his cruelty in separating mother and child. I beg him to send Dalip to me in Sheikhupura so I can see him at least once. *Or else end my misery by putting me to death.* I complain that my allowance is being withheld, that I'm having to sell my jewelry to receive basic amenities. I threaten to inform the English Queen of these wrongs. I write, *Shame on you for stealing my kingdom through underhand means. Show your true colors if you dare. Declare openly that you've made yourself king of Punjab!* He knows I'm powerless and pays no attention. Instead, he sends out notices everywhere that I, the corrupt and immoral "Messalina of the Punjab," had tried to seduce men into rebelling against the British.

When I'm almost crazed with desperation, the old woman who

cleans my cell falls ill and a younger woman takes her place. As she is sweeping under my bed, she whispers a password and adds that her name is Roshanara. She is one of Avtar's agents! In short, fragmented conversations spread over days so that the guards will not suspect us, she gives me some of the news I'm craving. Mangla has been banished from Punjab—no one knows where she has disappeared to. Avtar has gone into hiding. There's a high price on his head. I ask her to talk to Dalip, or at least get a message to him. But she tells me, sadly, that she cannot. He's closely guarded and never allowed outside the qila. He's well, though, and one of his old servants, Mian Kheema, is still with him. I'm a little relieved to hear this for Kheema has been with Dalip ever since he became king.

The next piece of news is infuriating. Dalhousie has justified his action of separating Dalip from me by announcing that I suffered attacks of madness. He claims I am an unfit mother who beat her child and terrified him; that is why the sweet-natured young maharaja refused to put the tika on Tej Singh's forehead. Even the Queen in England has been presented with this lie. Though Roshanara is quick to add that none of our subjects in Punjab believe this, I cannot hold back vexed tears.

When Roshanara wipes my eyes with her dupatta and asks how she might make my life more bearable, I can think of only one thing. "Give Avtar copies of the letters I wrote to Lawrence. Tell him to send them to our Punjabi papers. I want our people to know my pain as a mother and a queen. I want them to understand how unjustly the British have snatched away Punjab from my Dalip. I want to expose all of Dalhousie's lies."

Soon the letters make their way everywhere. Even my Hindustani guards whisper about them. A holy man, Bhai Maharaj, takes up my cause. He travels the country, exhorting large crowds to fight for the reputation of the Mother of the Khalsa, to come together and drive the British from their land. Nothing changes for the better in my incarceration, but at least my countrymen learn the depth of the perfidy of the British.

RETRIBUTION, IN TYPICAL BRITISH fashion, is swift. From Roshanara, I learn that Lawrence claims to have unearthed a plot to incite the native soldiers in the British garrison to rebel. He blames me as its author. The plot—of which I knew nothing until now—is clearly a fabrication. Three men accused of being my co-conspirators are hanged quickly, without a proper trial. But it allows Lawrence to decree that I am too dangerous to remain in Punjab. I must be exiled.

Even the courtiers, who have let me down so often, are shocked—all except Tej—and beg Lawrence to reconsider, but he is adamant. Once again, before the people of Punjab know what is being done to me, I'm bundled into a carriage and sent even farther away from my son. I do not even get the chance to say goodbye to Roshanara.

During the journey, my baggage is searched by the officers of the battalion escorting me; they rifle through even my few underclothes, claiming that I might be carrying dangerous articles.

"I've been imprisoned all this time," I protest, incredulous. "What could I possibly possess?" They ignore me. Nothing incriminating is found in the search but, as I discover later, several of my valuables go missing.

This time I've been imprisoned in Chunar Fort in distant Benares. The old stone qila, built on a barren hill, is even more bleak and desolate than Sheikhupura, and I have to use all my willpower to keep from spiraling into despair. What little jewelry I have is taken from me by my new warder, Major MacGregor. He claims it will be kept safely and returned when the government decides it is appropriate to do so—an ambivalent statement if ever there was one. My allowance is reduced to an unbelievably meager twelve thousand rupees a year, a fraction of what I had been promised by the Treaty of Bhairowal. Even MacGregor is embarrassed as he informs me of this. I don't bother to respond. What's the point? MacGregor, who seems to be a decent man, attempts to befriend me, but I reject his overtures. I make sure I'm veiled and mutinously silent whenever I'm forced to meet with him. The British are determined to break my spirit. But they don't know Jindan!

My only weakness is Dalip. I haven't seen him for almost a year now. I thought I would get used to his absence and the futility of my sorrow, but each time I think of him, it feels as though someone has cut away my heart and rubbed salt on the wound. I have wept so much this past year that I fear I have ruined my eyesight. Or perhaps my eyes have weakened due to the paltry prison diet, lacking in fresh fruits and vegetables.

Thank Waheguru for my faithful Avtar. The British continue to hunt him, so he must remain hidden. But he manages to get another assistant, a nimble, clever woman named Maahi, a job at the fort—this time as my seamstress. Through her, I send out more letters, making sure that my indignities are known to my people. All over Punjab, people grow enraged at my ill treatment. Revolts flare up across the kingdom. The Khalsa are particularly irate at their Mai's dishonor. Even Dost Mohammed, our longtime enemy, publicly censures the British for their cruelty. In distant Multan, Mulraj's mother champions me and pressures him until he rebels. Sher Singh Attariwala and his father, Chatar Singh, gather a substantial army and attack the British, routing them at Ram Nagar and, especially, Chillianwala. Dost Mohammed sends his Afghan cavalry, led by his son, to help them. It seems as though my beloved Punjab might yet regain her independence. I pace my room at night, too excited to sleep, praying.

But the British mobilize reinforcements from all across Hindustan. They have too many men and, more importantly, too many guns. My old nemesis, Gulab Singh, comes down from Jammu to aid them. Once again, we're betrayed by our own people. At Gujerat, the Sikhs fight valiantly. Three horses are shot down under Sher Singh; still he presses forward. When they run out of ammunition, our soldiers fight with swords and die as heroes. But finally the Attariwalas are forced to surrender. I weep with Maahi as she describes the veteran Khalsa soldiers being forced to hand over their swords.

"Aaj Ranjit Singh mar gaya," she says. Perhaps she's right. Perhaps the Sarkar's spirit has finally been killed.

I think Punjab has reached the nadir of her ill fortune, but I'm mistaken. Governor-General Dalhousie declares that because of the insurrections, the durbar's treaty with the British is now void. The British will therefore annex our kingdom.

Incensed, I tell Maahi, "But my poor Dalip—and even his incompetent court—had nothing to do with the rebellion! They've been paying the British all this while to protect them and keep peace in Punjab. How is this their fault?"

It's clear that Dalhousie is just making an excuse. Haven't the British done this, ultimately, to all their protectorates? It's part of their diabolic plan to crush Hindustan under their heels. I remember what my astute husband said so many years ago: *Sab lal ho jayega.* Indeed, my Punjab, her earth stained by the blood of patriots, has turned red now.

Even though I know what's coming, when Maahi brings me the news, it's like a punch to my stomach. Dalhousie has proclaimed that Punjab now belongs to the British. My son sits on his throne for the last time as he signs away his kingdom. He's only ten. Does he even understand what this means?

His courtiers—weak, treacherous sycophants—do nothing to protect him. Why would they? They'll retain their ill-gotten gains, their jagirs and titles. They'll be comfortable and safe. Dalip is the only one whose immense wealth—including the Koh-i-Noor—is seized by the British. He alone becomes their virtual prisoner. There is talk that soon, like me, he will be sent into exile.

I WAS AFRAID THAT I would break down when I learned what the British have done, but now that everything I cared for is lost, a strange calm descends upon me. Maahi, who has grown close to me over this year of imprisonment, weeps for me every time she visits, but my eyes are dry. I have made a decision, though. Maahi conveys my message to Avtar: *I refuse to remain the firangs' prisoner any longer. If ever you were faithful to me, arrange for my escape. I do not care if I die in the attempt.*

My loyal Avtar. He comes out of hiding at great risk to himself—the British have put a price on his head, and offered even more if he is captured alive—and devises a daring plan. Two weeks after the British have wrested my son's kingdom from him, in the privacy of my bedchamber, Maahi and I exchange clothes. We embrace each other and whisper our goodbyes. I thank her for all she has done for me, the trouble she is sure to face once the British discover our subterfuge. She repeats again the instructions Avtar has sent for me, wishes me Godspeed, and promises to come looking for me once the British release her. Then she lies down in my bed, covered with a quilt, pretending to be sick with a cough, while I veil myself and, carrying her sewing basket on my head, leave the qila. But first I cannot resist writing a taunting note for my warden to find.

You put me in a cage and locked me up. You surrounded me with sentries. You thought you could keep Rani Jindan imprisoned. But look, I got out by magic from under your nose!

THE SUN HAS SET by the time I find my way to the deserted spot on the banks of the Ganga where I'm supposed to meet Avtar. But no one is here. My heart sinks. I have only a few coins with me and no knowledge of the land. Suddenly a man steps out from behind a copse of trees and kneels in front of me. Avtar! I almost don't recognize him because he has grown so thin. He is dressed in a cheap kurta and shawl, like a peasant. His beard is long and unkempt. He touches his forehead to my hand and calls me "Maharani"—a title I had not thought to hear again. We are both too emotional for words, and besides, there is no time. Avtar has hired a little covered boat which was hidden among the river rushes all this while. Now, two boatsmen bring it forward. We climb in quickly. The boat will take us to Patna, a city distant enough that the British will not immediately think of searching for me there. I change into the clothing Avtar has brought: the saffron sari of an ascetic. In Hindustan, it is the safest disguise for a woman. I work river dirt into my uncombed hair until it becomes matted.

Avtar has planned well. In Patna, we stay in a gurdwara which offers free lodging to the poor. At night, after the others have gone to sleep, Avtar unfolds a crumpled map, and we try to figure out where I might find refuge. My prospects look grim. I cannot remain here; the British have too many garrisons in Patna. Nor can I go to Delhi and Bengal, which are in their chokehold. To the north-west, Wajid Ali of Awadh is a possibility, but he is a weakling, as is Raghoji of Nagpur in the south. If the British were to pressure them, Avtar fears they would hand me over without any qualms.

Despairing, I look in the only remaining direction: north. Amid the tiny tented symbols that signify the mighty Himalayas, I read a name. It evokes a memory: the Sarkar advising me in that golden time when it seemed he would live forever. *Our soldiers have fought side by side. Though his kingdom is a distant one, across the mountains, he has sworn to help me and mine if ever the need arises.*

I say, "I will go to the king of Nepal."

Avtar is concerned because it will be a long crossing through treacherous mountain terrain, and I am already weak. Still, he admits that politically Nepal is a better possibility than the others. It is a small kingdom and out of the way. It has a British Resident—which kingdom doesn't?—but he has heard that Prime Minister Jung Bahadur, an upright man and a powerful warrior, still makes the important decisions. "We will start as soon as I get us horses and supplies," he says. "I am afraid that very soon the British will discover that you're missing and start searching in every direction."

Avtar leaves in the morning, but he doesn't return. Afraid to go looking for him, or to ask questions, I wait in the gurdwara. I hear from other travelers that many firang redcoats are scouring the streets of Patna—for rebels, they claim. After three days of no news, I conclude with a heavy heart that some calamity must have befallen Avtar.

All night I pray at the gurdwara. At dawn I wipe my tears and embark on my journey. I will have to mourn my faithful Avtar, my staunch support for so many years, at another time. His sacrifice should not be in vain. I have only a few rupaiyas with me—Avtar had taken most of the money with him to buy horses. I tell the granthi at the gurdwara that I wish to go on a pilgrimage to the famous temple of Pashupatinath Shiva in Nepal. He gives me directions, an old blanket, some rotis, and what little money he can spare.

I take the path that leads north out of the city. I hope to find a group of pilgrims headed the same way, but I have no luck. Never mind, I tell myself, this is better. Since the Sarkar died, haven't I been on my own? Everyone that I depended on—Dhian, Jawahar, Lal, Mangla, and now Avtar—was taken from me. Perhaps we are always alone, from the time we leave the safety of our mothers' wombs until the time Waheguru gathers us to Himself.

I walk until my sandals fall apart. My feet bleed and calluses form. When the pain becomes too much, I comfort myself by imagining the look on MacGregor's face when he read my farewell note. Sometimes I'm able to buy a little milk, a few rotis, some puffed rice. When I run out of money, I beg. But once I leave the townships, there are few people to beg from. Often the route goes through forests where I must watch for wild animals. I collect stones to protect myself. A distant memory surfaces—didn't I do this in Gujranwala, when I was a girl?—but my mind finds it hard to hold on to things. At night I wrap myself in my blanket, tattered now, and sleep under trees or in caves. Days run into each other. I walk as though in a dream. One day I discover that I'm in the mountains. The nights grow so cold that in the mornings when I wake, my blanket is covered with chips of ice. My food runs out. I'm sure I will freeze to death soon, but I'm ready for it. Better death here, under Waheguru's open sky, than in a British prison.

Then miraculously, as I lie exhausted under an overhang of rock, a group of pilgrims comes across me. I fear I've conjured them out of my longing. But no, they are real. By fortunate coincidence, they, too, are on their way to Pashupatinath. Poor peasants from Bengal who have saved for many years to make this journey, they know little of the political upheavals in other parts of the country. They accept my story of being a fellow pilgrim, feed me, and sympathize when I tell them—not untruthfully—that the loss of my son has made me a sannyasin. They invite me to join their company and slow their pace so I can hobble along. They give me warm clothing, wrap my feet in rags, and make me drink an elixir for the wheezing I have developed. They restore, somewhat, my faith in humanity, though I am not sure if I will ever trust anyone fully again.

And so it is that, over a month after I escaped from Chunar, I find myself in Kathmandu, standing in front of Rana Jung Bahadur's mansion.

WHEN JUNG BAHADUR NOTICES me on his way to the durbar, he takes me to be a mendicant. A pious man, he stops his carriage and offers me some coins. But I refuse them. This intrigues him; he asks who I am.

I reply, "I am Rani Jindan, widow of Maharaja Ranjit Singh, who was once a friend of your kingdom." I know I should beg him for refuge, but the few shreds of dignity I have left will not let me. I would rather spend the rest of my life as a beggar outside the Pashupatinath Temple.

Jung Bahadur stares hard at me. Perhaps he perceives the truth on my face as well as the pride. Instead of dismissing me, he asks how I managed to get to Nepal. When I describe my escape and my journey, he steps down from his carriage and bows. "You are a brave woman, Mai Jindan. We remember the Sarkar with warmth and gratitude for the help he gave us in the past. And though we are far from Punjab, we have heard of the heinous manner in which the British snatched away your kingdom—and worse, your son. You are welcome in Nepal. You may live here for as long as you like. It will be an honor for me to provide you with a house and an allowance suited to your position."

Thus I find my sanctuary, a place to rest and recover, to watch from afar what the British are doing to my son. And to plan my next move. I may be injured; I may even be wounded to the heart; but I'm not defeated yet.

IV

Rebel

1860–1863

31

Kathmandu

I STAND ON THE BALCONY OF the small home loaned to me by Raja Jung Bahadur and look out over Kathmandu. All around me are the sloped and layered roofs of the city, the fluttering flags of the Buddhist shrines. In the distance, the golden spire of Pashupatinath gleams in the last rays of the sun; the Bagmati winds around the great temple complex like a slim silver chain. If I crane my neck, I can even see the small gurdwara I helped to establish, where, on the Sarkar's death day, the poor are fed. And where, from time to time, I secretly meet sympathizers who have traveled from Hindustan.

I shiver a little in spite of my thickly layered Nepali shawl, gifted to me by Jung Bahadur early on in my stay, before things began to sour between us. But I don't wish to go into the house yet. I strain my eyes to watch the dusty road. This is the time when messengers from Hindustan, who must traverse several mountain passes to get to Kathmandu, arrive. Every evening I watch for them, though I know they rarely have messages for me—and never the letter that I have longed for all these years, from my son, whom the British have taken halfway across the world to England. But still I hope.

My information comes from other sources. As I had feared, my faithful Avtar was shot by British soldiers in Patna. But a few of the spies he had trained had managed to hide themselves. Avtar must have shared my escape plans with them, because they searched until they discovered where I was, and now we are in regular touch.

When the spies sent me the details of Avtar's death—how he refused to give the British information about my whereabouts, how he was tortured before he was shot—I wept for months. I could not eat or sleep. Guilt weighed me down like a millstone. If I hadn't insisted on getting out of Chunar, if I hadn't sent word of my desperation to Avtar, perhaps he would still be alive. My health—already weak from my difficult journey to Nepal—worsened significantly. Jung Bahadur dutifully sent his physicians to care for me—though I think he secretly hoped I would die. I don't blame him. The British, displeased that he had given me sanctuary, pressured him in many ways.

With the British Resident in Kathmandu intercepting all letters officially addressed to me, I was even more thankful for Avtar's spy network. Without them, I would have been completely ignorant of my son's fate. But each message I received over the years was like a knife-thrust in my belly. First, the British sent my son away from Punjab, where he was loved and still had supporters, to faraway Fatehgarh, a godforsaken, mosquito-ridden village, where he was put in the care of an Englishman named John Login and his wife Lena. The Logins were overly kind to my lonely Dalip. Under other circumstances, I would have derived some comfort from this. But I couldn't help suspecting that their behavior was a ploy to usurp my place in Dalip's heart. To become his new parents and claim his loyalty.

Slowly the Logins sent away most of the people Dalip knew and loved, even his favorite attendant, Mian Kheema, who would have died to protect him. When he wanted to write to me, he was told that I had gone mad and run away, and no one knew where I was. What choice did my son have other than to cling to the Logins? They dressed him in English clothes, fed him their bland foods, and taught him their language. They took him to church and found him Christian playmates. Slowly he grew to be ashamed of Hindustani things, and even the part of himself that was Hindustani.

They got him a new servant, a Christian convert, Bhajan Lal, who wormed his way into my child's hungry heart. He read to Dalip from the Bible each night, brainwashing him and speaking ill of our Sikh traditions, until he agreed to convert. The British ignored the petitions of the few remaining employees from Lahore—Ram Singh, Dewan Singh, and the treasurer, Ram Kishen—who said Dalip needed to be taught more about his own religion first, that he was too young to make such a momentous decision. The Logins cut off my boy's beautiful, sacred hair, turned him away from the religion of his forefathers—and baptized him. They applauded him for seeing the light. I learned that Dalhousie even sent him his own Bible. And all the while, they told him stories of England, painting it as a magical land.

That was not the worst of it. When Dalip was barely sixteen, the British removed him from our country, so that the loyal Punjabis who were waiting for another opportunity to rise against the firangs would not have a king to rally around. They put him on a ship—ironically named the *Hindustan*—and sent him across the Kala Pani to England. And the most treacherous part of the scheme was that this exile was presented to him as a great and rare opportunity, a generous gift from Queen Victoria herself, so that he begged for it. When a secret messenger brought me this news, a terrible pain struck my chest and I slumped to the ground. The physician who was summoned said I had developed a disease of the heart, that I must not strain myself physically or emotionally. But how could I not? I raged again and again when I learned—for I have spies in England, too—how the firangs were making much of Dalip in their own country. How he had become a favorite of the Queen, who took him everywhere with her, dressing him up and showing him off—as though he were a pet monkey. How she had gifted him a locket painted with her picture, which he wore—did no one see the irony of this?—on a chain around his neck.

That was in 1854, six years ago. I have wept so much since then that I am now half-blind. Sometimes, strange fancies fill my mind.

Would it not have been better for Dalip to die in battle, like the noble Sham Singh and his soldiers at Sobraon? Then I realize my absurdity. My son was only eight years old then. The adults around him—including me—made all the decisions. Some, like mine, were foolish, shortsighted, and driven by vengeance. Some were greedy and treacherous, like those of Lal and Tej Singh—and ultimately, the other noblemen as well. Dalip alone had been given no options. Yet he was the one who was paying most dearly.

I spend much of my allowance, which Jung Bahadur reduces each year, sending letters in secret to Dalip in England. But I fear they are all intercepted because I have heard nothing from him. I cannot bear to think of the alternative: my anglicized son no longer cares for me.

I USE THE MONEY Jung Bahadur gives me for another covert purpose, one that would infuriate him if he learned of it: to help the freedom fighters in Hindustan.

For years, my chief contact was Raja Nahar Singh of Ballabhgarh, father-in-law of Dalip's cousin, Thakur Singh Sandhawalia. Nahar became one of the leaders of the 1857 War of Independence, gallantly joining Emperor Bahadur Shah's army in Delhi with his small force. I took pleasure in imagining that a few of his soldiers' rifles had been bought with my money. I prayed fervently that he—and his fellow warriors—would crush the might of the British. But he was defeated. I received a distraught message from Thakur Singh. *The British hanged him, like a common criminal, in Chandni Chowk. I will fight them until I die.* My heart ached for Thakur, who was only a year older than Dalip. *I have vowed to do the same,* I wrote back. *But we must be clever—and very careful.*

Nahar Singh, you have joined the ranks of my dear dead. I will not forget you, and I will not forgive your killers.

"My queen," Maahi says, stepping out onto the balcony. She walks with a limp—a gift of the British, who beat her severely when they discovered my escape from Chunar. She wraps me in a heavier shawl. "You must come inside now. Only a month ago you were ill with fever, and even now you have a cough."

Maahi arrived in Kathmandu about a month after me. Avtar had told her that we were going to the gurdwara in Patna, so when the British finally released her from Chunar, she had known where to start searching for me. It also helped that Jung Bahadur liked to boast about his generosity in giving a home to the destitute ex-queen of Punjab. She has taken care of me ever since, and that is a good thing, for in spite of my vow to not give up, there are days when I am too depressed to leave my bed. She coaxes and even bullies me at those times, reminding me of how much I mean, even now, to the people of Punjab. She contacted some of my old Lahori servants, who have joined me here. But we were unable to reach the one I loved most, my Mangla, who lives under close surveillance in Hardwar. Once, she almost managed to get to Dalip; but the British caught her and put her in prison.

Maahi brings me dinner. She knows my favorites and has had the cook prepare rajma-chawal. When I complain that I'm not hungry, she urges me to eat. "I have a surprise for you. But I'll not say what it is until you eat your food!" Such are the loving tricks she employs. After dinner is done, she says, "Jung Bahadur has summoned you to the palace tomorrow. The Resident has some news for you."

I am grateful to Jung Bahadur for granting me asylum when no one else would have dared to, but over the years our relationship has soured. The problems began soon after I arrived in Nepal. The British, knowing Jung Bahadur to be the strongest ruler in this part of Hindustan, began courting him. Perhaps my presence had something to do with it, too. Perhaps they were afraid that with my womanly wiles I would turn Jung Bahadur against them. After all, wasn't I the "Messalina of the Punjab'?

So when Jung Bahadur expressed a desire to visit England, Governor-General Dalhousie eagerly made the arrangements. In 1850, Jung Bahadur went to London, where he met with the Queen and was sumptuously feted by the court. When he returned to Nepal, he was sadly changed. Where before he had staunchly resisted the British, now he was in love with them. He spoke admiringly of the civilized elegance of their court. He began dressing like them and had his portrait painted in full European regalia, complete with the medals they had given him. He even changed the legal system in Nepal to follow England's. And he was distinctly colder toward me. It was clear Dalhousie had poisoned his mind. Or perhaps Jung Bahadur had realized that nothing was to be gained by befriending a deposed queen, whereas the British were offering him many rewards.

Things grew most tense between us in 1857, when the War of Independence raged across northern Hindustan, igniting the hope of freedom from the oppression of the firangs in the hearts of sepoys and civilians, poor and rich, Hindu and Muslim. From the eighty-one-year-old Bahadur Shah of Delhi to the twelve-year-old Birjis Qadr of Awadh, rulers declared war on the firangs who had stolen their kingdoms and wealth and disrespected their customs and religion. Every day I received news of gallant fighters who were risking their wealth and their lives to drive back the British army.

I thrilled to hear of the bravery of Nana Saheb, Tantia Tope, Kunwar Singh, Bakht Khan, Liyakat Ali—and Mangal Pandey, the soldier who sacrificed himself to light the first flame. And the magnificent women! Rani Lakshmibai of Jhansi and Begum Hazrat Mahal of Awadh, who fought not only for their people but also for their dispossessed sons. How I wished I could have joined them! I prayed for them deep into the night, and I cut down on every expense to send them money. I had hoped the Sikhs would join the fray—they were the best soldiers in the British army—but to my sorrow, they did not. Was it because they did not feel oneness with their Hindu and Muslim brothers? Was it because, during our Sikh wars, Hindu and Muslim soldiers, under British command, had killed their brethren?

This is the tragedy of Hindustan: our disunity. Our enemies have used it against us over and over.

WHEN THE BATTLE WAS at its peak and the British armies were being routed, I went to Jung Bahadur's home secretly one night and begged him to help the leaders of the War. We both knew that timeliness was crucial. More British soldiers were being sent as reinforcements by ship from England, but they were still far away.

"Your soldiers are the best trained," I said. "You've won every campaign you've undertaken, including a most difficult one recently in Tibet. Begum Hazrat Mahal's army—led by a troop of women soldiers—has just occupied Lucknow. If you join her, the British will never be able to defeat her. Do this for your people and your country. Rid Hindustan of the British, and be remembered as a patriot and a hero."

Jung Bahadur did not listen to me. He did, indeed, lead his formidable army to Awadh, but he joined forces with the British commander-in-chief, Campbell, instead. His fierce Gurkha soldiers wrested Lucknow from Hazrat, compelling her to flee with her son. Jung Bahadur's troops went on to wreak havoc against the Independence Army in Benares and Patna. I wept and raged as I heard how, one by one, the leaders of the revolution were killed, including the fearless Lakshmibai in a last stand near Gwalior.

When the remaining rebel leaders such as Nana Sahib, Khan Bahadur Khan, and Hazrat Mahal fled to Nepal, seeking refuge, Jung Bahadur led his army into the Terai region where they were hiding and killed or captured them. He planned to send the prisoners back to the British in chains.

After I'd learned about Jung Bahadur's treachery in Awadh, I had vowed in my fury never to see his face again. But I was forced to break my promise when I heard that Hazrat had begged him for asylum for herself and her son, and he had refused. I walked into the durbar where Jung Bahadur was being feted by the noblemen as the protector of his people, while the weak King Surendra sat watching silently, and I called him a coward and a traitor.

"Kill me for being the only one who dares to speak the truth!" I cried. "I don't care. Deep in your heart you know what a heinous and unpatriotic act you've committed by helping the British. Surely you've heard of their atrocities—even I know of them—since they crushed the resistance. At Kanpur, our soldiers were blown to bits from the mouths of cannons. Others were forced to lick the blood of the dead from building walls before they were hanged. At Fatehpur and Fatehgarh, entire localities were burned, the women raped, the children killed. Hindus and Muslims were force-fed beef and pork before being flogged to death. In Awadh alone, almost ten lakh innocent civilians were put to death. I don't know how, after your own demise, you will face Lord Pashupatinath, whose devotee you claim to be. The least you can do in reparation is to provide refuge to this courageous mother and son whose future you have destroyed."

Jung Bahadur stared resolutely over my head, ignoring me. His courtiers clamored that I, a woman and an outsider, knew nothing of politics and should not interfere in state matters. Hadn't the Hindustani armies also done atrocious things, they demanded. The guards removed me forcibly, and I was confined to my home for many months.

Perhaps, deep down, Jung Bahadur was ashamed, for he did, indeed, grant asylum to Hazrat Mahal and her son. And although I was never allowed to meet them, the young nawab—who was about the age Dalip had been when we were separated—sent me an Urdu poem in which he thanked me for being their savior.

I CANNOT SLEEP ALL night for wondering what kind of news the Resident, Colonel Ramsey—a man whose prime motive has been to spy on me and oppose me—might have. Is Dalip dead? Does Ramsey want to deliver the news in person so that he can gloat over my heartbreak? In the morning, I hide my worries and dress in my best outfit, a simple gray cotton ghaghra with a thick veil. I possess nothing nearly as fine as the silks and brocades I had to leave behind when I was imprisoned in Sheikhupura. But then, I'm a refugee, not a queen. I've also given up wearing white. It means nothing to the people here, and it's too hard to keep clean. My pearls were taken from me in Chunar, along with my other jewelry.

Entering the imposing royal palace with its fifty-five windows carved elaborately from black wood, I make my way to the court hall, where Jung Bahadur and I greet each other with wary politeness. Ramsey does not waste time. Bowing stiffly, he hands me a letter.

My hands shake as I open it. It is in English, a language I barely know, and it takes me a while to realize that it is written by my son. My weak eyes blur further with tears, and Ramsey takes it from me impatiently and reads it out.

> *Dearest Biji,*
> *Thanks to the kind intervention of my guardian, Sir John Login, I trust this letter will reach you safely. The British government has given me permission to visit India for a tiger hunt. I have missed you greatly and would very much like to see you again. We can meet in Calcutta, if you agree . . .*

I snatch the letter from Ramsey and kiss it over and over. I don't care what he thinks. My Dalip still remembers me! He wishes to see me!

"I will go to Calcutta," I say.

Jung Bahadur puts on a concerned face. "You must understand that if you leave, I cannot let you back into Nepal."

"I understand," I tell him. I have no wish to come back here. Once I hold Dalip close to my heart, I don't care what happens to me. There will be a hut somewhere beside the Ganga where I can spend the rest of my days. Or another British prison.

32

Calcutta

I HAVE NEVER SEEN A PLACE like Spence's Hotel, which is the venue the British have chosen for my reunion with Dalip. The hotel manager, who oversees the unloading of my luggage, tells me proudly that it is built like an English palace and is the best hotel in India—which is what the British call our country, as though by changing its name they can possess it more fully. The three-story exterior is flat and rectangular and built of gray stone, without a single turret or dome to relieve the monotony of its long line of windows. Even my hated prison, Chunar Fort, with pillars sprouting wherever the architect had fancied them and sudden doorways opening onto the river, had more character.

But perhaps it is also that I'm determined to hate all things British.

We pass by a lounge where many men sit smoking pipes, conversing or reading newspapers. Several are firangs who look like army men. I wonder if they've been placed here to keep an eye on Dalip and me. The manager throws open the door to our suite with a flourish, drawing my attention to the soft carpet, the velvet drapes, the lamps in bronzed sconces, the two separate bedrooms with large beds piled high with pillows. He announces that I've been given the best suite, courtesy of Governor-General Canning and the British government.

My first instinct is to retort, *As well they should, having snatched away my palace, my wealth, my kingdom, my freedom and my son.* But I remember what Rani Guddan taught me long ago: *Let your enemies think they've won.* So I merely say shukriya and tell Maahi to give baksheesh to the porters bringing my trunks.

In Kathmandu, I owned very little; I chose to use my dwindling allowance for more important things. But once I decided to come to Calcutta, Jung Bahadur had the court tailor make me some outfits. Perhaps he was happy to get rid of me, the troublesome mosquito always buzzing in his ear and sometimes biting. Perhaps he regretted not treating me better. Or he thought it would reflect badly on him if I went forth in rags. I was presented with two trunks filled with ghaghras, saris, salwar-kameezes, shawls, and shoes in suitably dull widow-colors. I didn't mind the drabness. How I dressed mattered little to me nowadays. At least I'd never have to buy clothes again. These would last me through the few remaining years of my life in whichever backwater pilgrim-town I spent them after my son returned to England.

I don't know how long I'll have to wait before Dalip arrives in Calcutta. The Resident gave me very little information. So I'm surprised and delighted when, in just a few hours, I receive a message stating that my son would like to meet with me, if it is convenient.

I want to laugh and cry at the same time. Convenient! After our long separation, I'd walk through fire to see Dalip. I'm nervous, too. It has been so long. I remember our last moments together: my sweet, plump-cheeked boy waving an excited goodbye from his carriage window, on his way to an excursion at Shalimar. I'd waved back, telling him I would see him in the evening. My last words had been, "Remember, too much sun gives you a headache."

Neither of us knew that we would be separated for fourteen years.

My mind churns with questions. What does Dalip look like now? What does he think about? What does he care for? How have his years with the Logins and the British Queen changed him? What—if anything—does he remember about me?

Then he's at the door, a vague shape in dark firang clothes. If Maahi hadn't alerted me, I wouldn't have known him. That's how weak my eyes have become, or perhaps how much he's changed.

"Biji?" His voice is deep, a grown man's. His Punjabi is strangely accented and halting, as though he hasn't spoken it in a long time. "Is that you? Ah, my beautiful Biji, what have they done to you!"

The shock in his voice makes me realize how much I've changed, how old and ugly I've become. I'm nothing like the fiery young queen he must have held in his mind's eye all these years. I shrink back, but the next moment he's kneeling in front of my armchair, kissing my hands, telling me how much he has missed me, how he feared that he'd never see me again, and how he wondered during all those lonely nights in Fatehgarh and London if I thought about him as much as he thought about me.

I run my fingers hungrily over his face, his shoulders, his arms, trying to comprehend that it's really my Dalip, so tall and handsome. And he still loves me! Joy chokes my throat, but I manage to say, "You're alive and safe, by Waheguru's grace! And we're finally together. What more could I want!"

Then my hands touch his head and, instead of the pagri that every Sikh man wears, I feel his short hair.

I knew that Dalip had become a Christian, but having the physical proof at my fingertips shocks me so deeply that I cannot hold back my tears. "The British took everything from you, beta," I lament. "Your throne, your kingdom, the Koh-i-Noor. I know you were too young to stop them. But your religion! How could you let them take that, too?"

Dalip does not speak, but I feel him stiffen and pull away. I bite my lip and silence myself. It was a mistake, to upset my son at our very first meeting, especially as the conversion was not his fault. How could any child have resisted the will of the British Empire? Or tamped down the urge to please his guardians, the Logins? How could I expect him to hold out when no one around him respected the customs of his people?

I turn our conversation carefully toward less sensitive matters. For hours we sit in my room, holding hands, reminiscing about happy times from his childhood in Lahore. He apologizes because his Punjabi is so poor, halting and peppered with English.

I tell him, "I'm impressed that you remember anything at all, after all these years of never speaking it. A few more days with me will bring it all back, I'm sure. Can one ever really forget one's mother tongue?"

Slowly, more memories return to him. The games and foods he'd loved. His horses and dogs and falcons. The pet cat that gave birth to nine velvet-black kittens, and for whom the qila cannons were fired in celebration. Riding his Arabian stallion, Veer, to meet the Khalsa army, and how loudly they cheered him . . .

Once he is comfortable with me, Dalip begins to tell me about his life in England. To my dismay, I see how deeply he admires the Queen and her husband. He tells me how kind they've been to him, according him the same rank as any European prince. I want to remind him that he had been far more important, the crowned king of the great kingdom of Punjab before Victoria's representatives snatched it from him, but I stay silent. Dalip, meanwhile, goes on to describe the coat of arms—a lion standing beneath a coronet—that Albert, the Prince Consort, had personally designed for him, and the portrait of him that Victoria had commissioned her favorite artist, a famous painter named Winterhalter, to create. Dalip is regularly invited to ride and hunt with the royal family on their estates. He plays with Victoria's children, who are very fond of him, and he often carries her youngest son, Prince Leopold, on his back. She has given him a seat of honor at court, and in the Parliament, too, whenever he visits it.

His admiration of the British Queen upsets me greatly. Does he not understand that she is responsible for our tragedies? To me, her behavior seems patronizing. I am particularly distressed to learn that Dalip carries her son on his back like a servant. It is not fitting conduct for a maharaja. But how can I tell him this without antagonizing him?

When Dalip proudly tells me that he is a fine hunter and an excellent marksman, one of the best in court circles, I am finally able to offer him some sincere praise. "You must get it from your father, who was the best hunter in Punjab." I describe the wild-boar hunts the Sarkar loved to go on, how he always rode in the front of the party, and how he faced his fierce quarry bravely—with a spear, never a gun.

As WE GROW MORE at ease with each other, Dalip and I begin to speak of darker things, sharing the pain of our separation.

"I was sent from one prison to another one farther away, outside Punjab. I was all alone, without even Mangla to comfort me. No one would bring me news of you, puttar. The worst part was that they didn't even let me say goodbye to you."

"I came back from Shalimar and you had disappeared, Biji, and Mangla, too. No one would tell me what happened to you. After that, I couldn't bear to set foot in the Musamman Burj, where we lived together. I had trouble sleeping at night without you. Kheema had to sit on the floor next to my bed and hold my hand."

"I was so desperate and lonely at Sheikhupura and Chunar. I tried very hard to send you news. I gave my jewelry to the guards so that they'd carry a letter to you—but I don't think they did."

"No, I never received anything. And then one day the Resident announced that I must move to Fatehgarh. I didn't want to go. I was unhappy there, bored and even lonelier. Whatever friends I had were still in Lahore. Though I didn't tell anyone, I felt angry all the time. Most of all with you, for going away—they told me that you'd left me. Sometimes they said you'd gone mad. I had no one to turn to except the Logins—and the British boys they brought to be my playmates. Slowly, I got used to that life. And then I wanted to be just like them."

"After they made you sign away your kingdom, I was livid. Maybe that fury made me determined to escape—and I did, in spite of all their guards. I disguised myself as my seamstress and escaped from right under their noses. I almost froze to death while crossing over the mountain ranges to Nepal, dressed as a sannyasin to evade my pursuers. It destroyed my health, but I don't regret it. At least I was free."

"You were so brave! I don't know if I could have done it. Once I learned that you were in Kathmandu, I sent you many letters. I even paid envoys to visit you. Finally I realized that you weren't receiving anything, and that envoys weren't allowed to see you. That's when I pretended that I was longing to go on a tiger hunt—and here I am!"

We smile conspiratorially at each other. How cannily we have tricked the firangs!

Three days pass. We laugh and weep so many times, I lose count. I call for laddus, which he says are still his favorite sweets, and feed them to him with my own hands, just as I used to when he was little. He sleeps on the sofa in my sitting room instead of in his own luxurious suite because he wants to be close to me.

"I want to hear you breathing in the night, the way I used to when I was a child," he says.

Most importantly, we make a decision: we're not going to be parted again.

OVER THE NEXT WEEK, Dalip visits Canning to tell him that we have decided that we will live together in India. The governor-general does not like this; he is afraid that our united presence in Hindustan will stir up trouble. He sends word to England and waits for the Parliament's response. Meanwhile, Dalip writes to the Logins every week, keeping them informed of our plans. I don't see why they need to know our business, but I say nothing. For many years the Logins were like Dalip's parents. I learn from Aroor Singh, the young Sikh who has been my son's attendant in England for a couple of years now, that he even calls Login *ma-baap*, mother and father, as a sign of respect. The blood rushes to my head when I hear this; I am incensed on behalf of both the Sarkar and myself. But I force myself to remain calm. The Logins' hold on Dalip is strong. It will take careful strategizing to dislodge them.

While Dalip is busy with the governor-general or off on bird-hunting expeditions in the Bengal countryside, I question Aroor, learning as much as I can about my son. He knows Dalip well, both his strengths and his weaknesses, and is loyal and protective. So it is natural that we become allies. Aroor, a devout Sikh, agrees with me that it was wrong of the British to manipulate a child into converting to another faith.

Speaking with Aroor makes me realize how the British have continued to dupe my son, hiding their guile behind a facade of kindness so craftily constructed that they probably believe it themselves. When Aroor tells me how happy Dalip is on his birthdays because the Queen remembers the occasion and sends him a gift, I grow indignant. She took everything from him! And now she has the gall to send him a horse, a dog, or a ring with a miniature of herself on it and act magnanimous. She has the audacity to name him "my Black Prince."

He's not yours, Victoria. And never will be, if I have my way.

Then I think, never mind. My son will remain with me in India now. I need no longer worry about the power the firangs wield over him.

BUT I'M TOO CONFIDENT too soon. The authorities in India confer with those in England as to what is to be done with us, this inconvenient mother–son pair. Telegrams are sent back and forth. Canning finally informs us of the government's decree: Dalip and I can be together only if we both go to England. Otherwise, he must return there alone—soon.

Dalip is upset and confused—upset at the government's high-handedness in deciding our lives for us, and confused because a large part of him feels British. Aroor has told me that he has been ill at ease in India among the "natives," as he sometimes calls our people, and longs to return "home." To complicate matters, Dalip senses that I hate the British and would be unhappy living among them. He knows, too, that as a Sikh, I don't want to die in a foreign land. It is important to me to be cremated by the Ganga, and have half my ashes scattered in our holiest river, and half placed with the Sarkar's in his Samadhi. As a loving son, he doesn't want to cause me any grief.

Dalip and I meet with Canning and try to reason with him. We tell him that he can send us to whichever part of India he wishes; we will live there quietly and simply. But it's futile. The British hold all the power.

After a week of useless discussions, I resign myself to going to England.

"I'll do it, Dula ji," I tell Dalip, calling him by the nickname I'd given him a long time ago, when he was a baby in Jammu, innocent and radiant and unafraid. "My love for you is greater than my hatred for the British."

His eyes well up. Sometimes I fear that my boy is too soft-hearted. When he kisses my cheek and throws his arms around me as he used to do when he was a child, I know I've made the right decision.

We get ready to capitulate to Canning. But then something no one expected happens.

A Sikh regiment returning from the China War is brought by ship up the Hooghly River to Calcutta. Somehow, the soldiers learn that my son is here from England, and that I have been allowed to return from exile after many years to meet with him. The news spreads among the troops like wildfire. Several hundred soldiers, battle-weary yet filled with enthusiasm, gather each day outside Spence's. They inform the frightened hotel manager that they will not leave until they have seen us. Their cheers and battle cries echo all over the hotel and send thrills through my entire being. Our people—dispersed, disinherited, defeated—haven't forgotten us. Though they had to take up jobs with the firangs after the Khalsa army was forcibly disbanded—or they would have starved—their true loyalty remains with their maharaja.

Dalip, however, is acutely uncomfortable with the attention and adulation. He does not know how to respond to the soldiers. This, too, pains my heart. My majestic, charismatic Sarkar's only remaining son has been made to forget the ways of royalty. I pull Dalip out onto the balcony, where I join my hands and bow to our people. I am pleased when he follows suit. The cheers reach a crescendo. I can see that the soldiers are deeply touched. Several have tears in their eyes. If we asked them, I know they'd risk their lives and revolt in an instant. For a moment my rebel heart stirs, tempted. Then I face reality. Such an uprising would mean certain destruction for them and further punishment for us. So I wave them goodbye and walk back inside. Still, the soldiers come back to see us, again and again.

Alarmed by this development, the officers in the British cantonment send hosts of firang soldiers to surround the hotel and keep things under control. And Canning decides that we must leave on the next ship to England.

To encourage us to depart peacefully, he offers to return the jewels the British had taken from me. "We will even give your mother a pension of three thousand pounds," he tells Dalip.

Dalip is elated and truly grateful; I am less so. Does Canning think I've forgotten that my pension, according to the Treaty of Bhairowal in 1846, was supposed to be one and a half lakh rupees per year? But I am not surprised. The British are used to wresting away everything and, afterward, returning a small portion to the dispossessed as though they are performing a great act of charity.

BEING ON A SHIP is a novel experience for me. I stand on the deck for a long time as we sail down the Hooghly toward the ocean. The palm trees and vegetable fields are so vibrantly green, even in my hazy vision, that I tear up. No. The tears come because I'm leaving my beloved country forever. When I was taken away from Lahore, tormented though I was, I had a small hope of returning. It was the same when I fled to Nepal. But as I look back at the receding shoreline of Gangasagar, I know this time it is final.

Waheguru, I pray that at least my ashes will make their way back home.

During the voyage, I spend much of my time on deck. I am the only woman who chooses to do so. The British ladies appear in the morning and evening for brief perambulations, protected from the sun by fussily decorated bonnets and scarves and sometimes parasols. The Hindustani women stay in their cabins, observing purdah. I don't care. I'm happy to be alone. I particularly love the aft end of the ship, where I can gaze for hours at the foam churning in our wake. When the ocean grows choppy, I revel in the excitement and sometimes find myself laughing out loud. Even the firang captain is impressed by what he calls my sea legs.

I tell him it is much like riding a spirited horse. "A great warrior once taught me that we have to move with the horse, to think of the two of us as one body. I'm doing the same with the ocean."

He nods and smiles. For the first time I see respect and wonder in the eyes of an Englishman. I smile back.

Aroor accompanies me on deck whenever he is free, but Maahi—so brave in other ways—is afraid of the water. And my poor Dalip, who became seasick as soon as we encountered our first squall, spends almost the entire voyage in bed in his cabin. I try to entice him upstairs, promising that the fresh air will make him feel better, but he groans and buries his head in his pillow. He cannot keep down any solid food at all. I, on the other hand, am made ravenous by the stinging salt air. Ship meals, geared to firang tastes, are sadly bland—an irony, considering they had first come to our country for our spices! But, forewarned by Aroor, I have armed myself with a trunk-load of pickles. These make my meals quite tolerable. Even my eyesight seems to be improving, and when I peer into my mirror, I'm happy to see that my face is less gaunt than before. This is good because I need to grow strong. There are many things I must do once I reach England, in the little time that I have left.

I order the cook to fix a shorba for Dalip with chicken broth, and this, along with the slices of ginger and sticks of cinnamon that I give him to chew, helps him to get a minimal amount of nutrition. He begins to depend upon me increasingly as we proceed on our journey, soliciting my advice, or requesting me to sit at his bedside and read to him out of my Punjabi books, for he has forgotten the Gurmukhi script. His favorites are the tragic–romantic qissas such as *Heer–Ranjha* and *Sohni–Mahiwal*. This suits me well as I, too, love these classic tales of love and loss. But in my trunk is hidden a very different book that I procured with much difficulty: Shah Mohammed's *Jangnama*, where the poet has depicted in heart-breaking detail how the glorious Lahore court was destroyed by the treachery of our own courtiers and the trickery of the British. I plan to read it to Dalip when the time is right.

Even as I worry about Dalip's health, a part of me is pleased at our resulting closeness. This is how Waheguru takes a storm sometimes and turns it into a rainbow. I'll need all of my son's trust if the hazy plan I'm beginning to formulate in my brain is to have any chance of success.

33

England

I STAND ON THE DECK OF the ship, wrapped in a long cloak, looking out at the grimy docks of London. Although it is summer, the day is unpleasantly cold—a damp gray unlike our dry Lahore winters, bright with sunshine. It has been two months since we left Hindustan. I shiver, but only partly because of the chill. There's a heaviness inside me. More than ever before, I feel the fist of the British government tightening around me. Now I am completely in their power. Except for my son and a handful of Hindustani servants that I've been allowed to bring, hardly anyone here knows who I am. And those who do, I'm sure, think ill of me. Rabble-rouser. Warmonger. Plotter. And of course, Messalina of the Punjab! Or do I flatter myself? By now, even the India Office must have written me off as old, blind, and decrepit. Why else would the authorities allow me to come here instead of shutting me up in a Hindustani prison?

I take a deep breath. Perhaps I can still surprise the firangs.

Excited to introduce his adopted country to me, Dalip has exerted himself and left his cabin. He stands beside me on the deck, his arm around my shoulders. Aware of my failing sight, he describes for me the tall port buildings, and the wharves that stretch as far as the eye can see, lined with tall-masted vessels, some belching smoke from their stacks. Hundreds of workers carry bundles and bales onto the docks—merchandise that has arrived from all over the world. Dalip recites names: Billingsgate, London Bridge, Legal Quays. He is especially proud to call my attention to the Tower of London, which he tells me is very old, almost eight hundred years, and has a most gruesome history of plots and executions. I want to tell him that our own qila in Lahore, originally built by Mahmud of Ghazni, is older. And in just my lifetime, I have seen plots and betrayals and deaths and executions that would raise the hairs on any British arm.

But I don't want to curb my son's enthusiasm. And more than that, I don't want to put him in a position where he feels he must defend the Britishers. There is time enough to educate him about our lost glory, our amazing and often tragic history. For now, I peer at the grimy English dockworkers sullenly unloading our trunks from the ship. What a far cry they are from the firangs who lord it over my countrymen in Hindustan as though they are gods. I watch a laborer coughing and spitting on the side of the filthy road and wish all Hindustanis could see what I am seeing: the ordinariness of the British. Perhaps it would empower them to hold their heads high and fight harder for our freedom.

WE'VE RENTED A TEMPORARY house in London—or rather, Login has rented it for us. Perhaps I would have disliked it otherwise as well, but knowing that it was that man's choice makes it even less palatable. It is dark and gloomy, just like the steel-colored skies. The windows must be kept closed at all times because of the cold, so the house smells musty and old. It is a sad smell—of old age and hopelessness. How I long for our bright Punjab sunshine, our airy havelis where the cooking was done in open rasoikhanas so that the smoke and the aroma of spices enticed but was never oppressive. In

England, my cooks must work in the basement, a dim room with sealed windows which fills with smoke, making us all cough. My servants complain that street urchins spy on them, making faces and jeering while they hang on to the railings outside. "Hindoos!" the boys cry in falsetto voices, not knowing how inaccurate their name-calling is: my staff is made up of Sikhs and Muslims. It infuriates the servants—and me, too—that they cannot run up and give the brats the well-deserved cuff on the ears they would have received in Hindustan to teach them to respect their elders. But Dalip has impressed upon us that such things are forbidden in England, especially for foreigners.

In this homesick household, my son is the only happy one. I am saddened when I see his relief at being back in this country—like a bird which, having been bred in captivity, feels comforted only in the safety of its cage. Aroor, who waits on Dalip when his English friends visit, reports to me—as he has taken to doing regularly—that he complains to them about how deeply he disliked Hindustan. He calls it a dirty, beastly place filled with deceitful, pandering natives. At such times, I feel hopeless and wonder what I am doing here.

It hurts me most when I learn from Aroor of Dalip's dismissive attitude toward our failed War of Independence. He knows so little about what really happened and shows no interest in hearing the facts. If anything, he sides with the British and is horrified by the stories of "rebel violence' and avarice which have been widely circulated in England. He has mentioned angrily, several times, that his Fatehgarh residence was burned down, his toshakhana looted, and Sergeant Elliott, the man who had been left in charge, killed by the "natives." I long to give him a different perspective, to tell him about the courage and gallantry of leaders such as Nana Saheb, Lakshmibai, and our own relative, Nahar Singh, and the men and women who followed them to their deaths for the sake of freedom. But when I bring up the subject once or twice, he tells me, quite definitively, that he does not wish to discuss it. At one time I would have argued. Now, weakened by age, illness, and—most of all—the fear of alienating my son, I remain silent.

WE HAVE TO WAIT in London for the customs house to release my jewels, which the British returned to me just before I left Calcutta. The customs officials are demanding a large amount as duty, which seems to be most unfair. Hasn't their government done enough harm, keeping my property from me for so many years? My life in Nepal would have been very different if I'd had jewelry that I could have sold instead of depending on Jung Bahadur's unwilling charity. Additionally, I discovered in Calcutta that several expensive pieces were missing from what they had returned. Who will pay for those? But Dalip declares that such arguments will not hold water. Instead, he asks Login—his ma-baap—for help one more time. Login the magician speaks to the right people in the right places, and it's decided that I can have my belongings back without further payment. Dalip cannot stop telling everyone, over and over, how influential and kind his guardian is.

Finally, I can't stand it. "Didn't you tell me that Login hasn't been your guardian since 1859?" I snap.

He merely smiles and says, "Dear Biji, you don't understand how it is."

When Dalip suggests we should invite the Logins over to thank them, I don't object. While he is the most respectful of sons, I am well aware that he is the master of this house. Besides, although I hate the Logins, I believe in the importance of giving thanks and expressing hospitality. I am, after all, a queen, even if the Logins' countrymen have treacherously taken away my kingdom. It will also give me a chance to flaunt my jewelry. But most of all, I'm curious to examine the couple who stole something more important than even the Koh-i-Noor from me: my only son—and from whose emotional clutches I plan to get him back.

WHEN THE LOGINS COME for dinner, I dress in my best salwar-kameez and wear my emeralds. Our cooks would like to show off their skills by making elaborate badshahi dishes—biriyani and parathas and chicken qurma—but Dalip asks them to keep the menu simple. Lady Login's stomach is rather sensitive, he informs us. I have redone the living room in Hindustani style, replacing the bulky furniture with a Persian carpet and silken cushions. Many items from my country are easily available in London, though they are of middling quality and criminally expensive. We invite the Logins to join us on the carpet. I am pleased to see Dalip sitting cross-legged with no discomfort. The Logins fidget as they perch on the cushions, trying to make polite conversation. Finally, at dinner time, I take pity on them and ask the servants to serve our meal at the table. I feel particularly virtuous because I resisted my baser impulses and told my cook to make the food blander than usual.

After a couple of glasses of wine, the dour Login opens up. He compliments me, in fluent Urdu, of looking well. It is a lie; my health and beauty have both been ruined, thanks to what his people did to me. But I manage a smile. He goes on to congratulate me on having weathered my first sea voyage like an experienced sailor, but I know what he's thinking: Is this poor, haggard, half-blind woman the once-dreaded Messalina of the Punjab, the one whom, even recently, Canning called a "she-devil'?

I swallow my anger and thank Login in Urdu for procuring this house for us, and for getting my jewelry out of customs. And for having taken such good care of my son when I was unable to be there for him. I add, "You are such a kind man, Lord Login. I am glad that my plot to poison you when you were in Fatehgarh failed."

I take pleasure in the look on Login's face, his hand stopped halfway to his mouth. It's not that the information is new to him. It had not been much of a plot. My resources—I was in Sheikhupura Qila by then, guarded day and night, my heart broken at my separation from Dalip—had been meager. Deep down, I had had no expectation that it would succeed, but I'd felt impelled to try. I could not just give up without a fight. Login had learned of the botched plot almost immediately, when my agent was put to death. But I think he's shocked that I'm so brazenly open about my misdeeds. He looks suspiciously at the food on his plate. Beside him, Lady Login—whom I dislike even more than her husband because when she came into the house she kissed Dalip on both cheeks and called him *my boy*—blanches and pushes her plate away.

I laugh and reassure them that I would never kill a guest in my home. The laws of hospitality forbid it. But the Logins make their excuses and leave soon after that, without waiting for the mango pudding my chef has created specially for them. I know I've disappointed Dalip by my bad behavior. But he's a good son and does not chide me. Perhaps he understands that seeing the Logins brings back some of my worst memories.

To make up for the less-than-successful dinner, I, along with Maahi, start taking English lessons from a woman whom Dalip enthusiastically hires for me. I think he is envisioning a near future in which I will be able to converse fluently with his dinner guests, before whom I currently choose not to appear. I learn many more words than I knew before, and common conversational sentences, but often our teacher's accent confuses me. Maahi, who is quicker at it than I am, helps me practise. I promise Dalip that as soon as I feel more comfortable with the language, I will visit Lady Login, and that I will be on my best behavior. Dalip has a tailor come to the house to fashion a dress for me because he thinks it would be good for me to be attired like an Englishwoman. I know I look much better in my Hindustani clothes, which drape elegantly and are far more comfortable, but out of love, I agree.

ON THE DAY OF the visit, I wear my new Victorian gown, a strange construct with a wide steel cage underneath—a crinoline, I am told—to spread out the skirt. I've never worn anything like this. The air swirling around my legs feels indecent, so I wear a ghaghra under it, and a bodice as well. For good measure, I put on gloves, a shawl, and a hat which sits on my head like a small bucket. For courage—though why should I need it? I'm a queen and Lena Login is just the wife of a doctor whose salary came out of my son's allowance—I wear the pearls the Sarkar gave me.

I'm nervous about walking on the street in my strange British finery, so Dalip hires a sedan chair for me, although they are rare in London nowadays. People stare as I'm carried to the Logins' home, which is only a few houses away from ours—no doubt so Login can keep an eye on us. Men stare; women whisper to each other behind their fans; and street urchins run after my chair, shouting. It seems as though everyone knows who I am—but the looks they give me are not the admiring, reverential ones I would have received in Hindustan. I wonder which of the many lies the British fabricated about me have been circulated here.

Lena Login tries hard to be a good hostess. She allows my servants to enter her house and help me to the drawing room, which is up a flight of steep, narrow stairs. She allows Maahi to remain in the room when I indicate that I might need her to translate for us. When I sit cross-legged on her overstuffed sofa instead of in the British manner with the legs dangling, she says nothing, though she cannot stop herself from raising her eyebrows. She tells me that she has had Indian tea with milk prepared for me. Her maid serves me what she claims are laddus, little balls that are a shocking shade of orange I've never seen. I would rather not have eaten anything at her home because firangs are overfond of beef and I suspect that their plates and silverware are contaminated with this taboo food. But I think of Dalip and make myself take a few bites of a laddu, which is rock-hard, and offer fulsome compliments. Lena Login insists that I also try a biscuit. The biscuit, though I hate to admit it, is rather delicious. I eat it slowly and methodically, memorizing the taste. I will describe it to my cook and ask him to make it for me.

Lena Login and I make an attempt to converse. I am interested in finding out how she thinks—it is good to know such things about one's enemy. But in spite of her having lived in Hindustan for many years, her Urdu extends mostly to words used for ordering servants around. So, after asking me about my health, and how I like London, she resorts to English. Her words, in her strange accent, waft over me like a fog. Even with the English lessons I've struggled through, I only understand a few words; I nod at what I hope are appropriate moments, but it is frustrating. I would have liked a more meaningful exchange, into which I could have inserted one or two innocent-sounding remarks about how changed my son is, thanks to her care.

My attention wanders as Lena Login drones on. Her home is stuffy, overcrowded and decorated with dull, though probably expensive, items. Tables and sofas take up much of the space. From the ceiling hang several chandeliers. Above the fireplace which has been lit—for my sake, she informs me, because I'm still not used to the British chill—sit many knick-knacks, urns, vases and the like. The paintings on the wall depict scenes of naval warfare. The only really beautiful item is the carpet, and I can tell from its design that it's from Hindustan. On a nearby table sit photographs of the Logins with their six children. I wish to know if Lena has arranged the marriage of their oldest son yet—he looks to be about eighteen, well past the age of betrothal. When Maahi translates, Lena Login laughs. Then she orders Maahi to be sure to correctly translate her words back to me.

"Oh no!" she says, speaking slowly so Maahi will get every word. "He is too young to make such an important decision. Besides, when the time comes, he will choose his own bride. That is our English way. I expect Dalip, having been brought up here, will do the same." She looks at me and adds, "It isn't good to interfere too much in the affairs of young people."

I do not respond to her statement, which is at once disrespectful of our customs and self-congratulatory. And untrue, since she and her husband continue to interfere in Dalip's life. I hope that Dalip will have enough sense—and filial respect—to consult with me when he decides to look for a bride, though I worry about what kind of woman he will find in London. As Lena drones on about her other children, I'm caught up in a memory from my days as queen regent—of the match I had arranged for Dalip—he was eight then—with Tej Kaur, the sweet and pretty daughter of Chatar Singh Attariwala, who headed one of our most important clans. The betrothal ceremony had been grand, with many gifts exchanged, and the celebrations in the qila had gone on late into the night, ending, at Dalip's request, with fireworks. Everyone had remarked what a perfect match it was.

But we lost the war, Lawrence became the British Resident, and I was thrown in jail. Lawrence prevented the marriage from taking place; the Attariwalas were too powerful, and he feared they might rise up against the British to restore the kingdom to their son-in-law. Chatar Singh did eventually fight the British—even in my faraway prison in Chunar, I had heard of the great victory he won in Chillianwala—but then the traitor Gulab Singh came down from Jammu, and the tables were turned.

I'm brought back to the present by Lena Login asking if I would like more tea. But I cannot bear to remain in this room any longer. My memories have depressed me, and in any case, I have done my duty. I rise and bow and she shows me out. At the door we give each other our first genuine smiles, both of us thankful that the afternoon's ordeal is over.

Later Aroor, who has cleverly made friends with one of the maids in the Login household, tells me that Lena described my visit at length to her husband at dinner, ridiculing my mix of Hindustani and English clothing, my poor language skills, and my strange, abrupt manners. She even asked him whether he thought I might have contracted syphilis in my youth due to my promiscuous lifestyle, if that is why I seemed "not completely there." I am infuriated to hear this, but not unhappy. It allows me to hate her wholeheartedly.

The visit has served its purpose, though. Dalip is delighted by the effort I've made. A few days later, when he is invited to dinner at Buckingham Palace, he proudly tells the Queen that I am adjusting very well, dressing like an Englishwoman, taking language classes, and going about town to pay visits to his friends. He comes back home elated and informs me that the Queen was most pleased to hear this.

"She has even promised to invite you to tea one of these days!" he ends.

I am saddened by his excitement. Does he truly not see what the British have done to him? Why is Victoria's approval so important to my son, whose kingdom would have been the equal of hers had it not been for the treachery of a select few? I hope she has spoken out of mere courtesy. I don't think I can force myself to be polite, even for Dalip's sake, to the woman whose henchmen so cunningly destroyed my kingdom. Aroor tells me that Victoria wears the Koh-i-Noor, which she has had cut to a smaller size, as a brooch on her bosom. That magnificent stone which used to grace my beloved Sarkar's arm, and later, on state occasions, my son's—I know I cannot bear to witness its diminished glory.

THE ONE JOY IN my miserable existence is that Dalip and I are growing closer. Aroor informs me that nowadays my son often refuses invitations from his friends to accompany them in the evenings to the theater or the music hall, or to join card parties at their homes. Dalip tells them that he needs to make up for our long separation by spending as much time with me as possible. We take our night meal together, authentic Punjabi food—rajma, chawal, karhi, parathas—which, thank Waheguru, Dalip still likes, and we reminisce about old times.

I am fascinated by the many incidents Dalip remembers, though often he has forgotten the names of the places and the people attached to them. He recalls feeding the white peacocks Dhian Singh had presented to him in Jammu when he was less than three years old. He remembers visiting the Golden Temple in Amritsar, watching the dome shimmer in the sunset while I told him that his father had had it covered in gold. He remembers his Uncle Jawahar with great fondness—how he would throw him up in the air, or let him ride on his shoulders. How they used to race each other on horseback, and how Jawahar always let him win. I smile, touched.

Then he says, "I remember the day he was killed by the soldiers."

My heart constricts. I'm afraid to ask him which details of that terrible day are imprinted in his mind. Does he recall me wailing in a tent all night, crazed with grief? Or begging the panches the next morning, with joined palms, to give me my brother's body so I could cremate it properly? Mangla had covered Dalip's eyes as a soldier brought his sword down on Jawahar's head. Still, what deep scars might the incident have left on his mind? Does he have any idea that the vow of vengeance I took on that day was what eventually led to the destruction of the Khalsa army—and the loss of his throne?

If he found out, would he ever forgive me?

But he doesn't say anything more, and I don't ask.

Dalip also recalls the day he signed away his kingdom, though he didn't understand what was happening at the time. "The British had taken you away already, so I couldn't ask you what to do, like the time when I refused to put the tika on that man's forehead—I've forgotten his name, though I remember his pockmarked face."

"Tej Singh," I say. Once again I'm overcome by guilt. Had I not insisted on using Dalip to shame Tej in front of the whole durbar, Lawrence might not have torn me away from my son, at least not for a couple more years.

"Before Dalhousie's secretary arrived in Lahore, the courtiers told me many times that I must do exactly what the British laat said. I remember all of us, dressed in our best, lined up at the qila gate to welcome him. We walked with him to the durbar. He read out a long proclamation in English. Then it was read out in Urdu, but still it made no sense to me. All the courtiers signed. They put the document in front of me and gave me a pen, so I, too, wrote my name there. Afterward, Kheema cried and told me I wasn't a king anymore."

So far I've been careful not to criticize the firangs to Dalip, but I can't help it now—I'm too angry. "That document was a mockery of justice. The British broke their word by making you sign it. Three years before, they'd signed a different treaty, establishing Punjab as a protectorate. They took away the richest part of our kingdom—the Jalandhar Doab—and in return they promised to guard the rest of it for you until you were old enough to rule. The British army was being paid twenty-two lakh rupees every year to defend the durbar and suppress rebellions. But they didn't abide by that agreement. Our country was too prosperous, and the British too greedy. When there was a rebellion—although the court had nothing to do with it—they leapt on it as an excuse to annex Punjab."

Dalip is silent for a long time, his brow creased in a frown. "No one ever told me this," he says finally.

"Why would they? It's to their advantage to keep you in the dark." I breathe deeply and take the plunge. "But I will tell you everything I know. If you choose to hear it."

There's a thoughtful look in his eyes, but he doesn't commit to anything. Instead, he wishes me good night and leaves the room without his usual affectionate embrace. I don't blame him. Knowledge—especially the painful kind that I'm offering—will bring all his comfortable beliefs about the British crashing down. They've been his patrons and friends ever since he was a boy. His ma-baap. He has remade himself in their image.

What would he be left with if I showed him their true face?

34

Koh-i-Noor

LONDON WEATHER, DAMP AND SOOTY even in the summer, does not agree with me. I cough and cough and have a hard time breathing afterward. Concerned, Dalip decides he must find a place that will be better for my health. In the autumn, he takes me to one of his favorite haunts, Mulgrave Castle in Yorkshire, up in the north of England. He shows me around the large stone fortress proudly, as though he owns it, when I know from Aroor that he is only a tenant who comes here for the hunting season.

The castle and the surrounding lands belong to a Lord Normanby, who is an ambassador somewhere in Europe. His wife, who lives nearby, spies on me whenever she can. Let her snoop all she wants! I wear my best clothes and climb up to the ramparts—though the stairs make me wheeze—so that she can see what a Hindustani queen looks like even after her kingdom has been stolen from her. Dalip, in his innocent way, has told the woman that she can come over to the castle whenever she wishes and she makes full use of his hospitality. I think she hopes to examine me up close, as one might an exotic animal that is now in captivity. Dalip makes much of her and offers her high tea, but I plead ill health and refuse to come out of my room.

"Why should I?" I tell Maahi when she tries to persuade me to be friendly. "I've no wish to create more fodder for her gossip."

I have to admit, though, that I like Mulgrave Castle. It is the best of all the places I've seen in England—and I've seen many in London, because Dalip likes to take me around in his carriage. There are fancier buildings—Buckingham Palace, the Tower of London, even Windsor Castle. But Mulgrave with its rough stone walls reminds me of our qila in Lahore, and the view from the ramparts is beautiful. The moors stretch out around us, and the woods behind the castle are filled with birds. Dalip is more relaxed here and spends much of his time outdoors, hunting. I think it is far better for him than those card parties in London. What he told me is true: he's an excellent shot. At the end of the day, he often brings back fifty or sixty grouse, which look to me like pigeons. It is a far cry from the boars and lions the Sarkar used to hunt, but I am glad that in the small ways that are allowed to him in this country, Dalip is following in his father's footsteps.

Like the Sarkar, Dalip, too, is generous. He gives whatever game we cannot use to the neighbors and never asks for anything in return. This makes them view him favorably. They refer to him—as usual, Aroor is my informant in this—as a jolly good fellow and a Christian to boot, quite different from the rest of the "heathens," a category in which I am sure they include me.

Login is particularly unhappy about Dalip's growing closeness with me. He has advised him to find me a separate house with some proper British servants, though I can, he offers magnanimously, still retain my "native' ones. He says he can get the India Office to pay for my residence. Though Dalip is usually most compliant where Login is concerned, in this case he has been stubborn.

Login comes all the way up from London to Mulgrave to inspect our domestic arrangements—and, I think, to see what mischief I might be up to. He tells Dalip that it is not considered proper in England for a mother to live with her grown son. Dalip needs to be around friends of his own age and have his own servants. Login particularly dislikes the affectionate familiarity with which some of my servants, who have known Dalip since he was a child, treat him.

Login takes Dalip aside for what he terms a "man-to-man' talk, but Aroor makes sure to eavesdrop on them. He reports to me afterward that Login tried to persuade Dalip to send me off to Lythe Hall, a mansion not too far from Mulgrave. He even offered to negotiate a very reasonable rent for him.

"What did Dalip say?" I ask Aroor, trying not to show my concern and my anger.

"The maharaja disagreed," Aroor replies with a fierce grin. "It is the first time I have seen him go against Login Sahib's advice."

Later, Dalip tells me more. "I told Lord Login, 'My mother and I have already been forced to live apart for too many years. I don't know how much time I have left with her. As you can see, her health is ruined because of the many hardships she has been put through.' Lord Login had the good grace to look ashamed, and he didn't try to persuade me any further."

I'm delighted to hear this. Delighted because of the love my son showed me. And because, finally, the lion cub is waking up.

BEFORE LOGIN LEAVES, HE and Dalip make up. They go riding and shooting and stay up late at night with their port and their cigars. I leave them alone at these times, but one evening after dinner, just as I am bidding them good night, Dalip requests me to wait. He asks Login if he might recommend a portrait painter, someone to create a fine likeness of me.

"I have several portraits of myself that Her Majesty commissioned.

Now I would like one of my mother, to hang next to mine in my permanent home—when I have one." He says after a pause, "As you know, Lord Login, I would very much like to buy an appropriate residence, once the India Office gives me my allowance, for which I have been asking them."

I can see that the mention of the allowance, especially in front of me, makes Login uncomfortable. I resolve to find out more about this at the first opportunity.

"Perhaps you should wait until the matter of the allowance is settled before incurring the expense of a portrait," Login advocates. "The best painters charge a rather exorbitant fee."

Or is his real issue that my son wants something to remember me by even after I am gone?

"Surely, Lord Login," I inquire sweetly, "now that Dalip has decided not to set up a separate establishment for me, there will be enough money for a painter?"

Login knows when he is beaten. He executes a stiff bow and says he will consult Lady Login on the matter.

After Login leaves, I ask Dalip about his finances. I am shocked to hear that the British, although they covered his living expenses, did not give him any money of his own until the age of nineteen. This after they had agreed to treat him as a major—according to Sikh law—when he turned sixteen. And the amount they finally gave him was a meager—

"Fifteen thousand pounds!" I exclaim. "I know you were promised far more when you signed away your kingdom. Avtar, who kept track of such things for me while I was in prison, told me of it when I escaped from Chunar. You were supposed to be given forty thousand pounds each year! Is there not a book in which such things are written down?"

Dalip replies, "I've heard of the Blue Books where the East India Company keeps all its records. They are stored in the British Museum, I believe."

"Ask to see the one for Punjab," I instruct him. "In addition to the money the British were supposed to give you in exchange for your kingdom, there are other properties for which they should have paid you. Your father had many ancestral estates that were his even before he became king. I used to collect a significant income from them every year on your behalf when I was regent. I don't remember all their names, but I want you to write down the ones that I can recall."

I reach deep down into my memory and pull up the names. Gujranwala, Chakowal, Wazirabad. Villages in Gujerat and Jhelum and Sialkot. And the rich salt-mines of Pind Dadan Khan. At the time of my regency, they had yielded rich revenue.

"What about your father's jewels?" I ask. "The British left you with a handful, but there were several chests' worth. You must ask about them. Not only are they valuable, they are also your legacy from your father. The first among them is the Koh-i-Noor. The Sarkar himself won it from the Afghan king Shah Shuja. It was not part of the Punjab kingdom. You *must* question the British, who like to pride themselves on their honesty, as to what right they had to take it from you."

Dalip lowers his eyes. "I gave the Koh-i-Noor to the Queen myself."

It pains me to see the shame on his face. "It's not your fault, Dula ji. You were barely ten years old. You did whatever the British insisted on. Your courtiers—a faithless bunch of namak-haraams, every last one of them—are the ones who should have ensured that you were treated justly. But they were too busy protecting their own jagirs and their own positions in the durbar."

"No, Biji," he says. "I gave it to her myself, again."

Then he tells me the story.

IT WAS IN 1854, the same year he—a boy of sixteen—had arrived in England, a country where he knew no one except the Logins.

How lonely he had felt in this cold climate, so far from everything that was familiar. But the Queen had been kind and gentle to him. She had invited him to dinners and festivals at her home in Osborne House and at Windsor Castle. She had invited him to spend time with her family, and encouraged him to get to know her children. They played together—he was not much older, after all—and became good friends. They made him feel like he *belonged*.

Additionally, the Queen commissioned a full-length portrait of him, to be done by the famed artist Winterhalter, who traveled all over the world, painting royalty. Winterhalter had just completed a lovely portrait of the Prince Consort, so it was a particular honor.

It was around then that Lady Login brought him a message from the Queen. Would he like to see the Koh-i-Noor again?

"Why?" I ask angrily. "Why would she want to taunt you with its loss?"

Dalip sighs. "The Queen isn't like that, Biji." But he sounds less certain than he would have earlier. "In any case, there I was, sitting for the portrait—standing, I should say, because it's a full-length portrait—in my royal costume, complete with sword and turban. Around my neck was a chain on which hung an ivory miniature of the Queen set in diamonds. I would like to show it to you some—"

"What happened then?" I interrupt.

I am on fire with anticipation and curiosity, and underneath it, a slow-burning rage. Besides, I have no wish to see Victoria's miniature. If I had my way, I'd throw it out with the kitchen rubbish.

"She came into the room and placed the Koh-i-Noor in my hand."

"She gave it back to you?" I ask, incredulous.

"No," he admits. "Though for a moment I was confused and excited. She said she brought it to me because I'd mentioned to Lady Login that I would like to see it again."

I sit up straight. "What did you do then?"

"I presented it back to her. And I said—but no, you would not like to hear what I said. Already to my own ears the words sound foolish, those of a fatuous boy dazzled by the glitter of the English court."

I touch his hand. "Tell me, Dula ji. I'll understand. And remember, no matter what you do—or have done—I'm always on your side."

"For a moment, Biji, I was so sad. She had cut up the diamond—made it smaller so that it would shine better, she explained. But she'd ruined it. As I held the Koh-i-Noor in my palm, I remembered my court, my kingdom, riding on the royal elephant with you, the people of the city cheering us so loudly I thought surely my father, the Sarkar, could hear it from heaven. All gone now.

"So I did the only thing I could, in order to maintain a show of dignity. I presented it back to her, saying it was my pleasure, as her loyal subject, to give my sovereign my greatest possession."

I close my eyes. *Ah, my son! You've given them another reason now to say that the Koh-i-Noor rightfully belongs to Victoria.*

Dalip hangs his head, looking stricken, so I put aside my own distress and hug him as though he is still the boy of nine whom I was forced to leave behind in Lahore. "It doesn't matter. The Koh-i-Noor was always bad luck. Let that misfortune descend on her! You focus on getting the government to pay you what is your due, here and in Hindustan."

He returns the embrace, strong and determined, his voice resolute as he says, "I will write to Lord Login tonight, asking him to bring me the Punjab Blue Book when we meet next. I'll mention the treaty which promised me forty thousand pounds. I'll bring up the subject of the Koh-i-Noor as well, and see what comes of it. At the very least, the British will know that I'm no longer ignorant of my rights—and for that, I have you to thank, Biji."

This is the happiest I've felt since I came to England, the most useful.

THE PRINCE CONSORT, ALBERT, has died suddenly of typhoid. I would like to think it is the effect of the Koh-i-Noor. Dalip, who was summoned to be one of the ten chief mourners at the funeral, says the Queen is devastated. I try my best to feel charitable, but alas, I am not very successful.

Enjoy your Koh-i-Noor now, Victoria!

Albert's death has put my son in a pensive mood. He talks of taking whatever the India Office gives him and returning with me to Hindustan. He says we can live simply there, in a small town by a river, dedicating our life to the destitute.

"Wouldn't that be lovely, Biji?"

My heart sings as I allow myself to imagine such a life. I agree heartily, but I am more of a realist than he is. The British will not let us out of their clutches so easily.

"I will open a Christian school where poor children will be given an education—and salvation," Dalip adds.

I sigh. His love for Christianity is a sore point between us, though we don't bring it up because neither of us wants the arguments it would lead to. He knows it hurts me to see him dress up and attend church on Sundays. But church is special for him, even here at Mulgrave, where there is only a small chapel. I imagine my "heathenness," which according to the doctrine of Christianity dooms me to an eternity in hell, pains him equally. He does not forbid it when the servants and I celebrate our holy days, but he makes sure to be elsewhere. I know that he'd love to discuss the Bible with me, to share its "truth," but in this one matter I have been stern and unyielding. I recite from the Guru Granth every day—with age, I've returned to my childhood practices—and Maahi, who has a lovely voice, often sings the shabads. Even though he barricades himself in the study with a drink, I'm certain he can hear us. Does it remind him of his childhood, when he had known some of these same shabads by heart?

Waheguru, help me bring my son back to the path of his forefathers.

DEATH IS A SHOCK, but after a while—in England, as in Hindustan—life goes on. Although Victoria continues to mourn the passing of her husband, her son Edward, the Prince of Wales, decides to get married. For the occasion, the royal family calls Dalip back to Windsor Castle, where Victoria wants him to be part of the wedding procession. Once again, he's mesmerized by her royal glory. Upon his return, he describes to me in minute detail how she was present for the occasion but shut herself up in a specially built box to keep herself apart. How, while everyone was clad in glistening finery, she wore only black. He is filled with admiration at her loyalty to her dear Albert, her unwavering love enduring beyond death. I bite my tongue to keep from asking him if she wore the Koh-i-Noor.

Dalip himself was dressed splendidly in full Hindustani attire, including a turban. He had taken out all his jewels from his bank vault for the occasion. He made sure to sport the Star of India, which the late Albert had presented to him. As he had imagined, it made Victoria very happy. He was asked to head the procession of foreign princes—a great compliment, he informs me—and was given a seat of honor in the front row, next to the royal family. The famous painter William Frith, who is creating a ten-foot painting of the event, has told him that he is going to be featured prominently in it. He has requested Dalip to visit his studio so that he can create an authentic likeness.

I can see the strategy the British are employing. They wish to charm Dalip again, to lure him back into the illusion they had created when they first brought him over: he is loved, he is valued, he is the best of the Queen's subjects. Why, he's almost as good as an Englishman, and far more exotic! This way, he will not create any trouble; he will forget the inconvenient facts his mother is inciting him to complain about.

I could point out their trickery to him, but it'll do no good unless he recognizes it for himself.

IT IS LATE NIGHT by the time he finishes telling me about the wedding. I expect him to excuse himself and go to bed—he returned from London just this afternoon, and it is a long, bone-rattling journey, even in his well-sprung coach. But he sits by me and fiddles with the edge of my shawl, a habit he had as a child. He has something on his mind.

"Tell me," I urge.

He blushes a little—he was always fair-skinned, and living under the pale England sun has only made him more so. "The Queen says I'm old enough to get married. She says I should look for a suitable wife."

My heart thuds in my chest. I understand her strategy. If he gets married in this country, to someone whose home and loyalty lie here, Hindustan will fade further from his mind. If he loves another woman, his allegiance to me will decrease. Still, I try.

"I don't know where we will find a suitable girl here."

"Oh! Don't worry about that. Lady Login was delighted when she heard this and made several suggestions."

Of course she did, I think irritably, *this woman who still competes with me for the role of my son's mother.*

Dalip continues, "But I did not want to proceed until you gave me your permission."

In the midst of my consternation, I feel a flash of joy. My son has chosen to keep our customs. He has shown his mother respect. I put aside my selfish concerns, place my hand on his head, and give him my blessing. I ask him if he already has a particular woman in mind.

"I do," he says shyly. "She's British. Is that all right with you?"

Waheguru! I shudder at the thought of an Englishwoman as my daughter-in-law. Not that she would care to have anything to do with me. I am sure she will establish her own separate household and keep Dalip there, away from me. And Login—along with the entire British government—will be delighted to have that happen.

"What about a Hindustani woman?" I venture. "I have heard that there are a few women from noble families, even one or two princesses, living here."

"There are," Dalip acknowledges. "For a while, the Queen was very keen that I marry Princess Gowramma, daughter of the king of Coorg, who has also converted to Christianity. She instructed Lady Login to take charge of her so that we could meet often. But I respectfully declined. I did not think we suited each other. In fact, I have not found any of the Indian women to my taste."

My heart sinks further. Even in this, the British have clouded his vision. Now, to him, his own race looks less attractive than his conquerors.

He grins and says, "None of them are as beautiful as you, Biji."

What can I do after that but kiss his forehead and wish him well?

I watch him leave the room with a new jauntiness to his step. There is a great fear in my heart, but also a small, cruel hope. The fear is of losing him forever; the hope—but I don't want to attract bad luck by naming it, not even to myself.

35

Prophecy

We return to glum, sooty London so that my son can go courting. He takes this project more seriously than anything else I've seen him do until now—except for going to Hindustan to meet me. Having observed his easy-going lifestyle for over a year now, I realize how difficult that journey halfway across the world, to a place he had no fondness for, must have been for him. That act of his, more than any awkward, halting words he might say, shows me how much he cares for me.

At significant expense, Dalip gets appropriate clothes, different kinds of attire for day and evening, for small soirées and large banquets. He has his tailor make him several of the short frock coats that have become fashionable recently. He buys the newly popular stovepipe hats to go with them—he likes them because they make him look taller. He gets a haircut, and a beard-trim in the latest mode, with side whiskers, and looks quite the English gentleman. He has his carriage refurbished and, because Lady Penelope Cunningham, the woman he is courting, likes to ride, buys two new horses. On horseback he is the equal of—or better than—any of her other beaus, as he well knows. She also likes entertainments, so Dalip often takes her, along with an entire party of her friends, to see plays at the

Princess's Theatre, or to an opera at Covent Garden. These outings are followed by lavish dinners.

Dalip is a good son. On occasions when he invites Lady Penelope's family to join them, he tries to persuade me to come, too. But I smile and say no. What would I do among all those firangs—I who still prefer to eat with my hands and speak in Punjabi? Better for me to spend my evenings in my comfortable bedroom, which Maahi keeps extra warm for me, reminiscing to her about the far grander entertainments arranged by the Sarkar in the Badshahi Qila. But more importantly, I don't want to be the reason an Englishwoman might turn my son down.

Lady Penelope is the daughter of a minor peer. In Punjab, she would not have been considered a suitable match for Dalip, but in England all the rules are upside down, and I suspect that my son sometimes wonders if *he* is good enough for her. I have not met her yet, though Dalip would like to introduce us—"The two most important women in my life," he says. I am glad that Lena Login has been demoted, but I tell Dalip I will wait until things are official between them. He is disappointed by my answer. He is certain I will love Penelope, who is very pretty and vivacious, with a sweet nature to boot.

Aroor has a different opinion. He describes Lady Penelope as plain-faced, with a long nose that is always up in the air. One day, when she visits Dalip, along with a party of her friends, I spy on her from behind a window curtain and decide that Aroor's description is closer to the truth than my besotted son's. I am also a bit concerned as Penelope seems as friendly—if not more—toward a couple of the other men in her entourage as she is with Dalip.

Aroor also confirms my other worry: Dalip is spending a great deal of money on entertaining Penelope. I am afraid the expenses are more than he can afford, especially as the Government continues to ignore his request to increase his pension. Here is another thing I have learned about my son: he is not very good at managing his money. Perhaps it is because he has never had to do it. Or perhaps it is because he feels that as a maharaja—which is what, ironically, Victoria calls him—he should not have to practice petty economies. I try my best to help by cutting down on household expenses. My faithful servants cooperate as much as they can. Though we keep it secret from Dalip, on days when he does not lunch at home, we eat leftovers. And when the housekeeping money runs out, I often dip into my own purse to pay the merchants.

THIS EVENING, DALIP COMES into my sitting room and throws himself despondently on the sofa. His clothing is wrinkled and his hair rumpled. And is that a streak of mud on his favorite trousers? This is unusual. Generally, he is elegant and, except for when he goes hunting, finicky about his appearance. I'm concerned, particularly when he refuses to answer my anxious questions. Not knowing what else to do, I leave him be and start my prayers, reciting from the Guru Granth. My eyes have grown worse, too weak to read our holy book. But fortunately I know most of it by heart. On another day, Dalip would have excused himself and gone to his study, but today he continues to lie on the sofa, his eyes closed. After I'm done chanting, he tells me that Penelope has accepted an offer of marriage from an Englishman. He is a friend of Dalip's; they have hunted fox and shot grouse on each other's properties. Dalip had introduced him to Penelope. Understandably, my son feels doubly betrayed.

"I was a fool. A blind, trusting idiot," he tells me. "I couldn't see the facts staring me in the face. Penelope wasn't really interested in me, only in the amusements I provided. For a while, perhaps, my exoticness fascinated her. It was fun to go around with the 'Black Prince,' as they call me in court. But when it was time to settle down, she preferred someone of her own kind. She had the gall, when she told me of her engagement, to invite me to visit their mansion once she was married so that we could all go hunting together."

My entire body aches with his sorrow. It is also heavy with guilt. Isn't this what I was hoping for? That he would be rejected by the Englishwoman he was so enamored of. That he would realize that Victoria's "maharaja' will never be considered the equal of the firangs, not where something as important as the intermixing of bloodlines was concerned.

"I should have known!" he cries. "I should have known better. Why can't I learn my lesson?"

"What do you mean?" I ask.

Dalip confesses to me that a few years back, he had fallen in love with a young woman, one of Login's wards and a distant relative. But even though he had begged the Logins for permission to court the girl, they had refused. They had come up with excuse after excuse. She was too young. He was a prince and she a commoner. The Queen would not like it.

"Lies, all lies. Even the Logins, whom I loved and thought of as my parents, didn't believe I was good enough to become a true part of their family. Even they, for whose sake I gave up my religion and my country, found me wanting at the end of the day. Ah, how foolish I've been!"

I'm incensed at the Logins, though unsurprised. I wish Dalip had told me about this incident earlier. I would have warned him then, even as he started courting Penelope, to guard his heart. I would have reminded him of his past failure, even though it might have angered him, for that is a mother's duty.

Are there other such secrets in his past which will emerge to torture him in the future?

"Dula ji," I implore, "forget about these firangs. Let us go back to our own land, where we will be loved and welcomed. In Hindustan, a hundred families will crowd around you, offering you their daughters and their loyalty. Every one of them will be proud to forge an alliance with a descendant of the Lion of Punjab."

At first, Dalip discounts my suggestion, but I keep bringing it up until, finally, it penetrates the gloom surrounding him. He informs the Queen and the Parliament that, disillusioned by the behavior of the Government and the India Office, he has decided to leave England for good and return with me to the land of his birth. Since the British have reneged on their promise of a suitable pension, which is his legal right by virtue of the treaties they signed, he would like them to return his personal properties in Punjab to him so that he may live as befits Ranjit Singh's son.

Taking my advice, Dalip adds that this time, if he is ignored, he will ensure that all the Indian newspapers—as well as any British papers with a shred of integrity in them—learn the full story of the dishonesty of their leaders. For my part, I write to our cousin in Punjab, Thakur Singh Attariwala, about the latest developments. I ask him to make a list of all the Sarkar's confiscated jagirs and mines that rightfully belong to my son, and to my delight he writes back with the requested information, expressing outrage at the perfidy of the British and promising to help us in every way.

"Do you really think the firangs will let us go back to Hindustan?" Maahi asks me. Though she is too loyal to me to complain about being in England, I know she is as homesick as I am.

I want to pretend confidence, but finally I tell her the truth. "I don't know, Maahi. But Dalip must learn to protest against injustice. Even if it gets him in trouble."

Maahi doesn't disagree, but her eyes fill with concern.

Now that he has been betrayed in so many ways by the Christians he trusted, Dalip seems less excited about their religion. He is no longer regular about attending church, not even when the Logins ask him to accompany them. This November, when we celebrate Guru Nanak's birthday, inviting to our home the handful of Sikhs I have met here courtesy of Aroor, he joins us in my rooms. He wears his Hindustani clothes, especially his turban, which he otherwise dons only on court occasions. He listens attentively as Maahi, my two Sikh servants, and I chant from the Guru Granth. He goes around the house, barefoot like us, helping to light the lamps. Afterward, he sits on the floor and eats the simple traditional langar with his hands, asking enthusiastically for seconds. That night, when I am about to go to bed, he wistfully inquires if it is ever possible for a man to return to Sikhism after he has given it up.

My heart leaps so hard that it hurts my chest. It does this often nowadays. Is it because, in my weakened state, emotions hit me harder? Or is this the sign of some hidden ailment? I take deep breaths to calm myself so that I will not sound overly eager and cause Dalip to shy away.

"It is possible," I say evenly, "but first a man must be certain that it is what he wants." He asks me about the requirements, and I tell him that the most important qualification is a willing heart, along with knowledge and respect for the teachings of the Gurus. The rest—five Sikh men to join in the pahul ceremony, the Gurbani to be read by a granthi, the amrit to be drunk and sprinkled on the head—can be easily arranged.

Dalip is impressed. "How do you know all this, Biji?"

I smile, hiding my decades-old sorrow. I don't tell him that I made it a point to learn these things soon after the news of his conversion reached me. That I've been praying and hoping since then.

Now that Dalip's romantic hopes have been dashed, we spend most of our evenings together. When his friends invite him to parties, or the Logins call him for dinner, or to accompany them to court, he turns them all down, though with his usual politeness. Aroor, who still has friends among the Logins' staff, tells me that there is much consternation in court circles about the change in my son. Letters have been exchanged between the Indian Council, Login, and Sir Charles Phipps, who writes to them on behalf of the bereaved Queen. The consensus is that I am an atrocious influence on the maharaja. Various plans about what should be done with me are being put forth. The British here would like to send me away, but the India Office is most reluctant to have me back!

Meanwhile, I use my time and my dwindling strength to describe the lives of the Gurus to Dalip. My favorites are Guru Arjan Dev and Guru Tegh Bahadur. I admire their courage and their decision to be martyred rather than be forced to convert. I describe how, as a girl, I visited Gurdwara Lal Khoohi, built on the site where Guru Arjan underwent horrifying tortures at the hands of Jahangir's agents, and the strong impression it left on my mind. Dalip listens thoughtfully. He doesn't say much, but I can feel the tales making their way into his being. Such is the power of stories.

There is one more tale I tell him, though it is more of a prophecy, a divination made by Guru Gobind Singh, our last spiritual leader. It is about a king named Dalip who will lose his throne as a child, be carried away into a foreign land, and live there for many years in deprivation. He will even marry a foreign woman. But finally he will return to Punjab, defeat his enemies, and lead his people to glory.

"What are you saying, Biji?" Dalip challenges me, his face flushed and feverish.

"Nothing," I say. But I hope he can read the message in my eyes. *Perhaps you are this king. Perhaps this prophecy is about you.*

Dalip must have frightened the British with his new determination, for the government comes back with an offer. They will raise his pension to twenty-five thousand pounds, almost doubling what they gave him earlier, but he must agree that this is in "satisfaction of all claims." They point out that asking for more than that would be "unreasonable," as even peers of the realm do not make as much.

"The overall income of the House of Lords," they point out, "is under ten thousand pounds."

There is a small addendum to the offer: Maharaja Dalip Singh must remain in England, though his mother will be allowed to return to India if she wishes. Where and when she will be sent will be known once the India Office makes a final decision. Meanwhile, she must set up an establishment of her own, with a suitable lady companion, so that the maharaja is free to attend to his own business, chief among which will be the purchase of a new estate, for which the government is ready to give him a loan.

I can see that Dalip is excited by these new developments. I, too, am happy for him, though I warn him not to grow satisfied too soon.

"Keep asking them for what is your rightful due," I tell him. "Keep bringing up the matter of our private properties, which they confiscated illegally." I remind him of the way in which the British reduced my pension—from one lakh and fifty thousand rupees to forty-eight thousand, and then to twelve thousand. And they stopped giving me even that paltry amount once they imprisoned me at Chunar Fort. I don't want my son to suffer the same way.

I concede graciously to the idea of establishing a house of my own. Though no one else knows this, Dalip and I have decided that he will stay with me most of the time, even if he maintains an apartment in one of the hotels. I am content with the pleasant and airy house Dalip finds for me in the quiet and dignified London neighborhood known as Kensington. The Logins recommend an English lady as a companion, whom I hire. I suspect she has been placed here to keep an eye on me, but to my surprise she is intelligent and good-humored and makes no effort to take control of my household, which is run efficiently by Maahi. Sometimes she accompanies me to a nearby park, but more often we sit together in companionable silence in the parlor, she knitting while I watch the flames leaping in the fireplace.

Dalip is often away these days looking for an estate. I realize now that this has been a longing deep in his heart: to have a home of his own, a piece of land within the boundaries of which he is truly the king. He is quite excited about a castle he is considering buying in Gloucestershire, a county not too far from London. He thinks I will enjoy it there. The weather will be better than at Mulgrave, as it is farther south, and it, too, has forests all around, filled with foxes for him to hunt. I caution him not to rush into a decision; perhaps other, better properties will come on the market. But he is too impulsive—a trait which worries me—and signs the papers without negotiating for a better price.

Dalip has commissioned a well-known artist, George Richmond, to paint a portrait of me. He takes great interest in the composition of the painting, which he plans to hang in his new castle. He personally chooses the clothes I will wear for my sittings: a blue silk ghaghra with a matching blouse, which he claims makes my skin glow. He complements it with a gold-bordered veil and arranges my jewelry, which he has brought out of the bank for this purpose, around my neck. Pride of place is given to my pearls, and to an emerald necklace which he remembers admiring from the time he was a boy. The painter, though undoubtedly good at what he does, is fussy and slow and sometimes irritates me, especially as I tend to tire quickly now. But I put up with the inconvenience because this is what my son wants, and make a stalwart attempt to look regal even when I'm exhausted. They say a part of the subject's energy finds its way into her painting, so I mentally recite prayers as I sit. I fancy the idea of my spirit—along with the blessing of the Gurus—watching over my son after I am gone.

I cannot tell anyone this, but I am afraid of what will happen to Dalip after my death. Though I love him dearly, I'm forced to admit that he has neither the strength of character nor the stubborn focus that his father—or even I—possessed. He's a sapling that bends in whichever direction the wind blows. One day, he is disgusted with the prevarications of the India Office as regards his pension and vows to go to India and dedicate his life to taking care of the poor. The next, his friends invite him to their estates and off he goes happily to chase after foxes. One day, he is angry with Victoria for the part she played in the loss of his kingdom and the Koh-i-Noor. The next, he accepts her dinner invitation and is thrilled when she presents him to visitors as the foremost of the foreign princes at her court. Right now, he is so in love with the estate he has purchased, Hatherop Castle, that he has quite forgotten his interest in Sikhism. He is creating fantastical and extravagant plans for remodeling the castle to make it look like the Sheesh Mahal. He has shown me architectural drawings of domes and cupolas, carved marble pillars, and walls inset with glass.

I can tell that a part of Dalip longs for the palace where he grew up, the palace which he will probably never see again. Re-creating it here will give him a certain comfort. When visitors admire his home, he will be able to tell them of the far greater Badshahi Qila where he was king. Perhaps then they will have an inkling of the glory that had been his. I sympathize, but I shudder to think how much it will cost. I beg him not to rush into things. At first my son hugs me and says I worry too much, but finally he promises to wait on some of the more elaborate parts of the project.

Who will curb his extravagant ideas once I am gone?

I CAN SENSE THE day of my death approaching. I find myself gasping even after the briefest of exertions. There is often a sharp pain in my chest. I have stopped going on walks, though sometimes I long to stand underneath the spreading canopies of the sweet chestnuts in the park. They remind me of the guava trees of my youth, though perhaps the resemblance exists only in my mind. On days when I find it hard to breathe, Maahi insists on summoning a physician, but there is not much the man can do for me other than prescribing some elixirs and recommending that I rest.

"I'll rest when I'm dead," I tell Maahi. "For now, let me spend my time with my son."

I have made all the servants swear not to tell Dalip about my illness. I don't want him to worry, or to feel that he needs to be at my bedside. He is just beginning to enjoy his new home and his more generous pension. I don't want to dampen his pleasure. Thus, whenever Dalip comes to town, I hide my tiredness and stay up late, listening to his ever-burgeoning plans for his estate and poring over architectural drawings, trying to make out, in spite of my blurry vision, the details he points to. He describes in triumphant detail the large shooting party of noblemen—including the Prince of Wales—who recently joined him there, and how impressed they were by the variety of game on the premises. He informs me with some pride that he was the best shot among them. And when he finally takes me to Hatherop, I draw upon every bit of my strength so I can walk around the grounds with him as he shows off his new home.

But within a year, Dalip has grown tired of Hatherop. He tells me that a far better estate has come on the market—Elveden, situated in Suffolk, quite close to London. It is near the ocean, to boot; the sea air will do me good. Most importantly, the hunting is superb, and it will be good for conservation of game as well. He plans to sell Hatherop and buy Elveden.

"How can you afford it?" I ask, worried.

"It will not be a problem!" he announces triumphantly. "The government has agreed to loan me the money."

It seems a strangely philanthropic action for the British, and indeed, after I question Dalip some more, I learn that they will charge him interest. Now I am even more worried. How will my son, whose only income depends on the government's generosity, repay them? I see their plan: this way, they will have him even more firmly in their clutches.

How can he now demand his rights, the properties in Punjab they cheated him out of?

I advise Dalip to be more prudent. I tell him that the Sarkar had never believed in living beyond his means. I recount to him how frugally I'd managed my household after I became a widow, to ensure that I wouldn't be beholden to anyone. Dalip listens politely to show me respect, but I can sense his impatience. As soon as I'm done, he asks the servants to clear the dining table. On it he spreads out a map of the lands around Elvenden Hall, and tells me how he plans to populate it with sand grouse, pheasants, and partridges, and how he plans to set up the only hawking establishment in that part of England. As soon as I've recovered from the ugly, racking cough which leaves me breathless, he promises, he'll take me up there so that I can see for myself why it is the perfect home for us.

DALIP IS AWAY ON a visit to a hunting lodge in distant Scotland when I grow dizzy while walking to the breakfast room in the morning. The room tilts around me and fades. When I regain consciousness, I find that I'm in my bed with my attendants hovering around me. I can see from Maahi's face that she has been crying. My chest feels as though a heavy weight is crushing it. The British doctor presses his icy stethoscope against my skin and looks grim. He gives me an elixir that he hopes will relieve the pain.

"Send for the maharaja at once," he tells Maahi.

I float in and out of consciousness. Sometimes there is a brightness behind my eyes, and dear faces from long ago linger, as though waiting to guide me to my next destination. I see the Sarkar's loving glance. Guddan doubles up with laughter at a joke. Pathani shows off a new set of jewelry, and Chand Kaur sits on a throne with a regal smile. My faithful Avtar, young again, bows and touches my hand to his head. Behind them stands Jawahar—not the bloodstained and terrified man who visited me in my nightmares, but the bright-faced boy I used to follow around Gujranwala . . . Was it only thirty years ago?

Suddenly Dalip is kneeling at my bedside, kissing my forehead, telling me I cannot leave him so soon, we've had such a short time together. His tears fall on my face as he says that he needs to show me his new house, which is almost complete.

"I need you to find me a good woman to marry, Biji, a woman who is honest and faithful and not British. I need you to teach my children all about our land and our culture, and to tell them all your wonderful stories. I need you to give me courage on days when life weighs heavily on me."

I put my fingers on his lips to hush him. I have very little time left, and I have an important decision to make, one that requires all my concentration.

I could give Dalip my dying blessing to carry on in his indolent ways, as though he were a minor English nobleman, unconcerned with the larger world as long as he's given enough money for his frivolous pastimes. He will be happy enough with his estate and his shooting parties, his hunting and his hawks, his invitations to lead processions in royal weddings and worship alongside Victoria in her chapel. He will be no trouble to anyone—and of no use. I could do that. It is, after all, what the British want.

Or I could try to remind him one last time of who he really is. But if I succeed, I'll doom him to restless unhappiness for the remainder of his life.

My Sarkar, which path should I take? What should I do, as his mother and as your queen?

His voice comes to me, as if from a long time ago, yet strong as it was the day he took me riding on the most beautiful horse in the world and told me about the battle he'd been forced to lead at the age of ten. How terrified he had been, and how resolute. How he had understood a truth that never left him for the rest of his life.

I beckon to Dalip to come closer. I whisper, "I am going, Dula ji."

"No, Biji," he cries. "You can't! Not so soon. We've only had two years together. There's so much more I need to learn from you. I haven't even shown you Elveden, how it's starting to look like our qila in Lahore . . . Now you can finally feel at home in this coun—"

With great effort, I raise my hand to touch his cheek. "Waheguru has decided that my time on earth is over. But before I leave, I want you to make me three promises."

"Anything! Just tell me what you want."

He means it right now. But will he have the determination to follow through? Nevertheless, I must do my part. I say, "The first is this: remember that the blood of the greatest king of Punjab flows in you. You are the only living son of Maharaja Ranjit Singh, the Lion of Punjab. He once said to me, 'What better way to die than in battle, with my loyal men around me? I would much rather go like that than be stuck in a stinking sickbed.' That is your heritage."

Dalip holds my hand tightly. "But I'm not brave like him, Biji. I'm not a daredevil. Nor a warrior. And the British are so strong, so crafty. Look how they've refused to give me even what they themselves promised in their treaty—"

The weight on my chest grows heavier. It's hard to speak, but I force myself. "Reach deep within, my son. You may be surprised by what you find there. You will not be alone in your quest for justice. Punjab is filled with men who long for your return. Contact your cousin, Thakur Singh. He will guide you. He will help you become a Sikh again, if you are willing. Who knows, perhaps you will fulfill the prophecy I told you about."

A cough racks me, and Maahi rushes up with water. I take a sip and continue. "I leave it to you to decide how you will live your life. And I bless you, no matter what you choose.

"But there are two things I request of you. Take my body back to Hindustan. I came to this land out of love for you, but my soul will never find rest here. Conduct my last rites in my own country, and place my ashes next to my husband's."

Dalip nods, too overcome to speak. I am glad he doesn't waste time in useless protestation. In the background, I can hear Maahi reading the Sukhmani Sahib to help my soul on its final journey. But from my son I need something different.

I draw on the last of my strength. "Do you remember what the

Sikh soldiers in Calcutta chanted when they came to Spence's Hotel to pay their respects to us? To show us that their spirit was unvanquished?"

I'm afraid he has forgotten the words, but he replies, "I do. The words are branded in my memory. At that time, they'd made me uncomfortable, but now I respect the soldiers' courage."

"I'd like to hear those words as my soul passes away."

His voice is hesitant, his intonation imperfect, but he says it, the victory cry that has kept our people resilient through centuries of persecution. "Jo bole so nihal, Sat Sri Akal."

I mouth the words along with him. *Whoever utters this will be happy: Eternal is the Great Timeless Lord.* It is Dalip's final gift to me.

It is also my final gift to him.

Epilogue

Nasik, 1864

THE SUN SHINES TOO BRIGHTLY in India, the young man thinks. It makes his head hurt, especially when it bounces, dazzling, off the river and into his eyes. Or perhaps it is the stench of the burning bodies, the pyres lined up next to each other on the funeral grounds, that is making him nauseated. One of the bodies is his mother's. Remembering her still hurts in the hollow space in his center that will perhaps never be filled. He will love no woman as he loved her. He will never admire anyone, male or female, as much.

She died last year in London, but it took the British an entire twelve months to give him permission to bring her body back to India for the Sikh rites she had requested. For an entire year, she was interred in an unconsecrated vault in Kensal Green Cemetery while they dithered. He used to wake up in the middle of the night, dreaming that she was pushing against the walls of her coffin, begging him to get her out of there. Over and over, he asked the British government, the India Office, and even the Queen, why it was taking them so long to consent to a simple journey for religious purposes. Login would have helped him, but he, too, was dead. He had no one in England anymore except Lady Login, and she was too mired in her own grief to help.

No, that was not true. He had Aroor. It was his faithful Aroor who found out—through his contacts in the servant world—that the British were afraid that if he went to Punjab, as he wished, so his mother's ashes could be placed with his father's, there would be an uprising. That the people would band together to place him on the throne once again.

He was astonished. "Do the people of Punjab really care so much for me? Do they still remember?"

Aroor said, "They will never forget their maharaja. Even the soldiers who have joined the British army are ready to desert and return to Punjab if you give them a sign. Thakur Singh has sent secret word that there are foreign powers who hate the British—the French, the Russians—who might be persuaded to take your side in such a battle."

The young man stored that information inside him. *The enemy of my enemy is my friend.* Perhaps he would use it some day.

Finally, when word of their cruel behavior seeped out to the public and letters of outrage began to appear in the newspapers—for the common men and women of England were more good-hearted than their leaders—the government gave reluctant permission. But they fettered him with conditions. He must not contact his relatives, particularly Thakur Singh with his militant tendencies. He must not check on the disputed properties that he claimed to own. In fact, he was not to go to Punjab at all. He must conduct the cremation close to Bombay, where his ship would dock. He must be accompanied by British troops throughout his sojourn in India. He must return immediately after the cremation.

He had no option. He had to give in, despite the fact that the blood of the greatest king Punjab had known flowed in his veins.

THE PRIESTS HAVE FINISHED chanting and left the ghats, but he waits, alone, except for the redcoats who are always watching. At the last moment, the British did not allow Aroor to accompany him, accusing the servant of being in touch with dissenters. There is no one to console the young man when he carries the earthen pot filled with the still-hot ashes of his mother to the river steps to scatter them in the Godavari.

He hears the sounds of hammer and chisel on stone, the voices of workmen. He is having a small samadhi erected for Maharani Jindan Kaur nearby, in a grove of trees near Panchbati. An urn with the rest of her ashes will be kept there. After the accursed British are driven from this country—surely it will happen one day, as it almost did in 1857—he will take the urn to its final resting place.

This was not what he had wanted, but the priests assured him that the samadhi was being built on a sacred spot. "The Godavari is not as holy as the Ganga, but it, too, is blessed." They'd told him the history of this place: Ram, hero of an ancient Hindu epic, had lived here for some time, along with his wife Sita, after he had been unfairly exiled from his kingdom.

The young man did not understand the story completely—his grasp of Hindi was rudimentary—but he felt an affinity, illogical though it might be, with the wronged Ram, who had also been deprived of his kingdom. And although he did not yet have a wife, as Ram did, he was making plans. He had decided not to marry an Englishwoman—painful experience had taught him the futility of making efforts in that direction; and he did not feel an Indian bride would suit him—they would have too little in common. Nevertheless, he longed for a helpmate, a companion to ease the loneliness of his nights. On the way back to England, his ship would stop at Cairo, just as it had on the way out, when he had met a girl in the Mission school there. Her name was Bamba. She was innocent and beautiful and looked at him with admiration. She would suit him well.

At times when sorrow at the loss of his mother, and fury at the compromises he had been forced to make regarding her last rites, threatened to overwhelm him, he thought of Bamba. She spoke no English, but he did not consider that a drawback. The young man imagined her receiving guests at his estate in Elveden, or going with him, dressed in her Abyssinian finery—for that was part of her heritage—to make her curtsy to the Queen. Wouldn't they be impressed by the bride he'd found, all by himself, on the other side of the world? Wouldn't they be envious of the young couple's perfect love?

ON AN IMPULSE, THE man leaves the last of the ashes in the pot and sets it afloat. He watches as it is borne along by the current—small yet defiant, he thinks, like his mother. How hard she had fought against the British, against her own treacherous courtiers. Though he'd never told her this, he remembered her standing up in durbar, a lone woman among all those men, the last queen of Punjab. Her beautiful face flushed—she had put aside her veil by then—she was entreating her noblemen to help her fight the firangs. They hadn't listened, the cowards, but she hadn't given up. She endured banishment and imprisonment and the many lies the British spread about her—oh yes, he'd heard the ugly stories even in England. She managed to escape and undertook a perilous journey by herself, through the mountain passes, into Nepal. Even when she was ill, she hadn't hesitated to accompany him across the black water, into the heart of enemy territory. She had spent the last of her energy trying to instill hope and patriotism into him, weak though he was.

All this she had done because she loved him.

The pot reaches a bend in the river. Just before it disappears, a ray of sunshine catches its rim, causing it to gleam. Or is the glimmer only in his tear-filled eyes? People revered his father as the Lion of Punjab, but his mother is the one they should have called Lioness. In her way, wasn't she braver than Ranjit Singh? Didn't she fight greater obstacles?

The young man steps into the Godavari. The current tugs at his clothes, which grow sodden and heavy. The soldiers watching him begin to shout. Do they think he's about to kill himself? The fools! He isn't going to make things that easy for them. He fills his cupped hands and sprinkles the water over his head.

"I will not forget you, Biji," he says. "I will not forget what you taught me. I will not allow the British to trick me anymore. I will return to my roots and my religion. I will be as brave as I know how to be, and as wily. And I will no longer settle, as I've done for so many years."

He takes a deep breath and says the words, even though he feels a bit like an imposter. *Jo bole so nihal. Sat Sri Akal.* They are awkward in his mouth, but after he has repeated them enough times, he knows they will become his own.

Acknowledgments

MY MOST SINCERE THANKS TO all listed below for their support, encouragement, suggestions, and blessings as I wrote *The Last Queen*.

My American agent, Sandra Dijkstra, and her team, especially Elise Capron and Andrea Cavallero.

My British agent, Caspian Dennis.

My editor and publisher at HarperCollins India, Diya Kar, and her team—Shatarupa Ghoshal, in particular. And thanks to Manpreet Singh for her careful read.

My friends Zack Bean, Nick Brown, Will Donnelly, Irene Keliher, Keya Mitra, Oindrila Mukherjee, Punam Malhotra, and Amritjit Singh.

Authors whose books were invaluable resources:

Michael Alexander and Sushila Anand, *Queen Victoria's Maharajah: Duleep Singh*

Peter Bance, *Sovereign, Squire and Rebel: Maharajah Duleep Singh*

William Dalrymple and Anita Anand, *Kohinoor*

Sita Ram Kohli, *Sunset of the Sikh Empire*

Lady Lena Campbell Login, *Lady Login's Recollections: Court Life, 1820–1904 and Camp Life*
Shah Mohammed, *Jangnama*
Amarinder Singh, *The Last Sunset: The Rise and Fall of the Lahore Durbar*
Khushwant Singh, *Ranjit Singh: Maharaja of the Punjab*
Khushwant Singh, *The Fall of the Kingdom of the Punjab*
Sarbpreet Singh, *The Camel Merchant of Philadelphia: Stories from the Court of Maharaja Ranjit Singh*

Special thanks to Ambassador Navtej Sarna, who gifted me his book *The Exile: A Novel Based on the Life of Maharaja Duleep Singh*, and encouraged me in my quest to write about the maharaja's largely forgotten mother.

The wonderful librarians at the University of Houston, especially Emily Deal, who procured numerous difficult-to-find books for my research.

My ever-patient and loving family: Murthy, Anand, and Abhay.

My spiritual guides: Baba Muktananda, Ramana Maharshi, and Nisargadatta Maharaj, who point me to That from which all creativity flows.

I am deeply grateful to each one of you.

About the Author

Chitra Banerjee Divakaruni is an award-winning and bestselling author, poet, activist, and teacher of writing. Her work has been published widely, in magazines and anthologies, and her books have been translated into twenty-nine languages. Several of her works have been made into films and plays. Her last novel was the bestseller *The Forest of Enchantments*, a retelling of the Ramayana in Sita's voice. She lives in Houston with her husband, Murthy, and has two sons, Anand and Abhay. She teaches in the internationally acclaimed Creative Writing program at the University of Houston. Chitra tweets @cdivakaruni and she loves to connect with her readers on her Facebook page: facebook.com/chitradivakaruni/.